Love Me Tonight

Love Me Tonight

by
Nan Ryan

A TOPAZ BOOK

TOPAZ
Published by the Penguin Group
Penguin Books USA Inc., 375 Hudson Street,
New York, New York 10014, U.S.A.
Penguin Books Ltd, 27 Wrights Lane,
London W8 5TZ, England
Penguin Books Australia Ltd, Ringwood,
Victoria, Australia
Penguin Books Canada Ltd, 10 Alcorn Avenue,
Toronto, Ontario, Canada M4V 3B2
Penguin Books (N.Z.) Ltd, 182–190 Wairau Road,
Auckland 10, New Zealand

Penguin Books Ltd, Registered Offices:
Harmondsworth, Middlesex, England
First published by Topaz, an imprint of Dutton Signet,
a division of Penguin Books USA Inc.

ISBN: 0-451-40483-1

 Topaz is a trademark of Dutton Signet,
a division of Penguin Books USA Inc.

Printed in the United States of America

Dedicated to:
My sister
Judy Henderson Jonas
January 14, 1942–July 16, 1993
In loving memory

Yes we'll gather at the river,
The beautiful, the beautiful river,
Gather with the saints at the river,
That flows by the throne of God.
—ROBERT LOWRY, 1864

Chapter One

This is what happened.

On a warm May morning in 1865, Helen Burke Courtney was alone on her farm near Spanish Fort, Alabama, a small coastal community on the eastern shore of Mobile Bay.

Helen was down in the south field, two hundred yards from the house. Her fair face was shaded with a stiff-brimmed sunbonnet. Her hands were protected by work gloves so old and well used the tips of her fingers had worn through the stiff fabric. The long sleeves of her cotton dress were blousy, the cuffs fastened at her wrists. The dress was gathered and full, the heavy skirts trailing the ground.

Helen had wisely covered herself from head to toe for the long hard day of spring plowing. But as the cool haze of early morning had burned away and the sun had shone through high and hot, Helen had unbuttoned the high-collared dress halfway down to her waist. And she had taken off her shoes and stockings, tossing them carelessly toward the northern edge of the field.

Barefooted, Helen guided the dull, rusting plow while old Duke, her faithful, aged saddle horse, wearily pulled it. Heavy leather harnesses draped over her slender shoulders, gloved fingers tightly gripping the plow handles, Helen made her slow, sure way from one end of the field to the other.

And back again.

The sun-heated soil felt good to her bare tender feet, just as it had when she was a child and skipped alongside her Grandpa Burke while he plowed this very same field.

Like her grandpa before her, Helen took great pride and pleasure in seeing the fertile soil of this lowland farm being turned into neat, furrowed rows. But she enjoyed no such feeling of satisfaction this year. There were few long straight rows to admire. Fewer tender green plants breaking through the rich soil. A large portion of the field was covered with weeds and johnsongrass.

Suppressing a sigh, Helen wished that the sea of sunflowers before her were tall stalks of tender green corn. She was late with the planting. There had been the long dreadful bout with influenza when she couldn't get out of her sickbed, much less do the work. And then when finally she was well enough, the heavy spring rains had kept her out of the soggy fields. Now she badly needed to make up for lost time.

Lord, if only she were twins.

Helen paused for a minute. She turned shaded eyes to the oak-bordered lane leading down to where her property fronted the bay. Helen had turned expectant eyes toward that narrow shady lane since the cool April morning in 1861 when her husband of six months had kissed her good-bye and rode away to war.

Will Courtney had mounted his spirited chestnut gelding that April day, smiled, leaned down to kiss her one last time, and promised he'd be home by planting time. She believed him. The war couldn't last long. Everybody said so. Will would be back before she hardly had time to miss him. The valiant Southerners would quickly vanquish the hated Northern enemy. Then the victors would return to their homes and loved ones and life would go on just as before.

Sure that it would happen just that way, Helen had started watching for Will's return soon after he'd gone. She had looked down that lane day in and day out as the days turned into weeks, weeks into months. And the months had stretched into years.

Missing him fiercely, lonely as she'd never been in her life, Helen had clung to her hopes and dreams and eagerly anticipated the glorious moment when Will would come riding down that lane and back into her arms.

Anxiously she planned for the homecoming. Each evening she set the table with her grandmother's fine bone china and fragile crystal, ready for the jubilant homecoming.

Helen had continued to look wistfully down that lonely lane long after word came that her husband, the brave William C. Courtney, C.S.A., had lost his life in battle.

Helen didn't belive it. She wouldn't believe it. Will wasn't dead. He couldn't be dead; not Will. Not her Will. It was a mistake. He promised he'd come back to her and he would. He had to. He'd come riding down the lane one day and they would have that long-awaited homecoming.

Helen had finally packed away her grandmother's fine china and crystal. She had placed all the delicate pieces in the heavy rosewood sideboard.

But even after the fine dishes had been put away, she didn't stop looking—several times each day—down that long shady lane where last she'd seen him.

Now Helen stared pensively at the silent, empty lane for a long moment before drawing a deep, slow breath and turning her attention back to the work at hand.

"Move it, Duke," she called to the half-deaf horse, "we have a lot of work to do."

Duke snorted and blew and trudged slowly forward. Helen gritted her teeth and bore down on the plow han-

dles, staggering under the heavy weight of the harnesses, her bare toes digging into the soft sandy soil.

Giving a tired whoop of joy when another row was
completed, she turned horse and plow about, rested a
minute, then started a brand-new row. She was halfway
across the long rectangular field when she again
paused to glance down the shady lane.

And so it was that Helen Courtney was looking directly at the tree-bordered alley when a stranger suddenly appeared. A man leading a shiny sorrel stallion
stepped out of the canopy of oaks and into the warm
May sunshine.

Helen felt a jolt of alarm slam through her chest.
Her hand reflexively went to the heavy revolver concealed in the folds of her gray work dress. The sight of
a small blond-haired boy astride the big stallion stayed
her hand.

Surely a man with a child meant her no harm.

Kurtis Northway meant no harm to the widowed
Helen Courtney. Or to anyone else. But he knew that
down here in the Deep South folks didn't trust him.
Didn't want him around. That had been made more
than clear to him.

Kurt Northway was a Yankee.

A dirty, no-good Yankee to these hot-blooded people. It made no difference that the war had ended. He
was still their bitter enemy and exceedingly unwelcome in this proud, defeated land.

Kurt was every bit as anxious to leave the South as
the South was to have him go. If it had just been him,
he'd have been riding home to Maryland this very minute. But he wasn't alone. He had a son to care for. A
son five years old. A son who didn't know him; a son
he barely remembered.

The day the war ended, Kurt had turned Raider—the
priceless sorrel thoroughbred he'd taken with him into

war—southwest toward the Mississippi Gulf Coast. He'd collected young Charlie Northway, the son who'd just been learning to walk when the first shot was fired at Fort Sumter. Within days of that fateful event, Kurt had ridden Raider into battle while his young wife took their baby son to her family home in Mississippi.

The summer before the long bloody conflict was finally over, Gail Whitney Northway died of the fever that took the lives of her entire family. Only the frightened, bewildered four-year-old Charlie was spared. Little Charlie had lost everyone.

Everyone but his absent father.

A kindly neighbor couple had taken Charlie in until Kurt could come for him. In gratitude, Kurt had given the destitute old couple all the money he had. He had none left. He and Charlie would have to work their way back to Maryland as best they could.

Kurt Northway shifted the long leather reins from his right hand to his left. Wishing he had a cigar, wishing he had a stiff drink of whiskey, wishing he had enough money to get the hell out of Alabama, Kurt rehearsed what he'd say to the young woman in the field. He hoped she would listen. She might not. She might order him off her property like so many others had in the past few days.

When Kurt reached the perimeter of the field, he dropped the sorrel's reins, looked up at his silent son, spoke gently to his obedient stallion, took a deep, spine stiffening breath, and started forward.

Never taking her eyes off him, Helen pulled up on Duke, slipped the heavy harnesses off her aching shoulders, and again touched her hidden weapon. Chin lifted defiantly, she observed with a look of keen inquiry the Yankee approaching her with long, determined strides. Eyes concealed beneath the stiff black visor of his blue kepi cap, the stranger was broad of shoulder and narrow of waist. A white cotton shirt and

faded blue uniform trousers appeared clean if some-
what frayed. His shirtsleeves were rolled up over
tanned forearms and his collar was open at the throat.
He was a tall, lean man with an easy, graceful stride.
As he neared her, his face broke into a warm, pleasant
smile.

Smiling with a confidence he didn't actually feel,
Kurt Northway saw—standing in the middle of the
rich, neglected farmland—a proud, unafraid young
woman in a faded gray work dress, lace-trimmed sunbonnet, and men's worn work gloves. She was moderately tall and virginally slender. Abruptly she removed
her bonnet, revealing hair of the palest shade of gold
pinned carelessly atop her head. She had a pretty, oval
face with skin remarkably pale and clear.

Kurt's smile became genuine when the wary young
woman suddenly remembered that her shirtwaist was
unbuttoned down past the swell of her breasts. A quick
look of dismay clouded her lovely face and she lifted
slim, nimble fingers to quickly button the dress. Then,
in an appealing, purely feminine gesture, she swept a
nervous hand over the pale gold hair and smoothed it.

Kurt Northway had reached Helen Courtney.

He removed his billed cap and, leaving plenty of
space between them, nodded his dark head and said,
"Kurt Northway, ma'am, late captain, Union army." He
extended a tanned hand.

Blue eyes riveted to his face, Helen slipped off her
right work glove, shook his hand, and quickly released
it.

She said, "Captain Northway, I'm Mrs. William
Courtney. You're trespassing on private property. If
you've lost your way, perhaps I can—"

"No, ma'am, Mrs. Courtney, I'm not lost. I was told
in Spanish Fort that you're looking for seasonal help
here on your farm."

His was a voice clear and pleasantly modulated. His

hair was a midnight black and his eyes, Helen noted, were a striking shade of deep, deep green, like the dark tropical foliage on the sloping coastal cliffs below the farmhouse.

Kurt Northway was equally aware of the large vivid blue eyes looking at him so fully and frankly and of the pale golden hair framing an arrestingly lovely face. He was charmed by the sound of her soft, cultured voice, even if he didn't like what he knew she was about to say.

"You heard wrong, Captain Northway. If it's honest labor you're seeking, try the loading docks over in Mobile. I need no help here. Sorry."

Chapter Two

"I'm sorry too, ma'am," he said in a low, soft voice.

Kurt Northway knew she was lying. Knew that the young widow desperately needed help working this remote coastal farm. But she looked on him as the enemy, was half afraid of him.

Careful not to make any quick, threatening moves, he said, "I tried the Mobile docks. The harbor's pretty quiet these days."

Blue eyes snapping, Helen nodded. "Yes, I know." Left unsaid was that *his* invading navy was responsible for destroying docks and warehouses and bringing shipping to a standstill.

Inclining his dark head toward the small boy astride the sorrel stallion, Kurt added, "Besides, ma'am, my son is too young to be left alone." He pinned her with his forest-green eyes. "I need farm work, so Charlie can be with me."

"Yes, well, I can understand that, but I'm afraid you'll have to find some other farm." Helen's tone was dismissive. "Captain, I'm presently alone here. My husband has not yet returned from the war."

Helen's husband wouldn't be returning and Kurt knew it. She was a widow. The aging gentleman who had directed him to her coastal farm had told him, "Everybody knows Helen Courtney's husband is dead. She does too. She just won't face it."

"I'm very sorry, ma'am."

As if he hadn't spoken, she went on, "It simply wouldn't do for you to . . . to . . . Let me repeat, I'm alone here, Captain Northway."

"I understand that, Mrs. Courtney," Kurt said evenly. "And if it were just me, I wouldn't dare propose such a questionable arrangement. But, ma'am, you do sorely need help and surely the presence of my son would make the difference."

Brow furrowed, Helen looked from the tall, dark Northerner to the small, blond boy. Then back again. Her blue eyes narrowed, she said hotly, "You actually expect me to hire *you*?"

"I was honestly hoping you might."

"You're a Yankee, Captain Northway!"

"Guilty as charged, Mrs. Courtney," he said, uncomfortably shifting his weight from one long blue-clad leg to the other. A tanned finger running unconsciously along the yellow cavalry stripe, he added, "But my boy Charlie's a good Southerner. Spent most of his life down here. His mama—rest her soul—was born and bred in Mississippi."

Helen's gaze left Kurt Northway, went again to the silent blond child. "How old is Char—your son, Captain?"

"Charlie's just five and he's a had a pretty rough go of it, ma'am. He lost his mother and both grandparents a year ago. I'm all he has left and I haven't the money to get him back home to Maryland." Helen's eyes again met Kurt's. He said with total honesty, "I have no money, ma'am. None. I'm not much of a father, I'm afraid. I can't even provide a bed or a meal for my son. But I've a strong back and am willing to work extra hard for any kind of roof over Charlie's head and whatever meager wages you can afford to pay."

Helen listened thoughtfully as Kurt Northway pleaded his case. He told her that he and the boy would be perfectly comfortable in the barn; they could sleep in the hay. Said they wouldn't expect to take their meals inside the house; they'd eat out in the fields or down at the barn. He promised to work tirelessly at any and all tasks needing attention. He vowed he'd keep his proper place at all times. He swore on his honor as an officer that he would show her nothing but the total respect she deserved. And he assured her she'd be as safe as a babe in her cradle with Charlie and him around to watch out for her.

Kurt at last fell silent.

Helen was more than a little tempted to take the tall stranger up on his proposition. Lord knows she needed help and she needed it immediately if she hoped to have a halfway decent harvest come autumn. But the idea of hiring a Yankee—allowing him to live right here on the farm with her—was not only distasteful, it was out of the question.

She'd be run out of town on a rail.

Helen lowered her eyes from his dark face. She looked again toward the tiny blond boy. But her narrow-eyed gaze accusingly touched the shimmering sorrel stallion the child was astride and her delicate jaw hardened. Helen knew horses. The big, fine-boned stallion was a thoroughbred—worth plenty of money to a discerning horseman.

"Captain Northway," she said sharply, "there are a number of wealthy gentlemen in Mobile who would pay you handsomely for your horse."

Kurt Northway's green eyes flashed with a sudden turbulence. He shook his dark head decisively. "Ma'am, that horse is the only thing in this world that I own. He got me through the war alive. I'd sooner sell my own soul than to sell Raider."

The simple heartfelt statement struck a sympathetic chord in Helen. She understood perfectly. Knew just how he felt. She felt exactly that same way about this secluded, run-down old farm with its bluff-front house. She was determined to hang on to it if it killed her, and sometimes she thought it would.

While there was breath left in her body she would never allow the rich, arrogant Niles Loveless to greedily gobble up her beloved land just to expand his own vast acreage.

"Captain Northway," Helen said after a long indecisive pause, "all I can offer are small, long-unused quarters adjoining the barn. And I couldn't pay you anything until harvest time in the—"

"That's fine by us, ma'am," Kurt interrupted, smiling. "Just fine."

Half skeptical, wondering if she was doing the right thing, Helen nodded and set her sunbonnet back on her head. "It's almost noontime, Captain. I imagine your son is getting hungry."

"I wouldn't be surprised, ma'am."

"I'll unharness Duke and take him on up to the barn," Helen said. "You can follow with Charlie and the thoroughbred." She turned away, stepped up behind Duke, and started to unhitch the heavy plow.

"Ma'am, let me get that," said Kurt, and he took her arm and gently moved her aside.

He made quick work of freeing horse from harness. Then, looping the heavy leather reins over Duke's back, he clucked his tongue to the old pony, coaxing him into motion. He turned, looked across the furrowed rows at his sorrel stallion, and gave a low, soft whistle through his teeth.

"Hold on tight, Charlie," he called to his son.

Helen watched, amazed, as the big thoroughbred turned in a tight semicircle and began prancing alongside the field's narrow green border, moving steadily in the direction of the farmhouse and outbuildings.

She looked at Kurt Northway and shook her bonneted head. "I certainly hope your beast doesn't decide to make a shortcut across the corner of this field. I've already started some planting in the northern end."

Without hesitation, Kurt Northway said, "Ma'am, Raider wouldn't dare trample your newly planted corn. His manners are impeccable."

Helen made no reply. She turned and walked away, giving old Duke a propelling slap on the rump. It was then that she remembered she wasn't wearing her shoes. She shot a quick glance at the tall man who had fallen into step beside her. Did the Yankee know? Could he tell that she was barefooted like some common peasant woman?

Taking great care not to allow her toes to peep out from her long gray skirts, Helen silently walked from the field, her grandmother's warnings echoing in her ears: "Young ladies should never be seen without their shoes and stockings. Why, having a fine gentleman encounter you barefooted is might near as bad as having him catch you in your camisole and pantalets!"

Helen clamped her jaw down tight. It was very doubtful that this tall dark Yankee was a fine gentleman; all the same, he wouldn't be catching her either in her underwear or with her feet bare. No sooner had she made the silent oath than Helen caught sight of her discarded shoes. There they lay, in plain sight at the edge of the field. Had the Yankee spotted them?

Helen's head snapped around. She looked up at his face and read the answer in his forest-green eyes. He *had* seen them. Well, he'd better not laugh if he knew what was good for him. No despised Yankee could make fun of her and get away with it. She wouldn't waste a second ordering him right off her property.

Kurt Northway said nothing. He didn't laugh. He didn't smile knowingly. He didn't cut or roll his eyes. He made no attempt to humiliate or embarrass her. He continued to walk alongside her as if nothing were amiss.

When they reached the shoes, the tall Yankee captain wordlessly bent down, plucked the cotton stockings from inside the shoes, and stuffed them into his breast pocket. He then knelt on the soft sandy soil, sat back on his heels, picked up Helen's shoes, and placed them on his lap.

He looked up at her and there wasn't a trace of teasing laughter in the depths of his green eyes. He patted his hard thigh and waited. Mortified, Helen sighed, lifted her gray skirts slightly, and placed her dirty right foot atop his blue-trousered thigh.

As if it were the most normal thing in the world for him to do, he gripped her slender ankle in his hand and carefully dusted the loose dirt from her foot with the tips of his long tanned fingers. Then gently he urged her foot into a shoe. He repeated the action with her left foot. When he was finished and both Helen's feet were firmly back on the ground, he rose to his own full height beside her, having said not one word.

Sure her hot face was telltale red, Helen needlessly cleared her throat, snatched the stockings from his shirt pocket, and said with as much dignity as she could muster, "If you'll kindly follow me, Captain, I'll show you to your quarters."

"Yes, ma'am, Mrs. Courtney."

Only after she had flounced away did the hint of an amused smile lift the corners of Kurt Northway's lips.

Chapter Three

"**M**rs. Courtney, I'd like you to meet my son, Charlie." Kurt plucked the boy from the saddle, set him on his feet. "Charlie, this is Mrs. William Courtney. We'll be staying here at Mrs. Courtney's place for a while."

Helen smiled down at the somber-looking child and thrust out her hand. But Charlie Northway was having none of it. He crossed his short arms over his chest, sidled closer to his tall father, and looked up at Helen from brown eyes filled with doubt and distrust.

"Charlie's a little shy," Kurt apologized, gently pulling Charlie around in front of him. Cupping the boy's head in his hand and brushing a wayward lock of blond hair off Charlie's forehead, he prodded, "Can't you say hello to Mrs. Courtney?"

"Charlie's probably too tired and hungry for much small talk right now," Helen said graciously. "Captain, take the horses on up to the corral." She pointed. "You'll find oats in the bin and a bucket on the peg by the door. The water trough is full. Meanwhile, I'll see what shape the quarters are in." She started forward, turned, and looked back at Charlie. "Want to come along with me?"

A violent shaking of his blond head was the response.

Helen didn't try again. She led the way, climbing the gentle slope from the flat field toward the outbuildings in the near distance. The silent trio, walking single file, reached the barn in minutes.

Kurt opened the corral gate and urged the horses inside. Helen went directly to the quarters at the far north side of the weathered barn. Charlie followed neither grown-up. The reserved little boy waited alone outside the plank corral, standing as still as a statue in the hot May sun.

Helen tried the door to the quarters. It wouldn't open. Rain-swollen and badly warped, the stubborn wooden door was tightly stuck. Helen shoved her sunbonnet off her head, allowing it to rest on her shoulder blades, held there by the loosely tied streamers beneath her chin. She tried the door again.

After several failed attempts, Helen leaned into the door and pushed with the full weight of her body. Shoulder and knee pressed against the rough wood, she shoved as hard as she could. The door didn't budge.

Frustrated, she was still struggling and groaning as if in pain when Kurt stepped up beside her, black leather regulation saddlebags draped over his left shoulder, a heavy canvas pack tucked under his arm.

"Wait, Mrs. Courtney, you'll hurt yourself if you're not careful."

"No ... I won't ... it's ... about to ..."

"Maybe I can get it," he said, and lowered the saddlebags and pack to the ground. Out of breath, Helen nodded and stepped aside.

Kurt gripped the doorknob, firmly turned it, and pushed inward with a strong forward thrust of his muscular arm. The door abruptly sprang open, flushing out a surprised blackbird. Exploding through the open door, the screeching bird swooped past Helen, its wings flapping wildly an inch from her face.

Badly startled, Helen shrieked, closed her eyes, and instinctively turned into the broad, sheltering chest of Kurt Northway. Helen's piercing shriek brought a frightened scream from Charlie and he lunged forward, wrapped his arms around his father's leg, and buried his face on Kurt's trousered thigh.

Kurt didn't move a muscle.

He felt the solid steel of Helen's hidden revolver press against his leg through the folds of her skirts. It struck him that such a lovely, vulnerable young woman living all alone had likely endured many long nights of fear. A sensation of empathy surged through him.

He would have laid a gentle hand on her back to soothe her, but knew she wouldn't hold still for it. She'd take it the wrong way. He was equally reluctant to clamp a comforting hand on his son. Charlie wouldn't like it either.

Helen's eyes opened, her head came up off his chest, and she forcefully pushed away from him. Flashing him a quick look of contempt as if she found him revolting, she said curtly, "Sorry. The bird scared me. It was silly of me."

"Not at all," Kurt said, shrugging.

Just as swiftly as Helen backed away, Charlie released his grip on his father's leg and moved back, his face screwed up in a frown. Kurt wasn't surprised by either reaction.

Collecting herself, Helen preceded them into the dim one-room quarters. She looked about, made a sour face, and quickly apologized for the total disorder.

"I had no idea the place was such a mess," she said. "No one has been out here for years."

She shook her head and moved about the close, shadowy room. The furniture—what little there was of it—was stacked against the far back wall. An iron bedstead and feather mattress, a tall scarred bureau, a couple of overstuffed easy chairs, a small table, and a half dozen straight-backed chairs with woven cane bottoms either badly worn or missing entirely were covered with cobwebs and dust and wasp nests.

Charlie sneezed, rubbed his nose, and sneezed again.

Helen sighed wearily. "You can't live here," she said.

"You're wrong, Mrs. Courtney. We can and we will," said Kurt, his tone level. He crossed the room, shoved rotted burlap curtains apart, and forcefully raised a dirty-paned window, allowing light and fresh air inside. "A little cleaning and it'll be home, sweet home." He smiled.

Charlie sneezed.

"Bless you," said Helen automatically. Then, "All this dust is getting to you, Charlie. Better scoot on out of here."

Charlie didn't move.

"Once the place has had a thorough going over," said Kurt, moving about the big room, opening more windows, "it'll be real comfortable. I'll get started right away."

"I'll help," Helen said, and headed for the door. Pausing, she added, "But it can wait a while. It's noontime. Draw some water from the well. I'll set out a basin, some soap, and a couple of clean towels on the back porch. After you've washed up, give me a few minutes. There's a shaded table out there on the porch. Take your places and I'll serve the noon meal."

"Will do," said Kurt as Charlie sneezed again.

Without another word, Helen turned and left. Lifting her heavy skirts, she walked hurriedly toward the house. A hundred yards from the barn, the farmhouse sat on a coastal clifftop directly above the wide mouth of Mobile Bay.

A sturdy but unimposing one-story structure in need of a coat of fresh paint, the dwelling had spacious rooms with high ceilings. A wide wooden veranda wrapped itself entirely around the house and each of the bedrooms opened onto the gallery, as did the front parlor and the kitchen in back. Weed-choked grounds surrounded the house, and directly below the big front yard, thick, junglelike foliage covered the sloping bluffs down to the water.

Helen neared the backyard.

Purposely blocking the open gate was her cat. A handsome Russian Blue breed with smoky blue-gray fur and a sleek, lean body, the haughty tom sat squarely in the center of the gate, his long tail curled majestically around him, his green eyes clearly registering reproach.

When Helen reached him, Dominic didn't make his usual soft purring sounds. Nor did he rise and brush affectionately against her skirts. He remained just as he was, eyes cold, mouth closed, a low, rattling sound escaping from deep down in his chest.

"Come on, Dom. Get out of my way," Helen coaxed the adored, aging tom her grandfather had given her when Dominic was just a kitten nine summers ago.

Dominic's answer was a turn of his regal head and a dramatic yawn. Helen smiled, went down on her heels, and stroked the soft downy fur under his chin. "Does this mean you've seen the Yankee and his son? Look, I had no choice. We need some help around here and you know it. So you can just grit your teeth and make the best of a bad situation, which is exactly what I'm having to do." She laid her cheek to the top of his head for a second, released him, and shot to her feet.

Stepping around the cat, Helen hurried into the yard. Curious, Dominic rose and leisurely followed. Woman and cat were immediately swallowed up in the deep shade cast by the tallest, oldest live oak on the farm. The low spreading branches of the ancient oak made a thick leafy canopy covering all but the farthest reaches of the big back yard.

A long wooden settee resting against the oak's thick trunk had once been Jackson Burke's favorite napping spot. Now it was Dominic's. Helen had never napped there, but she and Will had spent more than one romantic evening seated there, hidden from the day-bright moonlight, kissing in the hot darkness. Helen never passed the old settee with its peeling paint that she didn't think of Will and those warm, sensual nights.

At the back porch Helen took off her shoes. Shoes in hand, she rounded the corner of the wide gallery and padded toward the front bedroom at the northeast corner of the house.

She swept through the open French doors and into the dim coolness of her bedroom, tossing shoes on the floor and sunbonnet on the tall mahogany chest. Dominic followed his mistress inside, pausing briefly to rub back and forth on the satiny wood of the doorframe.

It took Helen less than ten minutes to wash up, brush her hair, and put on a clean checked gingham dress. It took the Russian Blue even less to leap up onto Helen's high feather bed, stretch luxuriously, place his chin atop his outstretched paws, and fall into a quick catnap.

Helen closed the door on the dozing Dominic and made her way down the hall to the kitchen. She carried towel, soap, and basin out onto the porch. She moved milk pails and crocks to the far end of the table. The table wasn't much. It was rough and splintery, but it would do.

Helen was in the kitchen slicing ham and cutting pieces of cold cornbread when Kurt and Charlie came into the backyard. She glanced out the window and watched their silent approach, wondering if they ever talked to each other. So far she'd not heard Charlie say a single word.

Helen served them their lunch there on the porch, but went back inside to have her own. She sat alone in the kitchen, just as she did at every meal. Just as she would continue to do.

Allow a Yankee to sit at her table?

Never in a million years.

Helen remained at the table for several long minutes after pushing her plate away. When she felt certain that the Yankee and his young son had had ample time to finish their meal, she went outdoors. Kurt rose to his feet.

"Sit down, Captain," she said. "This is as good a time as any for us to get squared away. I'll take this opportunity to tell you what's expected of you, as well as what I will and will not tolerate."

"A good idea," he said, pulling out a chair for her and reclaiming his own. "Charlie, you may be excused," he said to his son. "But don't get out of sight." Never looking at his father or Helen, Charlie slid off his chair, crossed the porch, and went down the steps into the shaded backyard.

In a businesslike manner, Helen quickly clicked off the dozens of tasks Kurt would be called on to do in addition to the all-important spring planting. She told him that to work a farm was to fight a never-ending battle. Said she was out of bed at sunup every morning and worked until sunset. And she would expect no less from him.

When she had carefully laid out all she wanted done and was assured he knew how to do all the things required of him, she then warned him about what she would not tolerate.

Casting a glance at Charlie where he sat silently on the long settee beneath the oak, his arms wrapped around his knees, she said, "You'll work six days with Sundays free. Your evenings are free as well and you may come and go as you please, but don't think you'll be leaving your son here in my care while you're out on the town. If I ever catch you drunk on my farm, you'll be told to pack up and go without the money owed you."

Kurt nodded and said nothing.

Helen again glanced at Charlie, lowered her voice until it was barely above a whisper, and added, "And, Captain, just in case you've made the foolish mistake of supposing I'm a weak, defenseless female, I assure you I am not. Nor, for that matter, am I a lonely, love-starved woman who'd be easy pickings for a strong, virile Yankee looking for a quick hour of pleasure. Let me warn you that I'm never without a loaded pistol and I know how to use it. I even sleep with the pistol under my pillow at night." Her blue eyes narrowed threateningly and her voice lowered a register. "Lay a hand on me and I'll kill you, Captain Northway."

Kurt had listened quietly throughout. His forest-green eyes had remained steadily fixed on her face. His intense scrutiny made Helen nervous, but to get her cool threat across, she felt obliged to staunchly hold his riveting gaze.

She felt a chill skip up her spine when, holding her with those forest-green eyes, his voice was seemingly unperturbed as he said, "I'm a Yankee, Mrs. Courtney, not an animal." He placed a hand flat on the table before her. "Take a good look at my hand," he quietly ordered, and she did so, noticing his fingers, which were long and slender as if molded by a sculptor.

Her eyes on the lean brown hand, she heard him say in a low, soft baritone, "This hand has *never* been on a woman . . ." he paused, and Helen's eyes lifted to again meet his, "who didn't want it there."

Chapter Four

Kurt withdrew his hand, pushed back his chair, and rose lithely to his feet. But he didn't move away. He stood there looming above, continuing to watch her with the patient stillness of a predatory cat. His deep forest-green eyes boring down on her with unnerving intensity, he extended his hand. The same suntanned, long-fingered hand which had lain on the table before her.

Swallowing with some difficulty, Helen automatically laid her slim white hand atop his smooth palm. The breath left her body when his hand closed around hers and she felt her fingers crushed in the warmth of his palm. With the firm pressure of his hand on hers, he gently, commandingly drew her to her feet.

Helen made a slight effort to withdraw her hand, but he held it—and her—fast. His strong tanned fingers sliding down to encircle her fragile wrist, Kurt lifted her hand up before his dark face and thoughtfully studied it.

His forest-green gaze touching each slim finger in turn, he said, "Is it necessary, Mrs. Courtney, for me to warn you to keep this soft white hand off me?"

Helen bristled. "Don't be ridiculous!"

"Is it? I don't think so. I respect the fact that you're a woman who loved and was loved by her husband." His wide shoulders seemed to slump minutely and his breath became a sigh. "Afford me the same consideration. I loved my wife with passionate devotion. And while the possibility obviously has never occurred to you, perhaps I don't want another woman's hands touching me. Can you appreciate that?"

"I ... I ... yes ... yes, I can." Helen, chastised, nodded.

He immediately released her hand. "Good. Then we understand each other a bit better. Sleep with your gun if you wish, but you won't need it to protect yourself." He smiled then and took a step backward. "At least not from me."

Eyes narrowed, Helen watched him turn and descend the porch steps. He crossed the yard with long, supple strides, his slow catlike movements radiating fluid grace and masculine confidence.

It was in that moment Helen decided she didn't like him. Not one bit. And it was more than his being the hated enemy, a conquering Yankee. She wouldn't have liked the tall, dark Kurt Northway had he been born and raised right there in Baldwin County.

It was his cool, self-assured manner, his ability to make her feel foolish and awkward that infuriated her. She was used to being the one in control. She was accustomed to feeling totally competent and capable of handling difficult situations and difficult people.

Especially men.

Since the day Will had ridden off to war, she had calmly, quietly discouraged numerous male approaches with fierce looks and flat-footed defiance. The nerve of this dark stranger asking if *he* should warn *her* to keep *her* hands off *him*. It would be a freezing day in Hades before she had any desire to touch the arrogant Yankee bastard!

"Captain Northway!" she called after him, her blue eyes flashing with indignity.

Kurt paused, turned, and looked squarely at her. "Yes, ma'am?"

"I . . . I . . ." Helen stammered, sighed, and shook her head. Irritably blowing a wayward lock of blond hair up off her forehead, she said, "We'll clean the quarters now, this afternoon. If we finish in time, you can begin plowing. Otherwise, you'll start all regular chores at dawn tomorrow."

"Good enough," said Kurt. "But there's really no need for you to help with the cleaning. I can do it."

But Helen did help.

Had it been only Kurt Northway who was to occupy the dingy quarters, she wouldn't have bothered. But since a five-year-old boy who had seen far too much tragedy in his short life was to live there for the summer, she wanted to do what she could to make sure the place was more habitable.

While the tired, displaced Charlie slept the afternoon away on the settee under the old live oak, Helen and Kurt busied themselves putting the quarters in order.

Kurt carried the dusty feather mattress outdoors for airing in the sun while Helen yanked down rotting curtains from the windows. Kurt whistled while he hauled the remaining furniture outdoors to be washed down. Her hair tied up in a white bandanna, the soiled gray work dress back on, Helen swept the wooden floors with a long-handled palmetto broom.

Kurt carried pail after pail of water from the well. Helen fetched homemade lye soap and strong-bristled brushes. On their hands and knees they scoured the wooden floor. Applying plenty of elbow grease, they crawled and scrubbed and swiped, making wide arcs with the stiff-bristled soapy brushes.

Laboring with single-minded intent, the two were unaware they were on a collision course. Working different sides of the room and facing opposite directions, they slowly, surely backed toward each other on all fours.

Inevitably they collided.

Helen's swaying bottom bumped soundly into Kurt's firmly muscled buttocks. Helen loudly winced. Kurt sharply inhaled. Both simultaneously levered themselves to their knees. Their shoulder blades banged together. Helen gasped. Kurt exhaled. Their heads snapped around. Their faces were mere inches apart. They found themselves looking directly into each other's eyes.

Helen's snapped with annoyance. Kurt's fixed gaze was one of apologetic solicitude.

"Did I hurt you?" he asked, turning swiftly on his knees to face her, his hands lifting to clasp her upper arms.

"No," Helen assured him, pushing anxiously against his chest. Shrugging free of his grip, she shot to her feet. "You finish this. I'll go to the house and gather up some towels and bed linens."

She snatched the bandanna off her head and whirled away. Kurt sat back on his heels and watched her storm out the open door. He shook his dark head. The lovely widow's aversion to him was intense. His young son's hostility was almost as acute. It was going to be one hell of a long, uncomfortable summer.

Kurt shrugged and went back to work.

Inside the house, Helen stood at the cedar-lined chest of drawers where the linens were kept. She crouched down on her heels, pulled out the bottom drawer—the drawer containing discarded linens which had been mended or were permanently stained or torn. She snatched up a yellowing pair of unbleached domestic sheets and a couple of mismatched pillowcases.

She closed the drawer, rose, and stood there with the less-than-exquisite bed linens in the crook of her arm, telling herself they were plenty good enough for a Yan-

kee's bed. She gave a quick, affirming nod of her head
for emphasis.

But what about the innocent little boy, a nagging inner voice asked. Should he have to sleep on such
coarse linens? Should he be made to lay that small
blond head on rough, ragged pillowcases because his
father fought on the wrong side in the war?

Sighing, Helen put the unbleached sheets back
where she got them. From a top drawer of the chest
she took out snowy-white, silky-soft sheets and a pair
of matching cases with delicate lace trim. Muttering to
herself, she returned to the quarters and Kurt
Northway.

Together they made up the bed with clean white
sheets which smelled faintly of fragrant cedar. Carefully avoiding his forest-green eyes, Helen ran a hand
over the downy soft bedding, then tucked a pillow underneath her chin and drew a lace-edged case up over
it.

She placed the pillow at the head of the bed,
plumped it up, felt Kurt Northway's eyes on her, and
stiffened.

"What is it?" she demanded, looking up in time to
catch an intensely wistful expression in the depths of
his green eyes. It vanished instantly and he smiled. She
didn't. She said, "Why are you staring at me, Captain?"

"I'm sorry, ma'am." His voice was very soft, very
low. "The last woman I saw tuck a pillow under her
chin to put a lace-edged case on it was my wife." His
wide shoulders lowered and lifted. "I'd forgotten it . . .
until now . . . until you did it just the same way."

"I'm sorry if it brought back painful memories,
Captain"—she picked up the second pillow, tucked it
under her chin, and began pulling the freshly laundered
case up it—"but this is the way I've always done it.
The way my grandmother taught me."

She tossed the cased pillow to him and turned away. He caught it, lifted it to his face, inhaled deeply of the clean, fresh scent, then carefully placed it at the head of the bed beside its twin.

Helen looked around and saw Charlie standing in the doorway, yawning, rubbing his knuckles into this eyes. She smiled at him, but her smile wasn't returned. In a warm, soft voice she asked if he'd like to help. Charlie said nothing. Finally he turned away, sat down on the stoop, and put his chin in his hands.

Concerned, Helen shot a questioning look at Kurt. He shook his head as if to say he didn't know what to do about the silent Charlie.

They themselves talked very little, an economy of words being all that was necessary to complete their tasks. When they finished in the late afternoon, the place was hardly recognizable as the same dusty, ill-kept room they'd first entered.

New blue-and-white-checked curtains graced the many windows. The battered furniture gleamed with polish and smelled pleasantly of lemon oil. A scarf lovingly crocheted by Helen's grandmother covered the scarred top of the highboy and a blue-and-white-checked cloth spread atop the small square table reached the clean wooden floor.

One straight-backed chair was pulled up to the table. The others, unusable since their cane bottoms had long since worn through, were neatly stacked out of the way at the back of the room. A large hooked rug lay on the floor beside the feather bed, ready for the touch of bare feet.

A blue glass bowl in the front windowsill was filled with yellow jonquils. And on the nightstand beside the newly made bed, a perfect pale pink rose rested in a sparkling bud vase.

Tired, dirty, their clothes damp with perspiration,

Helen and Kurt stood looking about, inspecting their handiwork.

"Charlie, come in here," called Kurt, "come look at our new home."

Turning, Helen waited expectantly, hoping Charlie would come inside. Maybe the sight of the clean, spacious room—so different-looking now with the luxurious sheets and the fresh window curtains—would cheer him. Would make him feel more at home.

Her hopeful gaze resting on the narrow back of the little boy seated on the stoop, Helen coaxed too. "Your father's right, Charlie. The place looks real nice now. Come inside and I'll show you where to put your things. You can have the bottom drawer of the highboy. Charlie?"

Charlie didn't budge. Nor did he answer. Just stayed where he was, as he was. Seated on the stoop, elbows on his knees, face in his hands, unreachable. Helen looked worriedly at Kurt.

Kurt smiled at Helen and said, "Well, it sure looks like a palace to me, Mrs. Courtney."

Helen didn't reply. She moved forward and fussily straightened the stack of white towels lying beside a large china bowl and water pitcher atop the highboy. Then, giving the room one last sweeping glance, she crossed to the door.

"Supper in an hour," she announced.

"We'll be there," replied Kurt, following.

Helen nodded, stepped past the uncommunicative Charlie, and started up the footpath toward the house. A few yards away, she glanced back over her shoulder.

Charlie still sat on the stoop, grimacing, appearing afraid and unhappy, his small, pale face screwed up in a terrible frown. His father stood behind him, smiling, appearing totally relaxed and in charge, his teeth gleaming white in the bronzed darkness of his face.

Helen whipped her head around and picked up her pace.

Lord, it was going to be one long, uncomfortable summer.

Chapter Five

"**D**ominic! Dommmminiiiiic! Dom, get yourself in here if you're coming!"

At bedtime that night Helen, barefooted and in her white batiste nightgown, stood on the side gallery just outside her bedroom, calling impatiently to her wayward tom. If she couldn't get him to come inside now, the inconsiderate Dominic would wake her in the middle of the night, scraping his sharp claws down the closed door and moaning pitifully.

"Dom, this is your last chance. Either you come in this minute or not at all!"

No sign of him.

Helen padded across the wide balcony and put both hands on the railing. She leaned over the waist-high railing and searched for the missing cat. Her sweeping gaze moved over the far reaches of the untended yard to the fruit orchard and pecan grove beyond. She scanned the big tree-rimmed pasture north of the house. Squinting, she peered toward the farm's thickly timbered wildwoods bordering the cleared fields.

She saw no flashing animal eyes.

No Dom.

Not in any mood for the spoiled feline's game playing, Helen turned away, started back inside, but paused. Suddenly she wondered, were her lodgers asleep? Was the dark Yankee sleeping peacefully? She started toward the back of the house.

After only a few steps, she stopped and shrugged slender shoulders. What did she care? Let the Yankee captain stay up all night or go to bed with the chickens, it made no difference to her. Just as long as he was up before the sun, discharging his duties.

Yawning, Helen returned to her bedroom.

Dominic sat there before the open door, the unusual green eyes inherent to his breed fixed admonishingly on her. Accusing her. As if she had been the one out tomcatting around.

"You green-eyed devil!" Helen scolded good-naturedly. "You'll wind up sleeping in the barn with the Yankee if you're not careful."

Dominic's reply was a bored closing of his green eyes and a wide yawn. Helen laughed, bent, scooped the cat up in her arms, and went inside. Once in the bedroom, Dominic squirmed out of her grasp, raced across the room, and leaped agilely up onto the high feather mattress. Stretching out at the foot of the bed, he flexed his front paws several times, extending the sharp claws, pulling at the bedcovers. Then he yawned again, laid his aristocratic head down, and allowed his lazy lids to close over the green eyes.

Dom was fast asleep.

Helen wished, and not for the first time, that it was as easy for her to fall asleep as it was for her cat. How wonderful to simply stretch out and be immediately lost in peaceful, dreamless slumber.

It wasn't that way for her. It was never easy to fall asleep, no matter how hard she had worked or how weary she was when she went to bed. Bed was a lonely—sometimes frightening—place to her. It had been since Will had gone away to war.

Sighing, Helen sat down on the side of the bed. From a carved wooden box on the night table, she took out an oval-shaped cameo locket. She opened the locket to the small photograph inside. A young, handsome Will Courtney smiled up at her.

Helen looked at the smiling Will for a long wistful moment, raised the cameo to her lips, and kissed the tiny photograph. She snapped the locket shut and placed it back inside the carved box. She reached for the loaded pistol. Tucking it under her pillow, she recalled the Yankee's words: "You won't need the gun to protect yourself. . . . At least not from me."

Maybe not. All the same, she'd feel better knowing the revolver was there within easy reach. Just like always.

Helen turned out the lamp and got into bed. She stretched luxuriously, sighed, but didn't bother closing her eyes. What was the use? She'd lie awake half the night. Just like . . . just like . . . just like . . .

Before the thought could be completed, Helen Courtney was sound asleep.

Kurt Northway wasn't.

While his son slept soundly beside him, Kurt was wide awake. He lay on his back, arms folded beneath his head, wondering why sleep wouldn't come.

This clean spacious room was the best quarters he had been billeted in since before the war. The bed where he lay was soft and comfortable, the sheets freshly laundered and smelling faintly of cedar. Shafts of moonlight made pleasing patterns on the floor and walls. A gentle breeze ruffled the blue-and-white-checked curtains. The night stillness was peaceful, lulling.

He wasn't hungry. He wasn't dirty. He wasn't cold. He wasn't hot. He wasn't lying on the hard ground somewhere. He wasn't listening for the whine of miniballs. He didn't have to wonder if he'd live to see the sunrise.

Still, he couldn't sleep.

A restlessness he couldn't curb made Kurt throw back the covering sheet and ease himself out of bed. He tiptoed across the room, slipped out the door, and sat down on the stoop.

A gentle night wind off the bay cooled his heated skin, lifted locks of his dark hair. The sweet scent of honeysuckle carried on the welcome breeze. High overhead a full moon sailed leisurely around the heavens, silvering everything below.

Kurt's brooding eyes slowly lifted to that romantic summer moon.

A deepening loneliness came over him. Inevitably he began thinking of another night. Another time. Another place.

With vivid clarity he remembered the lovely warm summer night when he and the young, trusting Gail had lain stretched out naked in the moonlight spilling across the bed in their honeymoon suite. Kissing. Talking. Laughing.

Making love.

Kurt felt a familiar squeezing in his chest and wondered if he'd ever be free of the pain. It was strange, but since the war had ended and he'd been reunited with Charlie, he missed his wife more than ever.

Hoofbeats.

The steady drumming of a horse's hooves striking the ground pulled Helen from a deep, restful slumber. Startled awake, she lunged up, grabbed the pistol from under the pillow, and raced across the darkened room. Heart pounding with alarm, she dashed anxiously out onto the gallery, ready to confront the nighttime intruder.

Pistol cocked and held straight out in both trembling hands, Helen crossed to the railing, prepared to quickly fire one warning shot, then take aim. She stopped short of pulling the trigger when she saw the horse.

The Yankee's big sorrel stallion was thundering around the tree-rimmed pasture north of the house. The Yankee was astride the mighty beast.

Helen slowly lowered the gun.

Framed against the pearl-gray light of the coming dawn, horse and rider were unquestionably a splendid sight to behold. The princely pair seemed to be more a mystical apparition than actual flesh and blood. Helen blinked to make sure they were real.

She'd never seen a horse move with quite the same swift graceful speed as the fleet-footed sorrel stallion. Nor had she ever seen a rider handle a big powerful thoroughbred quite as easily as the man on his back.

The Yankee was naked to the waist, his bare shoulders broad and well muscled. His faded blue uniform trousers rode low around his slim hips and hugged his hard thighs and long legs. His feet, shoved into the stirrups, were bare. His uncombed jet hair was flying wildly about his head and on his dark, handsome face was a look of pure, unadulterated pleasure.

He appeared to be enjoying the early-morning romp as much as the speeding horse. Forgetting herself, Helen enjoyed their fun as well. The heavy gun lowered and held at her side, her lips slightly parted, she savored a few stolen seconds of guileless joy. Hardly daring to breathe or move, she silently observed the superbly configured man atop the superbly configured stallion. Watching the daring duo, Helen caught herself smiling foolishly.

She promptly frowned when she caught sight of Bessie, the milk cow, standing out in the middle of the big pasture. Whirling away, Helen hurried back inside. All traces of the smile and the joy were gone.

Rising irritation replaced both.

The Yankee's first morning in her employ and he was exercising his damn thoroughbred instead of milking the cow! She had made it crystal clear that his very first chore each day was to do the milking. Obviously he'd paid no attention. He was out racing his stallion around the pasture like a carefree boy while she was left to do the milking.

Growing angrier with each passing minute, Helen washed up, dressed hurriedly, and started through the big, silent house. Reciting all the scathing things she'd say to the irresponsible Yankee, she burst into the kitchen and quickly skidded to a stop.

On the drainboard sat the big milk pail, a clean damp dish towel draped over the top. Curious but skeptical, Helen moved to the cabinet. Carefully she peeled back the covering dish towel.

The pail was rim-full of fresh, frothy milk.

Try as she might, Helen could find no fault with the Yankee's willingness to work or with his ability to handle the myriad chores which went with running a farm.

Still, she didn't like him, although she had to admit he was unfailingly polite and deferential. He seemed to be a gentleman and he projected an air of quiet intelligence. But he was too self-assured to suit her. Worse, he radiated a subtle animal magnetism that bothered her. There was something about him, something . . . dangerous. It was as if beneath that cool, polished veneer lurked the primitive, the savage.

She didn't like it when he stood too close or took her hand to help her from a chair or when he held her pinned with those forest-green eyes. In his imposing presence she felt flustered and uneasy; he made her uncomfortable.

Nonetheless, he *had* pitched in right from the first morning and had lifted a large part of the burden off her shoulders. He insisted that he be the one to do all the heavy plowing. And he'd had old Duke hitched up and was out in the field by the time Helen finished the breakfast dishes.

Helen was grateful and relieved to have such dependable help. Before he came, she'd been spending all her daylight hours in the fields and so many other projects had been neglected. Now she'd have the opportunity to do the washing and ironing, churn some fresh butter, gather fruit from the orchard, prune her rosebushes, weed the yard, tend the neglected flower beds, do a bit of baking, and give the house a proper cleaning.

The week seemed to rush by in a whirl of activity.

Late Friday evening Helen was in the kitchen fixing supper. While she stood at the wood cook stove frying chicken, she thought back over the past few days.

She was amazed at how much she and the Yankee had accomplished in the short time he'd been there. The corn was just about planted, a task that would have taken her at least another week had she been alone.

To give the devil his due, the man wasn't afraid of hard work. Uncomplaining, he toiled from sunrise to sunset, stopping briefly when she took his noon meal down to the field. Then he'd sit down under a shade tree, ravenously devour the food, and return immediately to work.

A hint of a smile played at Helen's lips as she turned a browning drumstick in the heavy black skillet.

No matter what she took the Yankee for his dinner or what she put before him at suppertime, he acted as if it were the finest meal he'd ever sat down to.

Her smile suddenly fled.

She only wished Charlie shared his father's healthy appetite.

Helen shook her head worriedly.

Little Charlie was sullen and withdrawn. He refused to talk. He never smiled. He hardly touched the hot meals she prepared. She felt sorry for Charlie. He was so young and so lost; just a baby, really. He badly needed his mother. His father was a stranger to him.

The expression she saw all too often in Charlie's big brown eyes brought back the vivid memory of a time when she was about Charlie's age and her grandparents had left her with friends while they traveled to New Orleans. She had clung to them for dear life when they returned, begging them never, ever to leave her again.

Poor Charlie. He must feel deserted, alone, frightened, just like she felt then.

Like she often felt now when she lay awake in the darkness of the night, worried and alone.

Chapter Six

I t didn't take long for the word to spread.

Within days the gentry of Spanish Fort were whispering that one of their own was guilty of unacceptable behavior.

"Have you heard?" asked the banker's pink-faced wife, Hattie Price, when the ladies of her weekly quilting bee gathered that Friday afternoon. "A dirty, low-down Yankee is living right there on the old family farm with Jackson Burke's widowed granddaughter!"

"Outrageous," fumed Mary Lou Riddle, middle-aged widow of the late Colonel Tyson B. Riddle.

"Unforgivable!" declared Rose Lacey, proud mother of two wounded war veterans.

"It simply can't be true," said dark-haired, glamorous Yasmine Parnell. Widowed in the war's closing days, Yasmine's quiet acceptance of her personal tragedy and the way she continued to discharge her social and charitable obligations was admirable.

Shaking her graying head and rolling her eyes heavenward, dressmaker Betsy Reed, noted designer of Mobile's fanciest Mardi Gras costumes, said, "Why, her husband, young Will Courtney, that fine Southern gentleman who laid down his life for the Cause, is surely spinning in his grave!"

Scandalous! Disgraceful! Shameful!

All unanimously agreed, their needles and eyes

flashing. A Yankee's presence on Helen's farm was unspeakable.

Yet the ladies spent the afternoon speaking of nothing else. Distasteful as the subject was, they couldn't let it go. They speculated about the shocking things which might be going on right there on the old Burke place.

Why, the man was a Yankee, after all, and so being, was certainly no part of a gentleman. Young Helen Courtney should have had the good sense to know that she'd be in constant danger of physical attack from a base, animalistic Northern brute.

"Perhaps she wouldn't mind a dollop of danger," said saucy newlywed Kitty Pepper with a wink and a toss of her dark glossy curls. "I hear the Yankee is quite handsome. Jet-black hair, Indian-dark skin, and so tall and lean."

"Kitty Pepper, hush your mouth this minute," scolded her blushing, outraged mother.

"Momma, I'm only repeating what I've heard." Kitty was undaunted. "My stars above, I thought you ladies would want to know."

Nodding, the women around the quilting frame focused eagerly on the young smiling Kitty. She giggled, and pressing a hand to full, high bosom, confided in a soft little-girl voice, "Now, I haven't seen the Yankee myself, but Grandma Baxter told Mavis King who told Beth Forrester who told Louise Downing who told me . . ." Kitty paused and drew a breath, "that there's 'a look of controlled savagery' about the Yankee!"

"Kitty Fay Pepper!" all scolded in unison.

"Hand me my smelling salts," murmured Mary Lou Riddle. "And Helen's such a pretty young thing, tall and slender with all that golden hair. What could she be thinking!"

* * *

The slender, golden-haired topic of their conversation soon learned what the sewing bee—and everyone else in Spanish Fort—thought about her sheltering a Yankee.

On Saturday afternoon Helen—waving away Kurt's offer to do it for her—hitched old Duke up to the wagon and drove the eight miles into Spanish Fort.

Helen always looked forward to her weekly trips to the village. Their purpose was to purchase needed supplies, but she generally stayed on for a couple of hours after her order had been filled. Other ladies were in town Saturdays and Helen enjoyed visiting with them. It was a deserved and welcome respite after a long, hard week of working alone at the farm.

On this particular Saturday, however, Helen had a nagging suspicion that the afternoon might not prove all that enjoyable.

Her palms grew moist when she guided old Duke up Main Street past the sheriff's office and the Baldwin County Jail. The Red Rose Saloon. Beekham's Furniture Store. The Spanish Fort newspaper office.

Helen gritted her teeth when she passed a many-windowed office whose glass-paned front door had LOVELESS ENTERPRISES written across it in fancy gold lettering. It was all too easy to picture the powerful, wealthy Niles Loveless inside, seated grandly behind his immense mahogany desk.

She was more than a little apprehensive as she pulled up on old Duke, wound the reins around the brake handle, and stepped down into the street outside Jake's General Store.

She'd told herself all the way into town that everything was fine. Just fine. More than likely no one yet knew about the Yankee and his son. But even if they did, they wouldn't think anything of it. She had always hired seasonal hands to help with the spring planting.

It wasn't her fault that she couldn't find local laborers this year. People would surely understand.

She was wrong.

As soon as Helen stepped inside Jake Autry's cavernous general store, she knew the word had gotten around. A knot of men loitering by a glasswares table saw her, nodded feebly, and immediately began talking among themselves, their voices lowered. Helen felt sure they were talking about her.

And the Yankee.

Ignoring them, she squared her slender shoulders, smiled, and proceeded directly to a wide counter behind which the skinny, bearded Jake Autry was unpacking sacks of chewing tobacco from a wooden carton.

"Hello, Jake. How are you this afternoon? Warm for early May, isn't it? Makes me dread August."

"Ma'am," mumbled Jake, and that was all.

This from a man who would talk your arm off if given half the chance. Never had Helen been in Jake's store that he hadn't filled her in on everything that had happened during the week. Furthermore, he had always good-naturedly passed along messages between her and her many friends and acquaintances.

Not today.

Jake had little to say, responding with a clipped "Yes" "No" or "I don't know" when she asked a question. Not only was he unusually closemouthed, he was also unusually quick in filling her order. He had never been either before.

Jake clearly wanted her out of his store as soon as possible. Pretending a nonchalance she didn't feel, Helen calmly bade Jake good day. She swept up her many purchases and turned to leave. Not one of the gentlemen offered to carry the supplies out to the wagon.

With a sigh and groan, Helen managed to dump

the heavy load onto the wagon bed behind the seat. She drew a breath, looked around, and caught sight of the Livingston sisters coming down the shaded wooden sidewalk.

Helen immediately smiled. She was genuinely glad to see the aged, eccentric spinsters. An idea popped into her mind. She would invite the fluttery, tremulous little pair to join her for a cooling lemonade at the Bayside Hotel dining room. Her treat. They'd be thrilled to death, bless their old hearts.

Helen started forward. The tiny, white-haired Livingston sisters looked up and saw her. They pointedly crossed the street, averting their eyes and twittering to each other as they went.

Stunned, Helen stopped short, feeling as if she'd been slapped in the face. She looked anxiously around. Had anyone seen the Livingston sisters openly snub her? If she ran into other friends, would they rebuff her too?

Helen stood there in the hot May sunshine feeling the icy winds of censure and ostracism chill her to the bone. It hurt. It hurt badly, but she understood. These gentle people had every reason to hate the Yankees. *She* hated the Yankees! She only wished the townspeople could understand her unique predicament.

Fighting back tears that made her eyes smart, Helen hurried to the security of her wagon. She lunged up onto the high leather seat, unwrapped the long reins, and immediately put old Duke in motion. Looking neither to the left nor the right, she turned the buggy about and uncharacteristically laid the whip to the old pony's backside.

Surprised, Duke pricked up his ears, neighed indignantly, and trotted down Main Street, moving faster than he'd moved in years.

Helen sighed with relief when the false-front buildings of Spanish Fort were left behind. On she drove. A scattering of houses bordered Main at the south edge of town. A face appeared in a front window of the Logan house—Francis Logan peering out at her from behind the curtains. Across the street, Myrtle Thetford stood on the porch, hands on hips, shaking her gray head accusingly.

The message couldn't have been made more clear. What she had done was considered traitorous and disloyal. A deed of such perfidy, the townspeople were horrified.

Helen gritted her teeth and told herself it didn't matter. It *couldn't* matter. She couldn't let it matter.

She had one main goal in life. To maintain—now and forever—ownership of the farm on which three generations of Burkes had lived and laughed and loved. And died. Since Grandfather Jackson D. Burke cleared the land and built the house for his bride in 1798, the Burkes had called the place home.

The farm, the adjoining timberlands, and the house—such as they were—were hers now. She was the last Burke left. It was up to her. That's why she had hired a Union captain. So that she could hold on to her home.

Helen's delicate jaw hardened and her chin lifted defiantly.

If it took a despised Yankee's help to keep from losing her land, so be it. Let people talk.

One native Alabamian and Spanish Fort old-timer who neither gossiped about Helen nor tolerated anyone else talking about her in his presence was widower Hamilton Minor Grubbs.

Still as spry and as active as a boy, Hamilton Minor Grubbs was fast approaching his seventy-first birthday. A man of medium height and sturdy frame, he was at least fifty pounds overweight from a lifetime's indulgence in fried foods and rich desserts. Nobody enjoyed a hearty meal more than Hamilton Grubbs, and he had the rounded belly to prove it.

That belly shook up and down and rolled like waves on the bay when he laughed, which was often. So often, in fact, he was called Jolly Grubbs for his happy, easygoing nature. The rotund Jolly had a full head of snowy-white hair, a ruddy complexion, apple-red cheeks, a ready smile revealing a mouthful of strong white teeth which were all his own, and a pair of blue eyes that twinkled constantly with devilment and fun.

The white-haired old gentleman, who lived alone on a little strip of cleared bottomland bordering the Burke farm, was Helen's closest neighbor. And closest friend.

Jolly Grubbs had known Helen all her life. He had paced the wide wooden gallery with Helen's nervous grandfather when Helen's father was born. He'd paced again with her father on the hot summer night in 1839 when she came squalling and red-faced into the world.

Jolly and his wife, Meg, were the first ones to the farm when word reached Spanish Fort that the Louisiana coastal steamer *Delta Princess* had gone down, taking Helen's young parents to watery, premature graves when she was just four years old.

Jolly had been there at his bedside when his dear old friend Jackson Burke drew his last wheezing breath. And when Jackson's frail widow—Helen's last blood relative—had followed him two years later.

He was there to give the bride away when a glowing twenty-one-year-old Helen Burke married the adoring, well-scrubbed Will Courtney. He was there again to comfort her when the young wife became a widow.

Jolly Grubbs knew more about Helen Courtney than anyone, save maybe Em Ellicott. Em Ellicott was Helen's best girlfriend. The two young women, who were the same age, had been as close as sisters since childhood. Jolly figured they shared all their best secrets.

But presently Jolly knew something about Helen

that Em didn't know. He knew that a dark-haired Yankee and his young son were living at the old Burke place. Em Ellicott was off in New Orleans spending a couple of weeks with some cousins, so she didn't yet know about the Yankee.

Jolly knew because he was the one who had steered Kurt Northway to Helen's farm.

Jolly prided himself on being an excellent judge of character. After only the briefest of conversations with Kurt Northway in Spanish Fort on Tuesday past, Jolly had known instinctively that Northway was a decent man who'd pose no threat to a fine young woman like Helen.

Northway needed work.

Helen needed work done.

So Jolly had sent the Yankee captain to the Southern widow.

He had sat there on the wooden sidewalk in a chair tipped back against the front of Jake's General Store watching the tall Yankee lead his sorrel stallion out of town and in the direction of Helen's farm.

Now on this warm Saturday Jolly's blue eyes twinkled as he contemplated paying a late afternoon visit to the Burke farm. He sighed suddenly and went in search of his old straw hat.

It was indeed a sad state of affairs that had brought together two such strange bedfellows.

Chapter Seven

Helen heaved a sigh of relief when she turned old Duke onto the tree-bordered lane leading down to her coastal property. Swallowed up in the thick cooling shade of the towering live oaks, she felt warm for the first time all afternoon. Much warmer than when she'd driven down Main Street in town with the bright May sun beating directly on her.

Helen's slender shoulders slumped with instant relaxation. All afternoon she'd held them rigidly erect. She had assumed a false air of utter indifference which she could finally discard. Never in her life had she been as glad to get back to the farm. She could hardly wait to reach the safe, welcome haven of home.

Wishing she never again had to leave the sanctuary of the old bay-front place, Helen looked eagerly forward to a quiet, peaceful evening alone on the gallery, seated in her favorite armless rocker. There she would stay to her heart's content.

As when she was a child, she'd watch the lights of Mobile twinkle brightly across the bay. And she'd follow the movement of the riverboats as they steamed out of port on the protected waters, bound for New Orleans, Biloxi, and Pass Christian.

Shielded. Sheltered. Safe.

Helen emerged from the canopy of shade deciding she needn't go back into Spanish Fort for at least two weeks. By then Em would surely be home from New Orleans. Em would stand by her just as she always did.

Emma Louise Ellicott was no fair-weather friend. She was a fiercely loyal confidante who could be counted on, had been since they were little girls together. The Ellicotts were highly respected members of the South's Old Guard. Em's mother was a Bankhead and the Ellicotts were blue bloods who could trace their ancestors to the thrones of both England and France.

But Em wouldn't give a fig what the townspeople were saying. She never had. She'd as soon thumb her nose at the gentry as not. The indomitable Em wouldn't question Helen's decision to hire a Yankee. She'd realize that it had been absolutely necessary and would accept it without passing judgment.

Helen turned Duke up the wagon path leading to the farm's outbuildings. Reining the old pony to a stop directly before the plank corral, Helen frowned when Kurt Northway ducked out of the barn and into the fading afternoon sunlight.

The sight of him always disturbed her. Today more so than ever. Because of him she had suffered hurt and humiliation, had alienated friends and neighbors. Seeing him now, she was filled with resentment and unrestrained loathing.

This tall, dark Yankee captain was going about on her property as if he owned the place. No wonder the townspeople were incensed.

Kurt started toward Helen, pulling on his work shirt, shoving long arms into the sleeves. He didn't bother buttoning the shirt. It remained open, exposing his bare chest. Helen couldn't help but notice the dense growth of thick jet-black hair that covered the hard flat muscles and narrowed into a thick line going down his stomach.

She stiffened as he approached. She quickly tossed

the reins aside, put one foot on the wooden passenger step, and turned about, preparing to back down to the ground. She was determined to alight before he could reach her. She didn't quite make it.

Kurt was too swift for her.

"Allow me," he said, stepping up directly behind her.

"No, really, I don't need any help, I can—" Helen winced when she felt his strong hands encircle her waist.

"—manage quite well alone," he finished for her. "Down you go," he said, lowering her to the ground directly before him.

Helen immediately felt a fierce warmth emanating from his tall body, caught the scent of sun-heated flesh. She felt like shouting at him to get away from her. Before she could order him to move, Kurt stepped back. She spun about to face him, inexplicably flustered and annoyed.

Turning cold blue eyes on him, she said, "Captain Northway, did you complete the plowing in the lower south field?"

"Yes, ma'am," he said. "All finished."

She nodded curtly. "I don't suppose you've gotten around to clearing the weeds from the grape arbor so I can—"

"Done. Took care of it shortly after lunch."

"Any corn shucked for the—"

"Bushel baskets full."

Helen's perfectly arched eyebrows lifted accusingly. "Stock been fed?"

"Every living animal on the farm, except old Duke here." He grinned boyishly then, and added, "Well, that is, besides you, me, and Charlie."

Frustrated by the man's undeniable efficiency, Helen snapped, "Then I suggest you get started mending the fence down by—"

"Was it that bad?" Kurt interrupted.

"What?" She gave him an inquisitive look. "Was *what* that bad?"

"Your trip into Spanish Fort."

"My trip into . . . I have no idea what you're talking about."

"Yes, you do."

"I most certainly do not! I thoroughly enjoyed my afternoon in town."

Kurt shook his dark head, placed a flattened palm on his naked belly, and allowed the tips of his lean tanned fingers to languidly slip down inside the low-riding waistband of his faded blue trousers. "You needn't pretend with me, Mrs. Courtney."

Guiltily realizing that her eyes had followed the slow, seductive movement of his hand as it slid toward his trousers, Helen jerked her head up, glared at him, and said, "You're absolutely right, Captain! There is no need."

"Then stop it," he softly commanded. "The townspeople were unkind to you. Because of me. I can see it in your eyes. I'm sorry."

Helen opened her mouth to deny it, closed it without speaking. Suddenly desperate to have him out of her sight, Helen rudely attempted to push Kurt out of her way. Her hands flattened on his hair-covered chest, she immediately found her wrists encircled with his imprisoning fingers.

For a long second they stood looking warily at each other, their gazes locked, Helen's hands trapped on his chest. The feel, the texture of crisp curly hair and smooth heated flesh beneath was so strange, so frightening to her sensitive fingertips.

For Kurt it was every bit as strange, every bit as frightening to have a pair of soft feminine hands resting warmly against the naked flesh of his bare chest. Her palms pressed warmly over each flat brown nipple, he felt his chest involuntarily expand against her covering hands, his belly tighten responsively.

Each waited for the other to make a move.

The spell was broken by the sound of Jolly Grubbs's rumbling voice shouting a loud, cheery hello.

Kurt and Helen sprang apart as if they'd been caught in some deviant act.

Her face red with anger, frustration, and embarrassment, Helen called to the approaching white haired-gentleman. "Hello, Jolly. How are you this afternoon?"

"No great complaints," came the shouted reply as Jolly walked toward them, fanning himself with a battered, big-brimmed straw hat.

Helen smiled in Jolly's direction, then turned to Kurt and snapped, "See to Duke and put away the wagon!" She whirled away, but looked back and hissed beneath her breath, "And for heaven's sake, Captain, button up your clothes!"

Jolly Grubbs had purposely waited the five days between Tuesday and Saturday before paying a visit to the old Burke farm. He figured he'd give the Yankee captain and his boy a chance to get settled in. And Helen a chance to get used to having the pair around before he came over to check on them.

Once there, he encountered three people who were noticeably ill at ease with one another. Helen was not herself. She had always been a lively, outgoing young woman, full of tomfoolery. Warm and friendly in the extreme. Now she seemed unusually anxious and strangely self-conscious, almost stiff. She went to great lengths to avoid any eye contact with the Yankee captain.

Captain Kurt Northway was polite, genuinely respectful, as perfectly behaved a gentleman as a son of the South. But he appeared to be tightly coiled, as if he were consciously holding himself in check. Despite the seemingly relaxed attitude of Northway's body, Jolly sensed a deep, underlying edginess, a watch-spring tension.

And the boy?

Well, little Charlie Northway was totally unreachable. The child was locked up within himself, unwilling to share his feelings with anyone. Fear, distrust, and sadness shone from the child's big brown eyes. Was present in the downturned curve of the babyish lips, the frequent sagging of his small chin on his narrow chest.

Jolly invited himself to stay for supper and promptly accepted his invitation.

Knowing that Helen most likely didn't allow the Yankee or his son inside the house, he further suggested—in Kurt's presence so Helen couldn't veto the notion—that they all share the evening meal out on the back porch where they could take advantage of the breeze.

His appetite as hearty as ever, Jolly smacked his lips appreciatively and ate with great gusto. After eagerly devouring several pieces of golden fried chicken, he joked that he had enjoyed the appetizer, now what was for supper, and his blue eyes twinkled with merriment.

Kurt courteously chuckled. Helen graciously smiled. Charlie's glum expression never changed.

Jolly polished off two thick slices of apple pie, pushed back from the table, groaned with satisfaction, and loosened his belt a notch. Sighing with pleasure, he withdrew a cigar from inside his shirt pocket, put it under his nose, and sniffed it. And caught the brief flicker of envy in Kurt Northway's green eyes.

"Join me in a smoke, won't you, Captain?" he said, and fished a second cigar from his pocket.

"Thank you, Mr. Grubbs," said Kurt, and took the offered cheroot.

"No need to be so formal, son. Call me Jolly. Every-

one else does." He looked at the clench-jawed Helen.
"Don't they, Helen, my girl?" Before she could reply,
Jolly asked Kurt, "Know what we used to call Helen
when she was a little shaver of two or three years
old?"

"Hamilton Minor Grubbs," Helen warned, "don't
you dare!"

Blue eyes still atwinkle, Jolly nodded sheepishly and
said no more, knowing that when Helen addressed him
by his full name, she meant business. He cleared his
throat and steered the conversation to safer topics. He
insisted Kurt tell them about his Maryland home.

Kurt volunteered little, but Jolly questioned him tenaciously. Showing little interest in what he had to say,
Helen nonetheless learned that Kurt Northway had
lived and worked on a large horse farm since he was a
boy. And that the farm's owner had taught him all
there was to know about training fine thoroughbreds.
Further probing questions from Jolly revealed that Kurt
was to be given property of his own by the man who
had been like a father to him. Their agreement was that
Kurt would give Willis Dunston five more years of service in exchange for a section of prime Maryland
grassland adjoining his own.

Jolly knew instinctively when he could get nothing
more out of Kurt, so he turned the conversation to the
weather, the crops, and the upcoming Baldwin County
Fair. As he spoke, he keenly observed and evaluated
each one of the uncomfortable trio seated at the table
with him.

Maybe there was nothing he could do about the obvious impasse between the two adults. That was their
lookout. Something they would have to work out—or
not.

But he *would* take the mute, moping Charlie
Northway in hand.

And the sooner the better.

Chapter Eight

Jolly Grubbs showed up at the farm again the next day.

The quiet serenity of the lazy Sunday afternoon was shattered when Jolly, mounted astride his big gray gelding, came galloping down the tree-edged lane yipping and shouting and waving his straw hat like a wild, unruly youngster.

Helen was out beyond the yard at the south side of the house, cutting roses and dropping them into a basket on her arm. She heard the racket, looked up, saw Jolly coming, and shook her head, smiling.

It had oft been said of Jolly Grubbs that he possessed "an excessive propensity for fun and foolishness." That statement had a great degree of truth. For a seventy-year-old man who had lived through more than his share of loss and tragedy, Jolly had managed to keep an amazingly cheerful disposition. His curiosity was unlimited, his optimism unshakable, his zest for living awe-inspiring.

Jolly thundered up to a clod-flinging stop a few yards from where Helen stood, climbed out of the saddle, and tossed the reins to the ground. Snorting and shaking his head, the gray gelding ambled off, his master paying him no mind.

Jolly hurried to Helen, flashing the sunniest of smiles, looking as if he harbored the juiciest of secrets.

"It's after three o'clock. You're a trifle late for dinner, Jolly," Helen told him.

"Then, by jeeters, I'll have to stay for supper," he said, enfolding her in a quick, bone-crushing bear hug as if it had been days instead of hours since last he'd seen her.

"Indeed," she said when he released her, checking to make sure her cut roses hadn't spilled from the basket. "So . . . what's on your mind? You're up to something; I can tell by the mischief in your eyes." She smiled at him.

Shoving his straw hat back on his head, he said, "I'll get to that, but first tell me how it went in town yesterday." His white eyebrows lifted questioningly.

"Why, it went okay," Helen said, continuing to smile. "Just fine." She saw no reason to burden this kindhearted man who worried about her far too much as it was. "Really."

"You sure, child?" He looked skeptical. "I know they've all heard about the Yankee being out here. Did anybody mention him to you?"

"Not a soul," she said with complete honesty, failing to further add that no one said a word to her. Period.

"Well, you have any trouble, you tell old Jolly. I won't hold still for anybody giving my girl a hard time. Why, when I was a young man, I called out a fellow for—"

"I know," Helen interrupted, having heard the story of the infamous Spanish Fort duel many times before. "There's not going to be any trouble, so relax." She tweaked his left ear. "And promise me you won't be fighting any duels to defend my honor."

"I promise. But anybody gets smart with you, just you tell me and I'll—"

"What brings you over here this afternoon with that devilish gleam in your eyes?" she again interrupted, anxious to get him onto another subject.

Jolly grinned, looked about to make sure they were alone. "Where's the captain?"

"I would imagine he's down at the corral currying that big sorrel thoroughbred," Helen said. "He spends every free moment there."

"Where's the boy?"

"If Charlie isn't lying listlessly on the settee under the live oak, he's sitting on the back stoop of the quarters." She sighed wearily. "That poor little boy. I'm afraid it's quite hopeless."

His smile back in place and as bright as the May sunshine, Jolly scolded, "Why, Helen Burke Courtney, you know better than that. There's not a single one of God's own children that's in a hopeless fix. Least of all a golden-haired little boy."

"I don't know," she said thoughtfully. "I've tried to draw Charlie out, honest I have. I'm sure his father has as well, but . . ." she shrugged.

Jolly hooted at her pessimism. "Why, what the devil do you two know about handling five-year-old boys? Not a damned thing. Just you leave it to me. I'll have that child laughing and talking a blue streak within a week." He bobbed his head for emphasis. "In two he'll be as rowdy as me."

Helen smiled fondly at the white-haired man who was so dear. "Well, Mr. Wizard, if you can actually perform such an unlikely miracle, I'll never doubt you again."

Confidently, "You just be thinking about what you're going to feed this wise old sorcerer for supper and I'll get to work."

"Fair enough," said Helen. She took his arm and walked with him to the back gate, where he left her, winked, and headed for the barn.

Helen stood for a moment, wondering what he had up his sleeve. Hoping he wouldn't be too disappointed when he learned, as he soon would, that Charlie

Northway would prove immune even to the persuasive charms of a lovable, outlandish man-child like Jolly Grubbs.

Jolly whistled happily as he strode down to the barn. He caught sight of Charlie sitting alone on the stoop and called out a warm hello. Charlie looked at him but didn't answer.

"Your pappy here, Charlie?" Jolly inquired.

Charlie refused to speak.

Undaunted, Jolly called, "Captain Northway, you around? It's Jolly Grubbs."

Kurt immediately appeared, greeting the older gentleman with the respect he deserved. Purposely speaking loudly enough so that Charlie could hear, Jolly told Kurt he needed to borrow Helen's saw.

"Sure thing," said Kurt. "I sharpened it just yesterday. I'll get it out of the toolshed."

Jolly followed Kurt, asking, "Any idea where I might find a smooth, thick piece of wood I can saw down till it's about yea long and yea wide?" He used his hands to measure.

"There are some odds-and-ends lumber stacked against the smokehouse," said Kurt. "I'm sure we can find something suitable there."

"Mighty fine," said Jolly. "Mighty fine. Now just one last little thing. I need a good long length of rope, new enough and strong enough to hold up a person's weight. A big person, mind you. Got anything like that in the toolshed or the barn?"

"I wouldn't be a bit surprised."

Kurt didn't question him as to what he intended to do with the saw, the lumber, and the rope. Jolly knew it wasn't because Kurt had no interest, but instead because he had already caught on to Jolly's scheme.

Within the hour a sturdy rope swing hung suspended from a low, sweeping branch of the big live oak tree in the backyard. And a portly, white-haired man was alone in the shady yard, seated in the new swing, swinging gaily back and forth, laughing as though he'd never had so much fun in his life.

From the cover of the plank corral, Kurt Northway crouched on his heels and watched Jolly swing, hoping the ploy would work. Inside the house, Helen stood at the kitchen window, looking anxiously out, the fingers of both hands crossed behind her back.

Finally, after several long minutes, the blond-haired little boy could stand it no longer. Curious, Charlie wandered up to the yard. He paused tentatively at the back gate. The dozing Dom, lying just inside, awakened and eagerly came to greet Charlie, wanting to be his friend. While Charlie half frowned, half grinned, the sleek blue-furred feline wrapped himself around Charlie's bare legs and made purring sounds in his throat.

Dom followed as Charlie shyly ambled forward toward the white-haired man in the swing. Jolly caught sight of the boy in his side vision and slowed the motion of the swing to a near standstill. Jolly didn't act surprised to see Charlie. Nor did he leap up and ask the little boy if he wanted to try out the new swing.

"Give me a push, will you, Charlie?" he called, and the child immediately came to stand directly behind him.

Charlie never saw the look of triumph that flashed in Jolly's blue eyes when Jolly felt a pair of small hands push insistently on his broad back.

"Wheeee!" squealed Jolly, shoving off with his feet, pretending it was Charlie's pushing that was sending the swing into motion. "Higher!" he called excitedly. "Make me go higher! I want to go higher!"

Charlie Northway said nothing, but he pushed and he grunted and he ran up and back, up and back, his short legs churning, pushing the laughing man seated in the swing.

After a time Jolly called, "Whoaaa! That's enough, Charlie," and brought the swing to a stop.

He got up out of the swing, drew a handkerchief from his pocket, and mopped his red face. From behind that handkerchief he watched slyly as Charlie sidled around and climbed up into the swing. Without a word, Jolly shoved the handkerchief into his pocket, stepped behind the boy in the swing, and gave him a gentle push.

Jolly purposely kept a tight rein on the movement of the swing, knowing that if Charlie was the typical boy, he'd soon long to swing faster, higher. Well, he was going to have to ask for it or he wouldn't get it.

Each played a waiting game.

The blond boy on the swing clutched the ropes tightly and pumped his short arms and leaned his upper body forward and back, straining to make the swing go faster, higher.

The white-haired man deliberately ignored the messages sent by the child's yearning body. He almost weakened when Charlie tipped his small blond head all the way back and looked straight up at him with big pleading brown eyes. But he was older and wiser than the stubborn little boy. He shook his white head and stuck to his guns. Frustrated, Charlie rocked his body back and forth, sighed, made faces.

And finally gave in.

"Will you make me go higher?" he said, again tipping back his head to look up at Jolly. "Please."

An understanding and comradeship between the two was born in the instant. The white-haired man's face broke into a wide, relieved smile. The little boy smiled back.

"Charlie, my boy," Jolly said, cupping Charlie's small chin for a moment in his veined, sun-weathered hand, "I'll make you soar."

Charlie Northway quickly took to the wise, permissive white-haired man who reminded him of his own deceased grandfather. On that warm Sunday afternoon, the two became fast friends.

From Jolly, Charlie was soon learning how to whittle and fish and swim and skip stones across the water's surface and a hundred other things a little boy needs to know.

Kurt Northway was grateful to the old gentleman. Kurt knew nothing about being a father. Jolly Grubbs did. He had raised three sons of his own.

Three loud, lovable, affectionate boys who grew up to be intelligent, dependable, well-adjusted men.

Fine men who earned their father's respect.

Honorable men who made him proud.

Brave men who lost their lives in the war.

Chapter Nine

Niles Loveless drew the diamond-and-gold-cased watch from his vest pocket and glanced at it. Three o'clock. He pushed the tall-backed leather chair away from the huge mahogany desk and rose to his feet.

Niles Loveless crossed the spacious office and lowered the shades over the many windows fronting onto Main Street. He locked the glass-paned front door on which LOVELESS ENTERPRISES was etched in fancy gold lettering.

Niles Loveless smiled then and reached for the finely tailored gray linen waistcoat hanging on the coat tree. He pulled on the waistcoat, tugged the matching double-breasted vest back down into place, and touched the gray silk cravat at his throat.

Niles Loveless took a wide brimmed planters hat from the coat tree, placed it on his blond head at a slight angle, and ran his thumb and forefinger around the front brim. He passed a well-tended, manicured hand over his smoothly shaven cheeks, licked the tip of his forefinger, and smoothed it along the closely clipped wings of his thick brown mustache.

Niles Loveless silently crossed the plushly carpeted office. He paused directly before the back door, took a small blue velvet box from inside his jacket pocket, and snapped it open. He withdrew the sparkling diamond-and-emerald necklace from inside, dropped the valuable bauble down into the right front pocket of his snugly fitted gray trousers, and tossed the velvet box aside.

He stepped out the back door into the narrow alley and his smile broadened. His fine brougham and matching blacks had been brought around just as requested.

Niles Loveless climbed into his fine carriage and drove around to Main Street. He headed north out of Spanish Fort, tipping his straw hat and smiling to friends and business acquaintances on the street. He had traveled less than a quarter of a mile when he spotted a couple of bobbing silk parasols ahead at the side of the road.

He drew rein on the blacks and stopped the brougham. He bounded down out of the carriage to greet the twittering, fluttery little Livingston sisters. The sisters were making their slow, sure way home.

Niles Loveless insisted he drive them the rest of the way and the sisters were thrilled. Both squeaked and trembled and giggled helplessly when the big blond man gallantly lifted each of them up into the claret-hued leather interior of the brougham.

Niles graciously inquired after their health and listened with interest as they listed their many complaints, interrupting each other often. When each ache and every pain had been discussed at length, he casually asked if they knew any "juicy gossip." And he winked at them when he said it.

After going into peals of high, rippling laughter, the sisters sobered and, their eyes flashing, said in unison, "Now, you know we don't like to tattle on old friends, but ... have you heard about the young Widow Courtney?"

He nodded, frowning sadly. "Sam the smithy told me that Mrs. Courtney hired a Yankee captain. Said the Northerner is living right there on the old Burke place with her!"

The sisters blushed and nodded their heads. "Isn't it scandalous?" said Caroline, the older of the two. "Why, proper folks will never associate with her again! I know sister and I certainly won't!"

"Can't say that I blame you," agreed Niles. "We're all awfully disappointed in the young widow." He shook his head. "She'll learn that such questionable behavior will not be tolerated by upright, God-fearing folks like us."

The Livingston sisters vehemently agreed. They went on and on about the dirty Yankee and the foolish widow until the carriage rolled to a stop before their once grand, but now run-down home a mile outside Spanish Fort.

When Niles Loveless left the pair, they waved madly, calling out to him to give their fondest regards to his sweet wife, Patsy. Smiling, nodding, promising he would, he drove away with them chattering gaily about what a fine, handsome gentleman Niles Loveless was.

"What a devoted, loving husband he is to Patsy," trilled Caroline.

"Yes. And such a doting father to his two little boys," added Celeste, the younger sister.

Holding hands, the sisters hurried up the flagstone walk to the house, still talking about the kind, upstanding Niles Loveless.

Niles Loveless continued on his way, the high-stepping blacks prancing proudly northward. When he'd driven another mile, Niles turned the big brougham off the main road and into a private drive, its entrance guarded by matching stone statues imported from Italy.

His destination within sight, Niles grew anxious to reach the big two-story dwelling at the end of the long pebbled drive that wound its way through the thick tall pine trees. For the first time since leaving town, he applied the whip, sending the horses into a fast trot. He circled the big white house and pulled to stop in the rear.

He bounded eagerly down, leaving the carriage to a waiting groomsman. Inside the manicured yard, he strode hurriedly toward the shaded veranda, climbed the back steps, crossed the wide porch, and let himself in the back door.

He was smiling with pleasure and anticipation by the time he closed and locked the door behind himself.

"Honey, it's me," he called, and started through the silent, spacious house, disrobing as he went.

He hung his planters hat and grey linen waistcoat in the marble-floored entrance hall. The matching gray vest was dropped on the carpeted stairs along with the gray silk cravat. Gold studs scattered as he stripped off his white shirt.

"Darling, where are you?" he called, reaching the wide upstairs landing. "Daddy's looking for his baby girl. Daddy's taking off his belt . . ." His grin broadened as he pulled the smooth black leather belt from the loops of his trousers and walked to the end of the cool, quiet corridor toward the last door, which stood open.

Eagerly he stepped into the open doorway, his face flushed, his broad chest heaving with excitement. And then he saw her across the dim bedchamber. She was seated at the dressing table calmly stroking her long dark hair with a gold-handled brush.

She wore a sweetly demure dress of pale yellow organza with frilly short sleeves and full ruffled skirts. On her small feet were slippers of soft yellow kid leather. Her full pink lips were naked of rouge, as was her lovely, flawless face. From across the dim bedroom she actually looked like a dewy-eyed young schoolgirl of no more than fourteen or fifteen.

Niles started toward her, dragging the tip of his long

leather belt back and forth across the deep carpet in a menacing manner. She quickly tied her long, flowing dark hair back off her youthful-looking face with a yellow satin ribbon, folded her small pale hands in her lap, and waited.

"Has my angel been a good little girl today, or must Papa punish her?" said Niles Loveless, approaching the seated woman.

She tossed her head and giggled. "I've been ever so good, Papa. I don't deserve a spanking."

"Are you sure?" He reached her. He paused, stood directly before her in a wide-legged, arrogant stance, continuing to flick the belt back and forth, back and forth.

Hands folded in her lap, feet crossed at the ankles, she lifted wide, innocent eyes to his and said, "Yes, Papa, I'm positive. I've behaved myself all day. Some days I'm a naughty girl and deserve a spanking. But today I deserve a present for being so good." Coyly she tilted her head to one side, licked her pouty lips, and lowered her heavily lashed gaze pointedly to his straining crotch.

Niles Loveless's wide smile turned to a salacious leer, his heart pounded in his naked chest, and hot blood coursed through his veins.

He said, "I'll give my angel a little present if she'll promise to give me something in return."

Smiling, she leaped up off the velvet vanity stool, clapping her hands and jumping up and down like an excited little girl.

"I will! I will!" she promised. "Give me my present. I want my present."

He laughed, wrapped a broad hand around the back of her neck, pulled her close, and kissed her. When the kiss ended, he brushed his mouth back and forth across her parted lips, purposely tickling her cheeks and chin with his thick, bristly mustache. He knew how she enjoyed having him tickle her—all over—with his mustache.

"Baby has to find it if she wants her present," he said, biting her bottom lip with his sharp white teeth, then lifting his head.

In a cloud of frothy yellow skirts and swishing glossy hair, she danced excitedly around the big man, patting and feeling his pockets with probing, playful hands. Giggling when he groaned and gasped and shuddered. From deep down inside the right trousers pocket, she found and withdrew a glittering diamond-and-emerald necklace.,

Squealing with delight, she hugged the tall blond man and whirled swiftly about so he could fasten the necklace behind her swanlike neck. She laughed giddily, pleased with her little present.

Almost as pleased as he was with what she promptly gave him in return.

Yanking the leather belt out of his big hand, she began flicking it back and forth just as he had done. She ordered him to finish undressing. When he stood naked in the shadowy room she teasingly looped the belt around his lean flanks and drew him close.

She put out the tip of her pink tongue and licked her lips wetly.

She asked, "Just exactly what kind of present does my big ol' sweet sugar daddy want from his baby girl?" She leaned to him and began licking his furred chest, making a wet, titillating little trail down the center of his torso to his tight belly, then slowly back up and around each straining brown nipple. "Tell me so that I can be a good little girl and my sweet papa daddy won't have to bare my little bottom and spank it."

His breath now coming in loud rasps, his naked body trembling with sensation, he murmured raggedly, "You know. Baby knows what I want."

She simpered and nipped his kiss-wet chest with sharp white teeth and lifted her head to look up into his passion-heated eyes. "If Papa won't say it aloud, Papa won't get his present," she whined in baby talk.

And so, knowing that it excited her to have him talk dirty almost as much as it excited him, Niles told her in the most graphic of language just exactly what he wanted her to do to him.

And momentarily he was sighing with deep carnal pleasure as he sat naked on the velvet vanity stool with her kneeling between his spread legs. She looked so cute, so sweetly innocent in the youthful yellow dress and matching hair ribbon.

Naughtily she held his heated gaze as she flipped her long dark hair back off her face, sank back on her heels, and bent to place her soft, unrouged lips over the pulsing tip of his straining erection.

There was nothing remotely innocent in the way she expertly made love to him with practiced lips and teeth and tongue, but it was sweet indeed. She drove him half crazy before finally bringing him to total fulfillment.

A half hour later a completely sated Niles Loveless was drawing his gray trousers back on while she fingered the diamond-and-emerald necklace at her throat. Making small talk, she asked if he'd heard the shocking news.

"You mean about Helen Courtney and the Yankee bastard?" he said, buttoning his pants.

"Mmmm. Won't he spoil your plans?"

"I'm sure that's what Helen thinks."

"Well, darling, with a man's help on the farm, mightn't she be able to produce a decent autumn harvest? Make enough money to pay the taxes and hold on to the—"

"I've no intention of allowing that to happen. I want that land, all of it. I am going to have it." He smiled then and added, "In case you haven't noticed, I'm quite adept at getting what I want."

"I had noticed," she said, smiling. "Have you seen the Yankee in town? What's his name?"

He shrugged. "I haven't seen him. Haven't even heard his name, but whoever he is, I have plans for him. Within two or three weeks, I'll see to it that he's left Alabama or is in the county jail. Either way, Helen will be amenable to my buyout offer before this summer ends."

"You're so clever, darling," she praised. Then, "I've heard the Yankee's quite handsome. There's sure to be gossip about the two of them way off out there alone."

"Of course there'll be gossip, as well there should." He shook a finger in her face. "You're to have nothing more to do with Helen Courtney, you hear me? I won't have people talking about you, dear."

"Niles, you're so protective, so solicitous."

With the tip of his little finger Niles touched the diamond-and-emerald necklace resting in the hollow of her throat. "I wouldn't be displeased if you mentioned to some of her friends you suspect Helen and the Yankee are . . . well . . ."

"But of course, darling." Her smile turned to a petulant pout. "Must you get dressed? We've only begun to relax."

He grinned and pinched her cheek. "While I agree that the three R's are more important than anything else in life, I really must hurry."

She gave him an innocent look. "Readin', 'ritin', and 'rithmatic? They're the most important thing in life?"

"No, pet," he said, and again drew her into his embrace. "Rum, riches, and rapture."

She laughed and said, "Well, darling, you have riches. Stay and I'll give you rum and rapture."

"It's tempting, but I really do have to go. The little

wife's giving an important dinner party for Senator Riggs—at my request. I promised Patsy I'd get home early."

"Mmmm." Yasmine sighed, locking her wrists behind his back. "Then I suppose I'll be seeing you again in a few hours."

"Oh?" His hands cupped her delicate rib cage. "You coming to Patsy's dinner party, my sweet?"

She smiled wickedly. "I wouldn't dream of missing the gala, darling," she purred.

Then Yasmine Parnell, the respected, glamorous, dark-haired thirty-three-year-old wealthy widow said to the esteemed, blondly handsome thirty-seven-year-old family man Niles Loveless, "After all, Patsy's one of my dearest friends."

Chapter Ten

Kurt Northway walked toward the corral as the first pale tinges of light streaked across the eastern sky. Perched on the corral fence's top plank, a towhee twittered his happy greeting to the new day. And from a budding peach tree far out in the fruit orchard, a mockingbird was singing.

Shirtless in the cool gray dawn, Kurt began to whistle softly, adding his own salutation to the coming sunrise. He felt surprisingly rested and fit, although he'd slept no longer than usual. Typically he had lain awake long past midnight, but this time it was from more than his normal restlessness.

It was amazement.

His son, the unreachable five-year-old, had for the past few days—since Sunday afternoon and the new swing—begun to talk and even to laugh with Jolly Grubbs. Jolly seemed to possess a special brand of magic that worked wonders on the withdrawn Charlie. Before Sunday, Kurt had never heard his son laugh. Now the wonderful sound echoed in his ears.

Feeling lighthearted for the first time in ages, Kurt approached the corral looking forward to his daily ride astride the powerful Raider.

Raider looked forward to it as well.

The big sorrel began to neigh and whicker even before he caught sight of Kurt. The stallion, restlessly prancing around the confines of the small dirt-

bottomed corral, knew that his master would soon be
there.

Raider whinnied loudly and trotted forward to greet
him when Kurt appeared in the pale dawn light to
throw open the gate.

"How about it, boy?" Kurt said, stepping inside and
stroking the stallion's sleek neck affectionately. "You
ready to run?"

Raider neighed and blew and shook his great head
up and down as if he understood perfectly what his
master said. And perhaps he did. Kurt had talked to
Raider as an equal from the day the prized stallion was
given to him as a newborn colt.

The excited stallion now nudged at Kurt's bare chest
with his velvet muzzle, ready and anxious to begin
their daily romp. He playfully bit Kurt's bare shoulder.
Shoving the stallion's head away, Kurt stepped around
him and headed for the tack room.

Knowing Raider was following closely on his heels,
Kurt said, "Now, you're not going to believe this,
Raider. Charlie has actually been laughing and talk-
ing."

His big head poking through the open doorway,
Raider snorted skeptically.

"I know. I told you you wouldn't believe it," Kurt
said.

He took the bridle down from the peg, slipped the
bit in Raider's mouth, and eased the restraint up the
horse's head, gently pushing Raider's erect ears outside the leather straps.

Then, fastening the buckle on the jaw strap, he said
into Raider's pricked ear, "Hey, I didn't claim he talks
and laughs with *me*."

Raider bared his teeth. Kurt smiled and slapped the
stallion's cheek, backing him out the door. He followed
with the worn saddle, threw it on Raider's back, and
tightened the cinch under the stallion's belly.

Raider turned his head and gave his master an impatient look. His big sleek body quivered all over and his long tail swished back and forth. The penned stallion was tired of wasting time. He wanted to run.

Kurt grinned, looped the long leather reins over the horse's head, put a booted foot into the stirrup, and swung easily up astride the big blooded beast. Raider immediately went into motion, prancing out of the corral, turning to the path that led directly to the large tree-rimmed pasture to the north.

The long, narrow path bordered the vegetable garden on one side, the fruit orchard on the other. The sound of the mockingbird's sweet song grew louder as the stallion passed the neat rows of tall fruit-bearing trees flanking the path.

Holding the reins loosely in one hand, Kurt turned a fleshly shaven cheek to the gentle breeze that blew in off the bay. In a sudden burst of high spirits, he laughed happily into the wind that washed over him like a cool clean stream. He was tempted to burst into song, to sing at the top of his lungs until the whole wide world awakened.

He didn't.

He threw back his head and smiled to himself. Raider picked up the pace, his heartbeat quickening like that of the man on his back. The breeze stiffened and Kurt's smile broadened. He bent his dark head forward, closed his eyes, and allowed the fingers of wind to play through his thick black hair.

When he raised his head and opened his eyes, he saw her.

Helen was in the vegetable garden at the end of a long row of green peas. She wasn't stooping to the vines, although the apron she clutched with one hand held her gathered bounty.

Kurt drew rein and silently watched her.

She stood as still as a statue, gazing into the rapidly

rising sun. The wind had caught the skirts of her gray work dress. The faded fabric pressed against the gentle feminine curves and billowed out around her slender body. Her pale golden hair was knotted atop her head and shining with fiery highlights.

Her face was in profile and for an instant it was unbearably sad. A wave of deep tenderness and compassion washed over Kurt.

He felt his heart kick against his naked ribs. Like a sudden blow to the solar plexus it struck him that this sad young woman had known far too little happiness. She was hardly more than a girl, yet she had no one to look after her. No husband. No family. Nobody.

Her fragile beauty was wasted. Hers should have been a carefree life filled with elegant gowns and fancy parties and summer picnics. Leisurely carriage rides in the country and moonlight kisses and heated passion.

Instead it was nothing more than survival. A harsh, struggling existence of threadbare clothes and backbreaking work and home-cooked meals. Bumpy wagons trips to town and solitary evenings and long, lonely nights.

Unaware she was being observed, Helen finally sighed, slowly sank to her knees, and continued with her task.

Drawn to her, Kurt quietly urged Raider forward.

Helen was bent over the English peas, snipping off the tender green pods and dropping them into her gathered-up apron. She heard the horse's hooves striking the ground. Her back stiffened. She raised her head and slowly turned it. She saw him.

Silhouetted against the pale dawn, he was less than fifty feet away.

He opened his mouth to speak, but said nothing. Nor did she. They silently stared at each other for a long, tense moment, he astride the stallion, she kneeling below.

Her breath curiously short, Helen cautiously eyed the dark, bare-chested man atop the enormous sorrel stallion. He didn't urge the horse forward, nor did he dismount. He sat there easily in the worn military saddle, his hand careless on the reins, his haunting forest-green eyes resting squarely on her.

Anxiously clutching the filled apron, Helen slowly rose to her feet. She could feel an odd excitement beginning to build in her. An almost imperceptible step took her closer to him. She didn't realize she had moved.

Kurt did.

He drew a quick breath and immediately nudged the responsive Raider with his knees. The stallion moved forward. Helen watched as the looming pair came closer.

She stood unmoving as if she were in some kind of strange trance. Her wide blue eyes focused fully on Kurt's darkly handsome face, she didn't reprimand him when he guided his big steed off the path and into her carefully tended garden.

Tender vines crunched under heavy hooves as horse and rider approached. Helen never noticed the destruction. The Yankee's intent so intrigued her, he had her undivided attention.

What did he want? What was he going to do? To her? With her?

Her heart beginning to throb with a bizarre mixture of fear and anticipation, she watched him closely as he bore steadily down on her.

The fleeting thought occurred that the big, powerful stallion and the dark man astride him were much alike. Both had the same offhand grace of movement, the same lean, rippling muscles, the same half-sleepy, half-hawk keen eyes. The same potency and power to thrill and please. Or frighten and conquer.

Kurt unhurriedly walked Raider toward Helen.

Helen stayed exactly as she was, unable to make herself retreat or advance.

Kurt reached her.

He looked down at her upturned face. Still neither spoke. Mesmerized by those forest-green eyes that held an expression she didn't understand, Helen couldn't look away.

After several heartbeats, Kurt abruptly leaned from his saddle and took firm hold of Helen's narrow waist. Throat gone dry, eyes locked with his, she thoughtlessly released her clutched apron and put her hands atop his bare, broad shoulders.

The carefully picked peas spilled forgotten to the ground.

Kurt smiled and lifted her from the ground as easily as if she were a small child. With cool authority he sat her sideways across the saddle before him. Still holding her questioning gaze, he reached down to her full, twisted skirts.

He flipped the cumbersome skirts and petticoat up over her knees, turned her forward, and urged a long, shapely leg over the horse's neck. When she was seated comfortably astride, he put the big beast in motion, never bothering to lower her raised dress.

Helen didn't bother either.

Nor did she object when—trotting down the path toward the northern pasture—Kurt reached up and withdrew the pins from her knotted hair. Instead she shook her head about, sending the locks cascading down around her shoulders like rippling falls of gold.

She didn't hear the sharp intake of air from the man in whose arms she was enclosed. Nor did she know that it took all of Kurt's practiced powers of self-restraint to keep from burying his face in all that fragrant golden silkiness. When his ally the wind tossed a long shimmering strand against his cheek, Kurt's bare belly contracted and he turned his face inward to inhale deeply.

In moments Raider had left the path, the garden, and the orchard behind and had reached the large tree-rimmed pasture. Without warning, the big stallion burst through the open gate and into a fast, ground-eating gallop. Caught off guard, Helen was slammed forcefully back against Kurt's hard chest. She laughed in startled surprise, half attempted to lever herself up, and felt the strong imprisoning band of his muscular arm slide around her waist to press her back in place against him.

She didn't try again.

She realized that she didn't actually want to move away from the welcome security of that sun-darkened arm. The stallion was racing so fast the ground flashed by below. Helen had never been atop a mount that moved so swiftly. A creature that could run with such heart-stopping speed.

It was alarming. It was dangerous. It was thrilling.

As the stallion thundered around the pasture, Helen's back was pressed closely against Kurt's broad chest. So close, the amazing warmth of his smooth bare skin seeped right through the thin fabric of her dress, enveloping her, but pleasantly so. She caught the scent of his heated flesh, so clean, so pleasing, so uniquely male. She anxiously inhaled and her lids almost closed over her shining blue eyes.

Strange as it was, she somehow felt gloriously safe and sheltered in this stranger's masterful embrace. It was as if the cold, threatening world and all that was in it could not touch her, harm her.

Helen deliberately closed her mind to everything save the stolen pleasure of the moment. She laughed delightedly as the Gulf wind stung her pale cheeks,

whipped her unbound hair about her head, and pressed
her dress against her shoulders and breasts. Her skirts
were carried higher, billowing up around her knees, exposing glimpses of her stockinged legs.

She didn't care.

She laughed all the more loudly.

So did the man behind her.

Kurt laughed into the strands of silky golden hair
tickling his face and his fancy. Charmed by Helen's
sweet, unexpected surrender to the simple joy of the
impromptu dawn ride, he savored the sound of her
laughter even as he laughed with her.

It was such a lovely, feminine, heartwarming laugh.
A golden, full-bodied laugh that divulged so much of
the real woman hidden beneath the usual stiff exterior.
A woman who laughed with the open, good-natured
abandon of this golden-haired widow was surely warm,
caring, uninhibited. A sensual, passionate woman who
had once known how to live life to the fullest, to love
deeply and with all her heart. Her gay, musical laugh
assured him that she'd not completely forgotten how to
do either. She was simply a bit rusty, as was he.

He hadn't done much laughing himself of late. Or
living. Or loving.

Their eyes shining with pleasure, the pair raced the
wind around the large tree-lined pasture. They were
behaving like a couple of carefree children, as indeed
they were for these few stolen moments. The joyous
sounds of their foolish frolic mingled with the thunder
of sharp hooves glancing on packed earth and the jin-
gle of stirrups and the blowing bellows of Raider's
powerful pumping lungs.

Helen was half afraid the wild, dangerous ride
would continue indefinitely. And half afraid it
wouldn't. The well-reasoned, thoughtful side of her silently cried out for the dark Yankee to pull up on the

big stallion, to bring him to a halt and lower her to the safety of the ground.

But her foolish, giddy, more daring side quietly pleaded with him to do just the opposite. With every pounding beat of her heart she mutely begged him to race on and on. To never stop the stallion. To go on holding her pressed against his muscled chest for eternity. To keep his long arm wrapped tightly around her. Forever and ever.

The man holding her in his protective embrace received the message as clearly as if she had spoken into his ear. Her slender pressing body transmitted her every desire and Kurt couldn't have been more pleased. His own desire was much the same. He too longed to ride forever, fast and free, with this golden-haired woman wrapped in his arms.

His morning rides were always a pleasure, but nothing compared with this one. Never half so thrilling. His heart thundered in his naked chest. He felt vitally alive, as if his blood were pumping and surging forcefully through his veins and out to every part of his body so that he tingled from head to toe.

On they rode.

The sun moved quickly up into the summer sky, its heat already growing fierce. Not nearly as fierce as the heat generated by two pressing, straining bodies atop a racing stallion. Raider's big, sleek body was wet with sweat. Kurt's bare back and long arms glistened with perspiration. Helen's fair face and throat were dotted with beads of moisture.

In their exhilaration, they never noticed the heat or discomfort.

But, just as stallion, man, and woman were having the time of their lives, Kurt Northway made a careless blunder. His arm tightening possessively around Helen's waist, he laughed and allowed his thoughts to surface.

"Ah, Mrs. Courtney," he shouted into the wind, "tell me true. Isn't this the proper way to watch the sun rise?"

Helen stiffened immediately.

Reality intruded with the sound of his deep, masculine voice reminding her who she was, who he was.

Without a word she let him know that their ride was at its end. Cursing himself for breaking the beautiful spell, Kurt dutifully drew rein.

Flushed and hot and breathing almost as hard as the winded Raider, they headed back to where they had begun. There Kurt gently lowered Helen to her feet and, smiling tentatively, started to dismount.

She stopped him.

The minute her feet touched the ground, Helen came fully to her senses. She threw up her hand in a halting, defensive gesture. The bright smile had left her flushed face. Her high brow was creased. Inwardly she shuddered. What had prompted such rash behavior? What on earth could she have been thinking?

"The sun's grown hot," Kurt said softly from atop the horse. "I suggest you wait until sunset to finish gathering the peas."

Helen looked at him sharply. His thick, too-long jet hair was in wild disarray and falling into his eyes. His naked torso gleamed wetly in the hot morning sunlight. Diamond drops of perspiration glittered in the crisp black hair covering his muscled chest.

The sight of him looming above, half naked, totally relaxed and in control, annoyed Helen. While he was quite obviously unaffected by the shared intimacy of their ride, her knees were weak. She felt half faint and trembly. Cold and hot at once.

"Captain Northway," she snapped irritably, "what prompts you to make suggestions to me? I regard any such advice as tactless and unnecessary. May I remind you that I've been running this farm alone for years. I don't need an interfering Yankee to tell me what I should or should not do." Helen's hands went to her hips. "I am in command here, not you. You may be a captain, Captain, but on this particular piece of property I'm in charge. I am not interested in your suggestions, proposals, or ideas as to how I should operate this farm. Do you understand me?"

"Sure," he said, wondering what had brought about such an overdone outburst.

"The proper reply, Captain, is 'Yes, Mrs. Courtney.'"

Half amused, half angry, Kurt said, "Yes, Mrs. Courtney."

"That's better. Now we both have work to do," Helen reminded him, her blue eyes snapping.

"Yes, ma'am."

"After you've finished with the day's plowing, you're to begin digging a drainage ditch for the stock pond. Think you can handle that?"

"May I respectfully remind the dubious lady boss that I have had considerable experience digging trenches."

Helen's jaw tightened. Her blue eyes narrowed. "I'm sure you have, Captain. Trenches from which to fire at unsuspecting Confederate soldiers!"

Chapter Eleven

Helen anxiously shoved her tangled, windblown hair out of her eyes—eyes that snapped with open hostility. She whirled away and marched off, anxious to put as much distance between Kurt and herself as possible.

Kurt watched her go, quietly analyzing her inflexible attitude toward him. He knew her resentment was not of him personally, but of the hated foe which he embodied. His conquering army had made her a widow, had spread destruction, had impoverished families. And now the defeated South was forced to live under Yankee rule. Mobile was an occupied city.

In Helen Courtney's mind, he was directly responsible.

Kurt sighed, shrugged, and told himself there was nothing he could do about it. For a few splendid moments the golden-haired widow had almost forgotten to hate him. Now she was sorry she had. She was ashamed that she had allowed herself to enjoy the ride with him. Conscience-stricken for forgetting and laughing and allowing a murdering Yankee to put his arm around her.

Kurt shook his dark head and turned the winded Raider back toward the corral.

All he'd wanted was to make Helen Courtney happy, but he'd done more harm than good. Now she'd be more on guard than ever. Barely civil to him.

Kurt was right.

Helen purposely steered clear of him the rest of the day. She made it a point to avoid him. She was deeply ashamed of her aberrant behavior and wondered at her temporary loss of sanity. What if someone should find out? She shuddered at the thought. And she promised herself she'd never again be guilty of such appalling conduct.

Helen was relieved when the long, tense day finally came to a close. The effort to evade the Yankee and at the same time not let Charlie know—she didn't dare risk upsetting the fragile little boy—had been wearing and difficult. Like walking a tightwire without benefit of a net. She was bone tired that night as she slipped on her nightgown. And it wasn't from hard work alone.

Yawning, she sat down on the bed's edge, took out the gold locket, and kissed Will's picture. She turned out the coal-oil lamp, stretched out flat on her back in the feather bed, and flung her arms above her head. Her wayward cat hadn't shown up, but Helen was too tired to care. Let him prowl all night—she needed some rest.

She closed her eyes, snuggled more deeply into the softness of the mattress, exhaled slowly, and waited for sleep. She could feel the tight, tense muscles in her arms and legs start to jump and uncoil.

Soon, floating in that pleasant semiconscious state somewhere between wakefulness and slumber, Helen was again astride a big powerful stallion and in the arms of a big powerful man. Racing the wind and laughing.

With a start Helen realized she was foolishly smiling. Her eyes came open and she shuddered. She slipped her hand underneath the pillow and felt the cold steel of her loaded revolver.

It was comforting to have protection at her fingertips just in case the Yankee had gotten any wrong ideas from this morning's wild ride. Let him make one false move and she wouldn't hesitate to use the weapon.

He came to her from out of the darkness.

He crossed the silent room while a gentle night breeze off the bay blew his raven hair back off his sculptured face. His green eyes gleamed with a hot intensity, and silvery moonlight touched the bare breadth of his smooth tanned shoulders.

He advanced with quiet, deadly determination and it was no mystery what he had come for. He had come for her. She had to save herself and do it quickly. But her limbs would not respond to the message frantically sent by her brain. She continued to lie there unmoving while her dark seducer bore steadily down on her.

Her eyes wide, her heart throbbing, Helen finally managed to slide her hand up under her pillow. Her fingers touched solid steel, but refused to grip the pistol.

He reached the bed and calmly finished undressing. When he had shed his clothes and was totally naked, he stood there for a long moment while she struggled to make her forefinger close around the revolver's trigger. The moon's illumination highlighted his tall, leanly muscled form, giving him a godlike appearance.

A masterful god of love come to take her to paradise.

Helen's heart raced madly in her chest when he sat down on the bed facing her. He caressed her cheek and she trembled at his touch. He leaned down and brushed her lips with his and she whimpered softly. His gleaming eyes held her gaze as he slowly, deftly undid the line of small buttons going down the center of her worn cotton nightgown.

With her hand still touching the pistol, she watched helplessly as he parted the opened gown, pushing it out of the way, bearing her breasts to his hot eyes. Her breasts immediately swelled and her breath began to come in anxious little spasms.

Slowly his handsome head lowered and he kissed her eyes, her cheeks, her mouth, her throat. And the first thing she knew, her fingers no longer touched cold solid metal, but warm smooth flesh.

Helen's sharp nails raked anxiously down his back as Kurt's hot lips moved over her flushed cheek to the sensitive spot just below her ear. Yielding to him, guided entirely by sensation, Helen forgot about the gun.

Her lips eagerly met his and her arms clasped him tightly. Kurt kissed a searing path along her neck as he lifted her off the bed and sat her on his lap. Their lips unerringly sought each other's while Kurt finished removing Helen's nightgown.

When she was as naked as he, he rose to his feet in the moonlight. Holding her in his powerful arms, he stood there kissing her until she breathlessly freed her lips from his and buried her face in his neck. She clung to him tightly, feeling as if all she had ever wanted was for this dark naked god of love to make her his own.

Kurt turned, put a knee on the mattress, and climbed atop the high feather bed with her in his arms. He sank back on his heels on the bed, gently laying Helen back across the pillows. He eased down beside her, his lips again seeking and finding, his hand touching her tingling body with a thousand deliciously different caresses.

Helen moved from one glorious level of ecstasy to the next as his warm wonderful mouth began an intimate excursion of her bare responsive body. Growing hotter and hotter with each touch of his sleek probing tongue, each nip of his flashing white teeth, Helen couldn't lie still. While his roving lips paid homage to her aching breasts, her jerking stomach, her quivering thighs, Helen gasped and moaned and thrashed wildly about.

With Kurt's dark face sinking steadily lower over her bare contracting belly, Helen became so excited her head tossed back and forth on the mattress. She savagely flung her arm out. Her hand struck something solid.

The carved wooden box on the night table crashed noisily to the floor, instantly awakening Helen.

Helen bolted upright, her heart hammering, her nightgown twisted around her waist. She lunged off the bed and fell to her knees on the floor. The contents of the wooden box had spilled out on the worn carpet.

A sob of shame escaping her trembling lips, Helen lifted the photograph of Will and pressed it to her wildly beating heart. Hot tears springing to her eyes, she sat there rocking back and forth on her heels, shivering with shame and mortification.

The graphically erotic dream had been so real, her face flushed hotly with guilt and frustration. It was as if the Yankee had really kissed her, touched her, feasted on her naked flesh. Still agonizingly aroused from the amazingly clear dream, Helen felt as if she had actually been unfaithful to Will. She hated herself for it.

She hated the Yankee even more.

Still badly shaken by the vivid dream, Helen stood unsmiling on the front veranda the next morning, a cup of hot black coffee in her hand. Thick morning mists shrouded the bay. The calm protected waters were completely veiled in dense, swirling fog. Across the wide inlet, Mobile Harbor was invisible.

Squinting fiercely, Helen couldn't even make out the tall turrets of Fort Gaines, the solid new fort built during the war to protect the entrance to Mobile Bay.

She frowned, disappointed.

If the choppy Gulf waters beyond the bay were
swathed in the blinding mists, there would be no riverboat arrivals or departures at the Mobile levee. Which
meant Em Ellicott wouldn't be getting home from New
Orleans this morning as planned.

Helen set her enameled cup on the veranda railing.
She withdrew Em's last brief note from the pocket of
her worn blue wrapper and reread it.

Dearest Helen,
I'm coming home as I can stand it here no longer! At
9 A.M. Thursday, June 1st, I will step down onto the
Mobile landing and so help me, if Coop is not there
waiting, I shall hang myself. Or him, when I finally locate him. I'll be out to the farm around noon. Unless
Coop missed me so terribly he has at last come to his
senses and can't wait another day to marry me!
                                        Love,
                                            Em

Helen folded the note and put it back in her robe
pocket. Her eyes again lifted to the fog-enveloped bay.
The thick haze might not burn away all morning. It
could be late afternoon or perhaps even tomorrow be
fore Em showed up at the farm. Might as well get
started on the laundry.

Helen moved to go back inside.

She heard something.

She stopped, turned her head, and listened. She
could see absolutely nothing through the blanketing
mists, but the sound of rapid hoofbeats striking the
earth carried in the early morning silence. She shook
her head in disbelief.

Northway and his stallion.

She shivered involuntarily.

The Yankee was exercising his blooded beast despite
fog so dense you could hardly see your hand before

your face. It was rash and reckless of him. A foolish,
daredevil stunt if ever there was one. Highly dangerous.

Helen's heart was pounding now. She swallowed and
put a hand to her tight throat. Quickly she told herself
it was concern for the priceless stallion's safety, not for
the man on his back. The disturbing dream had meant
nothing! He meant nothing. She didn't give a fig what
happened to the irresponsible Yankee captain. Let him
break his fool neck if that's what he wanted!

What she wanted was for Em Ellicott to get home.
Anxiously, Helen again gazed thoughtfully in the direction of the Mobile docks. Nothing had changed. The
bay was completely socked in. Em's arrival would def-
initely be postponed.

Helen started back inside and she began to smile
slightly. She'd bet everything she owned that Coop
was taking no chances. He was in Mobile, on the
levee, this very minute if she knew the sheriff.

A tall, lanky thirty-eight-year-old man with red curly
hair graying at the temples, deep set turquoise eyes, a
wide mouth, and a silver star pinned on his starched
white shirtfront waited on the foggy Mobile levee, nervously twisting his hat in his big, freckled hands.

His name was Brian A. Cooper. Sheriff Brian A.
Cooper. The tall redheaded sheriff stood alone in the
swirling gray mists, reluctant to leave his post despite
serious doubts that the morning paddle steamer from
New Orleans would arrive anytime soon.

If at all.

The sheriff was afraid to leave.

Sheriff Brian A. Cooper, back from the war for less
than six weeks, had been the most highly decorated Alabamian to serve in the Confederacy, a fact about
which he was reluctant to speak. His ruddy face

flushed blood-red with embarrassment when anyone else mentioned it.

But whether he liked it or not, Brian A. Cooper was an honored, revered hero in his hometown and the state of Alabama and throughout the entire South.

It was not from the closemouthed Major Cooper, but rather from his superiors—and his mates—that people had learned of his feats of derring-do. He had led charge after charge against the enemy. He was wounded three times. He was confined in a crowded Union prison before successfully escaping after five terrible months. He had suffered from hunger and cold in the winters, heat and malaria in the summers. Once he'd been left behind for dead when his defeated troops were forced to withdraw after a bloody battle in Chattanooga, Tennessee.

The commander of the opposing forces had found him and taken him to a Union field hospital, where his wounds were tended. When his health was restored, Major Brian A. Cooper was traded to the Confederacy, exchanged for a high-ranking Yankee prisoner being held by the Rebs.

The men who had served under Major Brian A. Cooper swore no braver man ever lived. Union officers who came up against the daring Southerner held much the same opinion of the dauntless redheaded calvary major.

When finally the long bloody war was all over, Brian A. Cooper had turned in his major's medals for a lawman's silver star and stepped back into his old position as high sheriff of Baldwin County. Folks warmly welcomed him home, slapped him on the back, and said now they'd sleep better nights.

Their big war hero was not afraid of any man, all proudly agreed. And they were right. The man didn't live whom Sheriff Brian A. Cooper feared. But the big, shy, soft-spoken sheriff was scared to death of one tiny, dark-haired woman.

Sheriff Brian A. Cooper had been "keeping company" with Miss Emma Louise Ellicott since the night they had met at an oyster supper in Bon Secour the summer of 1859. For the sheriff, the little fishing village of Bon Secour—"safe harbor"—proved to be anything but.

The sheriff had not been invited to the fancy summertime gathering for wealthy socialites. He'd been summoned to quell a mild disturbance. The trouble had ended before he arrived. But real trouble awaited the unsuspecting high sheriff.

He'd barely stepped into the light of the swaying Japanese lanterns before he found himself engulfed in swirling white organdy and dark flashing eyes and tantalizing perfume and feminine conversation.

He was a full head taller than Miss Emma Louise Ellicott and weighed twice as much, yet she managed to single-handedly surround him. The dark-eyed, dark-haired twenty one year old charmer had held him willing hostage all that evening.

And ever since.

So now Sheriff Brian A. Cooper stood in the thick fog on the Mobile levee and didn't so much as consider leaving. He wouldn't have dared. Sure as he did, the big white sternwheeler would come slicing through the mists with Em standing on the tall texas deck. If she didn't find him waiting, he'd be in the soup for sure.

Nine A.M. came and went.

The fog began to thin and blow out to sea. Patches of weak sun peeked through. Activity on the wharf picked up. Nine-thirty. Shafts of strong sunlight appeared. People started arriving from the hotels, some carrying luggage. Ten. Roustabouts began loading docked cargo vessels for shipment to northern ports.

At five past ten the *White Camellia* steamed out of the wispy mists and into the warm sunshine, its whistle blowing loudly, its passengers lining the railing.

Sheriff Cooper's squinty turquoise eyes lifted to the texas deck. Sure enough, there stood Em, blowing kisses and smiling. Minutes later she came racing down the gangplank and straight into his arms.

"Kiss me, Coop," she commanded, throwing her arms around his neck. "Kiss me like you missed me as much as I missed you."

"Now, Em, honey," he said softly, looking nervously around, an embarrassed grin on his reddening face, "mind your manners. We're not alone."

"No? Then let's go someplace where we can be alone." She locked her gloved hands behind his head and stood on tiptoe. "Say, perhaps the bridal suite of the Conde Hotel."

"Em Ellicott!" he scolded, his face flushing with heat. "You behave yourself or—"

"Or you'll what, Sheriff? Arrest me?" She laughed sunnily, withdrew her hands from around his neck, and lifted them together before his face. "Go on, lawman. Slap the cuffs on me and take me away."

"Shhhh!" Coop grabbed her arm, jammed his hat on his head, and propelled her to the waiting carriage.

Em never failed to shock and charm him. She was far too assertive for a genteel lady, yet it was that very quality which he found so irresistibly appealing. So downright scary. He never knew whether to run for his life or to never let her out of his sight.

Once they were inside the carriage, waiting for her trunks to be unloaded from the *White Camellia*'s hold, Em turned to him and plucked the hat off his head. She took off her gloves, ran her fingers through his thick red curls, and said, "Coop, if you don't kiss me, I'll hold my breath like a baby until I turn blue and pass out. So help me I will."

Grinning boyishly, the embarrassed, enchanted lawman gently cupped her pale left cheek in a big, freckled hand, leaned down, and started to press a quick
kiss to her right cheek. But the bold, eager Em was too
swift for the patient, gentlemanly Coop.

She quickly turned and lifted her face, so that it was
her waiting lips with which his wide mouth came in
contact. Before he could move away. Em had a tena-
cious hold on his shirt collar and her warm, soft lips
were moving persuasively on his. Coop didn't stand a
chance against this formidable flashing-eyed, sweet-
smelling, soft-skinned, lushly curvaceous female.
When Em kissed him, he was putty in her hands. Once
her honeyed lips took charge, he was no longer in
charge of his lips or his wits.

Em knew that.

So she kissed him now as if no one else were
around. She kissed him the way she knew he liked
best. She kissed him in an all-out effort to make him
stop stalling and start hunting down a clergyman.

Coop knew what she was up to.

But that didn't keep his toes from curling inside his
tall leather boots.

Chapter Twelve

The dense fog still had not lifted when Helen descended the back porch steps, crossed the big yard, and walked down to the quarters with Dom following closely at her heels.

She and Dom stopped several feet from the open door of the quarters and Helen called out, "Captain Northway! Charlie! It's laundry day. If you'll toss out your dirty clothes, I'll wash them for—"

Before her sentence was finished, Charlie appeared alone in the open doorway. His blond hair was tousled and he was in his knee-length nightshirt. Yawning, he rubbed his eyes, then scratched his tummy through the nightshirt's white cotton fabric.

He looked so small, so sleepy, and so adorable.

"Charlie, I'm sorry," Helen said softly, edging cautiously closer, "I woke you. Forgive me."

She expected no answer. While the beautiful little blond boy had begun to talk with Jolly, he still had nothing to say to her. Or to his father.

"Is Jolly here yet?" was Charlie's anxious reply as he squinted up at her.

Helen felt her breath catch in her throat. Eagerly moving nearer, she said, "No. No, not yet. Jolly's coming over again this morning?"

Nodding, Charlie opened his mouth to speak again, but Dom's antics distracted him. The spoiled blue-gray tom wanted Charlie's attention. Demanded Charlie's attention. To ensure getting it, Dom had turned and quietly strolled off into the moving mists, disappearing completely.

Only to come racing back, sprinting directly to the little boy, skidding to a stop scant inches from Charlie's small bare toes.

The Russian Blue fixed Charlie with his strange green eyes and made soft plaintive sounds in the back of his throat. The sleepy Charlie immediately grinned, squatted down on his bare heels, and rubbed a small hand back and forth over Dom's silky-furred back.

The cat loved it.

Dom meowed and purred and stretched out contentedly at Charlie's feet. He threw back his well-shaped head in an open invitation for Charlie to stroke him beneath the chin. Charlie caught on at once and did just that.

Dom was in ecstasy.

Charlie giggled, looked up at Helen with flashing brown eyes, and said, "She likes me!"

Helen smiled. "He. Dom's a boy cat. He likes you a lot, I'd say."

"So would I," came a deep, masculine voice from directly behind Helen.

Startled, she quickly turned around. Kurt Northway stepped out of the swirling mists. Smiling easily, he came up close beside Helen, his forest-green eyes focused solely on the small blond boy.

Helen's eyes remained on Kurt.

As usual, he wore nothing but his faded, low-riding calvary trousers. Helen found her nervous gaze following the lines of his hard sinewy figure from the wide, muscular shoulders to the scuffed black boots on his feet. Recalling yesterday morning's wild ride, she remembered all too well how it felt to be pressed close against that lean, hard frame.

She didn't remember the long scar she now saw so

clearly slashing downward from the small of his back and disappearing into the waistband of his trousers. Wondering how she could have missed something so visible, she had—for a fleeting second—the inexplicable desire to reach out and touch the white satiny imperfection marring the smooth tanned flesh.

Heat rose to her face. Hoping that the guilt over last night's dream didn't show on her face, she needlessly cleared her throat.

"Captain, if you'll gather up your dirty laundry and bring it up to the back fence, I'll wash it for you."

Kurt's eyes lifted from his son, cut to her.

Pinning her with his forest-green gaze, he smiled and said, "That's kind of you, ma'am. Only problem is . . . what will I wear while you're washing my clothes?"

Flustered, Helen gestured weakly. "Surely you have—"

"Two pair of trousers," he stated. "I'm wearing the good pair. The others are torn. Besides the trousers, I own exactly three tattered blue uniform blouses and one white shirt."

Listening, looking back and forth between the two grown-ups, Charlie announced proudly, "I have this many shirts." Rising to his feet, he held up ten spread fingers. "I think," he added, frowning, not quite certain. He tipped back his head to look up at Kurt. "Don't I, Captain?"

"You sure do," Kurt said evenly, displaying no emotion.

But his heart lurched wildly in his naked chest and the tips of his fingers felt numb. For the first time ever, Kurt Northway heard his only son directly address him. It was such an unexpected thrill, Kurt wanted to laugh out loud and shout for joy. At the same time he was momentarily speechless and his throat felt uncomfortably tight.

It mattered little that Charlie had called him Captain instead of Father. That was normal. To be expected. The child had only heard him called Captain. Both Jolly and Helen Courtney addressed him that way.

"Ten shirts," Kurt added, thinking it was true. Charlie did own ten shirts. But all were faded, frayed, and too small for the growing boy and he wished more than anything that he could afford to buy his only son new clothes.

"I think maybe they're all dirty," said Charlie, shrugging slender, nightshirted shoulders.

Helen said to Charlie, "If you'll bring them out, I'll wash and iron them today."

Charlie tilted his head to one side and said, "What will I wear to go fishing with Jolly?"

Helen leaned down, placed her hands gently atop Charlie's narrow shoulders and said, "Slip on a pair of trousers and gather up the rest of your things. It's summertime. You can go without a shirt today."

"Like the captain does?"

"Like the captain does," Helen confirmed. She dropped her hands away and straightened. "Now go on inside and gather up your soiled things."

Charlie hesitated as if thinking something over. Then shyly he reached out, took Helen's right hand in both of his own, and asked in a soft, hopeful tone, "Come in and help me?"

Helen was in a pickle.

She really didn't want to. Northway would surely follow and she didn't want to go inside with the Yankee captain. There was something disturbingly intimate about her being with him inside the room where he slept each night. Besides, it was downright improper. Her Grandmother Burke would surely have frowned on such libertine behavior.

But the last thing on earth Helen wanted to do was turn down the sweet, fragile child who by his very invitation was showing signs he was beginning to trust her.

Helen went inside with Charlie, Dom slipping in ahead of them.

Kurt followed.

But he purposely stayed near the open door. He stood unmoving with his back resting against the doorjamb, his long, lean frame in a relaxed attitude. Sensing that his presence in the closeness of the quarters might be somehow threatening to Helen, he deliberately maintained his distance.

Helen looked about the large room and could hardly keep from frowning. Consciously hiding her disapproval of the Northways' careless, typically male manner of housekeeping—or lack thereof—she immediately spotted a small, grimy shirt resting squarely atop the blue-and-white-checked tablecloth. The shirt was threadbare and faded from too many washings. The child badly needed clothes. Helen wished she could buy Charlie a whole new wardrobe, but she didn't have the money.

Helen walked over, plucked up the worn shirt, smiled, and said, "One down. Nine to go."

Watching her, Charlie grinned. He dashed across the room with Dom following, grabbed another soiled shirt from off a chair back, spun around, and held it up high for Helen to see.

"Two down!" She pointed at the raised shirt and held up two fingers.

And then it became a contest.

A lively, amusing game to see which one could find the greatest number of dirty shirts. The cat found the foolishness far too strenuous. Dom shook his regal head reproachfully, leaped up onto the unmade bed, stretched out, and closed his eyes as if to say, *Wake me when this nonsense ends.*

Momentarily forgetting Kurt's presence, Helen and

Charlie raced around the cluttered room, hunting, fishing, and yanking soiled shirts from the unlikeliest of locations. A triumphant squeal of delight went up each time either of them hit pay dirt.

Kurt stayed where he was throughout, watching the playful pair from beneath lowered lids, tempted to join in their fun, not daring to do so. No way would he intrude and risk bringing the rollicking game to a premature end.

Kurt kept quiet and thoroughly enjoyed being only a spectator. He watched the two chase madly around the room, squealing and laughing, Helen behaving as if she were the same age as Charlie.

Studying them in their abandon, Kurt wasn't certain which was the most charming. His small, blond, night-shirted son, or the slender, golden-haired, woman-child.

With his sculpted lips turned up into a smile of pure pleasure, Kurt eased down onto his heels in a crouching position, draping a tanned forearm across his thigh.

The spirited game continued.

Finally, when all but one of the shirts had been accounted for, Helen shouted out a loud, resounding "Nine down! Only one more to go!"

Face red from laughing, brown eyes flashing, Charlie turned anxiously about in a circle, searching high and low, eager to be the one to find the last shirt. To beat Helen to it.

From his vantage point across the room, Kurt spotted the missing shirt. Feeling much like a kid himself, he could hardly contain his excitement. Furiously attempting to catch Charlie's eye without alerting Helen, he was at last successful.

Frantic, Charlie finally turned big questioning eyes directly on his father. Kurt grinned at his son and almost imperceptibly gestured, pointing a lean forefinger toward the unmade bed. Charlie's blond head snapped around; he looked at the bed, saw nothing there but the rumpled white bedsheets and the dozing Dom. He quickly turned back to Kurt.

Kurt tapped the floor with his forefinger and again nodded toward the bed. Charlie put his hands on his knees, bent from the waist, peered under the bed, and spotted the shirt.

Bubbling with enthusiasm, he couldn't keep from laughing. His hands flew up to cover his mouth, but not before Helen whirled around, glanced at the grinning Kurt, then at the laughing Charlie.

The secret clearly written on his face, Charlie started for the bed. So did Helen. Screeching so loudly it stirred the dozing Dom, they raced each other across the room. Annoyed, Dom raised his head and glared at them as they fell to their knees beside the bed and hurriedly crawled under. Yelping and wiggling forward on their bellies, they lunged for the shirt.

They wrestled, they reached, and they giggled.

Kurt watched, applauded, and laughed.

Jolly Grubbs, having shouted a greeting several times without receiving an answer, appeared in the open doorway at the height of the fun and frolic. Puzzled, he dropped on the stoop the pair of heavy valises he carried, rapped loudly on the doorframe with his knuckles, and stuck his white head inside.

He couldn't believe what he saw.

Helen and Charlie were under the bed, giggling and scuffling, Helen's skirts and petticoats swirling up around the backs of her dimpled knees, Charlie's long white nightshirt twisted and riding up almost to his tiny heinie. Kurt Northway was watching, laughing, and applauding the lunacy.

" 'Pon my soul," Jolly called out in a loud voice, "have I come to the wrong farm?" He crossed his arms over his chest. "These can't be the folks I know."

Smiling, Kurt came lithely to his feet and motioned

Jolly inside. Shaking the older man's hand, he said, "No mistake, Jolly. This is the place."

"Jolly! Jolly!" Charlie shouted anxiously from under the bed. "It is too us!" He came scrambling out, the dirty shirt forgotten. "It' me, Charlie Whitney Northway!" he said, hurrying to Jolly.

"Well, so it is," said Jolly, nodding, arms coming unfolded, weathered hand going to Charlie's blond head.

Mortified, Helen too came scrambling out from under the bed, wondering miserably what Jolly must think. Face scarlet, she straightened her clothes, smoothed at her hair, and said a brisk, perfunctory good morning as she scooped up Charlie's dirty things and headed hurriedly for the door. There she paused briefly and, without looking at him, said, "Captain, kindly bring your laundry up to the back fence. I haven't got all day!"

Rushing out, she very nearly tripped over the two valises Jolly had left on the stoop and muttered loudly enough to be heard inside about men who never bothered to put anything in its proper place.

Jolly and Kurt exchanged sheepish glances.

Charlie tugged on Jolly's right hand and said, "Are we going fishing? Are we? Are we?"

"Soon as you put on some clothes," said Jolly. "Fish won't bite for a man in his nightshirt. Get your britches on and let's be off."

Charlie raced to the tall chest, fell to his knees, and drew a pair of short navy trousers out of the bottom drawer. "I'll hurry," he said, and, clutching the pants to his chest, dashed into the small curtained alcove they used for a dressing room.

Kurt smiled at Jolly and said, "I guess I'd better be getting my laundry up to the back fence if I know what's good for me."

"Wait a minute, son," said Jolly. "Bring in those two valises I left in Helen's way."

Kurt carried the heavy cases inside and at Jolly's direction placed them on the bed. Jolly unbuckled and unstrapped the valises, opened them. He said, "Jesse, my youngest boy, was about your same size, Captain. No need for all these good clothes going to waste. There's shirts and trousers and suits here. Even some cravats and shoes and . . . and . . ." Jolly paused, shrugged his shoulders.

"Jolly, I can't take—"

"Jesse, my son, won't be needin' 'em anymore."

Kurt caught the sadness that clouded Jolly's flashing blue eyes. He hadn't known, before now, that Jolly had a son.

"Jesse was killed in the war," said Kurt softly, and it was more of a statement than a question.

Jolly nodded. "Jesse and both his big brothers. Robert was the oldest. Danny was my middle son. And Jesse, the baby."

Kurt stared at the floor between his booted feet for a long second, raised his head, and looked Jolly squarely in the eye.

"I'm sorry, Jolly. Jesus, I'm truly sorry."

"I know you are, son." Jolly's fingers brushed fondly over the garments packed neatly in the open valise. "Take the clothes. Jesse had excellent taste. He was a dapper young man. You'll look good in his things."

"Thanks. It would be nice to have some decent clothes for a change," Kurt said, smiling. Then he laid a gentle hand on the older man's shoulder and said softly, "Jolly?"

"Yes?"

"How can you forgive me? Why don't you feel the same hatred for me as the rest?" He looked straight into Jolly's eyes. "You have every reason to hate me as much or more than the others." Kurt's hand dropped from Jolly's shoulder and he looked pointedly at the suitcases filled with a lost son's clothes.

Jolly sighed wearily and admitted, "I 'spect I've wasted more than my share of time ranting with rage and hate and grief. Know something? It never changed a thing. Not one damned thing." He smiled then and added, "I have no malice toward you, Captain. If Alabama was your home, you'd have fought for the Confederacy. Just as Jesse would have fought for the Union had we lived up North." Again he shrugged.

"Providence put you on one side, Jesse and his brothers on the other. The indiscriminate hand of fate spared your life, while my boys ..." He shook his white head and waved a big hand, indicating he didn't want to talk about it further.

"You're a wise man, Jolly Grubbs. And a kind one."

"I don't know about that," said Jolly, nonetheless pleased. Then soberly, "I wish I could say that the rest of the folks down here will be hospitable to you, Captain. I can't do that. These people are dyed-in-the-wool Southerners. The war's over, but they've been whipped, and whipped badly. Blue and gray don't mix any better now than it ever did."

"I understand," said Kurt. "I don't expect the townspeople to be friendly. It doesn't matter."

A worried expression came into Jolly's eyes. "Well, now, son, you might encounter more than just coolness from some of our citizens. We've got some hotheads in Spanish Fort, if you know what I mean."

"I'll watch my step."

"You do that. Just to be on the safe side, I'd—"

Interrupting, Kurt said, "I'm puzzled about something you can probably help me out with."

"I'll do my best," said Jolly.

"On my morning ride I came across three fairly fresh unmarked graves up past the northern field. I was wondering . . ."

Nodding, Jolly said, "Union soldiers with Farragut's fleet. They were on board an advance monitor when it hit a mine in the bay. The mangled bodies washed up on the eastern shore and I buried them. Been meaning to put up some kind of marker but—"

"I'm ready, I'm ready," Charlie interrupted, bursting out of the alcove. He rushed up to Jolly bare-chested in a pair of navy short pants, his shoes on his feet but not yet tied.

"Ready?" Jolly scoffed. "Why, you don't have a shirt on nor your shoelaces tied."

"Helen said I can go without a shirt," Charlie told him.

"Did she, now? Well, if Helen says so, then I guess it's okay. Tie your shoes and let's be on our way."

Charlie made a face. "I don't know how."

"You don't know how?" Jolly said as if astounded. "Well, by jeeters, it's high time you learned." He sat right down on the floor. "Come here to me. I'm fixin' to teach you how to tie your shoes."

While Jolly sat on the floor and patiently taught Charlie how to tie his shoelaces, Kurt unpacked the valises. From the neat stacks of trousers and shirts, he chose a pair of dark twill pants and a pale blue shirt. The trousers fit as if they had been tailored for him. The shirt was a trifle snug across the shoulders and chest, but the sleeves were exactly the right length.

The trio exited the quarters together.

Outdoors, Jolly and Charlie left Kurt, circled around behind the outbuildings, and picked their cautious way down a path in the hovering fog on their way to Jolly's favorite fishing spot on the pier at the bay.

Kurt watched until they were swallowed up in the

heavy mist. Then he turned, looked toward the house, and dutifully headed up to the backyard to take his dirty laundry to Helen.

As ordered.

Chapter Thirteen

Helen couldn't see Kurt coming toward her through the lingering morning fog. Nor could she hear his cat-footed approach. But when he paused a few yards away, she felt his presence as if he had reached out and touched her.

She knew he was there. She knew as well that he was looking at her with that frank male curiosity which she found so annoying, so unsettling. So could feel the heat of his direct green-eyed gaze move appraisingly down the length of her body.

Inwardly Helen shivered.

She whirled away from the steaming black wash pot over which she stood, a poking stick gripped tightly in her hand. "Captain, I don't like people sneaking up on me!"

"Ma'am, I apologize." Kurt immediately came forward, stepping into a patch of brilliant sunshine. "I should have called out to you."

"Yes, you certainly should have. In the future you will kindly remember to ... to ..." Helen stopped speaking and stared at him, her lips slightly parted in astonishment.

Gone was his faded blue army uniform, the only clothes in which she had ever seen him. He looked entirely different without them. He was fresh and well groomed and undeniably handsome in a pair of dark twill trousers and a pale blue summer shirt. The neatly pressed pants fit his slim hips and long legs perfectly. The blue cotton batiste shirt, open at the collar, strained across his broad shoulders and pulled tightly against the muscular biceps of his upper arms. The dark evidence of his virility was faintly visible through the delicate blue fabric lying flat against his chest.

He was potently masculine.

Holding his soiled uniforms balled up in the crook of his arm, Kurt turned slowly around before Helen, presenting his back to her, allowing her to fully examine him. When he pivoted, smiling, back to face her, she was frowning, her well-arched brows knitted together, her soft parted lips now thinned into a stern line.

Kurt was boyishly disappointed. He had expected her to be glad that he'd shed the objectionable union uniform which she found so offensive. Apparently he'd been wrong. It obviously made little difference what he wore. She looked anything but pleased.

In a low casual voice he said, "I'm disappointed, ma'am. I thought you would approve of my new appearance. Don't I look at least a little better?"

Thinking that he looked better than any man—and most especially a Yankee—should be allowed to look, Helen continued to frown. She purposely centered on the lengthy black hair curling down over his blue shirt collar.

"Captain, you need a haircut!" she said, wrinkling her nose with distaste. "Ride into Spanish Fort and visit the barber. Right now. This morning."

A tanned hand lifted to his hair. Lean fingers tunneled through the thick locks at his temple. He said, "It's eight miles to town. I'd lose a whole morning of plowing."

"It's too foggy to get any plowing done," Helen told him. "If you leave now you can be back by noontime or shortly thereafter."

Now it was Kurt who began to frown. "I can't. I can't do that, ma'am." He glanced off toward the distant horizon for an instant, then back at her. "I have no money. I can't even pay for a haircut."

"I can," she said, not looking at him. Turning back to poke at the clothes boiling in the heavy black wash pot mounted on legs over an open fire, she added, "I've a little money saved back."

"I don't want to take your money."

"Call it an advance on what I'll owe you at harvest time." She glanced at him, then at the small bunch of clothes tucked under his arm. She held out her hands. "Your laundry, Captain."

Kurt handed over the soiled, faded uniforms. Helen took them, turned back to the big wash pot, and stood poised as if she intended to drop the clothes into the boiling soapy water.

She hesitated.

She turned and looked at Kurt, defiance flashing in the depths of her blue eyes. Then she tossed everything into the orange flames beneath the wash pot.

She watched transfixed as the clothes caught and began to burn. She saw tongues of fire licking the hated yellow cavalry stripe going down a blue trousers leg. She squinted through the billows of rising smoke as the braided captain's bars decorating a tattered uniform blouse ignited and curled and blackened in the heat. With her poking stick she jabbed at the burning blouse, pushing the brass-buttoned garment more fully into the fire's fiercest flames.

She smiled triumphantly and looked pointedly at Kurt, daring him to object. Expecting—hoping—to see blazing anger or at least a touch of wistfulness in his eyes, Helen was disappointed.

Kurt calmly held her gaze and smiled back at her. In a soft, deep voice he said, "Thank you, ma'am. I'm grateful to you for doing that. Maybe now we can both start to forget all that has happened while I wore that blue uniform."

The wind taken out of her sails, Helen laid her poking stick aside, put her hands on her hips, and stepped closer to Kurt. Blue eyes now blazing like the fire consuming his tattered uniforms, she said coldly, "Captain Northway, in time you may be able to forget. I never will. I don't want to forget. I want to remember everything. I shall go on remembering for as long as I live. I'll take my hatred of your entire murdering army with me to the grave and beyond. Throughout eternity I will remember, Captain Kurtis Northway!"

For a long moment there was total silence. Then he spoke.

"No," he said calmly, "you won't, ma'am. I know how you feel now, but time heals the deepest of wounds. You're young and healthy and very beautiful. You will—"

"Don't you call me beautiful! I don't want to be beautiful to you or for you! You hear me, Captain? To you I'm not a woman, I'm your employer. And you . . . you're a hired hand only and . . . and . . . you're certainly no part of a man to me. Keep that in mind from here on out."

Kurt looked at her lovely face, now flushed with emotion. She was far more passionate than the present situation warranted. He was sure he knew the reason. The lovely, lonely young widow *had* thought of him as a man. And she didn't like it. She didn't like herself for thinking of him as anything other than a hated Union army captain.

A compassionate man, Kurt kept that knowledge to himself. He said, "I will, ma'am. I didn't mean to upset you."

"Upset me? I'm not upset!" she said hotly, then forced a laugh to prove it. "Believe me, you'll know it if I ever do get upset." She took a step backward, adding in a voice gone slightly shrill, "You needn't worry, Captain. *You* aren't capable of upsetting me."

Kurt took a slow step forward. "No, I don't suppose I am."

Helen retreated one more step. "I can assure you that you aren't."

Kurt languidly advanced another step, smiled easily at her. "I see. I guess I should be pleased."

Helen moved back, smiled back. "But instead your feelings are hurt, Captain?"

Kurt confidently moved closer to her. "A little, I'll admit."

Helen defensively moved farther from him. "Should I wonder why?" Her tone was derisive.

Kurt didn't take another step. He shoved his hands into the pockets of his tight twill trousers and fixed her with those riveting green eyes. "Mrs. Courtney," he said in tones so low and soft it was almost like a caress, "I've an idea that you already know."

She understood what he meant. She did know. His inflated male pride was wounded by the notion that he had no effect on her. She had little doubt that the vain Yankee army captain was accustomed to having women throw themselves at his handsome head. So he had arrogantly supposed that she would behave as foolishly as the others.

Well, he was wrong. Dead wrong.

She said, "Yes, Captain. I do know." Her blue eyes flashed the message that she was secure in the knowledge she was the one in charge here. "Go saddle your sorrel thoroughbred while I get some coins from the house. I don't want to look at that shaggy head of hair one more minute."

She turned and marched away. Kurt stayed where he was, admiring her queenly carriage, the seductive sway of her skirts, the flash of golden hair as she moved into and out of patches of bright sunlight.

His unblinking gaze followed her every step, and he stood there torn by two conflicting impulses. One was to inflict pain by going after her, grabbing her, and showing her the rude reality of his being a man, she a woman. The other was to protect and shield her from him and from herself.

Kurt slowly raised both hands, swept back his lengthy black hair, turned, and headed for the corral to saddle Raider.

He expected to see Helen back at the wash pot when he led the saddled stallion outside, but she was nowhere in sight. He dropped Raider's reins, told the stallion not to wander off, and started for the house. When he reached the back porch, he spotted the shiny coins lying on the top step.

Kurt bent from the waist, scooped up the coins, and dropped them deep down inside his trousers pocket. His eyes fixed on the back door, he turned his head, listened, heard nothing. He shrugged, went back to Raider, mounted, and left.

From inside the dim, cool interior of the silent sitting room, Helen watched him ride away. She watched as he cantered the big sorrel up the path alongside the house and turned him onto the narrow dirt rode. She watched as he rounded the corner and rode southward, disappearing into patches of fog. Then reappearing in shafts of radiant sunshine, his too-long midnight hair shimmering like shiny black silk in the dazzling light.

Helen unconsciously held her breath and watched until he finally turned the stallion into the shady lane and disappeared.

Only then did she release the heavy curtains, allowing them to fall back into place. Exhaling with relief, Helen walked through the house, rushed out the back door, and hurried anxiously down to check on her laundry.

At the big black wash pot, she picked up the poking

pole, stuck it into the bubbling water, and brought up a shirt. A small, little boy's shirt which had been badly soiled and now, miraculously, was snowy white once more. The sight of the spanking-clean shirt immediately gave Helen that sense of satisfaction which comes from a task well done.

The unsettling effects of last night's dream were beginning to leave her along with the worrisome man she'd just watched ride away. Like all dreams—the good ones and the bad ones—it no longer seemed so real, was already becoming harder to recall. Thank heavens.

Helen finally began to hum just as she always did on wash day.

Chapter Fourteen

Kurt anticipated a chilly reception in Spanish Fort. He knew how unwelcome he was in the still smoldering, Yankee-hating town. It didn't bother him a great deal. War-hardened and a natural loner, he had never sought nor needed any man's approval save his own.

In peacetime and in war he lived by his individual code of ethics. He had been on his own since age fourteen, had done the work of a man when he was no more than a boy. He'd kept his own counsel, settled his own scores, nursed his own secret hurts and heartaches.

He had served his country with pride and with honor. He'd killed men in battle with cool detachment and no scarring remorse. As a soldier serving his country, he had been given a job to do and he had done it to the best of his ability. That was all any man could do.

Raider tossed his big head and made snorting noises as the pair approached the scattered outskirts of Spanish Fort. Kurt laid a comforting hand on the stallion's sleek neck, patted the sorrel affectionately, and said, "It's all right, old friend. Settle down, boy. Easy, now. We made it through some mighty tough spots in the war. We can survive one afternoon in Spanish Fort."

Raider pricked his ears, whinnied, and immediately picked up the pace. As resigned as his self-controlled master, he pranced majestically up the road toward their final destination.

The first thing Kurt saw above the dense towering pines and ancient oaks was a Confederate flag, its edges trimmed with gold fringe. Topping a tall flagstaff pine pole, the Rebel flag fluttered proudly in the breeze blowing in off the bay.

His eyes on the rippling Stars and Bars, Kurt took a slow, deep breath, put a tight, cynical smile on his face, and rode into the sleepy Southern town.

Main street, leading into Spanish Fort, ran north and south. Residences lined both sides of the street south of the business section. Homes small and large faced each other across the wide thoroughfare. Kurt never turned his head to the left or the right, but he knew he was being watched.

On he rode, soon leaving the dwellings behind, reaching the commercial district. He passed a public bathhouse next door to a livery stable. The newspaper office was across the street, as well as the hardware store, the lumber yard, and the dentist's office. On his right a couple of well-dressed ladies, exiting a millinery shop, saw him and acted as if Lucifer himself had just ridden into their hometown. They shrank back, clutching each other's hands, as they stared open-mouthed at him.

Kurt nodded his dark head in their direction, then smiled when they gasped in stunned horror and rushed back inside the safety of the millinery shop. Men, lining the town's wooden sidewalks, didn't flee from him in fear. Instead they shouted insults and threats to which Kurt paid no attention.

At the freighting depot and stage line, a handsomely dressed lady alighted from the just-arrived Fairhope stage. As Kurt rode past, she looked directly at him. But unlike the pair of ladies at the millinery, she didn't gasp or recoil or hurry to get away. From underneath

her expensive bonnet worn atop a mass of dark, up-
swept curls, she looked at him with bold interest. Then
flirtatiously lowered her heavily lashed lids over a pair
of dark, flashing eyes.

Knowing she had captured his attention, the woman
glanced at him again, smiled almost imperceptibly,
turned, and slowly made her way around the parked
stage to the sidewalk. She was a glamorous, voluptuous woman. The stylish lavender-hued summer frock
she wore enhanced her pale coloring; the gown's tight
bodice was molded provocatively to her lush feminine
curves.

Kurt watched the woman step up onto the sidewalk,
managing as she did so to flash a pair of slender, well-
turned ankles encased in shimmering sheer silk stockings. She never turned back to look at him, but Kurt
knew she'd purposely exposed her lovely ankles solely
for him to admire.

She dropped her billowing lavender skirts and
moved grandly down the wooden sidewalk. The men
loitering on the street tipped their hats and smiled and
acted as if a queen were in their midst.

The woman paused directly before a many-
windowed office half a block away. She put her gloved
hand on the knob of a glass-paned door on which
LOVELESS ENTERPRISES was written in fancy gold lettering. Kurt's eyes narrowed as she swept inside and
closed the door behind her.

Loveless Enterprises.

It had to be the office of Niles Loveless, the wealthy
aristocratic landowner Jolly had told him about. The
same Niles Loveless who was determined to own Hel-
en's farm and timberlands. The lovely lady who'd gone
inside? Probably the pampered Mrs. Niles Loveless.

Kurt passed Jake's General Store. He pulled up on
Raider when he saw the colorful barber pole outside
Skeeter's Barbershop. Kurt swung down out of the

saddle, looped Raider's long reins over the hitching post, patted the big stallion, and said into his pricked ear, "I won't be long."

Hearing spirited muttering and feeling hostile eyes watching his every move from up and down the street, Kurt didn't so much as blink an eye. In no particular hurry, he mounted the sidewalk, headed directly for the open front door of the barbershop, and went inside.

The shop boasted two barber chairs. Both were filled. One customer was being shaved by a tall, skinny fellow in a white barber's coat. In the other chair a middle-aged man with only a horseshoe ring of fine wispy hair was having it painstakingly clipped by a short, pudgy fellow Kurt took to be Skeeter.

Skeeter looked at Kurt, gave him the once-over, and frowned. He said, "We're pretty busy this morning."

"So I see," said Kurt, smiling, and took a seat on the long wooden bench against the wall. "No hurry. I'll wait."

There he sat throughout the morning as men came in for haircuts and shaves and were promptly accommodated. It was nearing noon before both barber chairs were finally empty, both barbers idle.

Kurt rose from the hard bench, stretched, crossed the small shop. From a shelf on the wall he took a clean white covering cloth, whipped it around his neck, and tied it behind his head. He then took a seat in Skeeter's chair.

"Dinnertime," Skeeter said to his tall, skinny fellow barber, then looked pointedly at Kurt.

Kurt stayed where he was as the pudgy Skeeter hurried to the front door, looked back at Kurt, and indicated with a shake of his head that Kurt was to leave. "We both take an hour to eat dinner. You might as well—"

"I'll wait," said Kurt, and didn't move.

Skeeter's fleshy face reddened. He slammed the front door shut and hung up the CLOSED sign.

The barbers exchanged glances, shrugged, and fled to the back room, leaving Kurt alone in the shop, seated in the barber chair, calmly twiddling his thumbs beneath the white covering cloth.

It was nearing noon when Helen finished the last of the laundry. She was standing at the black wash pot, squeezing the excess water from freshly rinsed bed linen, when she heard a faint shout. She looked up expecting to see the newly shorn Yankee riding toward her.

A shiny black carriage was emerging from the oak-bordered lane below the house. Helen stood for a moment, the heavy sheet in her wet hands, squinting against the now brilliant sunshine.

A white-gloved hand furiously waving a lacy handkerchief shot from a curtained side window of the fine carriage, followed straightaway by a bobbing head of dark glossy curls.

"Helen! Helen, I'm back!" shouted Em Ellicott from inside the slow-moving conveyance. "Where are you? I'm back!"

"Em," Helen quietly murmured, then smiled, dropped the sheet back into the blue rinse water, and grabbed up her apron to dry her hands. She began running.

Em had the door open and was hopping out well before the aged, dignified Ellicott driver had a chance to climb down off the box and assist his spirited mistress. Em lifted her billowing skirts high and raced headlong to meet Helen, whooping and shouting as she flew.

When the two women met, they threw their arms around each other, embraced warmly, then broke apart. Holding hands, they jumped up and down, giggling and shrieking like a couple of schoolgirls.

Old Daniel, the Ellicott's faithful gray-haired driver,

scratched and shook his head, muttering to himself. "If you ask me, just might as well give up on Mistress Emma ever growin' up into a fine lady like her mama. Half the time she act like she don' have good sense and I ain't right sure she do. Squealing like a stuck pig, jest 'cause she see Miz Courtney." Daniel rolled his nearsighted brown eyes heavenward. "The good Lord alone know how she behaved herself when Mistah Coop go to meet her over at the Mobile levee. Likely she shamed the whole family, behavin' worse than some white trash woman, a huggin' and a kissin' on the sheriff right there in broad daylight. Why, I don't know what gonna' become of that—"

"Why, I'm bound straight for purgatory, Daniel," Em called over her shoulder to the censuring old family retainer as she and Helen started for the house.

"You is right 'bout that if you don't be mendin' your ways," huffed old Daniel before climbing up into the carriage to take a much-needed nap.

Em and Helen laughed and hurried to the house, arm in arm, both talking at once.

"... and I should have known my little scheme wouldn't work," lamented Em.

"... am positive everyone's talking about it," worried Helen.

"... had hoped Coop might realize he can no longer live without me ..."

"... but I simply had no choice, so I hired ..."

"... gone for four years in the war, so how could I expect ten days to ..."

"... and would do anything necessary to hold on to this land ..."

"... almost weakened, but then he came to his senses ..."

They had reached the front gallery. Em interrupted herself to ask, "Where's your Yankee?"

"He's not *my* Yankee!"

"Kitty Fay Pepper said she heard he's good-looking in a dark, primitive way." She arched her eyebrows. "Is he?"

"I guess he's not too unattractive." Helen shrugged. "I hadn't given it much thought."

"Well, where is he? I didn't see him down in the fields plowing as we drove up."

"He isn't here. He rode into town to get a haircut."

"The devil!" said Em. "I'll have to wait to look him over then? I was hoping to meet him today."

"Meet him?" echoed Helen, incredulous. "Good Lord, Em, you aren't going to meet him."

"Betcha I do," predicted Em, and laughed gaily when Helen shook her head, exasperated.

They were inside the quiet old house now. Helen led the way to her bedroom, where they could visit and enjoy the breeze off the bay. There she quickly changed out of her dampened wash dress while Em kicked off her slippers, climbed up onto the soft feather bed, and crossed her legs beneath her. Em peeled off her white cotton gloves and tossed them on the night table, loosened the lacy collar of her dress, and flipped her dark dancing curls back off her face.

Em talked a mile a minute.

She bitterly complained to Helen that her visit in New Orleans had worked no magic on her big, stubborn, redheaded sweetheart. Coop swore he had missed her terribly, but he obviously hadn't missed her enough to propose, as she had hoped.

She admitted she'd been foolish to suppose such a miracle would occur. After all, the big brave man she loved had been away from her throughout the interminably long war, seeing her only a twice in those four lonely years. Yet when the conflict had finally ended and he'd come back home for good, he hadn't asked her to marry him.

Em talked of her boring stay in the Crescent City

with a house full of obnoxious cousins. She admitted that when finally she got back home, she had shoved Coop inside the carriage and kissed him over and over, doing her darnedest to make him surrender. Said she blew in his ear and whispered that if they paid a quick visit to the justice of the peace, they could spend the rest of their day at the Conde Hotel doing more than just kissing.

"Em Ellicott, you didn't actually say that, did you?" Helen said.

"Sure as heck did," stated Em emphatically. "It almost worked too. I could tell by the pulse hammering on Coop's forehead. But alas, my big straitlaced, duty-first darling said he had to get back to Spanish Fort by noon to transport the jail's one and only occupant over to Mobile for trial." She laughed good-naturedly and added, "Can you believe it? I get beat out by a common thief!"

In time Em began to wind down, after filling Helen in on practically every moment of every day she had been away. Helen was sitting on the bed, her back against the tall mahogany headboard, arms wrapped around her raised knees. And she was laughing. Em always made her stories colorful and amusing, and just listening to her chatter made Helen feel good.

When finally Em's narrative on Coop and New Orleans was concluded, she said, "So now I'll shut my big mouth and you tell me what's been going on here. Tell me about your Yankee and—"

Helen abruptly stopped laughing.

"Em Ellicott, I told you, he is not *my* Yankee."

"Oh, you know what I mean. How did it come about? Jolly sent him out here, I'll bet? I understand the Yankee's got a young son. What's the little boy like? What's the Yankee like? Tell, tell, tell! Start at the very beginning." Em fell over onto her back, threw her arms above her head, and waited.

"You don't blame me, do you?"

"For what?" Em's head lifted from the mattress and she looked at Helen. "For hiring a strong-backed man to help you work this farm?" She laid back down. "I should hope not."

"I knew you'd say that," mused Helen gratefully.

She told her best friend about Kurt and Charlie Northway. About how Kurt was a hard worker and Charlie was the cutest little boy imaginable. Said the child had lost his mother and grandparents and he was so withdrawn, she'd been afraid he would never be normal, but that Jolly had taken Charlie under his wing and the two were the greatest of friends. Said they were down at the bay fishing together this very moment.

Helen talked at length about Charlie, said very little about Charlie's father. In midsentence, she interrupted herself, sighed, and said, "Oh, Em, you understand why I would hire a Yankee to help out. I had no choice. Why can't the others see it?"

"The others can't see beyond the ends of their long noses," Em snorted. "What do you care what they say or think, so long as you get to keep your farm?"

"I suppose I shouldn't."

"No, you shouldn't. I don't! Why, I'm certain the whole blessed town gossips constantly about me chasing after Coop. But so what? Think I give a tinkers damn?" Em laughed to show that she didn't. But abruptly she stopped laughing and levered herself back up into a sitting position. Swinging around to face Helen, she asked, "Have the busybodies been ugly to you?"

Helen shook her head. "No. Not really."

"You're lying to me, Helen Burke Courtney! Tell me the truth or I'll pinch you like I used to when we were kids."

Helen sighed. "I went into Spanish Fort last Saturday for supplies just like I always do. It was awful. Really awful." She closed her eyes for a second, opened them. "Jake didn't want me in his store. The Livingston sisters ... they crossed the street to keep from speaking."

Her face as dark as a thundercloud, Em reached for Helen's hand and held it firmly in both of her own. "I'm so sorry. I wish I'd been here. I wish I had been with you. I'd have told them all—the whole town—to go straight to blazes! I'd have had Coop arrest the entire lot of them and throw them in the pokey! I'd have made them sorry their mamas ever gave birth! I'd have seen to it that—"

"Lord, I'm glad you're home," Helen happily interrupted, smiling sunnily again.

"Me too. I just wish to high heaven Coop was as glad."

"You know Coop's happy to have you back."

"Mmmmm. Not quite happy enough to marry me."

Em dropped Helen's hand, clasped both of hers beneath her chin as if in prayer, closed her eyes, and murmured, "You hear me up there, Lord? I need some help down here getting a reluctant redheaded sheriff down the aisle. Think you can do something about it, please? And make it snappy." She opened her eyes, dropped her hands to her knees, and winked at Helen.

Grinning, she said, "You don't think the Almighty will strike me dead for being such a self-centered woman, do you?"

"Not if he hasn't already."

Both women dissolved into spasms of girlish laughter.

Chapter Fifteen

Kurt was still seated in the chair, the white cloth draped around his shoulders, when Skeeter and his helper returned an hour later. The two barbers were not alone.

A half dozen townsmen escorted the pair into their shop. All the men wore identical antagonistic expressions. All were armed. All were purposely exposing their weapons.

The short, pudgy Skeeter elbowed his way through the cluster of taller men, stepped up directly before Kurt, and said, "I ain't going to cut your hair."

"You're not?" Kurt replied evenly.

"No, I'm not!" Skeeter announced loudly, puffing out his chest and looking around at his audience of backup toughs. Chuckling, he bravely added, "You won't get a haircut in this town as long as I'm the barber."

"That a fact?"

"Yes, that's a fact." Skeeter took a menacing step closer. "So just what do you aim to do about it, Yankee?"

Kurt maintained his cool, casual manner. He lifted his hands up behind his head, untied the draped cloth, and pulled it away from his body. When he stood up, the blustering Skeeter took a defensive step backward. Kurt smiled. Then, taking his time, he folded the large cloth neatly and handed it to the barber.

He started to move toward the door. Six armed men stood in his way.

"Excuse me," he said, and pushed resolutely through the crowd. Grumbling and issuing threats, they allowed him to pass.

"Answer me, Yankee!" Skeeter wouldn't let it go. "What are you going to do about it?"

Kurt had reached the door. He paused, turned back, and acted as if he were thinking it over. Then he ran a hand through his unshorn locks and grinned.

"Not a thing." He exited the barbershop, unfazed by the shouted insults to his manhood and the loud derisive laughter which followed him.

As Kurt stood on the sunny sidewalk outside Skeeter's Barbershop, Niles Loveless, behind the locked door of his closed office half a block away, was scolding the forward Yasmine Parnell for taking such unnecessary risks.

"You're never to come here again," he said, buttoning his shirt. "I've told you before!"

"Never's such a long time, darling," said Yasmine, resting a bare foot atop his mahogany desk and seductively pulling a sheer silk stocking up her bare shapely leg. "Besides, you enjoy the added danger, just as I do." She slowly molded the transparent stocking up over her pale thigh and smiled accusingly at him. "Don't you?"

He couldn't deny it.

The beautiful Yasmine had been in his office for hours. She had breezed in at midmorning, looking incredibly desirable in a figure-hugging gown of lavender silk and matching bonnet, locked the door behind herself, and challenged, "Niles Loveless, if you're half the man I think you are, you'll make love to me this minute!"

She hadn't waited for a reply. She'd begun stripping immediately while he'd watched and begged her to stop and hoped she would and hoped she wouldn't. She hadn't. Wearing only her fashionable lavender bonnet, the rest of her clothes scattered about on the plush carpet, she crossed to him, swept his massive desk clean of all papers, pens, and framed photographs, climbed atop it, stretched out like a lazy cat, and purred, "I'm not leaving here until I have what I want."

Niles gave it to her.

Hands trembling, heart thudding with a mixture of hot desire and nervous trepidation, he took off his clothes and joined her atop the shiny desk. The door had remained locked all morning and on through the noon hour.

Now, at shortly after one o'clock, Niles was rushing her to get dressed, reminding her he had a business engagement at one-thirty and if she didn't hurry, they would get caught.

Yasmine wasn't worried.

She lowered her stockinged leg to the floor, slipped her foot into her kid-leather slipper, and dropped the billowing skirts of her silk lavender gown. Exhaling deeply, causing her ample bosom to swell against the low-cut bodice of her tight gown, she shook her bonneted head and laughed.

Picking up her reticule, she said, "Niles, darling, you worry too much. I made it a point to tell anyone who would listen that I had a scheduled meeting here in your office this morning. One which might prove quite lengthy."

"Good God, you didn't," said Niles, horrified. "And just exactly what was this so-called meeting to be about?"

"Why, the intricate, time-consuming handling of my assets," Yasmine teased, coming to him, straightening his cravat, pressing her assets against him. "Relax, my love. Everyone knows you promised dear Walter you'd take care of all my affairs."

"Yes, I did." Niles grinned then. "I've taken care of a bit more than old Walter had in mind." His hands slid down from her narrow waist and over the swell of her hips to possessively cup the rounded cheeks of her bottom through her rustling dress. Squeezing gently, he teased, "Do you suppose old Walter would approve of the way I'm 'handling your assets'?"

At times Niles felt almost guilty about their blazing affair. Walter W. Parnell had been an old and dear friend of the Loveless family, had grown up with Niles's father, Bennett Loveless. The two older men were partners in many business ventures, including banks throughout the South and a string of fine-blooded racehorses. With Bennett's untimely death when Niles was barely twenty, Walter Parnell became a father figure and mentor to Niles.

Niles remembered well the summer the widowed, forty-five-year-old Walter married the eighteen-year-old Yasmine, a milky-skinned Creole belle from New Orleans. That had been fifteen years ago. At the time, Niles had just turned twenty-two and had been married himself for less than a year to the pretty nineteen-year-old Patsy McClelland.

The moment he'd laid eyes on Yasmine, Niles had wanted her. But old Walter Parnell was nobody's fool. He'd locked the delectable Yasmine up in his pillared mansion, giving her no opportunity to dilly dally. She had gained the respect and admiration of the citizenry, who'd been skeptical when first Walter had brought home his beautiful young bride.

She had carefully maintained that respect when Walter Parnell rode proudly off to war at age fifty-six, leaving his trusted twenty-nine-year-old wife behind, making her promise she would call on Niles Loveless should she need anything.

Niles smiled now as he thought back on it.

Yasmine had needed something, all right. And he'd been just the man to give it to her.

The dust had hardly settled behind the departing Walter Parnell before Yasmine had summoned Niles to the big Parnell estate. In the soft feather bed she had shared with her husband, they made wildly physical love for the entirety of that cool April day. A violent meeting of bare burning bodies. An explosive coupling of hungry beasts, starving for the feasts of forbidden flesh.

The clever, provocative Yasmine had kept him wanting her with a white-hot passion ever since. A cruel creature, she loved showing up unannounced at his home on the pretense of visiting his unsuspecting wife, Patsy. She took a perverse pleasure from seeing him squirm as he played his role of faithful husband and contented family man while she lounged seductively in his drawing room, looking so lovely and sensual it was all he could do to keep his hands off her.

"Come by the house later this afternoon when you're finished here," said Yasmine, bringing Niles back to the present.

"Fine, fine. But now you really must go."

He opened the door, handed her out, and said loudly enough for any passersby to hear, "Don't mention it, Mrs. Parnell. Always glad to be of service."

"Good day to you, Niles. Give my best to Patsy."

She smiled, turned, lifted her skirts, and stopped short when her flashing eyes caught sight of a jet-haired man moving lithely toward a tethered sorrel stallion.

She heard Niles exclaim from behind, "Will you look at that magnificent beast!"

"Yes, isn't he," murmured Yasmine. She wasn't referring to the equine creature, but Niles was far too preoccupied to catch her meaning.

"I've got to own that thoroughbred!" Niles said, then stepped around Yasmine and hurried down the sidewalk toward Kurt Northway.

"Niles Loveless," he said, and put out his hand. "I don't believe we've met."

Before Kurt had a chance to respond, Yasmine Parnell stepped eagerly in front of Niles, offered her own small gloved hand, and said, "I'm the widowed Mrs. Walter Parnell. You must be Helen's Yankee."

"I'm Kurt Northway, Mrs. Parnell," Kurt said, unsmiling, as he gently shook her hand and released it. "My son and I hired out to do some seasonal labor at Mrs. Courtney's farm."

"So it's true," said Yasmine. "You're living with Helen."

She saw a muscle jump in his jaw, knew he was gritting his teeth. He said, "Mrs. Courtney has been kind enough to provide temporary quarters down at the barn."

Despite all the gossip she'd heard about the "crude, dirty Yankee," Yasmine detected the instinctive manners of good breeding. His impeccable manners were not all she noticed. He was tall and lean and aggressively male. Just looking at him made her feel small and soft and gloriously female.

"I wonder, Mr. Northway," she said, lowering her lashes slightly, glancing cautiously at Niles, then back at Kurt, "if you'd be interested in a little seasonal work at my estate. I'm always in search of good—"

"Thank you, ma'am. Mrs. Courtney keeps me pretty busy."

"Oh, I'll just bet she does," said Yasmine.

Kurt overlooked the snide comment. "If you'll excuse me, I should be getting—"

"Wait, wait," said Niles, running his hands appreciatively over Raider's big, sleek body. "How much do you want for your stallion, Northway?"

Kurt smiled. "Raider's not for sale, Loveless."

Niles finally looked up. "Don't be absurd. I'll offer you a pretty penny for the stallion. Step on down to my office with me and I'll—"

"The stallion is not for sale."

"Look, perhaps I haven't made myself clear. I'm willing to pay far more than the sorrel is actually worth. What would you say to one thousand dollars? Cash on the barrelhead. I'll give you this very—"

"No, thanks." Kurt unlooped Raider's reins from the hitching post and stepped into the street.

"Twelve hundred!" said Niles, anxiously following Kurt. "You can't turn down twelve hundred! I want this horse."

"So do I," said Kurt, and mounted.

Niles caught hold of the bridle. "Look, Northway, I thought . . . I was told you're only working at Helen Courtney's place in order to get the money to go back home."

"You heard correctly." Kurt nodded, slowly backed the stallion away.

"For twelve hundred dollars you and your boy can ride the train home and still have plenty left over to get started on a—"

"Good day, Mrs. Parnell. Mr. Loveless." Kurt wheeled Raider about in a tight semicircle and rode away.

"Fifteen hundred! Seventeen-fifty!" Niles frantically called, running a few steps after him, but Kurt didn't look back.

His eyes clinging to the shimmering sorrel stallion, Niles Loveless stood in the dusty street muttering to himself, "I must have that stallion! He's the finest thoroughbred I've ever seen in my life! I'd bet everything I own he'd be a shoe-in to win the race at the Baldwin County Fair! Dammit, he's exactly what I need to make my stable the envy of every discerning horseman in the South."

While Niles's covetous gaze followed the cantering stallion, Yasmine's interested gaze followed the jet-haired man astride. To herself she silently thought, *I must have that man! He's the finest specimen of masculinity I've ever seen in my life! He's exactly what I need to counterbalance my affair with Niles. With both I'd have a rich golden god to fill my warm, lazy afternoons. And a dark, dangerous devil to fill the sultry summer nights. The handsome Yankee's exactly what I need to make my boudoir the envy of every discriminating female in the South.*

"Look at that deep chest! The lean flanks! Those extraordinary legs," murmured a lustful Niles Loveless.

"I am," breathed an equally lustful Yasmine Parnell. "I am."

Chapter Sixteen

Helen stood in the sun waving good-bye as the Ellicott carriage slowly rolled away. Charlie was at Helen's side, waving too. He liked the talkative Em.

He and Jolly had returned from their fishing expedition around noontime, proudly displaying their catch. Now Jolly had gone home to rest.

It was the middle of the afternoon and all was very still. Not a hint of a breeze stirred the leaves on the trees or cooled the heavy air. And it was warm. Unseasonably warm for early June. Helen could feel her petticoat sticking to her legs and beads of perspiration forming at her hairline.

Helen waved until the big black carriage turned into the tree-bordered lane and disappeared. Then she looked down at Charlie. He was attempting to stifle a big yawn.

Helen smiled and said, "If I know Jolly, he's sound asleep in his favorite chair. Think you might like to take a little nap?" Charlie nodded sleepily. "I'll walk you to the quarters," said Helen. She held out her hand and to her surprised delight, the child placed his small warm palm in hers.

At the quarters Helen went directly to the bed, fluffed up the pillows, and smoothed the covers. Charlie put a knee on the mattress, climbed up, and stretched out on his back.

Flinging his short arms up over his head, he said,

"Wake me up when the captain gets back." He flashed that wide smile which enchanted her and at the same time broke her heart.

"All right," Helen said, tempted to kiss his smooth forehead.

"Helen," Charlie said softly, eyelids closing as he slipped toward slumber.

"Yes, Charlie?"

Helen's throat tightened painfully when the sweet little boy asked, "Will this be my home forever?"

Helen hadn't had to answer Charlie. He fell asleep instantly. But his words still rang in her ears an hour later as she completed the laundry. Struggling, she tipped over and emptied the wooden rinse barrel and the black wash pot. She was righting the heavy black pot when she heard the drum of hoofbeats.

The Yankee was back.

Helen's first impulse was to hurry and get inside before he spotted her. She changed her mind. She was mildly curious. She wanted to see how he looked with a decent haircut.

She began to frown skeptically when Kurt dismounted just outside the corral. Her jaw tightening, she started toward him, inspecting him closely, her gaze on his full head of gleaming black hair.

She heard him softly command his stallion to go on into the corral. The stallion obeyed.

Kurt turned to face her, but he didn't take one step. He waited. He let her come to him.

Growing angrier with every step she took, Helen doggedly approached, her blue eyes snapping with exasperation. She reached him, looked pointedly at his unshorn hair, then directly into his deep green eyes.

"Captain, are you bound and determined to annoy me?" She gave him no time to answer. "Must you stubbornly refuse to do what I ask of you? I specifically requested that you get your hair cut and you agreed! You took my money. You went into town. You've been gone the whole livelong day! You come riding back here in the late afternoon and your hair hasn't been touched! What on God's green earth have you been doing all this time? Drinking whiskey at the Red Rose Saloon? Gambling at Shelby's Poker Palace? You're either a fool or a hardhead or both! You can't expect to squander my hard-earned money and be allowed to remain here on this farm. I made that crystal clear the very first day, but you obviously weren't paying attention." She drew a quick, much-needed breath. "Just what have you to say for yourself?"

"Not too much," Kurt said in the same low-level tones he always used.

He reached down inside the front pocket of his trousers, withdrew the coins he hadn't spent, and held them out to her.

"I didn't get the haircut," he admitted. "But I didn't squander your hard-earned money either."

Puzzled, Helen looked at the coins resting on his palm. She didn't reach for them. She looked up sharply at him. "Why? Why didn't you have your hair cut?"

Kurt reached out, took her hand, and spilled the coins into it. "The barber refused."

"Skeeter Jones wouldn't cut your hair?"

"No, ma'am. Nor would his assistant."

"That's absurd. I've never heard of anything so . . . Why would he do a thing like that? I've never known Skeeter to turn down business. I can't understand . . ." Her words trailed off.

"It appears the town barber doesn't like Yankees any better than the rest of the good folks in Spanish Fort." Kurt shrugged wide shoulders.

Helen opened her mouth, closed it without speaking. She stared at him. She studied his dark, chiseled face with the too-long black curls falling over his forehead

and the deep forest-green eyes as calm as the quiet afternoon. He seemed totally composed. As impassive as
ever.

Helen felt her anger at him swiftly turning into anger
at the citizens of Spanish Fort. It was then, that moment, as she stood there in the warm sunshine on that
still June afternoon, that she felt, for the first time, a
vague kinship to the tall, shaggy-haired man before
her.

He was a Yankee, yes, but he was—to the best of her
knowledge—a law-abiding man who had gone peacefully into a place of business, not looking to cause
trouble, offering money in exchange for services rendered. He didn't deserve to be turned away any more
than a well-behaved Southerner would deserve to be
turned away in some Northern establishment.

"Captain," Helen said finally, a hint of kindness in
her voice, "I'm sorry for what happened at the barbershop. And I'm sorry as well for all the unkind things
I said to you. I apologize."

"Apology accepted. I understand."

"I'll cut your hair."

His green eyes immediately widened.

"I'll do it right now. This afternoon."

Kurt smiled then. "I've never had a lady cut my
hair."

Helen didn't smile, but her face had lost its tightness
and her eyes softened. "Then we're even, Captain. I've
never cut a man's hair." She turned away, paused, and
said, "Unsaddle Raider and give him his rubdown.
Charlie should be awake by then. The two of you come
on up to the house. I'll meet you on the front porch."

"We'll be there," said Kurt.

Helen waited for the pair on the shaded front veranda. All was ready. She had spread a worn sheet on
the porch's wooden floor. That done, she had placed a
straight-backed kitchen chair squarely in the center of

the spread sheet. On the chair seat lay a folded white towel, a pair of scissors, a soft-bristled brush, and a round hand mirror with a long silver handle.

As she waited for the pair, Helen leaned against a solid porch pillar, her arms folded, and looked out over the calm blue bay. All traces of the morning's thick shrouding mists had long since evaporated. The sun shone down from a cloudless sky, its fierce glare making tiny reflecting mirrors of the outgoing tide's gentle waves.

Across the wide bay rose the buildings of Mobile, shimmering in the afternoon sunlight. Just south of the city, at the entrance to the bay, were the tall turrets and huge cannons of Fort Gaines. In the harbor one lonely passenger steamer, a couple of shrimp boats, and a few scattered timber barges moved easily in and out of the port.

Helen sighed.

She recalled the time before the war when the harbor of Mobile was one of the busiest in the entire country. Huge cargo freighters bound for England, Spain, the Caribbean maneuvered cautiously through the heavy traffic of sleek sailing vessels, majestic riverboats, burly tugs, and huge barges.

Back then the active port with its constantly bustling levee was an exciting place. So incredibly thrilling to stroll down the wide wooden wharf through the milling crowds. Banjos playing gaily. Smiling youths tap-dancing while people tossed coins at their feet. Vendors selling fresh flowers and sugary pralines and sun-ripened fruit. Elegantly gowned ladies and handsomely dressed gentlemen promenading to see and be seen. Well-heeled passengers disembarking from wedding-cake-trimmed sidewheelers.

It was over. The good life. The old life. The golden days and nights. Gone. All gone. It would never come back again.

"Mrs. Courtney." Kurt Northway's deep voice from very near pulled Helen from her wistful reverie.

Blinking away the past, she turned to see Kurt round the corner of the house. Alone. Before she could question him, he said, "Charlie was sleeping so soundly, I hated to wake him."

"He's had a busy day," Helen replied, nodding.

But even as she calmly made the statement, she was frantically wishing that Charlie was awake, was going to be with them. Or that she had not offered to cut Northway's hair. Never in a million years would she have made such a proposal had she known he would come alone. Now she couldn't very well back out.

Kurt walked up beside her, stood looking out over the wide expanse of the calm blue bay. Sensing her edginess, he made a special effort to put her at her ease. Smoothly engaging her in casual conversation, he commented on the breathtaking view from the wide shaded gallery.

His gaze fixed on the buildings of Mobile, he told of his and Charlie's day-long stay in the gleaming old city across the water. He asked the names of the myriad sweet-smelling bushes and flowering trees filling her big front yard. He pointed to the thick maze of lush green foliage below them, bordering the yard.

Helen explained that the dense junglelike growth totally enveloped the bluffs where the headland fell away and sloped down to the bay fifty feet below. Pointing, she told him that once there had been stairs leading from the yard's front border all the way down to the water's edge. Her Grandpa Burke had built them before she was born.

"And you used to skip down those stairs, counting the steps as you went," said Kurt, smiling, his eyes remaining on the dramatic landscape spread out at their feet.

She looked at him. "Yes, yes, I did. But that was a

long time ago. The steps have all fallen down or rotted
from the rains. The swampy jungle had reclaimed most
of the path Grandpa cleared to build the steps." Helen
turned away. "It's Dominic's domain now. We'd better
get started on that haircut."

"You're right," Kurt said, and began unbuttoning his
blue cotton shirt as Helen walked away.

From the straight-backed chair, Helen picked up the
scissors, brush, and long-handled hand mirror. "Captain, I've laid out a towel for you to—" she turned
quickly, practically bumped into his broad, bare chest,
and stopped speaking.

Kurt reached out, touched her waist, steadied her.
"You okay?"

"Well, yes, I ... I ... didn't know you were so
close. . . . I didn't expect ... Captain, you've taken off
your shirt."

"Did you want me to leave it on? I thought since ...
I can get it ... put it back on."

"No. No. Of course not," she said, quickly lifting
her eyes from his naked torso.

But not quickly enough to avoid noticing that his
waist, as slender as a young boy's, was corded with
muscles which stirred with the rise and fall of his
breathing, or that the crisp black hair covering his
chest was damp with perspiration. "I ... ah ... sit
down, please."

Kurt nodded, picked up the folded towel, and took a
seat on the chair. He dropped the towel across a knee.
"Just tell me how you want me," he said. "What you
want me to do."

Curbing the urge to shout *I want you to put on your
clothes and leave,* Helen said, "Drape the towel around
your shoulders so you won't get hair all over your ...
on your . . ."

"Will do," he said. He shook out the towel, leaned

up, and swirled it around his bare shoulders. "Ready when you are."

"Hold these," ordered Helen, handing him the mirror and the brush.

Knowing she could put it off no longer, Helen swallowed hard, stepped around behind him, nudged his head forward, lifted a handful of long, curling black hair, and was amazed to find its texture so pleasingly soft and silky. The thick jet locks were so luxuriant she found herself half longing to lay the scissors aside and fill both her hands with the abundance of beautiful black hair.

"You have so much hair," she commented, needing to break the silence, her hand closed around a lush thick wedge of inky-black curls. Her throat felt dry. She ran her tongue over her lips.

"Take as much off as you want," he said, wondering why she was stalling.

He didn't see her fight for a breath, or momentarily close her eyes and shake her head to clear it. Nor did he see the appealing half-tender, half-sad expression that came into her blue eyes when finally she raised the scissors and snipped away a lock of his hair. He didn't see the way she reluctantly opened her hand and allowed the severed hair to slide from her soft palm and flutter to the spread sheet beneath them.

Kurt had no idea she was striving hard to stay poised and aloof as she cut and clipped and turned his head this way, then that. But when she had worked her way around and stood directly in front of him, he noticed she'd caught her upper lip between her teeth and that she was struggling to keep her hand completely steady.

In a matter of seconds Kurt was as tense as Helen.

And it wasn't because he was afraid she might cut him.

As she worked, she moved steadily closer, unconsciously stepping in to stand directly between his spread knees. While she ordered him to "Hand me the brush" and "Now take the brush back" and "Hold still, please" and "Close your eyes now," he caught the faint scent of the lilac soap she used for her baths and fought the impulse to inhale deeply. Her slender arms were lifted, her hands in his hair, the scissors clipping and snipping.

He tried to keep his eyes shut for two reasons. He didn't want to get hair in them and he didn't want to openly stare at her.

But he couldn't manage it.

His eyes opened to slits. Guiltily he watched the gentle bounce and sway of her perfectly formed breasts—inches from his face—as she reached and stretched. He felt the muscles of his inner thighs bunch and jump beneath the tight-fitted trousers, his bare belly contract involuntarily.

Meaning only to venture a stolen glance at her face, his gaze slowly lifted, but got only as far the open collar of her pastel summer dress. Her slender neck was glistening with dewy moisture. A single bead of perspiration trickled slowly downward toward the delicate hollow of her throat. As he watched the shimmering droplet slide seductively down the slender column of her throat, he was rocked with the insane desire to lift his hands to her back, press her gently forward to him, and lick away the tiny diamond bead from her pale heated flesh.

Kurt's hands were on his thighs, the mirror on the chair between his legs. His long fingers moved nervously, gripping the trousered flesh above his knees, then stiffening, like the claws of a cat.

A sudden flash of heat from Kurt's body, so near to hers, assaulted Helen, burned through her summer dress, raised her own temperature. She felt as if she were pressed flush against his naked chest. She could feel her heart—or was it his?—pounding, pounding. Her breath was growing short.

Kurt saw the throbbing pulse in Helen's slim throat, knew his own was hammering out of control at his temple. Rivulets of perspiration dripped down his heaving chest, pooling on his rigid stomach.

Helen paused for a moment, scissors in hand, to press a forearm to her shiny brow.

Kurt felt he must say something to ease the crackling tension.

"Awful still today," he said.

Her breath shallow, she nodded. "No breeze whatsoever."

"Might mean rain later this evening."

"I wouldn't be surprised."

Their bodies taut, warm, and wet, they talked about the weather, the coming storm season, carefully avoiding each other's eyes. Her hands ice-cold despite the worrisome heat of her body, Helen continued to clip the coal-black locks, hurrying now, anxious, frantic to be finished.

"There," she said at last, stepping back, exhaling with relief. "Done. All done."

"Is it?" he said softly, and she knew he was not referring to the haircut. He rose to his feet before her, allowing the white towel to slide from his bare brown shoulders.

"Yes, it is," she said emphatically. "Of that I'm absolutely certain!"

Chapter Seventeen

While Helen was nervously clipping Kurt's silky black hair on the front veranda of her home, Niles Loveless was also getting a haircut. Niles didn't trust Skeeter Jones or Skeeter's young apprentice to snip his prized golden locks.

Each week a Mobile barber in whom Niles had total confidence arrived at the palatial Loveless mansion at an appointed hour. He came to cut Niles Loveless's hair, to clip and buff his nails, and to give his handsome face a shave and a special skin moisturizing treatment.

Seated in the comfortable, tufted-backed barber's chair in his private barbershop, Niles, as usual, was conducting business as his foppish little Mobile barber carefully trimmed his pale gold hair.

Three of Loveless's employees stood dutifully still before their boss, as subjects might stand before their monarch. They never sat in Niles's presence. Here there were no chairs, save the one in which Niles half reclined, his wide shoulders draped with a fancy striped barber's cape, his expensively shod feet crossed and resting atop a tufted footstool.

It was here, in his own personal barbershop, that Niles conducted the kind of business he wouldn't want known by the townspeople. Or by his wife. The men standing patiently before him were a trusted, hand-picked trio who could be counted on to carry out any and every assignment. And then to keep their mouths shut about it. The Mobile barber wouldn't consider blabbing anything he overheard. Niles paid him handsomely for his services and for his silence.

Halfway through the haircut, Niles lifted a hand, signaling the barber to stop. The flashing clippers instantly stilled. Niles yanked the flowing barber's cape off, snapped his fingers, and pointed to his discarded vest and suit coat, which lay across a heavy black walnut chest against the wall.

"Bring that vest here to me."

It was done in the blinking of an eye.

Niles draped the vest across his knee, reached down inside a small front pocket, and brought forth a gold-and-diamond-cased pocket watch with a heavy gold chain. He tossed the vest back to one of his faithful three, lifted the watch by its gold chain, and began to methodically swing it back and forth.

"Boys, have you any idea what this watch is worth to me?"

"Hundreds," said one.

"Thousands," proclaimed another.

"I've no idea," admitted the third.

"It's priceless," said Niles.

He stopped swinging it back and forth, scooped it up into his palm, stuck a thumbnail under its outer rim, and flipped the gleaming back open. He gazed at the sentimental message etched inside.

"My wife gave this watch to me as a wedding present." The men nodded, said nothing. They had seen the watch many times. Knew it meant a lot to their boss. "My sweet Patsy," murmured Niles, almost reverently, "the adored mother of my children."

He snapped the back shut. "Catch!"

He threw the priceless gold-and-diamond pocket watch at the three unsuspecting men and chuckled when all anxiously leaped for it, terrified lest it slip through their hands and crash to the marble floor.

"Got it, boss," said big Harry Boyd, pleased to have come up with it. The other two, husky Jim Logan and balding Russ Carter, sighed with relief and exchanged glances.

"One of you—just one—ride out to the old Burke farm after midnight tonight," instructed Niles. "Make certain everyone is sleeping when you get there. Hide the watch somewhere in the outbuildings. Conceal it well enough so the Yankee or that snot-nosed kid of his won't stumble onto it. But don't hide it so well that a thorough search conducted by the proper authorities won't quickly turn it up."

The man holding the gold-and-diamond-cased pocket watch frowned skeptically. "Boss, it's a good idea. But how you gonna make it stick? You said yourself today was the first time you'd seen the Yankee. He doesn't even know about the watch, much less have had an opportunity to swipe it from you."

Niles grinned, self-satisfied. "You're wrong, Boyd. When I ran into the Yankee in town this afternoon, I shook his hand. Then I foolishly turned by back on him to admire his stallion. Obviously the sneaky bastard picked my pocket when I wasn't paying attention."

The men laughed and shook their heads, approving of their clever boss's scheme.

"By this time tomorrow, Helen Courtney's Yankee will be in jail," Niles confided, eyes sparkling. "And being the kindhearted man I am, I'll gallantly agree to drop charges if Northway will agree to get out of Alabama. Immediately." Niles leaned back in his barber chair, clasped his hands behind his half-shorn head, and smiled smugly. "Now, since the poor fellow hasn't the money to get across the county line, much less to

Maryland, I'll graciously offer to purchase his sorrel stallion, thereby supplying the cash for his journey."

Again the three men laughed and nodded their approval.

Niles's hands came down from his head. He leaned forward, looked at each man in turn, and said, "I want the Burke farm and timberlands. I want that blue-coated bastard out of Alabama *before* he makes it possible for Helen to hold out for another year. I want to own that Yankee's fine sorrel stallion. I want to run that magnificent thoroughbred at the Baldwin County Fair." He paused, smiled without warmth, and asked, "Am I going to get my way, boys?"

"Yes. You bet. Count on us, boss!" all quickly assured him.

Again Niles leaned back. He summoned the patiently waiting little barber to step back up to the chair. He said, "If that dirty Yankee is not in the Spanish Fort Jail within twenty-four hours, one of you is going to be mighty sorry I've been crossed."

Out of breath, a troubled expression on his fair face, Niles Loveless rushed across the street and into the outer office of the Spanish Fort Jail at half past nine the very next morning.

Sheriff Brian A. Cooper, seated behind a paper-cluttered desk, looked up.

"Mornin', Niles," Coop said, not bothering to rise. "Where's the fire?"

"It'll be under your skinny ass come election time if you don't arrest that thieving Yankee living out there with—"

"Whoa! Hold on a minute," said Coop. "What's this all about? Have a seat. Get your breath."

"There's no time for that! Helen Courtney's Yankee hired hand stole an extremely valuable pocket watch from me! I want justice done, dammit!"

"Have any proof this Yankee stole your watch?"

"Proof? How's this for proof? I've had that gold-and-diamond watch since the day I married sixteen years ago! You've seen it. The whole town's seen it. The Yankee must have known I owned an expensive watch and . . . ." Niles went on to explain about meeting the Yankee, admiring his stallion, and foolishly turning his back on the man, who was apparently an adept pickpocket.

His tale told, he pointed a finger in Coop's face, "Go on, Sheriff! Get out there to Helen's farm and arrest the worthless Yankee thief!"

"I'll look into it," said Coop, and returned to his paperwork.

"Look into it? You'll look into it?" Niles said, incredulous, his face growing beet red. He pounded his fist down on Coop's cluttered desk. "I want that bastard in jail!"

Coop didn't flinch or so much as blink. Cocking his head to one side, he looked at Niles and said, "I thought you wanted the watch back."

"I do! Of course I want the watch, but I—"

"I'll ride out to Helen's farm when I finish up here. Talk to the man. See what I can find out."

"That it? That's all you aim to do?"

"That's it."

"You listen here, the law states that—"

"In Baldwin County I am the law," Coop quietly interrupted.

Growing angrier by the second, Niles said sarcastically, "Get this straight, Coop, you may have been a big hero in the war, but the war's over. Now you're nothing more than an elected servant, a high sheriff of Baldwin County. I pay your salary; I call the shots. Get my watch and bring in that dirty Yankee son of a bitch!"

Niles turned and stalked out the door while Sheriff

Brian A. Cooper, still seated, tranquily watched him go. A half smile touched Coop's wide lips. He shook his curly red head, half in pity, half in disgust.

Niles Loveless couldn't push him around, but Niles didn't understand that. Couldn't possibly understand.

In Coop's opinion, Niles Loveless was a spineless coward who had shirked his responsibility as a son of the South during the war. The wealthy owner of a hundred slaves, Loveless had been exempt from conscription, so he hadn't served, hadn't fought for the Confederacy. While every able-bodied man from sixteen to sixty rode into battle, Niles Loveless never left his plantation, never heard a shot fired in anger.

Niles Loveless knew nothing about hospitals and stockades and dungeons. He knew nothing about pain and starvation and suffering. He hadn't learned what it was like to be constantly hungry and tired and either freezing cold or sweltering hot. He'd never held in his lap the head of a dying comrade, precious life waning away from lack of proper care and medication.

Niles Loveless would never understand that once a soldier had been through the unspeakable horrors of a bloody, four-year-long war, he could not be threatened by any man.

Sheriff Brian A. Cooper had more respect for the Yankees than he had for Niles Loveless. At least they had fought for what they believed in, just as he himself had done.

The lanky sheriff finished his paperwork, stacked it all neatly, and shoved it into the middle drawer of his desk. He pushed back his chair, rose, and went for his hat.

He walked down to the livery stable for his chestnut gelding, mounted, and rode out of town.

South toward Helen Courtney's coastal farm.

Chapter Eighteen

Helen poured more of the hickory ashes she'd collected into the weathered clapboard hopper. She decided the hopper was full enough. She would make her lye soap today and it was none too soon. She had only a couple of bars left.

Each day for weeks Helen had added ashes to the hopper, then poured in clear water to make a depression until lye had begun to drip from the grooves in the platform down into the big stone jar she had placed underneath.

Satisfied the stone jar held an ample amount of the lye, Helen went to the woodpile, gathered up an armload of kindling, and returned to the hopper. She built up a small fire, waited until it was burning nicely, then went up to house to get the grease drippings she'd saved from cooking.

When she returned she saw Kurt coming in from the fields. Charlie trailed him. Dom followed Charlie. She immediately spotted the rusting plow bit in Kurt's right hand and sighed.

"Hit a rock," Kurt called to her, holding up the damaged bit. "Broke the point off the bit."

Charlie left his father, came dashing eagerly toward Helen. "What are you doing?" he asked. "What's the fire for? What's in the bucket? Are you cooking dinner?"

She smiled down at the curious little boy. "No, I'm

making lye soap." To Kurt she called, "So you'll have
to ride into town to the blacksmith's? Miss the whole
day of plowing?"

"Can I help make lye soap?" asked Charlie, tugging
at Helen's sleeve to get her attention.

"No. I'm pretty sure I can fix it," called Kurt. "I'll
file it back down to some semblance of a point.
Shouldn't take more than an hour. Charlie, don't you
be bothering Mrs. Courtney."

"Good," she shouted. Then, "He's not bothering
me." To Charlie she said, "You may help, but you must
be really careful. I don't want you getting burned."

Eagerly Charlie promised, "I will. I'll be reeeally
careful!" He looked down at Dom, who was giving
him a quick ankle rub, and said to the cat, "I can't play
right now. We have to make soap!"

The Russian Blue made a rattling sound, closed his
eyes, butted his head against Charlie's knee, then
turned and walked away.

"Dom's mad, but he'll get over it," Charlie told
Helen.

She nodded, agreeing, and they went to work. While
Kurt sat on the steps of the toolshed and vigorously
filed on the damaged plow bit, Helen and Charlie
mixed together the grease drippings and the painstakingly collected lye drippings. They cooked the strange
concoction over the fire. While it was boiling, Helen
added a dash of salt so that when the bubbling liquid
cooled, it would harden properly.

They took turns stirring and Helen watched with her
heart in her throat when it was Charlie's turn. She
made a conscious effort to hold her tongue. She could
still remember how aggravated she used to get when
she helped her Grandma Burke at some small task and
she shouted and cautioned and carried on the whole
time they worked. She didn't want to behave like her
dear, overly protective grandma.

But first thing she knew, Helen was anxiously warning the little boy to "Stop stirring so fast, you'll splash
yourself" and "No, Charlie, no, don't ever lean over
the pot" and "Here, give me the spoon, you're going to
be scalded alive!"

Exasperated, Charlie shrugged narrow shoulders,
handed her the long-handled wooden paddle, and told
her earnestly, "I'm not a baby."

Helen wanted to hug him. She didn't. But she smiled
and said, "I know you're not. I'm sorry. I suppose I
worry too much."

Charlie cocked his blond head to one side. Thoughtfully he said, "Girls worry a lot, don't they? My
mommy worried too. Sometimes she cried." With his
eyes fixed on Helen's face in a direct gaze that rivaled
his father's, he told her, "My mommy's up in heaven
now." He pointed short fingers toward the sky.

"I know," Helen replied softly. She laid a tentative
hand on his small golden head. "She'll never worry or
cry again."

"That's what the captain told me," Charlie said, and
turned his attention back to the bubbling pot. "It needs
stirring," he announced. Helen agreed, handed him the
spoon, and allowed him stir.

And she worried.

When it was almost done, Helen—much as she
hated to—called on Kurt for help. She needed a tub
filled with water. She could have drawn the water herself, but she was afraid if she left Charlie to watch the
bubbling mixture, he might accidentally get burned.
Yes, she did think of him as a baby—a precious, innocent, golden-haired baby—she couldn't help herself.

Kurt immediately laid aside the plow bit and came.
He drew the water for her, measured a few quarts out
into the waiting wooden tub, and then insisted he be
the one to add the lye-and-grease mixture into the water.

"Get back," he warned both Helen and Charlie.

"Be careful," cautioned Helen.

"Always," Kurt said, and expertly ladled the boiling liquid into the cool water. He turned and said, "Now what?"

"Now we just spread a cloth over the tub and—"

"Somebody's coming!" Charlie interrupted, whirling around at the sound of approaching hoofbeats. "Jolly! Jolly?"

Helen and Kurt both turned and squinted.

"It's not Jolly," said Kurt.

"No," said Helen, first recognizing the chestnut gelding, then the red-haired man on its back. "It's the Baldwin County sheriff. I wonder . . . what . . . he . . ."

Helen felt a curious uneasiness instantly swamp her. This was no social call. Not at this hour. Had it been, Em would have been with Coop. He was alone. The silver sheriff's star, pinned to his shirtfront, glittered in the sunshine. His Colt .44 was in its leather holster on his hip. His wide-brimmed straw hat was pulled low over his eyes.

Something was wrong.

"Charlie," Helen said anxiously to the little boy, "will you take the empty grease pail back inside the house for me?"

Charlie didn't want to. He wanted to stay and get a close look at the armed sheriff, but his father said softly, "You heard Mrs. Courtney. Go inside."

His bottom lip stuck out in a pout, Charlie snatched up the empty grease pail and went into the house. Helen glanced briefly at Kurt. He didn't look at her. He made no move to turn and leave. She wondered if he knew the purpose of Sheriff Cooper's visit. If so, his face gave nothing away.

"Coop," she called, putting a friendly smile on her face, lifting her skirts, and hurrying to meet the approaching rider.

The sheriff swung down off his chestnut gelding, tossed the reins to the ground, swept off his hat, hung it on the saddle horn, and covered the space between Helen and himself in four long-legged strides. He put out his big right hand. Helen took it in both of her own, shook it warmly.

"I'm always glad to see you, you know that, but . . . what is it, Coop? Has something happened? What's wrong?" Helen asked bluntly, still clinging to his big freckled hand.

"Nothing's wrong. Not a thing. Just need to have word with your . . . ah . . . with . . ."

He looked from Helen to Kurt and stopped speaking. His lips fell open in surprise. Helen followed the direction of his gaze. He was staring at Kurt and Kurt's green eyes were fixed on the tall, lanky sheriff.

"I don't believe it!" exclaimed Coop. "I just don't believe it!" He pointed a long forefinger at Kurt. "If it's not the softhearted Union captain from the Battle of Chattanooga! Captain Northway, I'd know those eyes anywhere!"

Starting to grin now, Kurt came forward, his hand outstretched. "The wounded redheaded Rebel major! My God, you made it, Cooper! I've wondered so many times if you had."

Nodding his head, Coop said, "Thanks to you I'm very much alive and kicking! Glad to see you survived the conflict too."

"You're looking a lot healthier than when last we met," said Kurt.

"So are you!" declared Coop.

Both men laughed.

Astounded, Helen stood there speechless, watching the exchange. Finally Sheriff Cooper turned to Helen and said, "Helen it's a small world we live in. This fellow here saved my life in the war."

"I wouldn't go that far," said a modest Kurt
Northway.

"You must tell me all about it," Helen said, looking
from one man to the other. She was more than a little
curious. Her old friend Coop knew Northway? It was
incredible. "Come on up to the back porch. I'll brew
some fresh coffee and see about some food. It's almost
noontime. You'll stay for dinner, won't you, Coop?"

"Why, thanks, Helen," Coop replied, "I am getting a
little hungry."

Chapter Nineteen

At the table on the back porch, the two men drank hot black coffee, ate sliced ham and potato salad, and reminisced over the fateful occasion that had brought them together. While both Helen and Charlie listened attentively, Sheriff Cooper recounted the events leading up to that cold November day in 1863 when his Confederate command came face-to-face with Captain Kurtis Northway's Union troops.

"It was the 'Battle Above the Clouds,' " said Coop, telling of the fierce fighting which took place atop Lookout Mountain up in Chattanooga, Tennessee.

He spoke of the thick fog and mist that had settled around the crest of the mountain, making it nearly impossible to tell friend from foe.

"You tell it," Coop prodded Kurt. "Tell what happened that day, Captain Northway. How we chanced to meet."

Kurt looked embarrassed. His face actually flushed a little beneath his dark tan. Helen couldn't believe it. She had never seen him appear to be even the tiniest bit uncomfortable. It was almost endearing.

Looking into his coffee cup, Kurt said softly, "We had been ordered to take the Confederate rifle pits at the base of Missionary Ridge." His eyes lifted from the cup, but he continued to idly run the tip of his forefinger around the cup's rim. "We found ourselves up against some mighty heavy fire from the main Confederate defenses above."

"That's where I was," put in Coop, pointing up.

"We had no further orders to do it, but somehow . . . for some reason, all of us . . . all at once, stormed up the slope. We managed to rout the Rebs and capture the crest." He shrugged. "That's about all there was to it."

"Not quite," said Coop, looking from Helen to Charlie. "Our flank collapsed totally and was forced to retreat. In the melee, I was left behind. The captain here found me. I'd been slightly wounded."

Kurt shook his dark head. Now Coop was being the modest one. "Major Cooper was badly wounded, near death when I got to him. Propped up against a fallen tree trunk, he was attempting to make a tourniquet with his belt. He'd lost a lot of blood; I didn't expect him to live another hour."

"And I wouldn't have," Coop assured Helen and Charlie, "if he hadn't taken me to a Union field hospital in the valley below."

"So he actually saved your life." Helen was thinking aloud, moved by the story.

"He did indeed," said Coop, "and him badly wounded himself." He shot a quick glance at Kurt. "I vaguely recall the back of your blue uniform blouse being soaked with blood. What was it? Artillery fire? Minié ball fragments?"

"A little nick from a Reb's saber," Kurt said, and quickly changed the subject.

Into Helen's thoughts flashed the sight of Kurt, shirtless, the evil-looking scar slashing downward from the small of his back and into the waistband of his trousers. A little nick? It had to have been a near mortal wound to have left such a nasty scar.

Helen glanced at Kurt from under lowered lashes. She was seeing him in a new light. Near death himself from a blow dealt by a soldier's slashing saber, Kurt had further risked his own life to save that of a Confederate major. There had to be *some* good in a man who would do such a noble thing.

Even a Yankee.

The conversation turned from the past to the future. Coop's interest was genuine when asked what Kurt's plans were. His tone level, Kurt said he and Charlie would be staying in Alabama until after the autumn harvest. Then what? prompted Coop. Kurt told him about the Maryland horse farm back home and how one day he would own his own place, raise his own thoroughbreds.

"Guess you're getting anxious to get on back up there," said Coop. "Sounds like a mighty good life."

"It is," said Kurt. "You'll have to come up for a visit sometime."

"I might just do that," said Coop, smiling.

When the meal was finished, Charlie was the first to leave the table. Asking his father if he might be excused, he bolted down the porch steps calling Dom's name, ready to make amends to the sensitive feline who might have his feelings hurt.

"I have to be going myself," said Coop, pushing back his chair.

Helen and Kurt saw Coop out the back gate. They fell naturally into step on either side of the lanky sheriff, walked him toward his grazing chestnut gelding.

It was Helen who said, "Tell us the truth, now, Coop. Why did you ride all the way out here today?"

Coop made a face, kicked at a small stone with the toe of his boot, and exhaled.

He looked up, straight at Kurt. "Niles Loveless, one of our community's more vocal citizens, has accused you of stealing a valuable diamond-and-gold pocket watch."

Kurt said nothing.

"That's utter nonsense! A mean, malicious lie!" Helen quickly spoke up. "The two have never even met!" She snapped her head around, looked at Kurt with flashing eyes. "Have you?"

"I'm afraid we have," admitted Kurt. "When I was in town yesterday, Loveless came out of his office, introduced himself, and offered to buy Raider."

"Anybody with him?" asked Coop. "Or was it just the two of you?"

"A Mrs. Yasmine Parnell was with Loveless," said Kurt. "She happened to be coming out of his office just as I was ready to leave town. Loveless was bidding her good day, saw me, and came out to admire my stallion. That's the one and only occasion I've ever seen Loveless. Talk to Mrs. Parnell. She'll tell you that I had no chance to take Loveless's watch. I didn't even see the watch, didn't know he had one." Kurt shrugged. "Don't get me wrong, Sheriff. You're more than welcome to search—"

"No need for that," said Coop, reaching for his hat. He frowned. "I imagine Helen's told you that Loveless would do just about anything to get his hands on her farm and timberlands." Kurt nodded. Coop went on, "You're a new burr under his saddle, Captain. Before you came, he figured Helen wouldn't be able to hold out another season."

"He wrongly accused me of theft to get rid of me?" asked Kurt.

"That's the kind of man Loveless is. Ruthless. Greedy. Determined." Coop draped a long arm over his gelding's back and chuckled, but it was a scornful laugh "And one of the most respected citizens of Spanish Fort." He sighed, shook his head, and then climbed up into the saddle. "What's the Bible say? 'The wicked shall flourish'? Loveless flourishes, believe me. Good to see you again, Northway. Helen, thanks for the delicious meal."

Kurt and Helen watched the sheriff ride away. When he had turned the big chestnut into the shaded lane and disappeared, Kurt turned to Helen.

"Mrs. Courtney."

"Yes?" She looked up at him.

"Aren't you going to ask?"

"Ask what?"

"If I did it. If I stole Loveless's pocket watch."

"No," she said, then reached out, impulsively touched his forearm for a fleeting second, and felt the muscles bunch and tighten under her sensitive fingertips. "I don't have to ask. I know you didn't."

The clock mounted in the spire of the First Methodist Church tower was striking four P.M. when Sheriff Brian A. Cooper rode back into Spanish Fort. The sheriff went directly to his office, took off his straw hat, hooked it on a wall peg, and ran a hand through his curly red hair.

Idly wondering how long it would take before Niles Loveless showed up, Coop grinned, crossed the small office, circled his scarred desk, dropped into his swivel chair, and leaned back. Without looking down, he pulled the yellow string dangling from his breast pocket and withdrew a small white cotton sack of tobacco.

With fore and middle fingers he plucked a single wheat-straw cigarette paper from a packet inside the pocket. He held the paper between thumb and middle finger, opened the sack with his other hand, and shook some tobacco out onto the paper. He tightened the yellow drawstring with his teeth, put the tobacco back into his pocket.

Then he carefully rolled the paper around the tobacco, put out the tip of his tongue, and moistened the edge of the paper, sealing it. He stuck the cigarette between his lips, struck a match with his thumbnail, and lit it. Drawing the smoke deep down into his lungs, the sheriff sighed, leaned way back, and lifted his booted feet atop his desk.

Before Coop could take a second long, relaxing pull on his newly built smoke, Niles Loveless walked in the door.

"Where is he?" said Niles, frowning, looking down the short hall toward the two jail cells. "Where's the Yankee? He back there in a cell?"

"Nope."

"No? Why the hell not? Didn't you arrest him? Bring him in? I want the bastard locked up for stealing my watch!" Niles Loveless was not used to being thwarted.

Coop slowly lowered his feet to the floor, but remained seated. He placed his cigarette in the corner of his mouth, allowed it to dangle there as he spoke.

"Looks like you got the wrong man. I know Northway. He's no thief. I'm not locking him up." Coop squinted against the cigarette smoke drifting up into his eyes. Lowering his voice, looking the other man squarely in the eye, he said, "Nice try, Niles, but no cigar. And no jail cell for an innocent man."

"He's not innocent! He's thieving Yankee trash and—"

"The case is closed," said Coop with resolute finality. "Now get out of here before I arrest you for bringing false charges."

Eyes flashing contempt, Niles glared at the stubborn go-by-the-book sheriff. Seething, he said, "The watch! What about my expensive diamond-and-gold watch? My watch has been stolen!"

"You're wasting your time and mine, Niles," Coop said, and rose to his feet. "I'm on to you."

"Why I . . . I don't know what you're implying . . . you . . . you have nothing on me!" sputtered Niles

Loveless. His face flushed red, he finally whined, "Dammit, how am I supposed to get my watch back?"

Coop lifted on eyebrow. "I'd suggest you have the lackey who planted it for you go back and get it."

"Damn you to eternal hell!" muttered Niles, and he spun about and stormed angrily out the door while Coop chuckled.

Chapter Twenty

As late spring waned toward early summer, the days steadily lengthened. Each dawn the June sun rose a little earlier. Stayed in the sky a little longer. Burned a little brighter.

The balmy, longer days suited Helen fine. More work could get done. More fertile fields could get plowed. More corn and sugar cane and wheat could get planted.

There were no cotton fields on Helen's coastal farm. Hadn't been since Will left for the war. For the past four years there'd been no one to help chop and pick the cotton. And now, with the new punishing federal cotton tax of $15 a bale in place, there was no profit to be made from a small cotton crop.

Necessity had made a practical woman of Helen. She was bent on raising only those crops which would bring the highest price or else would grace her table at mealtime. With Northway plowing and planting the money crops, she had time to weed and tend her garden and to pick the ripened fruit from her orchard.

Helen was out in the orchard on a fine Friday morning in mid-June. She was gathering golden peaches. Her spirits were unusually high. The day was breathtakingly beautiful, the sun warm and welcome on her face. Life seemed good again, worth living. Almost normal. She was half content. She felt safe after years of being constantly afraid.

From up at the backyard came the welcome sounds
of shouts, squeals, and laughter from a newly outgoing
Charlie as Jolly pushed him back and forth in the
swing beneath the old live oak. And, if she turned,
lifted her head, and squinted real hard, she could catch
glimpses of Northway, wearing a shirt as requested, up
at the northern field, expertly guiding the plow down
long straight rows behind old deaf Duke.

Helen began to hum softly.

Maybe she'd make a big fresh peach cobbler for
supper. Jolly loved peach cobbler, so Kurt and Charlie
likely would as well. When the cobbler was baking,
she could set up the ironing board between two
straight-backed chairs and iron Charlie's little shirts.
After that, she'd churn some fresh butter. And then
perhaps later this afternoon she'd lay out a dress pattern on that bolt of fabric Em had brought over several
weeks back.

The generous Em had pretended she'd purchased the
bolt of material for herself and then hadn't been able to
use it. Helen knew better, but she didn't let on. She
pretended along with her best friend as Em thrust the
bolt at her, frowned, and said, "The color's all wrong
for me. I declare, I don't know why I ever bought it.
I'd hate to see it go to waste. It would be perfect for
you, Helen, bring out your eyes. Take it, make yourself
a dress for the Baldwin County Fair."

Helen decided she would make herself a new dress
out of the crisp sky-blue cotton piqué, but she wouldn't
be wearing it to the Baldwin County Fair. She had no
intention of going to tomorrow's fair.

Everyone in Spanish Fort, and for miles around,
would turn out for the fair. It would be the first county
fair since the carefree days before the war. The last one
had been a lively celebration back in June of 1860. She
and Will, not yet man and wife, had gone to the fair together and stayed to the very end.

Helen stopped humming. She stopped plucking peaches from the bough.

Her dress for the fair had been yellow, Will's favorite color. Yellow with delicate white lace around the low-cut neck and short puffed sleeves. Throughout the long, lovely June day Will had held her hand as they strolled among the bunting-draped booths. At the late afternoon horse race which was always the high point of the fair, she had complained that she couldn't see over the press of people ringing the track. Will had promptly shocked and delighted her when he'd wordlessly lifted her up to sit on his strong right shoulder.

Helen shivered, remembering.

As if it were yesterday she could recall how intensely thrilling it was to feel his muscular arm clamped firmly over her yellow-skirted knees, anchoring her in place. Laughing, she had clung to the thick blond hair of his head as the field of thoroughbreds flashed by on the oval track and the crowd screamed with excitement.

Abruptly, Helen stopped smiling. She made a sour face. One of Niles Loveless's blooded beasts had won the race that day. No doubt this year it would be the same. One of Niles's many expensive thoroughbreds would win again. As if he needed the $100 purse prize money! Well, so what? She wouldn't be there to see it.

Let Niles win. She didn't care.

Em Ellicott came to the farm that warm Friday afternoon. Pretty and youthful-looking in a cool summer dress of white muslin and sprigs of green and pink flowers decorating bodice and hem, she wore her dark glossy curls loose and flowing, held back out of her eyes with a pearl-encrusted barrette.

She spotted Jolly and Charlie on the front gallery and rushed forward to meet them. She gave Jolly's fleshy cheek an affectionate pinch and then she put her

hands on her knees, leaned down, and said to Charlie,
"How you doing today, Charlie? You and Jolly been
having a good time?"

"Uh-huh," he said, then giggled when Em reached
out and tickled his belly.

"You're my friend too, aren't you?"

"Yes," said Charlie. Then, "Do you know the captain?"

"Not yet, but I'd like to meet him. Is he around?"

"Down at the field," Charlie told her. "He works all
day."

"Does he?" said Em. "Well, perhaps I—" She
stopped speaking, looked up. Helen stepped out onto
the porch. "I'm here to help with the sewing," Em announced, giving Helen a hug. "I'm going to make sure
that new blue dress is ready for tomorrow's . . ."

Her words trailed away when Helen gave her a
quick, cautioning shake of her head, her blue eyes signaling Em to say no more. It wasn't until the two
friends had retired to Helen's bedroom and were seated
on the floor, laying out a dress pattern on the blue cotton piqué material, that Em asked why she was not
supposed to mention the Baldwin County Fair in front
of Charlie Northway.

"Because he isn't going," said Helen.

Em made a face. "I suppose that means you don't
intend to go either."

"Wild horses couldn't drag me to that fair."

"Helen Burke Courtney, you promised me six weeks
ago you would attend the fair!"

"Yes, well that was six weeks ago. That was
before . . ."

"Before the Yankee?"

"Yes."

Em gave a loud sigh of exasperation. "You've got to
stop this foolishness."

"What foolishness?"

"Hiding out because of your Yankee," Em said. "You've done nothing wrong, so stop acting guilty. Come to the fair. You'll be with Coop and me the whole time. You'll see, people will start to thaw toward you before the day ends."

"Maybe," Helen admitted, bending over to cut along the edge of the pattern they'd laid out on the spread blue piqué. "I really don't care anything about going to the fair."

"But you should!" Em scolded. "You should care. It's high time you started caring about things again. Look at me when I'm talking to you!"

Helen sighed, stopped cutting the fabric, and looked up.

Em smiled and said gently, "Helen . . . the war's over and Will's never coming back. He's dead, Helen. Will is dead!"

"No," said Helen, stubbornly shaking her head, just as she always did. "No, don't say that . . . don't . . ."

"I will say it! He's dead. You have to face it, you must! Will is dead. You are not. You have to go on living."

Helen sighed wearily. "I am living."

"No, you're not. You're breathing and eating and sleeping, but you aren't really living. Oh, Helen, don't you understand? Your whole life's ahead of you and I can't bear to see you waste it."

Helen finally smiled at her dearest friend. "Let me get this straight. If I don't go to the Baldwin County Fair I'll be wasting my entire life?"

"No, no, that's not what I meant and you know it. Lord, you're pigheaded at times," Em said, frowning. "Just think it over, will you? And let's get this dress finished in case you change your mind!"

The two spent the afternoon working on Helen's new dress. When finally Em announced she had to leave—that she should have gone an hour ago—the blue piqué dress was as good as finished, save for being hemmed. Thanking Em for coming and for helping make the dress, Helen walked her down toward the barn where the waiting Ellicott carriage was parked.

Helen frowned and stiffened when she caught sight of Kurt coming around the barn. What was he doing back from the fields? There was still a good two hours of daylight left. It wasn't quitting time.

Em saw Kurt too.

"Your Yankee?" whispered Em. "Introduce us."

"Now, Em."

"You heard me," Em hissed.

Helen had little choice. She called out to Kurt. He came forward to meet them.

"Captain Northway, I'd like you to meet a dear friend of mine, Miss Emma Ellicott. Miss Ellicott is engaged to Sheriff Cooper." She turned to Em. "Em, Captain Kurtis Northway. He and Coop know each other from the days of the war."

"Miss Ellicott," Kurt said, took her hand in his and shook it warmly. "Coop's a lucky man. It's a pleasure to meet you."

"The pleasure's mine, Captain," said Em, smiling. Then, immediately, "I was just saying to Helen, you both should come to the Baldwin County Fair tomorrow. Coop and I will be there. We could all get together and—"

"Em, the captain's not interested," Helen interrupted, scowling at Em. She flashed warning eyes at him. "Are you, Captain?"

"We all stay pretty busy around here," said Kurt.

"Everyone needs a day off now and then," said Em, as Helen firmly clasped her arm and propelled her to the carriage.

"Good-bye, Em." Helen practically shoved her inside. "Give my best to your folks."

"Sure enough," said Em. She stuck her head out the

window and said, "Captain, has Helen told you about the fair's horse race? Coop and the rest of the men seem to enjoy the race more than anything else. Some fine thoroughbreds compete. The prize money's not much—a hundred dollars, winner take all—but big side bets are made, I'm told. If you don't care for horse races, there's all kinds of good food, and then tomorrow night there's a dance at the . . ."

The carriage pulled away with Em still waving and carrying on about the Baldwin County Fair.

When at last the black brougham turned into the tree-bordered lane, Helen turned to Kurt.

"What is it?" she asked. "Why are you back so early? Something's wrong." It was a statement, not a question.

Kurt frowned. "I'm afraid so. Old Duke just died."

Tears immediately sprang to Helen's eyes. "No!"

"I'm sorry."

Helen sadly shook her head. "It's my fault. I worked him to death. He was too old and—"

"Horses are like people, ma'am," Kurt gently interrupted. "They don't like being thought of as old and useless. They'd much prefer to stay active to the end. To go the way your old pony Duke went."

Skeptically, Helen looked at him, unshed tears glistening in her eyes. "You really think so?"

"Yes. Now you go on back up to the house and I'll take care of Duke."

She sighed, then nodded. "Duke's momma is buried up there in that far corner where the timberlands begin." She pointed to the northeast. "There's an old wooden marker, but it's all covered with johnsongrass and—"

"I'll find it," said Kurt.

"Jolly's here," Helen said. "You want him to help?"

"No. I'll borrow Jolly's gray gelding to take Duke away. I'll bury him by his momma. Let Jolly keep

Charlie occupied. I'd rather Charlie see no more of death right now, even that of an aged horse."

"I understand," she said, for once in complete agreement with him.

Chapter Twenty-one

It didn't last long.

Within hours the two were in complete disagreement.

The sun was setting across the bay and the night's meal had just been finished. Jolly and Charlie had already gone around the house to sit in the old cane-bottomed rockers on the front gallery and watch the sporadic traffic on the water.

Helen, clearing away the supper dishes, looked at Kurt and said, "Captain, while you're plowing in the morning, I think maybe I'll . . . that I . . ." She stopped talking. He was looking at her strangely, shaking his head. "What? What is it?"

Kurt leaned up to the table. He braced himself on an elbow and propped his chin in his hand. "Has it already slipped your mind? Old Duke is now in his grave."

"No, of course it hasn't slipped my mind."

"How am I supposed to plow without a horse?"

"Well, since Duke's gone, you'll just have to harness up Raider," she said in innocent earnestness.

Kurt's face came out of his hand. He shoved his chair back and shot to his feet with a swiftness that so startled Helen she dropped the gathered dishes back to the table with a loud clatter. Openmouthed, she stared at him. Dangerous sparks shot from the depths of his forest-green eyes and the tendons in his neck were taut and standing out in bold relief.

His voice was curiously soft, but not pleasant, when he said, "Raider is a thoroughbred."

"I know that."

"Thoroughbreds do not pull plows, ma'am."

"Oh, really? Well, I don't think it will hurt Raider to do a little work," Helen said, and turned her back on him.

Kurt grabbed her arm and whirled her around to face him. "Raider does not pull a plow."

Helen wrenched her arm free of his encircling fingers. "Get this straight, Captain. The plowing *must* be done. Raider will do it!"

"No," Kurt said stubbornly, "Raider will not."

"He will if you expect to be paid come autumn!" Helen warned.

"I'll pull the plow myself before I hook Raider up to it," he said firmly.

"Don't make such asinine statements," she snapped at him.

"I am dead serious."

He was and she knew it.

The space between them crackled with open hostility. It was the first time she'd ever seen him lose his studied control, show any real emotion. She was halfway frightened by it. And, at the same time, oddly thrilled by it.

As she looked anxiously into the stormy green eyes in his handsome, sun-darkened face, she sensed there was something wild and dangerous just beneath the surface. Was certain that at this very minute his tall, lean body was taut with leashed passion. Knew that if she said much more, all that carefully reined-in force might be let loose.

Perversely, she was tempted to see if she could make him explode. She felt the almost overwhelming desire to see all that scary, bottled-up potency liberated. She wondered what he might actually do if she pushed him too far.

She couldn't stop herself. She knew it was irresponsible to say one more word, but she did.

Swaying a hair's breath closer to him, she said, "Either hitch up that pampered stallion and get on with the plowing or else!"

"Or else?"

"Else you . . . you pack up and get off my farm!"

She braced herself for the outburst.

It never came.

She studied his angry, handsome face, watched it change before her very eyes. Suddenly she saw in it the young, vulnerable boy he had once surely been. She felt a peculiar tightness in her chest.

"Fine. Give me twenty-four hours," he said calmly, then stepped around her and walked away.

Helen was horrified.

She was stunned. She couldn't believe what was happening. Already she was sorry for what she had said. She had stupidly told him to get off her farm and he was calling her bluff. Why had she shot off her big mouth? Why had she issued such an insane threat? She had given him no choice! He would never in a million years have considered using his beloved racehorse for that kind of labor and she knew it.

He was actually going to leave. Leave her with the plowing half done and crops in the field.

Helen felt panicky.

She had to stop him before this went any further. She couldn't let it happen. She couldn't let him leave.

"Captain, wait!" she called, and hurried down the porch steps after him.

Kurt stopped as he reached the back gate, but he did not turn around. Genuinely distressed, Helen hurried to him. When she caught up, she grabbed his forearm,

turned him to face her. She had every intention of telling him she was sorry, that she didn't mean it, that she
took it all back.

Her fingers tenaciously gripping his arm, she swallowed anxiously, but before she got the chance to
speak, he looked at her indifferently and said, "Will
you watch my son tomorrow?"

"Watch your . . . why?" Her brows knit. "Where will
you be?"

"I'll be gone all day," he coolly told her. "I have important business in town."

The minute he said "important business," it dawned
on Helen. She knew exactly what he was up to. He was
going to the Baldwin County Fair. He was going to the
fair to enter Raider in the race. He meant to win the
$100 prize money. With the money in his pocket, he'd
pick up Charlie and leave immediately for Maryland.
That's why he had asked for twenty-four hours.

Helen's reeling brain raced. She had to think fast.
Had to use her head. Had to keep him from going to
the fair, from winning the race. He couldn't possibly
leave if he had no money.

"Captain." She used her most authoritative voice in
an attempt to mask her fear. "If the business you have
in town is to enter Raider in tomorrow's horse race,
you can just forget it." She drew a shallow breath, took
her hand from his arm. "I will not look after Charlie
while you traipse off to the fair!"

Kurt shrugged. "Then he'll have to come with me."

"No! You can't do that to Charlie! You know very
well that the townspeople might forbid their children to
have anything to do with the son of a Yankee captain!
Think how badly he would be hurt. I won't let that
happen, I won't! You are not going to the Baldwin
County Fair!" Her voice had become shrill.

"You're wrong," he said unemotionally. "I am going."

Desperate, certain if he got his hands on that prize money he would leave her, Helen tried again. "I'm your employer, your boss. I won't allow it."

"You won't allow it? I'm bigger than you, ma'am," he said, a trace of amusement in his tone, and he moved in a step closer to prove it. Helen had to tip her head back to look at him.

"You're right, Captain. You are bigger than I. But fortunately I have an equalizer."

"Really? Show me."

"Gladly!"

Swiftly Helen shoved her hand down into the pocket of her work skirt, forgetting, until that moment, that she didn't have the pistol. Too late she remembered that since a few short days after Kurt and Charlie had come to live at the farm, she had stopped carrying the weapon. It was in the top drawer of her bureau, not in her pocket.

He must have known. Of course he did. His hands had been on her the morning of their wild ride atop Raider; he'd known since then that she no longer carried the pistol. Damn him!

Helen warned impotently, "I have a gun. It's loaded!"

"I know you do."

"I'll draw it and—"

"No, you won't."

"I will . . . I'll—"

"You wouldn't shoot me, would you?" His chilly green eyes warmed slightly. He reached up, touched a wayward strand of silky golden hair lying against her flushed cheek. Gently tucking it behind her ear, he looked directly into her eyes and warned in a low, flat voice, "Never draw on me unless you mean to kill me."

"Don't worry!" She slapped his hand away, angry and upset. "If I ever pull a gun on you, I *will* kill you!"

"Fair enough," he said, then smiled an absolutely dazzling smile and softly told her, "And killing me is the only way you'll keep me from going to the Baldwin County Fair."

Chapter Twenty-two

Kurt went to the fair.

Charlie stayed home with Helen.

Secure in the knowledge that any disagreement between Helen and himself would not affect the way she treated Charlie in his absence, Kurt left his son behind with her.

The little boy knew nothing about the Baldwin County Fair. The grown-ups had carefully avoided mentioning it in Charlie's presence. Had he known about it, he would have pitched a fit to go. Helen, Kurt, and Jolly were all of the same mind. It would be far too risky for Charlie to go into Spanish Fort and the fair.

Which was a shame.

Under different circumstances Charlie would have had the time of his life. Swarms of children showed up at every fair for the day-long celebration. Charlie had changed so much in the past few weeks, he would have fit right in with the other rowdy boys his age. Unless those little boys were not allowed to play with the son of a hated Yankee. It wasn't worth taking the chance.

Kurt slipped out of bed before sunrise on that cool Saturday morning. He sat on the edge of the mattress, ran his hands through his hair, and looked back over his shoulder at Charlie. Lying on his stomach, short arms flung up over his head, face buried in the pillow,

Charlie slept the deep, peaceful sleep of the truly innocent.

Kurt smiled and carefully spread the covering sheet
up over Charlie's narrow shoulders. He touched his
son's small head, gently running affectionate fingers
over the silky golden hair at Charlie's crown.

Then he quickly rose, shaved, dressed, and went to
the corral. He fed Raider a bucket of oats, curried him,
checked his big, sleek body for any abrasions. And,
one at a time, he lifted the hooves and keenly inspected
them for thorns or pebbles. He talked to the stallion
throughout, explaining that their usual morning ride
must wait until later in the day.

When he was satisfied Raider was fit as a fiddle,
Kurt saddled the big stallion, but left the cinch loose
under his belly and tied the stirrups up. He led the stallion out of the corral as the first pink and gray tinges
of dawn lightened the eastern sky.

In the darkened house, Helen was awake. She had
spent a long, fitful night, getting little rest, worrying,
wondering what was going to happen. Yawning tiredly,
she got out of bed in time to see Kurt leaving.

Wearing only her nightgown, she stood at the
kitchen window as he led his horse out of the corral.
Her face screwed up into a worried frown, she hurriedly moved from the kitchen window to the tall ones
in the dining room as man and horse moved past the
side of the house, just beyond the yard. Finally she
slipped out on the south gallery, being quiet as a
church mouse, taking care not to be seen.

Clutching her long white nightie up around her
knees, she stood barefoot in the summer dawn. Watching Kurt Northway. Princelike, he moved with a slow,
fluid grace which prompted the inane thought that he
was most likely smooth and graceful on the dance
floor. She would never know, of course.

Helen's discerning woman's eye quickly noted that

Kurt's tanned face was smoothly shaven, his jet-black hair neatly brushed. He wore a freshly laundered white shirt and a pair of snug-fitting navy trousers. Like a mother fussily checking her child's appearance, Helen was pleased. He was as clean, well-groomed, and handsome as any man she'd ever seen, so at least her old friends couldn't fault him on that score.

Helen clicked her tongue against the roof of her mouth, silently chiding herself. She was silly to care one way or the other. Immaculate or slovenly, he was still a Yankee. That fact alone was cause enough to get him shunned by the throngs of fairgoers. She herself would probably shun him if she could afford such a luxury.

Just as the tall, lean man and the big, sleek horse reached the entrance to the tree-shaded lane, both paused. Kurt stopped, slowly pivoted, and looked directly toward the house. Helen gasped in horror and jumped back when he lifted a hand and waved to her. Had he known all along that she was there?

Feeling foolish and guilty and irritated all at the same time, she rushed back inside wishing she had never gone out. Wishing he hadn't caught her. Wishing things could be different.

Wishing that she and Charlie were going with Kurt to the fair. Wishing that the three of them could walk among the many booths and buy foolish nick-nacks and win prizes and eat spiced shrimp and laugh and have a good time like all the other men, women, and children in Baldwin County.

She wished she and Charlie could see Kurt win this afternoon's big race. Wished the two of them could be there, leaning over the rail cheering wildly when Raider flashed across the finish line ahead of the pack.

Wished Kurt's reason for entering the race was not so he could leave.

Helen closed her eyes and bit down on her trembling bottom lip. She made one last wish.

With all her heart and soul, she wished that the powerful Raider would somehow lose the race.

Kurt led the big stallion into the dark tree-bordered lane. They emerged at the other end and turned north. Toward Spanish Fort.

Kurt didn't mount his horse. He had no intention of riding his thoroughbred the eight miles into town. He would walk alongside Raider, setting a slow, leisurely pace. It mattered little if he himself was worn out come race time. He didn't want Raider tired.

He and Jolly had talked it over and had carefully laid their plans last night. Jolly was to be waiting for him at the edge of town. At that time, Jolly would take charge of Raider. The town's livery wouldn't refuse extending service to Jolly Grubbs; it might turn down Kurt. So Jolly was to be the one who'd see to it the big stallion was stabled, guarded, fed, watered, and well rested by race time.

Helen waited until eight A.M.

The sun was high in the sky when she went down to the quarters to wake Charlie. Realizing today would probably be the last one Charlie spent on her farm, Helen was resolved to keep her worries to herself, to make it a happy day for them both.

She knocked softly on the door and spoke Charlie's name. She went inside, tiptoed toward the bed, and smiled when she saw him, sound asleep, lying on his tummy, hugging his pillow.

Her gaze rested on the angelic-looking Charlie for a minute, then shifted to the empty pillow beside him. The white, lace-edged pillow revealed the deep indentation where a head had recently rested. Impulsively, Helen picked up the pillow and lifted it to her face.

She pressed it to her nose and caught the clean, unique scent of the man whose dark handsome head had lain on it.

Inhaling, clasping the pillow to her, she looked at the empty side of the soft feather bed and tried to picture Kurt Northway there. Did he sleep on his back or his stomach? Were his arms at his sides or folded beneath his head? Did he sleep as peacefully as his beautiful son? Or did he toss and turn restlessly?

What did he sleep in? Did he wear a knee-length nightshirt similar to Charlie's? Or nothing but his white linen underwear? Did the darkness of his broad bare chest and trim waist and leanly muscled limbs contrast sharply with the snowy-white sheets beneath him?

A chill skipped up her spine and Helen quickly placed the pillow back on the bed.

"Charlie," she whispered, and circled to his side of the bed. "Charlie, it's time for breakfast." She knelt down beside him.

A small blond head came up off the pillow. Charlie rolled over onto his side, grinned at her, then flopped onto his back and sat up. Weight supported on stiffened arms, he asked, "The captain already gone?" He had been told that his father had important business in Spanish Fort, that he would be gone all day.

Helen nodded. "Left bright and early."

Charlie swung his short legs around and slid off the bed, stood there facing the kneeling Helen, his back against the mattress, his short fingers twisting on his nightshirt. "You 'member what you promised?"

Helen smiled and lifted her hands to his tiny waist. "I sure do."

Charlie squirmed free of her hold. "I get to eat breakfast in the house."

"That's right. We'll eat at the kitchen table."

"And . . . and . . . then . . ." his eyes grew big and round, "we make gingerbread men!"

Helen said, "This afternoon. We bake cookies this afternoon. First we do our chores. Then after dinner we'll rest a while, maybe take a little nap, and then we'll bake the gingerbread men. Okay?"

Helen rose to her feet.

"Okay." Charlie clapped his hands. "Okay!" Charlie immediately frowned and, racing over to the bureau, he asked, "I got to do this first. Will you help?"

"Sure." She supposed he wanted her help in choosing something to wear.

But Charlie jerked open the bottom drawer and scooped up an armload of his clothes.

"Wait," Helen said, smiling tolerantly. "You only need one shirt and one—"

Charlie furiously shook his golden head. "No, see . . . see, the captain told me to . . . to . . ."

"To what Charlie? What does the captain want you to do?"

"To have *all* my clothes together when he gets back," Charlie told her.

The little boy's statement jolted through Helen like a harsh physical blow. She swayed on weak legs, sat down on the unmade bed, and attempted to sound nonchalant when she asked, "Why? Did the captain tell you why he wanted you to have all your clothes together?" She held her breath.

Arms wrapped around a bunch of little faded, frayed shirts, Charlie lifted his shoulders in a shrug. "I don't know."

Helen smiled, nodded, and said, "I'll help you. We'll have everything ready by the time the captain comes home this evening."

She came to kneel down beside Charlie, her hands trembling slightly as she lifted the worn, carefully folded little-boy clothes out of the drawer. When the drawer was empty, when all Charlie's clothes were stacked together atop the blue-and-white-checked tablecloth, Helen said anxiously, "Boy, I'm starving, aren't you? Get dressed and let's go up to the house and have ourselves some flapjacks and ham."

Charlie started to yank his nightshirt up over his head, remembered his modesty just in time, and said, "You have to turn your back!"

Helen smiled, "I'll wait for you outside." She slipped out the door, grateful to have a few seconds alone to fully compose herself.

In seconds Charlie came bounding out the door. He raced up the path toward the house in front of Helen, frantically calling Dom's name. The Russian Blue, lazily stretched out on the far side of the water well, heard him but calmly waited until Charlie was even with the well. Then the cat came prancing out from behind the well, meowing a greeting.

Charlie spotted him.

Squealing with uninhibited glee, he tore out after the blue-furred cat. Playful, Dom shot away, but soon stopped and waited for Charlie. Charlie caught up. He squatted down, scooped the big tom up off the ground, and rose to his feet, pressing the cat to his chest, Dom's four paws dangling against the little boy's body.

Charlie wagged the remarkably docile Dom toward the house while Helen followed, laughing despite her troubles. The lovable Charlie had won even the heart of the independent Dom.

RACING ENTRIES—SIGN UP HERE

The sign was posted above a temporary plank table just outside the fairground's oval racing track. Groups of men loitered about under the nearby shade trees. The talk was of nothing but the afternoon's mile-long race. Bloodlines of the entrants were discussed. Side bets were being placed on long shots.

Most of the men agreed it was a one-horse race. Niles Loveless was, for the first time, racing the costly black he'd purchased last spring in Louisville. The four-year-old thoroughbred had been sired by one of the fastest horses ever bred in Kentucky. While a couple of other speedsters with respectable bloodlines were entered in today's contest, the black looked to be the clear winner.

At shortly before noon Kurt made his way toward the oval racetrack, purposely skirting the busy fairgrounds. Weaving through the growing clusters of men, he ignored the questioning looks he drew and stepped up to the entry table.

A fleshy, pink-cheeked man with bushy eyebrows and sideburns looked up and frowned. "This is Baldwin County, Alabama, Yankee! We don't want your kind here at our fair around our women and children."

Loud conversations dropped to a low hum. Then silence fell as all eyes turned on the tall, dark man standing before the table.

"I'm not at the fair with your women and children," Kurt said. "I'm at the track and I see only men. I'm here to enter my horse in this afternoon's race."

Jeffrey Stark, the overweight, pink-faced man behind the table snorted. "You what?"

"I'm entering my thoroughbred stallion in the horse race."

Stark grinned nastily up at Kurt. Playing to his audience, he said sarcastically, "You may as well go on back to the farm and take your nag with you. You ain't runnin' him in this race."

"The Spanish Fort newspaper said the race is open to anyone," Kurt reminded him.

"Anyone but a Yankee," said Stark, and he looked

around and laughed. The watching men nodded and laughed and waited for Kurt to turn and leave.

Kurt stayed where he was. "My name is spelled N-o-r-t-h-w-a-y. Write it on your list. I'm running my stallion in this race."

Stark stopped laughing. "No, you're not."

"Yes, he is." The voice of quiet command came from beyond the crowd.

Heads turned as Sheriff Brian A. Cooper walked through them, stepped up to the table beside Kurt, and repeated the statement.

"Yes, he is," the sheriff said softly. "Now add his name to the list and let him draw a starting position."

Stark's pink face grew pinker. His bushy eyebrows wiggled. "What the hell are you doing here, Sheriff?" he growled.

"Upholding the law," said Coop laconically. He hooked his thumbs in his low-riding leather gun holster and slowly turned about to face the crowd of men. "Anybody got any problem with another entrant in the horse race? If so, let's hear it right now and let it be the end of this discussion."

Nobody did.

But Niles Loveless, arriving just after the incident, was far from happy with this turn of events. Niles stood on the fringes of the growing crowd, surrounded by his minions, frowning with displeasure.

Later, he shot Kurt a look as Kurt passed by him.

Kurt paused, extended his hand, and said, "I believe we've met. Loveless, isn't it?"

Niles reluctantly shook Kurt's hand. "So you're going to run that sorrel in today's race?"

"That's the plan."

"Who's going to ride him?"

Kurt shrugged. "I am."

Niles chuckled. His hangers-on laughed uproariously. "You're a little large for a jockey, aren't you?"

"Raider doesn't think so."

"Sell me the sorrel, Northway. Do it now before the race. Before my black beats him so badly I'll no longer want to own him."

"Raider's not for sale, either before or after the race." Kurt started to walk away. He stopped, turned back, and said, "By the way, Loveless, you have the time?"

Without thinking, Niles reached into his vest pocket for the watch that was not there. He looked up and caught the knowing grin on Kurt's dark face and his own flushed angrily.

Kurt turned and walked away, chuckling softly to himself.

Teeth gritted, Niles Loveless said under his breath, "Damn that insolent Yankee son of a bitch!"

Chapter Twenty-three

Helen sat across the kitchen table from Charlie for the second time that day. She listened distractedly to his excited, rambling little-boy talk. And all the while she was wondering where Charlie's father was this noon hour. Had he found a place that would serve him food? Or would he be forced to go hungry all day? And what did she care if he starved to death?

"Finish your milk," she interrupted Charlie.

When Charlie had cleaned his plate, he tore away the linen napkin tucked under his chin, and said, "Is it time yet?"

Helen laughed and shook her head. All morning he'd been asking if it was time to bake the gingerbread men. Once again she reminded him of the chores they had to complete before any baking was begun.

"After while," she told him for the umpteenth time. "Won't be long now."

Helen knew how Charlie felt. Much as she savored these final hours together, she couldn't help wanting the time to pass, the hours to hurry by. But for a different reason than Charlie's.

She wouldn't know, until day's end, whose thoroughbred had won the race. The waiting was enough to drive her crazy. The last thing she wanted was for Northway to collect the prize money, yet she vacillated on wanting Raider to win and wanting him to get beat.

One minute she couldn't help but consider what a

sweet, rewarding victory it would be. In her mind's eye she could see the mighty stallion flying around the oval track, leaving all the others far, far behind, streaking across the finish line in a blaze of glory.

And Niles Loveless standing there brokenhearted!

The very next minute she would change her mind. Much as she'd like to see Niles Loveless's thoroughbred get soundly beaten, she would catch herself hoping—praying—that Raider wouldn't win. If the big sorrel won the race and Northway collected the prize money, he and Charlie would go back home to Maryland. Taking with them any hopes she'd had of holding on to her farm.

Helen grew increasingly tense as the day progressed. She jumped each time the tall cased clock in the foyer struck the hour or half hour.

Twelve noon had come and gone. Helen and Charlie did the dishes. Twelve-thirty. This was pure torture. One o'clock. Helen wished she had gone to the fair. One-thirty. What, she wondered miserably, was happening in town this very minute?

Two o'clock.

The clock in the tall spire of the Methodist church struck two o'clock.

Kurt Northway lounged lazily in a chair tipped back against the wall outside the Red Rose Saloon. The saloon was closed. The town was deserted. Everyone was at the fair. Kurt was alone on Spanish Fort's silent Main Street.

Full from the big meal he'd shared with Sheriff Cooper and Em Ellicott, he sat in the sun and dozed, totally relaxed, confident that the upcoming race belonged solely to Raider. The prize money was his.

And he knew just what he would do with it.

The day's warmth and the silence lulling him, Kurt

fell asleep with his fingers laced together across his stomach and his long legs stretched out before him.

A carriage rolled slowly down the empty street. A lady was inside. She spotted the lone man on the wooden sidewalk and recognized him. She tapped the top of the coach and ordered her driver to pull over.

Catnapping, Kurt sensed a presence. His eyes slitted cautiously open. Shimmering rose silk filled the entire scope of his vision.

Slowly his eyes climbed upward from the voluminous rose skirts. His narrow-eyed gaze appreciatively touched a waspish, nipped-in waist, slid languidly up to a full, magnificent bosom which was not entirely covered by a tight rose silk bodice. His frank, lingering stare resting on the expanse of bare, womanly flesh revealed by the gown's low-cut bodice caused those voluptuous breasts to swell against the restraining silk as if their proud owner were struggling for a breath.

Kurt's gaze finally lifted to a lovely face framed with elaborately dressed dark hair.

She smiled at him. He started to rise.

"Don't." Yasmine Parnell lifted a hand. "Stay just as you are."

"You shouldn't be here, Mrs. Parnell."

"Why not?" Yasmine smiled down at him. "Am I in danger, Captain?"

"Yes." Kurt smiled. "In danger of coming out of your dress."

Yasmine laughed. "So you have noticed that I'm a woman."

"I've noticed."

"I'm glad." She looked cautiously around. "I hoped you had. I'm on my way to the fair. I understand you're racing your thoroughbred this afternoon." He nodded. "Think you'll win?"

"I know I'll win."

"Such masculine confidence. I like that." She smiled

at him and added, "I like winners. If you win, come call on me at my home. We'll drink champagne toasts." She put out the tip of her pink tongue and licked her red lips wetly. "To the victor go the spoils, Captain."

Kurt lifted a dark eyebrow. "You'd risk crossing Niles Loveless?"

Yasmine's flirtatious smile evaporated. "I don't know what you're talking about!"

"Yes, you do, Mrs. Parnell."

"You dare insinuate that I . . . that Mr. Loveless . . . why, he's a married man and I . . . I don't have to stand here and listen to such farfetched, filthy accusations!"

"No, ma'am, you don't," said Kurt.

Yasmine's hands went to her generous hips. "Listen to me, Yankee, if you so much as hint to anyone that—"

"Your secret is safe with me."

"I don't like you, Northway," she spat venomously. "You're a cocky Yankee bastard and you suppose that all women want you. Well, here's one who doesn't!" Yasmine whirled away and hurried to her carriage, stung by his rejection, determined to get even.

Bristling with anger, she went to the fair. And she wasted little time in whispering to the ladies of Spanish Fort that she had every reason to believe that "Helen's Yankee" really was "Helen's Yankee." In the most intimate sense.

Yasmine didn't actually believe she was spreading lies. She took it for granted that since the darkly handsome Northway turned her down, it was surely because he was having a torrid affair with the love-starved Helen Courtney. Damn that hypocritical, long-suffering Helen. She ought to be ashamed of herself.

Sleeping with a dirty Yankee!

At race time Yasmine joined her friend, plump and pretty Patsy Loveless, at the oval track. They linked arms and anticipated Niles's big win. Niles joined them, stepping between them just minutes before the starting gun. Yasmine possessively took his arm and smiled adoringly up at him. Niles nervously cleared his throat and put his other arm around Patsy's waist.

Crowds of people were pressed eagerly around the track. The excitement rose as the minutes ticked away toward four o'clock.

Jolly Grubbs stood with his arms folded over the railing directly before the finish line. He said a little prayer as the field approached the starting line.

Fourteen nervous, high-strung thoroughbreds were led into position. Raider had drawn the number ten slot. In the number one post position was Niles Loveless's blooded black, a ninety-five-pound jockey on his back.

Seconds ticked away. The crowd roared. The clock in the Methodist church tower began to chime. A pistol shot rang out. The horses streaked away from the starting line.

The race was on.

Chapter Twenty-four

Helen's heart lurched when the tall cased clock in the hallway struck four. She beat the batter in the big pottery bowl faster, harder, her eyes staring sightlessly, her teeth clamped tightly together.

"You're splattering!" Charlie shouted.

Charlie sat atop the kitchen cabinet, a dish towel tied around his waist, a freshly baked gingerbread man in his hand, its head and arms eaten off. Barefooted, Charlie had flour on his nose and one ear, grease on his shirt, and flecks of cookie batter all over his dish-towel apron, his face, in his hair, on his legs, and between his toes.

He had been allowed to beat the first batch and had repeatedly heard "Charlie, watch it, you're splattering" from Helen. He thought it was terribly funny that he could now say it to her.

"Helen, you're splattering!" he squealed again, and then laughed.

Helen came to her senses and laughed with him. She *had* made a mess. Flecks of batter covered her apron and dress. She winked at Charlie and set the big bowl down beside him. Dipping a finger into the batter, she touched it to the tip of his nose. He giggled and wiped it off. And, of course, he immediately stuck his finger into the batter and smeared a dab on Helen's chin. She tried to lick it off with her tongue while Charlie clapped his hands and laughed.

It was well past five when the two of them had finished baking and decorating several dozen gingerbread men. It took another half hour to clean up the kitchen. And still more time to clean up themselves.

It was when everything had been done that time really dragged for Helen. She had no idea when she could expect Kurt. If Raider won the race, Kurt might feel like celebrating the victory. He might go to a saloon and drink. Or gamble. Or worse.

What difference did it make, really? If he was leaving tonight, it mattered little what he did with his last evening in Alabama.

As the shadows lengthened, Helen anxiously paced the worn carpet of the parlor. She was so edgy Charlie noticed and asked her if something was wrong. She assured him that everything was fine. Said nothing was bothering her, but it was a little stuffy in the house, would he like to go outdoors?

He was out the front door in a flash, followed quickly by the tense Helen.

The June sun was setting over the bay. Helen was rocking nervously in her favorite cane-bottomed rocker on the front gallery. She watched Charlie catch lightning bugs in the big front yard. Every few minutes she'd get up, walk around to the south side of the house, and look toward the tree-bordered lane. Then sigh and go back to her rocker.

At last she heard the faint drum of hoofbeats. Charlie heard them too.

"The captain's home!" Charlie shouted, and he set his jar of fireflies down, told Dom to guard them, and sped around the house.

Heart beating erratically, Helen followed.

Kurt Northway rode into sight. The last rays of the dying sun fell on his beautiful black hair. He was smiling.

Raider had won.

Helen felt sick.

Kurt reined in Raider and dismounted. He held in his right hand a brand-new traveling valise. He nodded almost imperceptibly to Helen and her hand went to her throat.

He smiled down at Charlie and asked, "Did you remember to get all your clothes together?"

Charlie nodded furiously. "Helen helped me."

"Good," Kurt said. He set the traveling valise down on the ground and told Charlie, "I brought you a present."

Charlie stepped eagerly forward. "A present for me? What is it?"

Kurt turned, took a box from his worn black saddlebags, and handed it to his son. Charlie ripped off the lid, looked inside at the brightly painted toy soldiers, and gave a loud shout of happiness. He quickly turned and showed the soldiers to Helen. She made the proper reaction.

Turning back to his father, happiness shining out of his big brown eyes, he said, "Thank you, Captain."

He looked so sweet and cute standing there holding the box of toy soldiers to his narrow chest, Kurt wanted to reach down, pluck him from the ground, and hug him tightly.

"You're very welcome," said Kurt.

"Can I go spread them out on my bed?"

"Yes, you may. Take the valise with you."

"Okay, Captain!" Charlie started to pick up the traveling case, but his father stopped him.

Kurt lifted it from the ground, turned to the stallion, and quietly told Raider to take the valise and follow Charlie down to the barn. Charlie laughed when Raider whinnied and shook his great head, then firmly clamped his teeth over the valise's handle when Kurt held it up to him. Carrying the valise in his mouth, the big stallion obediently followed the happy little boy, who wagged his box of new toy soldiers tucked underneath his arm.

Helen and Kurt were left alone. They faced each other.

"Aren't you going to ask?" he said.

"There's no need," she said cheerlessly. "You won. Congratulations."

His handsome face broke into a broad grin. "Raider left his closest opponent—Niles Loveless's black—ten lengths behind. Won it without breaking a sweat."

Helen tried to smile. Failed. "That's wonderful." Her tone was far from convincing.

"You don't sound like you think it's wonderful."

"Sorry." She drew a breath, looked him straight in the eye. "So . . . when will you be leaving?"

"When do you want me to leave?"

Helen hung her head. She nudged at a stone with the toe of her worn slipper. "Raider won the race. Now you have enough money to go to Maryland."

"Actually, I don't," Kurt said with a smile in his voice. Helen's head snapped up.

"You can't get to Maryland on a hundred dollars? Families live for an entire year on less."

"I don't have a hundred dollars."

"You don't have . . . You've spent it?"

"Yes, ma'am."

"All of it?"

"Just about." He crossed his arms over his chest and leaned back from the waist, waiting for her to speak. When she stood there silently staring at him, he said, "Don't you want to know what I spent it on?"

"No. It's none of my business."

"A good team of plow horses to replace old Duke. Got a pair of sturdy grays for seventy dollars. They're being delivered in the morning."

Her lips falling open in astonishment, Helen stared at him, unable to believe she had heard him correctly.

"But . . . I thought . . . the traveling case . . . telling
Charlie to get his . . ."

" . . . old worn-out clothes together," Kurt finished
for her. "So we can burn them. I bought Charlie some
new clothes today with the money I had left over after
paying for the team." He laughed, a rich, warm laugh,
and told her, "I'll be back in your fields plowing by
noon tomorrow."

Helen was speechless.

She felt like laughing and crying at the same time.
He was staying! He'd spent his prize money to buy
plow horses to help her hold on to her farm. He could
have taken Charlie and left her high and dry, but he
wasn't going to do it. She felt her heart throbbing in
her chest. She was tempted to throw her arms around
his neck and squeeze him.

"I don't know what to say," she finally spoke. "I
thought . . . I supposed that you . . . I made a foolish
threat and I . . ."

"You didn't mean it. I know you didn't. You never
meant for me to leave and I never meant to leave." He
smiled then, uncrossed his arms, and said, "You do understand, don't you, why I could never allow Raider to
pull a plow?"

She nodded. "Yes, I do." She smiled then. "I'm very
grateful to you for what you've done. You'll never
know how grateful. Thank you." He nodded. Helen
was so overwhelmed with relief she couldn't trust herself to say more. Awkwardly, she murmured, "Well . . .
you . . . you must be tired. I'll say good night now."
She turned to leave.

"Wait," Kurt said, and he caught her arm, gently
pulled her back. He reached into his shirt pocket and
pulled out a small box. "I brought you a little present."

Her eyes grew as wide as Charlie's had. "A present
for me?"

"It's not much," he said, almost apologetically.

Helen eagerly opened the box and took out the delicate mother-of-pearl hair clasp. "It's something to wear in your hair," he said. "I noticed your friend Em had one in her hair the other day, so I thought you might like it." He shrugged wide shoulders. "But you don't have to wear it if you don't want to, I just ..."

Helen handed the box to him, slid the barrette up into her hair and fastened it. "It's beautiful. Thank you, Captain."

She looked so sweet and lovely standing there in the fading dusk wearing the new clasp in her golden hair, Kurt felt like plucking her off her feet, pulling her into his arms, and hugging her close.

He smiled. "You're very welcome, Mrs. Courtney."

Chapter Twenty-five

Come Monday morning, Niles Loveless was in a bad mood.

He sat behind his massive mahogany desk in his spacious office on Main Street. The big room was dim. He had not raised the shades over the many windows, nor had he unlocked the front door. He didn't want to see anyone and he didn't want anyone to see him. Sullen, he sat there in the gloom nursing a headache. A bad headache.

The sting of seeing his finest thoroughbred beaten in Saturday's race still smarted badly. A loss to any of the entries would have hurt. But to lose to the Yankee captain's sorrel stallion had been devastating.

The race had been such an embarrassing disappointment, he had taken Patsy and left immediately. Using the excuse that he had a mountain of work do to back at his office, he had dropped Patsy off and went straight to Yasmine Parnell's place. And was furious to find she wasn't there waiting for him! He had let himself in, poured himself a stiff drink, and went upstairs to wait.

He was drunk and angry when finally she came in at seven that evening. He got drunker and angrier still when she repelled his amorous advances, telling him she wanted only to rest and change before going to the fair's dance. As if he were a naughty child, she sent him home to his wife. Once there, Patsy soundly scolded him for being late for dinner and for smelling of liquor. Then she frowned, flounced up the stairs, and locked him out of his own bedroom.

So instead of celebrating sweet victory in a crowd of well-wishers and admirers, Niles had spent Saturday night drinking alone in painful defeat.

And most of Sunday as well.

Muttering oaths, Niles leaned back in his swivel chair and gripped his throbbing temples. Eyes shut, he cursed everybody and everything he could think of to curse. He finally opened his eyes, sighed wearily, and wondered if it was too early to pour himself a good stiff drink.

He automatically fished inside his vest pocket for his diamond-and-gold watch. And cursed anew when he remembered it was not there. Furious, Niles swiveled his chair around, rose to his feet, crossed the plushly carpeted office to the back door.

There he paused to compose himself.

Niles Loveless appeared totally serene when he stepped out the back door to confront the three men waiting patiently in the alleyway. Looking pleasant, Niles nodded to them all in turn and the tense trio collectively breathed a deep sigh of relief.

Smiling, Niles said, "Boys, come on in for a minute."

He turned, went back in, and they all eagerly followed.

Inside, Niles asked, "Which one of you rode out to the old Burke farm and hid my watch?"

Harry Boyd threw back his thick shoulders. "It was me, boss! I did it. The sheriff been out there yet and found it?"

The words were barely out of Boyd's mouth before Niles was on him. All traces of his former fake smile now gone, Niles grabbed the big man by his open shirt collar, jerked Boyd's startled face down a couple of inches from his own, and said, "No, the sheriff didn't find it and you'd better damn well remember where you hid it."

Blinking with confusion and surprise, Boyd began furiously nodding his head. "I remember. I know exactly where I hid the watch and I—"

"Good. Ride back out there tonight and get it," ordered Niles, yanking on the man's collar for emphasis.

"But why? I thought—"

"Just do it!" snarled Niles. He released his hold on the big man's shirt, again clutched his own banging temples, and added contemptuously, "And get out of my sight, all of you! I can't stand to look at you!"

The chastened Harry Boyd waited until well past midnight. Then he rode alone onto the Burke property, thanking the fates for the new moon which gave so little light. Deep into the dense pine forest Boyd rode, dodging tree branches and thick undergrowth in the darkness.

Boyd drew rein when at last he came out of the woods and into the open. Before him lay the silent farm with its level fields, old bay-front home, and sprawling outbuildings. The big house was dark. Boyd was relieved. His gaze went to the barn. Then to the connecting quarters. No lights shone. Boyd exhaled with released tension.

"Piece of cake," the big man silently assured himself.

He dismounted, tethered his horse to a tall pine, and started toward the distant outbuildings. Under the cloak of darkness he approached the barn, tiptoeing as he neared the corral where the big sorrel stallion was penned. He stopped every few steps, expecting the horse to catch his scent and put up a racket.

No sound came from the darkened corral.

Boyd reached the old barn's open front door. He

slipped inside, paused, and blinked sightlessly. It was pitch-black. He could hardly see his hand before his face. He would have to feel his way to where he had hidden the watch.

Boyd swallowed hard, put his hands out before him like a blind man, and slowly advanced deeper into the dark interior of the barn. Getting his bearings, he remembered where the ladder was which went up to the corncrib. He quickly headed in that direction.

In seconds his searching outstretched hands came in contact with the splintered ladder and Harry Boyd shook his head happily in the darkness. Hoping the rickety rungs would hold him one more time, he began his climb. He grunted softly when he reached the landing and levered himself up.

A glassless window near the top of the barn's steep roof allowed a small degree of moonlight to spill inside, but it wasn't enough to be of any great help. Fortunately, Boyd remembered exactly which stack of corn he'd hidden the watch under. All he needed to do was get over to it, move a few cobs aside, pick up the watch, and then get the devil out of there.

On hands and knees the big man crawled past several neat stacks of corn, feeling suddenly as if he might sneeze at any second, knowing that he couldn't let that happen. He stopped, lifted a hand up to cover his nose and mouth, squeezed his eyes tightly shut, and waited for the sensation to pass. When it did, he set out again, grinning in the darkness when he reached the neatly stacked mound of corn directly to the right of the high window.

Eager now to get the watch and go, he crouched on his heels and began scooping up ears of corn, rearranging those which were left. He reached a large hand into the hiding place and spread his fingers, expecting to touch cool smooth gold.

He felt only corn shucks and rough wood. He

shoved his hand farther inside, patted anxiously, came up with nothing.

He tore into the stacked corn like a madman, tossing ears this way and that, clawing furiously, forgetting the need for silence. Like a raging bull he snorted and blew and crashed around, frantic to locate the watch.

On all fours, the wildly charging Harry Boyd ripped the crib apart, slinging corn and loose husks everywhere. Out of breath, heart hammering, he rose up on his knees, feeling for all the world as if he were going to cry.

The cry died in his throat and he stiffened with shock when a hand abruptly shot out of the darkness and clamped down hard over his mouth. His eyes wide with fright, he almost choked on his tongue.

"This what you're looking for?" came a low, deep voice from directly behind.

Diamonds winked in the dim light as a gold-cased pocket watch, suspended by a glittering gold chain, was slowly lowered in front of his face and made to swing back and forth, back and forth before his startled eyes.

Afraid to breathe, afraid to move, certain that the next thing he would see or feel would be the steel barrel of a gun, the trembling Harry Boyd froze. His big, muscular arms hung useless at his sides. His eyes flashed with fear.

Kurt withdrew his hand from Boyd's mouth. He stepped from behind the kneeling man, moved around to face him.

"I asked a question," Kurt said softly, dangling the pocket watch inches from Boyd's nose. "Answer me."

Nodding furiously, fighting to swallow so that he would have enough saliva to speak, Harry Boyd finally managed to croak, "You can keep it. You can keep the watch. I'll tell—"

"I don't want Loveless's watch. I don't want anything Loveless has." Kurt reached out, unbuttoned the man's breast pocket, and dropped the watch inside. "Take his watch back to him. And take this message with you: I will personally see to it that he *never* gets his filthy hands on a single acre of Mrs. Courtney's land." One-handed, Kurt rebuttoned the kneeling man's shirt pocket. "Think you can remember that?"

"Yes, sir," gasped Harry Boyd. "I'll tell him."

"Get up."

Harry Boyd struggled to his feet. "Anything else?"

"Yes. This is private property. You're trespassing. If I ever catch you on it again," said Kurt coldly, "I'll kill you."

Chapter Twenty-six

Yankee soldiers lie here in peace,
Guests of strangers,
Far from home,
They too died for their country

K urt stood in the early morning silence studying the epitaph he had carved on the new wooden marker. He bowed his head respectfully and offered a brief prayer for his fallen comrades-in-arms.

At his feet were the graves of the three Union soldiers Jolly had buried at the edge of Helen's property. Union soldiers with Farragut's fleet who had lost their lives in the Battle of Mobile.

Kurt raised his head.

Eyes squinted, he gazed toward the distant northern horizon ... toward home. Come autumn, he would leave this place. He would finally go back home to Maryland. But these men would never go home. This rich Alabama soil was their final resting place.

Kurt turned away from the graves now marked by the carved wooden headstone. The sun was coming up and he had plenty of work to do. He wouldn't leave Alabama until all the work was done. He couldn't, in good conscience, go back to his home without first making sure Helen wouldn't lose hers.

He was determined that she would keep her beloved land. He worked tirelessly from sunup to moonrise to finish the plowing and planting. With the team of strong-bodied grays pulling the heavy blade before him, he plowed long straight rows until his arms ached so they felt as though they were being jerked out of their sockets and his legs grew so tired he could barely walk. He worked until he felt he couldn't grip the plow handles another minute, couldn't possibly take one more step.

And found that he could.

On he went, the broiling Alabama sun beating directly down on his tired back. All through the long hot day, he was so soaked with sweat his clothes stuck wetly to his heated body. And he was thirsty. Always thirsty. So thirsty he felt as if he were "spittin' cotton," as Jolly would say.

It didn't matter.

The only thing that mattered was getting the crops planted as quickly as possible. He was totally focused on one and only one goal: To see to it that Helen Courtney had a bountiful autumn harvest. A harvest which would provide money enough to take care of the exorbitant land taxes, pay his wages, and leave her able to live comfortably. To live comfortably without the constant worry of losing her farm to Niles Loveless.

His unflagging dedication to his backbreaking chores was not lost on Helen. A quiet admiration for him grew daily as she witnessed him toiling uncomplainingly in the sun-blistered fields. It was twilight each evening before he came in, hot, tired, and dirty.

She would look out the kitchen window and see him at the well, taking the dipper down off the hook to get a drink. Several drinks.

She'd seen the total exhaustion written on his handsome face, watched him lean wearily against the well post as he drank thirstily of the cool water. She'd noted as well that there was not a dry thread on his tall, lean body. His work shirt clung stickily to his back and chest and biceps. His face was always covered with the powdered red earth. Beads of sweat slipped down his cheeks to his bare throat. His jet-black hair was wet and clinging to his head.

Now on this warm June evening, Helen was watching when Kurt Northway ripped off his dirty work shirt and draped it over the side of the well. He lifted a dipper full of water, turned away from the well, bent down, and poured the water over his dark head. His eyes shut, he lifted his head and smiled as the cool water streamed over his dirty face, clinging to his long dark eyelashes and sluicing down his bare chest. It was such a purely masculine gesture, Helen couldn't keep from smiling. A woman would never—no matter how hot—pour water over her head.

Only a man would do that.

Her smile widened when he lifted his hands to wipe the water from his eyes, then shook himself like a great dog and pushed his wet hair straight back off his face. She could almost hear his deep sigh of satisfaction. When a tanned hand went to his hard abdomen, spreading water over smooth taut flesh, Helen felt suddenly as if she were looking in someone's window. It was an invasion of his privacy.

She quickly turned away, guiltily admitting to herself that she had derived a disgraceful degree of pleasure from spying on him. It worried her that she had so enjoyed it. What had gotten into her?

Helen frowned.

Was she forgetting who this man was? Had it momentarily slipped her mind that he was a Yankee? She almost wished she hadn't burned his uniforms. Wished he still wore those cavalry trousers with their yellow stripes so there'd never be any doubt about who he actually was.

Helen ground her teeth savagely. Had it been only weeks since she'd hotly assured him that she would *never* forget he'd worn the uniform of the hated enemy? That she didn't want to forget. Ever. That she would go on remembering for as long as she lived. That she would take her hatred of him and his murdering federal troops with her to the grave and beyond.

Dear God, was she already forgetting?

No!

No, she wasn't. And she never would.

The work load eased a bit when all the fields had finally been planted with crops. There was still much to do, but Kurt managed to find the time to tackle a new project. It was to be a surprise for Helen. He conferred with Charlie and Jolly and warned them not to let the cat out of the bag.

Quietly he went about tearing down the rotted stairs leading from the front yard down to the bay. When every last stick of old wood had been hauled away, he took a scythe and cleared the badly overgrown path of tangled vines and choking weeds and brushy undergrowth. When he'd successfully hacked a clean wide path through the dense jungle foliage, he rounded up all the loose lumber he could get his hands on. Jolly donated to the cause, sneaking planks down to the building sight, taking special care not to be seen by Helen.

Charlie was beside himself with excitement over the proposed stairway. He'd been repeatedly cautioned not to tell Helen and spoil the surprise, but it was all he could do to keep the secret.

Something was up; Helen knew it. Charlie's big brown eyes sparkled constantly with impishness and he did a lot of whispering to Jolly and cutting his eyes at Helen and clamping his hands over his mouth to keep himself quiet.

The secret was finally out one early morning when the sound of hammering awakened Helen. Curious, she quickly dressed and went out back to investigate. She looked toward the barn, saw nobody. Puzzled, she realized that the sound of the rhythmic hammering was not as loud as it had been when she was in her bedroom.

She went back inside, walked through the house, and stepped out onto the front gallery.

The hammering grew louder, closer.

"What the . . . ?" She descended the porch steps and hurried across the big front yard, zeroing in on the report of the unseen hammer. It was coming from below. From down on the sloping bluff. She strolled toward the edge of the bluff. To the spot where the old rotting wooden gangway once stood. A new top step was now there in place of the old. Helen stepped cautiously onto it, looked down. Directly below her knelt Kurt, hammer in hand, nailing a piece of carefully measured wood into place.

He was rebuilding the stairway!

A new, wide path had been cleared all the way down to the waters of the bay. The old rotted ladder had been torn down and carted away. Lumber had been sized and cut to build new newel posts and steps. And it had all been done without her knowing. That's why Charlie had been bursting with excitement of late. He knew about the construction of the stairway and he'd been dying to tell her.

Overwhelmed, Helen stared down at Kurt.

He wore no shirt. No shoes. His naked torso gleamed with sweat. The sleek muscles in his bare back slid and bunched with each lifting and lowering of his arm as he pounded with the hammer. In his mouth were several long nails. Stacked beside him were a half dozen precisely cut pieces of wood.

"What are you doing?" she heard herself ask stupidly.

He looked up and smiled around the nails in his mouth. He rose to his feet, the hammer in his hand, carefully took the nails out of his mouth, and said, "Take a wild guess."

"Rebuilding Grandpa Burke's gangway down to the bay." He could tell by her expression she was immensely pleased.

He nodded. "Soon you can skip down the steps, counting as you go, just like when you were a little girl."

Amazed that he'd remembered her telling him about that, she flushed. "I doubt I'll do much skipping, but it'll be grand to have the stairway again." She sat down on the top step. "Such a wonderful surprise. I had no idea."

Kurt crouched back down on his heels below her, still holding the hammer.

"You mean Charlie actually managed to keep from telling?"

"He did, bless his little heart. Now I feel bad. I've spoiled the big surprise, haven't I?"

"You could always pretend you didn't know."

"I'll do that," she was quick to agree. "We'll let him be the one to tell me. To show me."

"I appreciate that," said Kurt. His hand idly flattened on his chest and he realized he wasn't wearing his shirt. He immediately dropped the hammer and reached for the discarded shirt. Looking sheepish, he said, "Sorry, ma'am. I know I promised I'd quit going around here bare-chested and I—"

"Captain, forget what I said." Helen took the shirt from him, laid it on the step beside her. "If you're cooler working without a shirt, then I see no harm in you being bare-chested." She quickly changed the subject. "Will it take long to rebuild the steps?"

Kurt shook his dark head. "Two or three more days at the outside."

"I can hardly wait," she said truthfully.

"They'll be real handy for us all," he said, lifting a forearm to blot his perspiring forehead. "Charlie and Jolly will make good use of them. They'll no longer have to walk so far out of the way to get down to their fishing pier."

She nodded, smiling.

"I imagine I'll be slipping down for a nighttime swim now and again."

"Mmmm," was all Helen said.

"And you . . ." he ventured, looking out over the calm body of water reddened by the rising sun, "you might enjoy an occasional afternoon stroll by the bay."

The new stairway was soon finished.

But Helen made believe she had no idea. She did it for Charlie. And for Jolly as well. A big, overgrown kid at heart, Jolly was every bit as excited as his five-year-old playmate.

On the day the project was completed, Charlie jumped up as soon as supper was finished, went to his father's chair, and whispered in Kurt's ear.

"Yes," said Kurt. "You may."

Charlie flew around the table to Jolly. Kurt and Helen exchanged a quick conspiratorial glance. Charlie never noticed. Neither did Jolly because Charlie was whispering to him that he needed to borrow his red bandanna.

A good sport, the blindfolded Helen was soon being led—Charlie held one hand, Jolly the other—across the front yard toward the bluff.

"Just a few more steps," Charlie told her.

"Nearly there," Jolly backed him up.

Smiling, hands in his trousers pockets, Kurt followed the trio.

"Stop!" Charlie shouted. "Stop right here, Helen."

She stopped and waited. Jolly reached up and removed the bandanna blindfold. Helen's eyes grew wide and her hands went to her cheeks.

"A new stairway!" she declared loudly. "I can't believe it! It's wonderful, wonderful!"

She went on and on excitedly about what a "terrific surprise" it was and said that she had "no idea" and she was "too happy for words." Charlie clapped his hands and squealed with delight. Jolly shook his white head and laughed happily. Kurt grinned and silently applauded her for her acting ability and for giving pleasure to a sweet little boy and a kind old man.

Genuinely happy to have the new gangway, Helen spontaneously turned to hug Jolly warmly and thank him. No sooner had she released him than she fell to her knees, hugged Charlie swiftly before he had the chance to object, and said, "It's the best surprise I've ever had in my life. Thank you so much!"

She rose, smiling.

Charlie, cocking his blond head to one side, innocently asked, "Helen, aren't you going to hug the captain too?"

Helen stiffened immediately. So did Kurt. They glanced anxiously at each other. The awkward moment passed. Finally Helen extended her hand. Kurt took it.

"Thank you," she said, and for one fleeting instant it seemed to her he looked hurt that she had refused to embrace him.

Charlie loved the new wooden steps as much as Helen had when she was a child. The energetic little boy raced up and down them dozens of times each day, always with the shouted warning from a grown-up echoing in his ears: "Charlie, watch your step!" "Charlie, slow down, you're going to break your neck!" "Charlie, don't go near the water!"

Jolly found the new steps to be a godsend. He no longer had to hike nearly a half a mile, circling around behind the barns and angling down across the bluff, to get to the fishing pier directly below Helen's house. Now he was just steps away.

Fifty-two to be exact.

Charlie had counted them. With Jolly's help; Charlie couldn't count that high by himself. Jolly was more than glad to teach him.

The new stairway came in handy when the Fourth of July rolled around. Helen, with Charlie's help, fixed a fancy picnic lunch and the four of them trekked down the wooden steps. At sunset they sat on a blanket spread beside the water's edge and feasted on fried chicken, sliced ham, fresh black-eyed peas, stuffed eggs, yeast rolls, and strawberry shortcake with thick cream.

As darkness descended, they climbed back up the stairs and spent the evening on the front gallery watching the fireworks display across Mobile Bay. Charlie squealed and clapped each time a colorful explosion lighted the night sky. Jolly clapped and shouted with him. A couple of happy kids caught up in the wonder of the incredible pyrotechnic exhibition.

But between the bursts of colored light, Jolly quietly noticed—as he had so many times—that Kurt Northway and Helen Courtney continued to behave like polite strangers. They were graciously civil in front of him and Charlie, but the chasm between them was as wide as ever.

Jolly could tell.

They consciously avoided each other's eyes. They never directly addressed each other. They had chosen to sit as far apart as possible to watch the fireworks display. Helen was in her armless rocker at the northeast corner of the gallery. Kurt lounged on the porch steps.

Jolly noticed, but said nothing.

Jolly Grubbs was not only clever at handling impressionable five-year-olds. He was pretty good at dealing with complicated adults as well.

Never once did Jolly make an attempt to draw Helen and Kurt closer together. If they chose to remain un-communicative strangers giving each other a wide berth, or if in time they became the best of friends, it was their lookout, not his.

Besides, most likely he'd never be able to persuade either of them that living in the past or clinging to old hatreds was a terrible waste of time. That was something they would have to discover for themselves. Let them learn about life from the living of it.

They were intelligent, sensitive, decent people.

They were also young, healthy, and handsome.

And undoubtedly lonely.

Chapter Twenty-seven

Summertime had come to Spanish Fort.

Long scorching days. Endless steamy nights. The sticky, stifling heat was now a constant. It had taken firm hold and would blanket the Deep South for the remainder of the summer. It was muggy even at sunrise. By noontime each day the Eastern Shore was sweltering under a high, blindingly white sun.

As the interminable afternoons dragged torpidly toward a late summer sunset, thunderheads would often boil up and the sky would darken drastically. Heat lightning would flash in jagged lines across the blackness of the heavens and booming thunder would rattle the windows of the old farmhouse.

Occasionally the huge white thunderheads generated enough energy to produce a brief rainstorm. When that happened, the whole sky opened up and a violent downpour lashed the land, pelted the house's slanted roof, and dripped off the moss-hung oaks.

A fleeting respite from the oppressive heat.

But as soon as the storm passed and the sun popped out again, it was hotter and steamier than ever. It was hard to draw a breath, much less get the work done.

As the wilting humid heat settled over the southlands, Helen found herself becoming increasingly short-tempered.

Not with Charlie.

Never with the sweet, lively Charlie. Already she

loved—too much—the small blond boy whose laughter warmed her heart.

Her flashes of temper were directed solely at Charlie Northway's darkly handsome father. Lately she lashed out at Kurt Northway with ever-increasing frequency. But it never fazed him, which frustrated her no end.

No matter how angry she got or what hateful words she flung at him, the Yankee's cool self-discipline remained intact. He never raised his voice. Never argued. Never took her to task. Just continued to go about his work with quiet diligence, weeding, hoeing, thinning, pruning—laboring long hours under a broiling summer sun.

Uncomplaining. Unexcitable. Unperturbed.

With one exception—that memorable day she had suggested hooking Raider up to the plow—she had never seen Northway show any real emotion. None at all. Which of course could only mean one thing. The big, beautiful thoroughbred was of significant importance to him. And she, of course, was not, so her hostility didn't bother him in the least.

Not that she cared.

She sure didn't.

Still, for the life of her she couldn't understand him. Couldn't figure him out. He remained a man of mystery. He kept silent, but he fought to make the farm prosper. He suffered quietly and worked hard. Much as she hated to admit it, he worked harder than was necessary. He did far more than was asked of him. He couldn't have done more had the place belonged to him.

He seemed to take quiet pleasure in fixing things. He had painstakingly fashioned a flagstone walk leading across the front yard to the new steps he had built down to the bay. He had seen to it that the shrubbery was trimmed and thinned. That the lawns were neat and free of weeds. That the overgrowth of boxwoods bordering the front yard was pruned and shaped into a low well-shaped hedge.

Helen had to admit that her long-neglected place was beginning to look like it had in days of old.

The Yankee was always busy at some project and Helen often looked up from her own chores to quietly observe him.

Naked to the waist. Suntanned. Gleaming with sweat. An unsettling sight, and one which never failed to capture her attention.

More than once she had allowed her rapt gaze to travel slowly downward from his full head of glistening jet-black hair to the strong tanned column of his neck and smooth broad shoulders. Then to the wide chest covered with crisp black hair. Midnight hair that thinned into a line going down his flat belly and disappeared into the dark trousers that clung to his slim hips and long legs.

He was as sinuous as a panther, handsomely virile, exuding a potent maleness. And she was attracted. Helplessly attracted. Dark and seductive, he was the kind of man who stirred shameful thoughts in ladies who should know better. A man who had but to walk into view to disturb the equilibrium of any female present.

The sight of him—all rippling muscles and strong animal magnetism—made Helen's pulse quicken, her face feel hot, and her throat to go dry.

And that made her feel terribly guilty. And angry.

Angrier than ever.

Damn the cool, controlled Yankee and his dark, threatening masculinity!

Kurt was not quite as cool and controlled as Helen supposed. From that very first morning, the morning she had snatched off her bonnet and the sun had made a halo of her long, golden hair, he had felt a faint, unwanted stirring of desire.

As the weeks had gone by and the sultry heat had descended, that faint stirring had grown steadily into full-blown hunger. Manfully he had fought the ever-present yearning, but without complete success. Helen Courtney was young, beautiful, and very desirable. He desired her. More than she'd ever know.

He had told himself, time and again, that it wasn't actually Helen Courtney he desired, only that which she embodied. Lush, warm femininity. A lissome, slender body. Pale alabaster skin. Silky golden hair. Dazzling blue eyes. Lips a soft, full promise of pleasure.

Yet no matter how many times he told himself it wasn't Helen he wanted, but a woman, a beautiful woman, he knew that was not the truth. The glamorous Yasmine Parnell had brazenly offered herself to him the day of the Baldwin County Fair. She was his for the taking. Should he choose, he could ride to her home in the dead of the night—this very night—and Yasmine would welcome him into her bed. Even if Niles Loveless had been there only hours earlier.

Kurt was not even mildly tempted.

He had known scores of women like Yasmine Parnell. When he was very young, very naive, and very reckless, he'd spent many nights in the arms of such women. Naughty married women. Urbane single women. Pampered rich women. The horsey set. In their beds he'd learned the art of lovemaking. They had taught him how to give a woman pleasure, had shown him the most sensitive spots to touch, to caress, to kiss. And exactly *how* to touch, caress, and kiss. He had been an apt pupil. He had learned his lessons well.

But in all those years with all those sophisticated women, he had never known the sweet yearning which was awakened in him by his very first glimpse of the

young, beautiful, and totally innocent Gail Whitney.
The trusting young girl who had become his wife.

Now that same sweet torture, that same burning desire was upon him again. He wanted the youthful, exquisite, virtuous Helen Courtney. He would find
himself thinking of her in unguarded moments when
she was out of his sight. At night as he lay awake in
the hot darkness beside his sleeping son he thought of
little else. He would see her clearly in his mind and
that glorious vision aroused him. He wanted to make
love to her. To make love to her in every way imaginable. To shock her and thrill her and please her. To
look directly into her beautiful blue eyes while he took
her to new heights of ecstasy.

He wanted to hold her naked in his arms. He wanted
to feel her pale, satiny skin against his own hot flesh.
He wanted to have her intimately close, so close that
the womanly scent of her would make him dizzy with
burning desire and fierce hunger. He wanted his name
on her lips as he swept her away into an erotic eupho-
ria.

He wanted to grab her up out of her garden again
and spirit her away on Raider. To leave the farm and
Charlie and Jolly and the hard work and the intrusive
world far behind and forgotten. To find a lush hidden
spot in the dense tropical growth below the bluffs
where the two of them could shed all inhibitions along
with their clothes and share the kind of joy known only
to lovers.

Yes, he wanted Helen.

And he strongly suspected that the reason for Hel-
en's increasingly dour disposition had more to do with
him than with the sultry summer heat. She too felt the
strong, forceful pull of raw physical attraction. He was
sure of it.

But she denied it. She was unwilling to admit, even
to herself, that she was starved for affection. And she

couldn't possibly allow herself to admit that she could feel anything—even elemental lust—for a Yankee deserving only of her contempt and hatred.

Late July.

Another hot, steamy night on the eastern shore of Alabama's Mobile Bay.

Kurt made no pretense of going to bed. What would be the use? Why bother lying down only to thrash about and risk waking Charlie?

A smile touched Kurt's lips. Charlie had a new way of getting cool at bedtime. Jolly, naturally, had taught him.

"Want me to show you?" Charlie had asked Kurt.

"By all means."

"Okay! Now watch me, Captain, watch me," Charlie demanded. "Then ... then ... you can do it."

Quick as a wink, Charlie had stripped off his hot nightshirt. Wearing only his brief underwear, he climbed into the bed, stretched out on his back, and reached for a saltshaker which he'd placed near him on the night table.

The shaker did not contain salt. It held water. Charlie generously sprinkled himself with the water, laughing as the cooling drops peppered his arms and legs and chest. Kurt laughed with him.

And when Charlie handed him the shaker, Kurt sprinkled his own chest and arms.

"Feels good," Kurt said.

"Told you!" said Charlie.

"Yes, sir, I believe that'll do the trick," Kurt said, and blew out the lamp.

It didn't do the trick.

He'd known all along that it wouldn't. While Charlie was asleep almost as soon as the light went out, his father was not so fortunate. The droplets of water al-

ready evaporating, Kurt went outdoors, sat down on
the stoop. He drew a deep, slow breath.

The night air was hot and humid. And fragrant with
the heavy perfume of magnolias. Almost overpoweringly sensuous. The seductive potency of this semi-
tropical place was intensified by the knowledge that
Helen slept alone in the big darkened house. At his fingertips, yet out of reach.

Temptation he couldn't touch.

Kurt ground his teeth. It was too easy to imagine
himself on the gallery outside her open bedroom doors,
slipping noiselessly inside. Getting into her bed. Making love to her in the sticky moist heat. Feeling her
hot, damp body move sinuously against his own slippery sweat-drenched frame.

Kurt shot to his feet.

His hands clenching into tight fists at his sides, his
belly involuntarily tightening, he started toward the
backyard.

Sweltering, Helen lay awake in the seductive darkness. The still night air was heavy with heat and hu-
midity. The almost overwhelmingly sweet scent of
magnolias permeated her close stuffy bedroom. It was
too hot to sleep. Her nightgown stuck to her body and
her skin felt prickled and itchy. No breeze from the bay
fluttered the limp curtains or stroked her burning skin.

She was miserable. So restless and uncomfortable
she felt she couldn't lie there for one more moment.

Adding to her misery was the knowledge that Kurt
Northway lay sleeping in the quarters. Helen's hot face
grew hotter still as she imagined what it might be like
to kiss him. It was not the first time she fantasized
about it.

His was a marvelously masculine mouth and she had
no doubt it could give a woman great pleasure. Would
his kiss be soft or savage? Or an exciting combination

of both? Suddenly she felt as if she had never wanted anything in her life as much as to be kissed by Kurt Northway.

No, she breathed in fierce denial. *No, no. I didn't mean it, Will, I didn't mean it.*

Helen sat up and reached for the carved wooden box resting on her night table. Anxiously she withdrew the oval cameo locket and pressed her trembling lips to the tiny photograph inside. Then she sat there for a long time clasping the cameo containing Will's picture to her breast.

But when she returned the locket to its resting place, another object on the night table caught her eye. A delicate mother-of-pearl hair barrette lay framed in a wedge of bright moonlight.

A half sob, half sigh escaped Helen's lips as she reached for the gleaming hair clasp. Remembering the way Kurt had smiled the evening he had handed her the gift, Helen allowed her fingers to trace the configuration of the dainty barrette. Impulsively she swung a large section of her loose blond hair forward over her face, then pulled it back and secured it with the mother-of-pearl clasp.

She shut her eyes and shook her head, but it did no good. No matter how hard she squeezed her eyes shut or how desperately she tried to push the wicked thoughts of a Yankee's kisses out of her mind, she still imagined the darkly handsome Kurt's fiery lips covering her own.

Kurt kissing her. Kurt kissing her over and over again while she begged him to stop and hoped he never stopped.

Gritting her teeth, Helen jumped up from the bed.

Barefooted, wearing only her perspiration-dampened nightgown, she walked straight out the bedroom doors onto the moon-splashed gallery.

* * *

Kurt moved quietly, circling the darkened house. He crossed the front yard to the new bay stairway. Taking the steps two and three at a time, he anxiously descended the bluff down to the water.

There was the moon shining big and bright. The bay, stretched out before him, was silver and black. Kurt was unbuttoning his pants by the time his bare feet touched the small strip of sandy shoreline between the base of the bluff and the water's edge. He hurried down the narrow stretch of beach, stopping when he reached an outcropping of vine-covered rocks twenty-five yards from the steps.

There he stripped down to the skin, nimbly climbed higher up the jutting boulders, and dived into the deep waters of the bay below.

He swam until his breath was short and his arms and legs ached and tingled with exhaustion. Then he turned and swam tiredly back to shore. He pulled himself up on the jagged rocks, dripping, naked. He stretched out on a smooth slanting pillar of stone to rest and catch his breath before getting dressed.

He lounged there on the rocks in the moonlight, looking out at the sparkling waters, the sky full of stars, the distant lights of Mobile twinkling far across the bay.

Head resting in his folded arms, he turned to look down at the silvery sands below. His head came up and his wet-lashed gaze widened when he saw her. . . .

Helen stepped down from the wooden stairway.

Kurt frantically grabbed his trousers and covered his groin. His first impulse was to call out to her, to start apologizing for his nakedness. Then he realized he was hidden from her view, out of sight above her. If he shouted he might frighten her. The best thing to do was to keep quiet and never let her know he was there.

With his eyes riveted on her, Kurt quickly saw she was in her nightgown and her feet were bare. Her glorious golden hair was brushed out loose around her shoulders, gleaming silver in the moonlight. She turned her head and the moonlight glinted on an object in her hair. Kurt's heartbeat quickened when he realized it was the hair clasp he had given her.

From his vantage point on the rocks above, he stared at her, asking himself if any woman could really be that lovely, or was it only an illusion, the magic of the moonlight.

She walked across the sand toward the water's edge and it dawned on him that her intent might be to take a cooling midnight swim. Anticipation rose as he watched her move gracefully toward the lapping waters of the bay.

When she stood directly at the water's edge, she gathered her long white nightgown up to her pale thighs and Kurt's heart hammered in his naked chest. Afraid she was going to strip the nightgown off, and equally afraid she wasn't, he muttered under his breath, "Don't. Don't do it, lady. Please don't do this to me." In the very next breath he was begging, "Please, baby, please. Jesus, sweetheart, take that gown off. Take it off."

Holding the gathered nightgown up with one hand, Helen waded out into the shallows. There was the immediate sound of her sharp intake of breath, and then a long sigh as if she had been suffering and had now found a measure of relief. She waded about, kicking at the water, while Kurt watched her, mesmerized. He blinked in shock when all at once she gave a girlish little yip, and, moving quickly out from shore, dived into the deeper water and began to swim.

Still wearing the white nightgown.

In seconds she came splashing back to shore. She walked out of the water and Kurt's heart pounded. The saturated nightgown hid none of her feminine charms, only tended to accent them. Kurt stared shamelessly, eagerly taking in the miracle of her beautiful body.

Her breasts were firm and high. The nipples, taut from the cold of the water, pressed provocatively against the soggy fabric, as clearly visible as if she wore nothing. Her waist sank in to a breathtaking slenderness. And then that graceful swell outward to her flaring hips.

His heated gaze was helplessly pulled to the shadowy triangle between her pale thighs and he felt the blood thicken in his veins. She stood in the moonlight as if she had been placed there by the gods of love solely for his own personal pleasure.

She was facing him, with the brilliant moonlight striking her full on. Her wet golden hair spilled down around her shoulders, and with the thin batiste gown plastered to her lush body, she looked nakeder than naked.

The primitive thrill of it was hammering at his temples, beating in his blood, throbbing in his groin.

He knew what he did at this moment was crucial. He could go to her now, this minute, while she was undoubtedly vulnerable. Forcefully he could hold her, kiss her into submission, make love to her on the sand before she had time to realize the import of what she was doing.

If he did, it would either live on pleasantly in his memory. Or he would regret it forever.

While Kurt was agonizing over the fateful decision, Helen quietly turned and walked slowly away.

Saving herself from him.

Saving him from himself.

Saving them both from a fleeting ecstasy that would lead to lasting remorse.

Chapter Twenty-eight

Helen stripped off the soaked nightgown and tow-
eled herself dry. She pulled out the drawer of the
bureau, but shut it without removing a clean nightgown. She climbed naked into bed and decided then
and there that in the future she would have little or
nothing to do with the Yankee.

There was no need for her to talk to him on a daily
basis. No reason even to see him every day. The man
worked well unsupervised. He didn't need her to tell
him what had to be done.

Furthermore, she would stop constantly stealing
looks at him. She would never look at him. She was
well aware that he rarely wore a shirt, so if the sight of
him naked to the waist upset her, then the intelligent
thing to do would be to *stop* looking.

So she would.

She wouldn't talk to him. She wouldn't look at him.

Except when it was absolutely necessary.

For the next few days Helen's plan worked amazingly well. She stayed mostly inside, keeping herself
busy giving every room in the old house a thorough
cleaning. She spent an entire afternoon in the bedroom
next to her own, the main guest room.

The guest room was spacious and bright and, just as
in her bedroom, a pair of tall French doors opened out
onto the wraparound gallery. Helen threw those doors
open wide to give the room a needed airing.

She polished the woodwork and changed the bed linens. She kept the room ready for guests at all times, just as her Grandma Burke always had. Granny had told her, time and again, "Sweetums, remember that a proper Southern hostess must always be prepared to put up overnight guests. Anyone who comes for a visit should be invited to spend at least one night."

When she'd finished her cleaning and the spotless room smelled pleasantly of lemon oil, Helen carefully plumped up a couple of shiny pink silk pillows which rested atop the pale blue velvet chaise lounge. Then she crossed to the high, canopied four-poster to tie back a loose panel of the fading blue velvet bed hangings.

After finishing the guest room, Helen tackled her own bedroom next door. Then the parlor and the kitchen. Finally the never-used dining hall with its impressive candle-and-glass chandelier and long dining table and massive rosewood sideboard where Grandma Burke's fine china and crystal were stored.

Helen carefully polished the huge sideboard and the gilt-framed mirror mounted above it. Last she lovingly rubbed and buffed the long dining table at which no one had sat since Will went away to war.

Saturday afternoon rolled around and Helen realized with dismay that she would have to see Kurt briefly. There was no way around it. Every other Saturday he rode into Spanish Fort for supplies.

This was the Saturday.

He had, from the beginning, taken over the responsibility of going into town for needed supplies. Knowing that Helen's feelings had been badly hurt when she'd gone into town alone, he announced that he wouldn't allow it to happen again. He would go for her.

At first she had scoffed at the idea, said that was no solution and she wouldn't hear of it. She told him the last thing she needed was him complicating matters by getting into street brawls. Why, he had asked, would he be getting into brawls? Because, she had warned him, if he walked down Main Street in Spanish Fort he would be insulted and challenged before he'd gone one block.

Kurt assured her he would not rise to the bait, no matter what was said to or about him. From here on, he had calmly declared, he would be the one who went to town.

The citizens of Spanish Fort could hurt her. They couldn't hurt him. Besides, he'd be leaving right after the harvest. Maybe then, with him gone, the townspeople would cool off and come to their senses. Start treating her with the respect she deserved. Until then, he would handle the chore.

Finally Helen had agreed, and Kurt had been making the Saturday trips into town ever since.

Helen tensed now as she heard the soft knock on the back door. She knew it was Kurt. She buttoned the high collar of her faded calico dress, smoothed back her wayward hair, and picked up her carefully thought out list. She composed her features into what she hoped was a bland, businesslike expression.

She opened the back door.

There he stood, backlit by the sun. Tall, tanned, and undeniably handsome. He was well scrubbed, his hair was neatly brushed, his face closely shaven. He was dressed today in black denim trousers, a gray chambray shirt, and black cowboy boots with a shiny inlaid silver design on the toes.

"Afternoon, ma'am," he said in that rich baritone.

Helen's attention was immediately drawn to his sensual mouth, and that ludicrous yearning to be kissed by him returned full force.

"Captain," she replied, dropping her gaze, anxiously

thrusting the list at him. "Get just these things I've
written down!"

Kurt carefully folded the paper once, then once
again, and slid it into the breast pocket of his gray
chambray shirt. "Have I ever gotten anything other
than what you requested?"

"Well, no. No, you haven't."

"Any reason to think I might?"

"Captain, it's getting late," she said, wanting him to
leave. Wanting him out of her sight. Wanting him
to . . . oh, Lord, wanting him! "You'd better be on your
way if you're to get back by suppertime."

He nodded, but didn't move. He leaned a forearm on
the doorframe and gave her a thoughtful, heavy-lidded
look. "I haven't seen much of you lately," he stated
flatly.

"So?" Her well-arched brows shot up.

"So, are you okay? Feeling all right?"

"Feeling fine, thank you very much." She was pointedly flippant.

"Good," he said. A long pause while his eyes studied her face. Then softly, "I've missed seeing you."

"I have work to do," she snapped, and slammed the
door in his face.

A slow smile lifting the corners of his lips, Kurt
turned and left.

Kurt encountered the usual catcalls and curses that
afternoon in Spanish Fort. He was accustomed to it; he
hardly noticed. He walked into Jake's General Store as
if he had no idea he wasn't welcome there. He turned
Helen's list over to the scowling proprietor, smiled,
and told Jake he would be back in an hour to pick up
the order.

He walked out of the store, looked up the street, then
down. He headed for the county jail to see if Sheriff

Cooper was in town. When Coop was around, Kurt shared a cigar and a cup of coffee with him.

The high sheriff wasn't in, so Kurt recrossed the street, strolled leisurely down the wooden sidewalk, killing time, gazing in shop windows.

He passed by the small emporium for ladies where he had found the mother-of-pearl hair barrette for Helen. He stopped, looked at the items artfully arranged in the shop's widow display.

A pleated ivory satin fan trimmed in tiny little pearls. A stoppered crystal vial of expensive French perfume. A dainty linen handkerchief and a pair of long white kid gloves. A trio of smooth matching gold wrist bracelets. A carefully folded white lacy undergarment so sheer and fragile it looked like it would dissolve if touched.

A muscle worked in Kurt's lean jaw. The delicate underwear conjured up improper thoughts and visions. Immediately he pictured Helen in the wispy little bit of gossamer and lace. The vision was so real he swallowed hard and turned quickly away from the window.

But the image stayed on in his mind.

Kurt walked slowly back toward Jake's General Store, again disregarding the mocking and ridicule of the town locals. When one of the men stepped directly into his path, daring Kurt to say something, Kurt stepped down off the sidewalk and walked on in the dusty street.

The loud laughter and shouts of "That Yankee's the biggest coward I ever saw" didn't upset Kurt. He had heard it all before.

He was loading the provisions in the wagon when Niles Loveless came out of his office and started toward him.

Before Niles could ask, Kurt smiled and said, "No, Loveless, Raider is not for sale."

"You'll change your mind once you've heard my new offer," said Niles confidently.

"No," said Kurt, "I won't."

"I'm willing to pay three thousand dollars for that sorrel stallion! Think of it, three thousand dollars! We can walk over to the bank right now and I'll draw out the cash. That's a lot of money, Northway. You and your boy can be on your way north to your home by tonight."

Kurt agilely swung up onto the wagon seat, grinned, and said, "I'm on my way home right now."

Helen frowned when she saw the wagon emerge from the tree-lined lane. She'd been anxiously looking toward the lane for the past hour, expecting his return. And, admittedly, halfway looking forward to it despite her resolve to stay away from him.

But now that he was within sight, she wished she could hide out somewhere. Wished she didn't have to see him, talk to him, be in the same room with him. In his compelling presence she felt quite powerless and it was a feeling she disliked immensely.

Helen went to the front door, glanced anxiously out at Charlie and Jolly, hoping they'd go to meet Kurt and save her from being alone with him. They didn't budge from their spot on the top step of the new bay stairs. Helen shook her head. They weren't going to be any help.

She sighed, then rushed into the silent dining room and nervously checked her appearance in the gilt-framed mirror above the rosewood sideboard. She pinched her cheeks, bit her lips, and ran her fingers through her loose blond hair.

She jumped when Kurt called to her from the back porch, then immediately chided herself for being a nervous Nellie. She threw back her slender shoulders and, taking her own sweet time, marched into the kitchen and opened the back door.

Both his arms filled, Kurt waited for her to step back. Thoughtlessly, she stood there in the way. So Kurt turned sideways and, facing her, eased through the open door with her in it. Their bodies were dangerously close. So close, there were only scant inches of daylight between them. Helen's full skirts brushed against his trousers legs and, unbeknownst to either of them, the intricate silver work on the toe of his boot snagged the underside of her skirts.

"Excuse me," she said, face flushing, realizing she was at fault, that she should have moved out of the doorway. With her hands lifted in a defensive manner, she quickly made a move, only to be jerked back. "You let me go!" she said, thinking he had pulled her back.

"Ma'am, I'm not holding you," Kurt said, gesturing to his arms, which were filled. "My hands are full."

Her eyes flashing blue fire, Helen yanked on her skirt, saw that it was caught, and said coldly, "Captain, you are standing on my skirt. Kindly lift your foot and set me free."

They both looked down as Kurt lifted his right foot. Nothing happened. When he lifted his left, her skirt rose with it.

"Stop!" she warned, pressing both hands to the folds of her skirt. "Lower your foot," she ordered.

She raised her head at the same time Kurt raised his. Their faces were inches apart. Too close for comfort.

"I'm caught," he said, and smiled.

"Well, get uncaught!" she hissed, reflexively leaning back away from him, turning her head to one side.

Kurt tried. He really tried. He twisted the toe of his boot to the left, then the right. But he couldn't free the snagged boot from her skirts.

"Ma'am, I'll have to set these sacks down so I can use my hands."

Helen made a face. "Well, go ahead. What are you waiting for?"

"You'll have to go with me."

"I know that, Captain!"

"Here we go, then," he said, and grinned sheepishly.

Kurt turned and edged backward into the kitchen while Helen moved forward with him. Kurt went very slowly, taking care not to yank her off balance. Since her skirts were caught by his left foot, Helen had to carefully match her steps to his. When his left foot stepped backward, her right one stepped forward, and so on as they awkwardly made their way into the kitchen.

Facing him, obliged to move with him, forced to be uncomfortably close, Helen found herself in exactly the kind of troublesome fix she'd been trying so hard to avoid.

At last Kurt's lean buttocks bumped up against the kitchen cabinet. He inclined his dark head, indicating that they were to switch positions. Teeth gritted, Helen followed his lead as they turned about in a tight semicircle.

Her back now to the cabinet, she bridled with indignation as he was forced to lean closer in order to deposit his armloads of provisions onto the countertop behind her. His tall lean body was briefly pressed to hers as he set the heavy bags on the cabinet, one on either side of her.

It took only seconds; it seemed like hours.

For one uncomfortable instant she was trapped inside his long encompassing arms, crushed flush against his, her breasts touching his chest, her temple brushing his chin. He was so close she could feel the heat emanating from him and it sent her senses reeling.

His burden unloaded, hands finally free, Kurt anxiously leaned back. When he did, Helen felt the pull on her skirts. And on her heart.

"I'll have you free in a second," he said, and crouched down on his heels directly before her.

With both hands, Helen gripped the cabinet behind her. "Please hurry!"

"I will," he said as his hand went beneath her skirts. "It's not your dress after all. It's your petticoat. The lace on your petticoat is snagged in the silver trim on the toe of my boot."

"Dress! Petticoat! Who cares? Just get it loose!"

"Yes, ma'am. Right away."

Kurt couldn't get it loose. He tried. Taking care not to tear the lace, he worked at it, but to no avail. Attempting to make light of the situation, he grinned up at her and said, "Hope your evening is free, Mrs. Courtney. Looks like you'll be spending it with me."

Not on your life! she thought. *I'll rip the petticoat up first!*

"Oh, for heaven's sake!" she said aloud. Then, "Move back," and as a last resort Helen sat down flat on the floor facing him.

"Here, I'll do it!" she said in exasperation, slapping his hands away.

Muttering angrily to herself, she worked feverishly at getting the caught lace unhooked from the boot's silver trim. She worked and worked, making unhappy faces, the tip of her tongue caught between her teeth, her nose wrinkled.

All at once she heard deep, rich laughter. She stopped working, raised her head, and glared at Kurt.

Leaning lazily back, propped on a stiffened arm, he was watching her and laughing as though he found their awkward predicament terribly amusing. She saw nothing funny about it. Nothing! Damn him. He seemed to delight in making her feel foolish and self-conscious. She wanted to wring his neck.

"It isn't funny!" she told him hotly.

Continuing to laugh easily, Kurt agilely rolled back up into a sitting position facing her. "Ah, but it is. Very funny. Ironic, actually." He reached out and playfully tugged at a wayward golden curl.

"Ironic?" She shoved his hand from her hair. "Just what the devil is that supposed to mean?"

"For days you've assiduously avoided me," he said, his forest-green eyes shining with devilment. "And here you are bound to me, unable to get away."

"I have no idea what you're talking about!"

But even as Helen spoke, her own sense of the absurd brought the faintest of smiles to her lips. He was right, of course. She had purposely avoided him and now here she was, trapped on the kitchen floor with him, unable to free herself of him.

It *was* funny.

Despite her best efforts not to, Helen began to laugh. Suddenly the whole thing seemed hilarious and she laughed at the utterly preposterous fix the two of them were in. Once she gave in to it, she laughed with delight and total abandon. She laughed as she hadn't laughed in ages.

Kurt was laughing too. Laughing so hard his wide shoulders shook and his stomach jerked. Tears of mirth soon rolled down Helen's hot cheeks and she was fighting for breath and hitting at Kurt, begging him to stop it, to stop laughing, to stop making her laugh.

Her caught petticoat was forgotten in the frolic. They laughed and laughed until they were both as weak as newborn kittens and no longer knew what it was they were laughing about. When Helen sagged helplessly toward Kurt, he put supportive hands on her upper arms and gently rested his forehead against hers.

And still they laughed.

Until a piercing scream abruptly ended their laughter.

Chapter Twenty-nine

Neither Jolly nor Charlie had paid any attention to Kurt's arrival. Theirs had been a busy Saturday afternoon and they were too tired to go meet Kurt.

At least Jolly was too tired.

The two of them had been playing cowboys and Indians, taking turns being the cowboy. Shooting each other, groaning and falling to the grass, then leaping up and running again.

Finally, puffing and out of breath, Jolly had made it over to the new wooden staircase leading down to the bay. He dropped wearily down on the top step to rest.

Fanning himself with his battered straw hat and wiping his flushed face with a handkerchief, Jolly grinned over his shoulder at Charlie and said, "Pardner, you can put away your six-shooters. This old Indian chief is a goner. Just carry my bones back to my people."

Charlie giggled, shoved his imaginary twin pistols back into their imaginary holsters, and dropped down on the wooden step beside Jolly. Barefooted and wearing nothing but a pair of short trousers, he was dirty from head to toe.

He sat still for only a second, then asked, "Want to play hide-and-go-seek now?"

Jolly smiled at the rambunctious boy. "Chappie, I'm afraid I'm at the end of my tether."

Charlie made a face. Then quickly smiled again. "Want to see me turn somersaults?"

"Do flowers bloom in Alabama in the springtime?"

"Does that mean no or yes?" Charlie, puzzled, cocked his head to one side.

"Yes," Jolly said, ruffling Charlie's blond hair and laughing. "I would sure enjoy seeing you turn some fancy somersaults."

Charlie was up off the steps in a burst of new energy. Shouting to Dom to stay clear, he raced out onto the lawn, then abruptly fell forward to place head and hands on the soft grass and flip over onto his back.

Jolly enthusiastically applauded, so Charlie leaped up and repeated the stunt. Again to loud applause. Charlie kept at it, turning somersaults all over the expanse of the grassy front yard, getting so caught up in the exercise, he never noticed when Jolly stopped clapping.

In a dizzy upside down world all his own, the dirty little boy tumbled and rolled and flopped about all across the big yard, perfecting his acrobatic skills, enjoying himself immensely. Losing all track of time and place, he repeatedly turned somersaults, until at last he lay woozily flat on his back in the grass directly in front of the house. Far away from the wooden steps and Jolly.

Charlie had finally had enough. He rose, brushed grass blades off his chest and legs, turned, and saw Jolly lying stretched out beside the boxwood hedge bordering the yard. Charlie immediately clapped his hands together and laughed. Jolly was playing cowboys and Indians again! Jolly was playing like he'd been shot.

Jolly was playing dead.

Clapping his hands in delight, Charlie said, "That's good, Jolly!"

Laughing, he took a couple of eager steps toward the dead Indian chief, expecting Jolly to jump up and laugh. But Jolly didn't jump up. Jolly didn't move.

Jolly didn't laugh. Jolly continued to lie there sprawled out on the lawn, playing dead.

"Jolly?" Charlie quit laughing and his blue eyes clouded a little. "Jolly, get up," he called softly, tired of the game now, ready for Jolly to quit being a dead Indian. Ready to play something else. "Jolly, stop it," he said, beginning to get angry at his playmate. "You just stop it!"

Jolly didn't stop it. Jolly paid no attention. Jolly didn't move. Jolly continued to lie there, refusing to get up.

Charlie stopped when he was still several yards away. He stared at the white-haired old gentleman stretched out on the grass with his eyes closed. So quiet. So still. So lifeless.

"Jolly," Charlie said in a soft, uneasy whisper. "Jolly, answer me."

Charlie was frightened now. Suddenly he remembered another summer day, another house with a big front yard, another white-haired man lying still and quiet back in Mississippi. His Grandpa Whitney wouldn't answer him either, wouldn't get up, wouldn't move.

Charlie tried hard not to cry. He didn't want to cry. Jolly never cried. The captain never cried. Only girls cried. And babies. He hated to cry, but tears were stinging his eyes. His throat hurt really bad and he was shaking like it was cold.

He couldn't move any closer to Jolly. He tried to make himself go out to where the white-haired man lay so still and quiet, but he was afraid. Instead of going forward, Charlie started backing away. He kept backing up until he reached the steps of the front porch.

Charlie began to scream.

Helen and Kurt heard the scream, stopped laughing, froze, and looked at each other in horror. Then in an instant Kurt had pulled the boot from his foot and

Helen had jerked off her petticoat. One boot off, one on, Kurt raced through the house with Helen right on his heels. Outside, Kurt snatched his screaming son up from the ground and into his arms.

"Charlie, what is it? What is it, honey? Are you hurt?" Kurt's tone was anxious, his heart hammering.

Face chalk-white, Helen rushed to the pair, threw protective arms around both man and boy and pressed her cheek to Charlie's little bare back.

"Jolly's dead! Jolly's dead!" cried Charlie, his short arms gripping his father's neck, tears streaming down his face.

Charlie's scream had roused Jolly from his nap. Alarmed, he came hurrying across the yard, a worried look on his face.

"No, Charlie," Kurt consoled him, "Jolly's not dead. Jolly's right—"

"He's dead! He's dead," cried Charlie, his small body jerking with sobs. "I saw him! I saw him dead on the ground like Grandpa Whitney!"

"No, Charlie, darling," cooed Helen, pressing her lips to Charlie's warm grass-stained back. "Jolly's all right. Shhh, shhh."

"Hey, sport," called Jolly, lumbering up out of breath, "here I am! Look at me. Look here, Charlie."

Helen stepped back then, placed a hand over her rapidly beating heart, and drew a long, shaky breath.

"You see," said Kurt. "What did I tell you? Jolly's right here and he's just fine. See for yourself."

Sobbing and gasping, Charlie's blond head came up off his father's shoulder. He looked around, saw Jolly smiling at him, and reached anxiously out to touch his weathered face.

"You . . . you sc-scared me . . . Jolly," blubbered Charlie, his body still jerking.

"I'm sorry, Charlie, my boy," murmured Jolly, covering the small fingers resting on his face with his own large hand. "Old Jolly was just taking a nap, that's all."

"I . . . I . . . thought you . . . were dead," sniffed Charlie, his tears leaving twin paths down his dirty face.

Jolly drew Charlie's small hand to his mouth, kissed it, and placed it back on Kurt's shoulder. "I didn't mean to scare you, Charlie. Forgive me."

Jolly stepped back beside Helen, put an arm around her. She touched her head to his shoulder and sighed with relief. Kurt smiled at the pair over Charlie's head and sat down on the porch steps.

Holding Charlie close in his arms, Kurt said against the fine feathery blond hair of the little boy's head, "Charlie, sweetheart, Jolly isn't going to die. Not for a long, long time."

Charlie lifted his head, looked into his father's eyes. "Grandpa Whitney died."

"I know. But he was very sick. Jolly isn't."

Charlie's short fingers clung to the collar of Kurt's gray chambray shirt. "He's not going to die like Grandpa Whitney?"

"No, he's not."

Charlie gasped for a breath. "Will Helen?"

Kurt shook his head. "No, Helen isn't going to die either."

Charlie gasped for a breath. "Mommy died."

"Yes, I know. She was real sick, like Grandpa and Grandma Whitney."

"They died and left me by myself," Charlie sadly told Kurt.

"That won't happen again, Charlie."

Wiping his tears on the back of his hand, Charlie looked directly into Kurt's green eyes. "You sure? I'm afraid that—"

"Don't be afraid. Jolly and Helen aren't sick. They aren't going to be sick."

"Are you?"

"No. No," Kurt said, looking his son squarely in the eye. "Why, I'm so big and strong I bet I can carry you on my shoulders all the way down to the quarters for a bath." He grinned reassuringly at Charlie.

Charlie didn't smile, but his narrow shoulders slumped with relief. He cupped Kurt's tanned cheeks in his small hands and affectionately patted his face.

Earnestly he asked, "You won't ever leave me, will you, *Daddy*?"

"Never," promised Kurt, his voice gone rough with emotion.

Chapter Thirty

Moved by the touching scene she'd witnessed between father and son, Helen couldn't put it out of her thoughts. All that evening she could think of nothing else. In her mind's eye she kept seeing the usually cool, imperious Kurt Northway badly shaken by his son's scream. Then lovingly holding the crying, frightened Charlie in his comforting arms. Gently cradling Charlie's small blond head to his chest. Softly assuring the little boy that no one else he loved was going to die and leave him.

The warm, caring way in which Kurt had handled Charlie revealed a gentleness she hadn't known was there. A gentleness made all the more appealing because it was in such stark contrast to his dark, dangerous good looks. To see a man so ruggedly attractive and sexually threatening show such uncommon sensitivity made Helen more curious than ever.

In her woman's romantic heart, she couldn't help but wonder about him as a lover. All this time she had supposed he would be passionate and exciting. Now she was convinced he would be caring and gentle as well. The idea of the handsome, hot-blooded Kurt being an infinitely patient lover brought heat to Helen's face, caused her pulse to flutter.

She shook her head and dismissed such indecent notions.

She put aside the book she'd been holding unread,

turned out the parlor lamp, and rose. It was past bedtime. Almost midnight. She should try to get some rest.

Helen went dispiritedly to her bedroom. She didn't
feel tired. It was so hot and sultry she wouldn't be able
to sleep. Besides, the moonlight streamed in through
the double doors and fell directly across her bed.

Restlessly she roamed the silent bedroom. She
looked at herself in the beveled glass atop the bureau.
She frowned, plucked the pins from her hair, and
picked up her hairbrush. Pulling the soft-bristled brush
through the heavy golden locks, she walked over to the
night table beside her bed.

She smiled, laid the brush aside, and picked up the
delicate mother-of-pearl barrette. She held the clasp in
the palm of her hand and ran the tip of her forefinger
fondly over the smooth surface. After a minute, she
started to place it back on the table, changed her mind,
grabbed a thick wedge of flowing hair at the right side
of her head, and slid the clasp up into it. When she'd
fastened the clasp, she ventured back over to the mirror.

She liked the way she looked with her hair swept
dramatically back on one side, her right ear and throat
exposed. She grinned impishly, reached up, and tugged
the wide boat neck of her faded work dress down off
her right shoulder. She smiled foolishly at herself in
the mirror, then immediately sighed and turned away.

Helen was outside before she knew that was where
she meant to go. Exiting the open French doors of her
bedroom, she casually glanced in the direction of the
quarters. Seeing no lights, she shrugged and strolled
leisurely around the wide gallery to the front of the
house.

Hesitating, she stood at the front railing looking out
at the bay. The night was almost achingly beautiful. A
near full moon silvered the calm protected waters and
gilded the tall pines. A myriad of night sounds rose

from the dense jungle foliage decorating the bluffs, and somewhere in the distance a panther called plaintively to his mate. A gentle but warm breeze off the bay lifted wisps of Helen's loose hair and stirred the ivory magnolias, heavily perfuming the sultry air.

Helen drew a deep, slow breath.

Every sight and sound and smell registered as if her senses were unusually keen on this hauntingly beautiful summer night. The splendor of it was breathtaking. The yearning it inspired was sweet pain. The physical longing it aroused was as elemental and as old as time itself.

And then, as if the fates had heard the silent calling of her lonely heart, Kurt Northway suddenly appeared. Softly speaking her name so that he wouldn't frighten her, he stepped out of the nighttime quiet and into the moonlight. Her hands gripping the white gallery railing, Helen watched, speechless, as he walked directly below her.

Strangely, his presence did not surprise her. It seemed natural. As if the two of them had planned to meet here in the moonlight on this bewitchingly beautiful night.

Kurt came unhurriedly toward the porch steps, moving with that natural fluid grace. The moonlight glinting on his jet-black hair left his tanned face in shadow. He wore a freshly laundered shirt of snowy white, open at the throat, the sleeves rolled up. His trousers were of fine black linen, crisply creased and falling just to the instep of his polished black leather shoes.

Helen suddenly wished that she had changed. That she had worn something pretty and fresh. She was in an old work dress of faded calico with narrow skimpy skirts, the low loose neck sagging down on her bare shoulder. And she had left her shoes in the bedroom.

Should she yank her dress back up on her shoulder and go inside for her shoes?

It was too late. He'd already caught her.

Kurt slowly ascended the porch steps, nodded his dark head, smiled, and said simply, "Evening, ma'am."

"Captain," she replied.

He stood in shadow, looking at her, the power of his eyes undiminished by the darkness. "I like your hair swept back that way," he said.

"Thanks," was all she could manage.

Moving into a wedge of bright moonlight, he explained he was concerned his restless thrashing would disturb the slumbering Charlie. Then he asked, "Mind if I join you? Just for a minute."

"No. Certainly not," Helen said, bending her knees slightly so that her skirts would hide her bare feet. Anxiously she tugged the dress back up on her shoulder.

Kurt smiled and said, "I liked it better the other way."

She gave no response. Instead she asked how Charlie was. Kurt told her Charlie was fine, that the two of them had spent the evening together talking, Charlie asking many questions, and Kurt answering as best he could. She said she was glad to hear it. For the next few minutes they discussed Charlie and the events of the afternoon.

At a lull in the conversation, Kurt dropped down on the top porch steps, draped a tanned forearm over his bent knee, and said idly, "Too hot to sleep."

"Isn't it," Helen agreed, and sat down in her armless rocker directly across from him.

"It's a beautiful night, though," Kurt quietly observed.

"Yes, it is. I came out here to ... I ... yes," she said, feeling suddenly self-conscious, as if he somehow knew what she had been thinking as she stood in the moonlight looking out at the silvered bay.

Longing to put her at ease, Kurt inhaled deeply of the flower-scented air and said conversationally, "Reminds me of the summer nights back in Maryland when I was a boy."

And he began to talk about those days. In a low, rich baritone he told her he had gone to work on a big horse farm when he was barely fourteen. Said it was a beautiful place, rolling hills that looked like soft green velvet. Said he'd learned everything he knew about horses from Willis Dunston, the man who owned the farm. Told her it was Dunston who had given Raider to him the night Raider was born.

He fell silent, brushed imaginary lint from his black linen trousers, and leaned his back against the solid porch column.

"Please, Captain, do go on," Helen urged. "What about your parents? Tell me about them."

Kurt said his mother had died when he was an infant, his father was killed in a knife fight when Kurt was fourteen. That's when he had gone to the Dunston farm. Said Dunston trusted his judgment, treated him like a man, it had been a good life. Smiling then, Kurt told her it had become an even better life in the spring of '59 when a Mississippi gentleman came to Maryland to buy horses. He had brought with him his beautiful young daughter.

"Gail Whitney was just seventeen, I was twenty-eight," Kurt said. "We married that summer and barely nine months later Charlie was born."

With ease and no self-consciousness, Kurt talked of the happy times and Helen soon relaxed completely. Kurt spoke of the past and of his plans for the future. He told of Willis Dunston's promise to deed him a section of fine Maryland grassland in exchange for five years of labor. Charmed by the sound of his deep, low voice, Helen found his narrative compelling. But she experienced the slightest twinge of dread when he talked about leaving Alabama.

At last Kurt paused, laughed self-deprecatingly, and said, "Forgive me, Mrs. Courtney. I haven't talked so much in years. You must feel you know more about me than you ever wanted to learn."

"Not at all," Helen quickly assured him. "No, no . . . go back to the time when you—"

Kurt raised his hand and shook his dark head. "It's your turn, ma'am. Tell me about yourself. Tell me everything."

Helen laughed softly and said that would take all night.

Kurt laughed. Then he said, "I have all night. Don't you?"

She didn't say yes, but she didn't say no.

Kurt waited and soon Helen began talking. At first she spoke haltingly, wistfully of the days gone by. She began by telling Kurt of the handsome young man whom she'd known for as long as she could remember. Said that it had always been understood that when she grew up, she would marry Will Courtney, and of course she had. Said the two of them had spent only six short months as man and wife before Will went away to war.

Helen hesitated then, as if she had decided to say nothing more, but at Kurt's gentle urging, she was soon talking again, telling about the days when she was a child. She said she too had lost her parents—both of them—when she was just four years old. They had been killed in a storm at sea. She barely remembered them. Said hers had been a happy childhood because of the dear grandparents who had raised her. Said both spoiled her rotten and she loved them for it.

She told Kurt of the wonderful times the three of

them had spent together. She talked of their trips into town on Saturday afternoons, of drinking lemonade at the Bayside Hotel with Grandma Burke, of Christmas parties at the church and Fourth of July celebrations over in Mobile. She told of the wonderful summers when they would go all the way down to the Gulf Shores and stay in a white cottage on the broad white beach.

Smiling, she told of how they waded in the surf and went crabbing and built fires on the beach at night. She described the beauty of the sugary white beaches with the sea oats bending in the prevailing winds off the sea and the spectacular sunsets over the Gulf, turning the ocean pink and gold.

She stopped speaking for a moment. Then, her voice rising slightly with excitement, Helen told Kurt about Point Clear, the fancy resort a few miles down the coast from her farm where for decades wealthy families had come to spend their summers.

Her eyes sparkling, she said, "There were grand dances every evening under the stars on a big white dance pavilion built right out over the water. An orchestra always played and sometimes when the night was very still, I could hear the music as I sat here on the porch." Helen smiled dreamily and charmingly admitted, "I'd pretend that I was at the dance wearing a beautiful white dress and whirling about the floor in the arms of a handsome beau."

She laughed suddenly, the musical sound pleasing to Kurt. She stopped laughing and confessed, "Of course, I was never really there, but I always wanted . . . I used to . . ." She fell silent, sighed softly, and shook her head.

His gaze fixed steadily on her, Kurt rose lithely to his feet. Crossing the moonlit porch, he went directly to her. He bowed formally from the waist and put out his hand. Looking up at him with wide, questioning eyes, Helen placed her hand in his. His firm fingers closed warmly around hers and effortlessly he drew her to her feet.

Smiling at her, he said in a low persuasive voice, "Miss, I couldn't help noticing you across the pavilion. You're very beautiful in your white summer dress with your pale golden hair stirring in the breeze off the water." He drew her hand up to his chest, clasped it there with his own. "I'd be truly honored if you would favor me with this dance."

Kurt smiled warmly and winked at Helen. Silently urging. *Play the harmless game with me.*

She did.

Enchanted, Helen smiled shyly up at her darkly handsome suitor and said softly, "Why, I do declare, sir, you'll turn this poor little farm girl's head if you're not careful."

Chapter Thirty-one

Charmed, Kurt threw back his head and laughed. His teeth flashing starkly white in the darkness of his face, he slid a long arm around Helen's narrow waist and drew her up into a loose embrace. He began to hum a lively tune in a low baritone.

Helen placed her hand lightly on his right shoulder. She felt the smooth fabric of his white shirt and the steel-hard muscle beneath. The texture of both was pleasing to her sensitive fingertips.

His hand resting lightly at her back, Kurt applied the gentlest of pressure and the pair began to dance there on the moonlit gallery. Soon Helen's delighted girlish laughter carried on the humid night air as they spun and swayed and lost themselves in the sweet foolishness of the moment, enjoying the lovely summer night.

And each other.

Her temple resting comfortably against Kurt's cleanly shaven chin, Helen felt giddy and lighthearted, as if she actually were a young starry-eyed girl being romanced at a summer dance by a dark exciting stranger.

A smile in his voice, Kurt teased, "Miss, I do believe your dancing slippers are the prettiest I've ever seen."

Helen pulled back a little, looked up at him, and saw the devilment flashing in the depths of his forest-green eyes. He knew she was barefooted! Oh, well, what did

she care? She laughed, made a fist, and playfully hit
him on the shoulder.

"Of all my fine dancing slippers," she said coquet-
tishly, "these are my very favorites, so mind you, sir,
don't step on them."

"My dear, if I do, you may shove me into the deepest waters of the bay."

"You can't swim?" she inquired politely.

Kurt grinned. "Actually I'm a better swimmer than
dancer."

Helen smiled saucily. "So then you're an excellent
swimmer."

"I didn't say that."

"Well, aren't you? Maybe I shouldn't wonder,
but—"

"Maybe you shouldn't," he interrupted, his eyes
gleaming. "Maybe we should go swimming together so
I can show you." His dark brows lifted.

"Maybe you shouldn't make such bold proposi-
tions," she warned haughtily.

"Maybe you shouldn't say no until you think it
over."

"Maybe you shouldn't hold your breath while I do."

"Maybe I shouldn't." He grinned at her.

"Maybe you shouldn't." She smiled back at him.

They both laughed.

Helen's girlish giggles mixed with Kurt's low
chuckling and impulsively she leaned her forehead on
his chest. They were having fun, kidding each other,
flirting a little, laughing over nothing at all, as carefree
as two kids. They teased each other about being
hooked together on the kitchen floor earlier in the day.

Helen let him know he had looked ridiculously
funny racing through the house wearing just one boot.
Kurt got her back by inquiring as to whether or not she
was now wearing a petticoat or had she given up the
practice for good. She most certainly was wearing one,

she quickly set him straight. He shook his head doubt-
fully; how could he be certain unless she showed him?
Then he'd have to wonder forever, she quickly re-
joined.

The breezy banter and easy laughter continued as
they spun dizzily about, moving into and out of the
patches of moonlight dappling the broad gallery.

The mindless merriment continued for several minutes and neither could ever pinpoint exactly when or
why the frivolous tone of the evening changed. But after a while Helen's bubbling laughter softened and died
and Kurt's spirited humming became a slow, melodi-
ous refrain. They no longer spun and whirled madly
about, covering wide expanses of their porch dance
floor. The dancing became more subdued, the tempo
more languid.

They quieted. They slowed. They barely moved.

The mood changed dramatically.

The seductive heat of the summer night and the seductive nearness of their swaying bodies became almost overpoweringly sensual. Kurt released Helen's
right hand, wrapped both his arms around her, and
drew her closer. Sighing, Helen's left hand slid up
from his shoulder to the back of his head. Her fingers
tangled in the silky jet hair curling appealingly over his
white shirt collar. Her other hand rested on his chest.
She could feel the heavy beating of his heart.

They no longer talked. There was no need. Their
pressing bodies communicated far more effectively
than words. Her lids closing over her shining blue
eyes, a little smile touched Helen's lips. She had imagined that Kurt would be a good dancer, since he moved
with such catlike grace, but she'd never dreamed he
would be quite this smooth and masterful. She could
follow him with absolutely no effort. She sensed his
every movement before it was made, without him lead-

ing her into it. It was almost like she was a part of him, as if their two gliding bodies were one.

Maybe, she dreamily mused, it was because they fit together so well. Which was surprising. Kurt was a tall man—at least six-two—and while she was by no means short, she was only moderately tall at five-six. Yet magically in his embrace, she felt completely comfortable.

Almost too comfortable.

Dancing on bare tiptoe, her breasts were pressed against the warm solid wall of his chest and through the folds of her skimpy skirts she could feel the slow, erotic movements of his pelvis against her own. Their legs were entangled and so were their heartbeats.

Sighing softly, enjoying every langorous step of the slow, exciting dance, Helen told herself that this sticky summer heat was responsible for her feeling so warm.

But she knew better.

It was the powerful heat of Kurt's lean body that caused her pulse to pound, her face to flush. Cooling off would be simply a matter of moving out of the strong arms surrounding her. Or was it the opposite? Would she never cool off again unless she *stayed* in his arms? Unless she—

Those forceful arms drew her closer still and Helen felt new waves of warmth envelope her. Every inch of her body strained to be nearer to the searing strength of his. She no longer cared if she was ever again cool. She wasn't sure she even wanted to be cool. All she knew was she wanted to stay in this dark man's arms, to move with him, to breathe with him, to be so warmed by him she would never again be cold.

Helen pressed her face against Kurt's tanned throat and wrapped stroking fingers around the back of his neck. Every few seconds, when she could no longer stand not seeing his handsome face, she lifted her head. Each time she raised her glance it was met by a pair of glowing dark green eyes.

Helen's breath caught when Kurt placed a hand to the bare curve of her neck and shoulder. His fingertips touched, toyed, spread new heat up to her exposed right ear and down to the sensitive hollow of her throat. Helen stopped breathing entirely when that warm caressing hand casually tugged the low neck of her dress off her shoulder.

She felt the fabric slowly sliding down her upper arm as his low, rich voice just above her ear said, "Isn't this how you were wearing it?" He added, "I like it this way best." A tiny shudder went through Helen when his hand, so warm, so gentle, possessively cupped her bared shoulder. She felt an answering shudder surge through his tall lean frame.

His senses stirred to the limit by the sweet closeness of her soft willowy body, Kurt stopped moving altogether. He set Helen back a little. His hand captured her chin. He gazed at her oval face, aglow in the silvery moonlight. She was breathtakingly lovely, every feature perfection. The large, luminous eyes. The high, well-defined cheekbones. The delicate nose. The proud, stubborn chin. The full-lipped mouth. It was a beautiful face. A flawless face. A face he would never forget.

"What is it?" Helen asked anxiously, unnerved by his intense scrutiny. "What are you doing?"

"Looking at you," Kurt said honestly. "That's all. Looking at your amazingly perfect face. Have you any idea how beautiful you are, Helen?"

At the sound of her name on his lips, Helen's heart pounded. It was the first time he had ever called her Helen. He said it again, as if he liked saying it as much as she liked hearing it.

"Helen. You're exceptionally beautiful, Helen."

Kurt abruptly put both his hands into her hair. His

gaze dropped to her parted lips as his fingers tightened in the heavy golden locks and he tilted her face more fully up to his.

He looked deeply into Helen's eyes, his lips curled in a seductive half smile. The timbre of his voice deep and soft, he said, "Was this the face that launched a thousand ships, and burnt the topless towers of Ilium?" Slowly lowering his dark head until his lips were nearly touching hers, he finished in a whisper. "Sweet Helen, make me immortal with a kiss."

Helen's eyes were fixed on his mouth, now dangerously close to her own. Kurt was going to kiss her. She knew he was. She knew as well that he was giving her ample opportunity to stop him if she didn't want to be kissed. Helen didn't pull away. She didn't say no. She wanted to kiss him. Had to kiss him.

Kurt hesitated for another heartbeat, then covered her trembling mouth with his own. It was the briefest, the tenderest of kisses, his lips lightly brushing across hers, then lifting, hovering close. His fingers entwined in her hair, he gently urged her head back a little farther, and whispering her name, he slowly kissed her face, admiring each perfect feature with the faint, fleeting touch of his adoring lips.

When his mouth returned to hers, Helen softly sighed. He kissed her again and this time his lips lingered longer on hers. Spellbound by his amazingly chaste yet pleasing kiss, Helen stood on tiptoe against him. His lips were incredibly warm and smooth and infinitely gentle. Such a surprisingly guarded kiss from a man who looked so dangerous. Enthralled, Helen felt as if she wanted the sweetness of this slow, soft kiss to last forever. She relaxed completely against him, loving the way he was molding her mouth to fit his with such subtle ease, exerting very little pressure, yet skillfully inducing her lips to cling to his.

Kurt's lips dallied expertly against Helen's, soft, pliable, cautiously teasing. Playful plucking little kisses soon became punctuated with longer, more insistent ones. His tongue brushed along Helen's lower lip and she made a small sound of protest. But her lips parted a little. His tongue skimmed over her teeth as his hand left her hair, went around her waist. Kurt drew her closer against him and in seconds his kiss became hot and demanding.

Helen trembled, wrapped her arms around him, clung to his long, deeply clefted back. His tongue explored the inner recesses of her mouth and Helen gloried in the dazzling intimacy. His tongue touching hers set off explosions of sensation which sent her senses reeling. Her body blazed with a new kind of heat and she snuggled closer to the hard-muscled frame of the man so expertly kissing her, holding her. His teeth gently tugged on her full bottom lip before his mouth slid down over her cheek to the side of her throat.

Helen couldn't stifle the little gasp of ecstasy that escaped when his mouth—that marvelous, experienced mouth—pressed a kiss to the sensitive spot just beneath her ear. Her eyes helplessly closed when his searing lips slowly traced along her throat and down over her shoulder. Tingling excitement raced through her when he opened his mouth and spread biting, sucking kisses over her hot bare skin.

Helen felt her bare toes curl, her stomach flutter wildly, her nipples tighten into aching points of feeling. When his mouth returned to hers, Helen kissed him with unrestrained passion, her mouth opening wide to him, her tongue as bold as his. Her fiery response rendered Kurt helpless against the total, involuntary arousal of his body. His heart thudded against his ribs and the hot heavy blood began beating in his temple as well as in his groin.

Cradling her closer to him, one arm tight around her as though he would never let her go, Kurt kissed her again and again, each kiss becoming wetter, hotter, longer. Helen whimpered softly when his searing mouth left hers, but she sighed and shivered when he kissed the hollow of her throat. She squirmed with pleasure when his lips began a slow steady slide downward. When his mouth reached the fabric of her low-cut dress, he tugged on it with his teeth, carrying it lower until Helen murmured softly, "No . . . no."

Kurt's dark head lifted and Helen saw the raw passion in his eyes, knew it was mirrored in her own. He turned her more fully to him and they came together anxiously, their kisses now fierce, savage, devouring tongues meeting, mouths fusing with impatient hunger and release of pent-up loneliness and need.

"Helen, Helen." Kurt whispered her name in voice heavy with desire. "Sweetheart, let me love you," he murmured, his lips again on her soft white shoulder, his hands pressing her closer to the throbbing erection straining against the confines of his black linen trousers.

"Kurt." Helen excitedly whispered his name, sought his fiery lips, kissed him hotly, and for only a second allowed herself the illicit thrill of feeling the power of that hard male flesh throbbing insistently against her responsively thrusting pelvis.

Breathless, shaken, Helen finally came to her senses. They must stop and stop now. She tore her burning lips from his and murmured against his tanned throat, "No. No, Kurt—"

"Oh, baby, please." Kurt's lips were in her hair. "Sweetheart, let me—"

"Captain Northway," Helen anxiously interrupted, "let me go." Shaking with emotion, she struggled to free herself.

The strong arms wrapped tightly around her immediately loosened and reluctantly released her. Forcefully Helen pushed him away, turned, and fled into the safety of the darkened house, hot tears of shame, guilt, and frustration stinging her eyes.

Trembling, his heart pounding, Kurt stood there alone on the moonlit porch. His dark face was hardened with disappointment and passion, his hands balled into tight fists at his sides. He ground his even white teeth and his lids closed over eyes filled with pain.

At last he drew a long, ragged breath, opened his eyes, turned, and walked down the steps and into the moon-silvered yard. Kurt harshly reminded himself that he should never have come up to the house in the first place. She hadn't invited him here. Hadn't wanted him here.

In mental and physical agony, Kurt returned to his place in the barn.

Chapter Thirty-two

The summer grew hotter and so did they. Kurt fought his agonizing hunger for Helen the way men have fought it for centuries. He worked himself half to death, falling into bed each night physically exhausted, the edge taken off his burning desire.

Utter fatigue helped curb his troublesome carnal appetite, but the deep longing lingered, never fully left him. Tired as he was each night, he lay in the darkness seeing Helen's face awash in the moonlight. Wishing he could feel her there beside him. Wishing he could hold her again for just an hour, or a moment even. Wanting to pull his fingers through her long golden hair. Wanting to hear her laugh. Wanting to hear her breathe. Wanting her . . . wanting her.

Helen fought too.

She stayed away from Kurt as much as possible. And each night at bedtime she took out the cameo and gazed at the picture of the husband whose face was growing dimmer in her memory with every passing day.

Repeatedly she reminded herself that the dark man sleeping in the quarters down at the barn was one of the murderous devils responsible for the deaths and destruction which had forever changed her life and her beloved Southland.

But that didn't work anymore.

She could no longer make herself think of Kurt as a

hated Yankee. The label didn't fit the man she'd come to know. Kurt Northway had proven himself to be a decent, hardworking, kind, and sensitive man.

That's what made it so hard.

If he were mean and callous, a no-good, worthless through and through, it would have been so much easier. Then at least she could console herself with the sure and comforting knowledge that she didn't belong in his arms.

And he didn't belong in her heart.

Confused, torn between the endless yearning to be held by him and the growing guilt she suffered because of it, Helen lost sleep. She tossed and turned in her bed, seeing Kurt's dark face silvered by moonlight. Wishing she could feel him there beside her. Wishing he would hold her again for just an hour, or even a moment. Wanting to run her fingers through his silky midnight hair. Wanting to hear him laugh. Wanting to hear him breathe. Wanting him . . . wanting him.

The sleepless nights left Helen so listless she moved through the long hot summer days in a somnambulent daze. She welcomed the exhaustion; it helped dampen the unwelcome fire that burned within her. Still the sweet yearning never fully left her and Helen was afraid it never would.

Young Charlie unwittingly and unknowingly saved Kurt and Helen from themselves and from each other. The tireless, full-of-life little boy was everywhere at once. It would have been nearly impossible to put anything past the bright, inquisitive, big-eyed Charlie.

At times Kurt guiltily wondered what might happen if his son were not always underfoot.

Helen never allowed herself to consider such a possibility. She was eternally grateful that the little boy who had become such a happy, curious, lovable child—thanks to Jolly Grubbs—was rarely out of sight.

The adorable Charlie was either trailing after his fa-

ther or helping her. Even when he went fishing with
Jolly—which was often—he was liable to turn up at
any minute, proudly holding up his catch.

Helen was relieved that there were enough obstacles
in their way to prevent anything from happening between Kurt and herself. To further ensure safety, Helen
no longer risked sitting on the gallery in the evenings
after dark.

She avoided going outdoors at nighttime once and
for all after a dangerously close call one sweltering,
muggy night when she'd slipped down to the bay.
Hot, miserable, feeling as if she couldn't stand one
more second in her stuffy bedroom, she had stolen out
onto the gallery, around the house, and down the front
steps.

She had dashed across the front yard and hurried
down the wooden bay stairs, savoring the occasional
gusts of night wind, anticipating a cooling walk in the
shallow waters along the shore. But she had barely
stepped down onto the sand when she stopped short.
She saw something. Something that was not a part of
the natural landscape.

A statue to rival the beauty of Michelangelo's David.

A solitary figure on the solitary beach, Kurt Northway stood unmoving on a jutting cliff of rock, gazing
transfixed at the bay, unconscious of her presence.

As naked as the day he came into the world.

His lean dark body glistened wetly in the moonlight
and his raven hair was plastered to his well-shaped
head. Helen openly stared, overwhelmed by his un-
adorned male beauty. She was totally awed. Everything
about him was perfection. His imposing height. His
wide smooth shoulders and deeply clefted back. His
drum-tight belly. His powerful thighs and long legs
well muscled, but supple.

Proud, naked, he was the embodiment of all that is

male and the sight of him caused her heart to miss several beats.

Helen was tempted as she'd never been tempted in her life.

It was all she could do to keep from calling his name and running to him. Nearly impossible not to strip the hot choking nightgown from her burning body and give herself up to the passion which threatened to consume her.

She could almost feel those strong wet arms come around her, that magnificent naked male body press her insistently close. Could almost taste the heated kisses, feel the caressing hands, experience the swift melding of his hard hot flesh with the waiting softness of her own, the two of them coming together in primitive ecstasy there on the slippery, sea-sprayed rocks.

Helen turned and fled in fear of the dark Adonis on the rocks, telling herself he must surely be an appealing, irresistible form of Satan risen up from the depths of hell to lure her to everlasting damnation. Well, she was just too smart for him. She would not yield to the powerful pull of his dangerous allure. She would not behave in a manner totally at odds with the way she had been raised, with the way in which she had always conducted her life. She would not sacrifice self-respect and decency for one night of stolen rapture.

But most of all, she would not—could not—stand the prospect of spending long, lonely months or even years ahead missing the dark careless lover who would all too soon be gone.

And she would be forgotten.

After that one near-disastrous occurrence, Helen didn't go outdoors at night. She was afraid. Afraid she might see Kurt. Afraid Kurt might see her. Afraid he might come to her. Afraid she might go to him. Afraid he might take her in his arms again and kiss her and kiss her until she begged him never, ever to stop.

Chapter Thirty-three

"Owwwww!" howled Charlie.

"What is it?" Helen called, a worried expression on her face.

It was a blistering hot Thursday afternoon, the very last day of a long, sweltering August. Helen sat on the front steps of the sunny gallery shelling peas. Charlie was out on the lawn, attempting to teach the Russian Blue to fetch a stick he kept throwing. The dignified Dom refused to play such a senseless game. He had no use for the stick, so why would he want to chase after it? He looked at Charlie with those strange green eyes and didn't stir. So Charlie had to retrieve the stick each time. On the last go-round his bare foot had come squarely down atop a grass burr.

"A sticker," Charlie shouted. "I stepped on a sticker."

"Come, let me see," Helen instructed. She set her pan of shelled peas aside.

Hopping on one foot, Charlie sprang over to her, pulling terrible faces, making sure she knew he was in excruciating pain. "Owwww, oooh, mmmmm," he grunted and groaned.

"Give me your foot," Helen ordered when he reached her.

Charlie put his hands on her shoulders and stuck his bare, dirty foot in her lap. "Looks like a nasty old goathead," Helen said, and gingerly caught it between thumb and forefinger and swiftly plucked it free. "There!" she said, and held it out for Charlie to see. "Got it. It is a big one, isn't it?"

Charlie studied the sticker thoughtfully, frowned, shook his blond head, and said, "Well, by jeeters, no wonder it hurt so bad!"

Dissolving with laughter, Helen tossed the sticker away and impulsively hugged the dirty, boisterous little boy who almost daily skinned a knee, an elbow, or his chin, bumped his head, fell from a tree or out of the swing, stubbed a toe, stepped on a burr, or got stung by a yellow jacket or a red ant.

Helen was proud of herself. She had gotten used to Charlie's calamities and no longer panicked at the sight of blood freely flowing from one wound or another on his small body. She had learned to remain calm, or at least to appear so. It wasn't easy. Charlie was all boy and a real handful. And she had come to love him too much not to worry a little. Well, all right, more than a little.

"Charlie, you're awfully warm," Helen commented, brushing back the sweat-dampened blond hair from his dirty forehead.

"I'm as hot as a road lizard," he said, again sounding a lot like Jolly Grubbs.

"Why don't you sit down here for a while and help me shell peas?"

Charlie shrugged. "All right." He dropped down on the steps.

The two of them were still there half an hour later, Charlie enthusiastically helping Helen shell peas while Dom dozed peacefully beside him, one furry paw resting near Charlie's scabbed left knee.

In the dazzling Southern sun, inertia had set in and Helen was almost as sleepy as Dom. Idly nodding yes or no to Charlie's countless questions, it was all she could do to hold her eyes open.

She was quickly pulled from her lethargy when Charlie announced loudly, "Somebody's coming to see us! In a big black buggy."

Smiling, expecting to look up and see the Ellicott brougham, Helen frowned when she recognized the fancy leather-hooded carriage and high-stepping steeds pulling it. Niles Loveless was paying one of his unexpected, unwelcome calls.

Helen offered a silent blessing for Charlie's presence. Thank heavens he was right here with her on this particular afternoon. And thank heavens that his father was nowhere in sight. Niles Loveless would have liked nothing better than to be able to report to his plump, spoiled wife Patsy that he had caught the widowed Helen Courtney alone with her Yankee hired hand.

The Loveless carriage rolled to stop at the south side of the yard and Niles climbed down. A big black mastiff jumped out, barking excitedly, and accompanied his master toward the house.

Niles Loveless was impeccably dressed in one of his expensive, custom-cut summer suits of crisp white linen. He reached the porch, removed his white straw planters hat, and bowed grandly to Helen.

Smiling broadly, he nodded to Charlie. "Hello, young man. You must be Northway's son."

"Captain Northway," Charlie corrected, and proudly confirmed, "He's my daddy."

Niles smiled. Then he said to Helen, "Mrs. Courtney, you're certainly looking well. I do believe you just get prettier every time I see you. Having tenants living right here on the place must agree with you."

Helen stayed as she was, where she was. Seated on the porch steps, shelling peas. "What's on your mind, Niles?" she asked in a tone less than cordial.

"Why can't a gentleman pay a visit to a dear lady of

whose family he's always been fond?" His teeth
flashed in a widening smile and he winked at Charlie.

"Save the small talk, Niles. What do you want?"

"As you wish." Niles's smile faded only slightly. "I
come forward in a frank and friendly manner to lay my
cards on the table. The purpose of this visit is the same
as all my previous calls. I want to buy this property.
I'm *going* to buy this property. From you or from the
tax court when you default. Sell it to me and you will
get some small equity. I mean to own it, Helen, one
way or the other."

Frowning, Helen dropped her unshelled peas, rose to
her feet, and put her hands on her hips. Charlie quickly
mimicked her, leaping up, placing his small hands on
his hips, and glaring at Niles Loveless.

"I have told you, Niles," Helen said with deliberate
slowness, "this farm is not for sale."

Niles shook his blond head, tapped his white straw
planters hat against his trousered thighs, and chuckled
patronizingly. "Now, my dear, I am only trying to help
you. Why, it's out of the goodness of my heart that I'm
prepared to pay you far more than this place is worth.
You're a smart woman—act like one. Take my generous offer and put an end to this ugly talk that's going
around."

Bristling, knowing he meant unkind stories were being whispered about her relationship with Kurt Northway, Helen hotly ordered Niles to leave.

Dom had come out of his stupor and moved down
the front steps. He crouched down flat to the ground,
lowered his head, and hissed warningly at the intrud
ers. Niles's big black mastiff yelped like he'd been
wounded, turned tail, and bounded out of the yard.

But Niles made no move to leave.

Charlie shouted at Niles, "You go away!"

Niles Loveless merely laughed, reached out, and ruffled Charlie's blond hair.

But then a deep, commanding voice from behind
him said, "Where are your fine Southern manners,
Loveless? The lady asked you to leave."

Niles Loveless turned, grinned at the approaching
Kurt, and said, "I was just leaving, Yankee." Niles put
his white planters hat back on his head. "Thought any
more about selling me that sorrel thoroughbred?"

Kurt moved past Loveless. In no particular hurry he
climbed the front steps. He turned to face Loveless,
crossed his arms over his chest, and leaned a muscular
shoulder against a solid white porch column.

Gently, he said, "The stallion is not for sale." There
was a note of authority in his voice, as if he were a
man accustomed to giving orders and to being obeyed.
"Nor, says Mrs. Courtney, is this farm. Good afternoon, Loveless."

Kurt, Helen, and Charlie watched as Niles, no longer
smiling, muttered under his breath, turned on his heel,
hurried to his carriage, and quickly drove away. When
he had turned into the tree-bordered lane, Helen turned
to the tall silent man standing beside her.

"Thank you," she said, wanting to say more, wanting to touch him.

Kurt merely nodded. Then said to his son, "Charlie,
anytime that gentleman shows up, you're to come get
me immediately."

"I will, Daddy," Charlie promised eagerly. Then, as
Kurt pushed away from the porch column, Charlie
asked, "Where are you going?"

"Time to milk old Bessie."

"Can I come with you?"

"Have you finished shelling the peas?"

"Oh, I forgot!" Charlie said, making a face. "Almost. Will you wait for me?"

"You go on," Helen told Charlie. "I can finish this."

"Helen can finish this," Charlie told his father. "Can

I milk Bessie? You think she'll let me? Will she mind me pulling on her—"

"Let's go find out," Kurt smoothly interrupted. "Want to ride piggyback to the barn?"

Charlie was jumping up and down and stretching his short arms up to Kurt before the sentence was finished. He squealed with joy when Kurt effortlessly plucked him up off the ground, swung him around, and settled him gently on his back.

Smiling, Helen watched the pair walk away, Charlie clinging tightly to his father's neck, laughing merrily and calling to Dom to follow. The Russian Blue raced ahead. When they had disappeared around the house, Helen slowly sank back down on the steps.

She reached out and touched the white porch column. The column which Kurt had leaned against just moments ago. The tips of her fingers gliding over the weathered wood, Helen reviewed the brief but pleasing little scene in her mind.

Kurt had come to her defense. He had stepped up onto the porch and stood protectively close beside her. He had coolly ordered Niles Loveless to leave. One word from him and Niles had turned tail and fled. Just like his big cowardly mastiff!

Helen laughed aloud. As long as Kurt Northway was around, she needn't worry about Niles Loveless bothering her again.

He wouldn't dare.

Nor, Helen realized gratefully, would anyone else. She was, she knew, safe here on this remote coastal farm as she hadn't been in years. She had almost forgotten what a good feeling it was to have a fearless man to watch out for her, take care of her.

Picking up her pan of shelled peas, Helen sighed. She'd better not get *too* used to the security. It was, she reminded herself, only temporary. The summer was slipping away. It was already the last day of August.

Tomorrow September began. Soon the leaves would start to fall and the sun would come from a different angle.

And by the first frost of October, the crops would be in and the Northways would be gone. Helen didn't want to think about it. She went inside to start supper.

Jolly showed up by the time Helen reached the kitchen. When she told him they were having fried catfish and black-eyed peas and flour gravy for supper, he said, "Well, what are you dilly-dallying for? Put on the skillet and I'll set the table."

They were all glad to see him, glad to have him stay for the evening meal. Charlie because he hadn't seen his best friend all day. Helen and Kurt because they now wouldn't risk being alone together once Charlie finished his meal and rushed off to play.

Besides, Jolly was never at a loss for words. He welcomed the opportunity to pontificate and his steady, spirited monologue kept Helen from having to talk to Kurt. And vice versa.

His first bit of news was that storm warnings had been hoisted eastward from Pensacola across the Panhandle.

Hearing that, Helen immediately tensed. "Awfully early in the season, isn't it?" she said, concern clearly written on her face. "Should we take precautions?"

"No. No need for it this time," Jolly said quickly, wishing he hadn't brought it up. No one knew better than he just how frightened Helen was of hurricanes. Since a surprise storm had killed her parents at sea when she was only a child, she had been terrified of wind storms.

"Are you sure we're not in danger?" With effort Helen kept her voice calm, but Kurt noted her anxiety.

"No danger at all, child," Jolly reassured her. "Might get a little rain out of it, nothing more. Really."

Jolly tucked his napkin into his shirt collar and

quickly changed the subject. He told, between bites of catfish, of the latest goings-on in Spanish Fort and Mobile. The Livingston sisters had been tut-tutting about Em Ellicott shamelessly chasing after Coop. The widowed Yasmine Parnell was away on holiday; she had gone down the eastern shore to that fancy Point Clear resort for a couple of weeks. The famed actor Tyrone Power was appearing at the Water Street Theater in Mobile. And on and on.

"And I almost forgot," said Jolly, halfway through the meal, "Tom Blake's opened a sawmill over in Bay Minette."

"Really?" Helen's eyebrows raised. "Now, Tom Blake ... isn't he the ..."

"Old Vance Blake's only grandson. Vance and your granddaddy were the best of friends. Vance married a little gal from Bay Minette and moved over there so she could be near her folks," Jolly said. "I think Tommy the grandson might be on to something with this sawmill idea. Lord knows there's a big demand for building lumber."

Agreeing, Helen asked question after question about Tom Blake's new sawmill. She and Jolly discussed it at length while Kurt politely listened, surprised by Helen's keen interest in the subject.

Concluding, Jolly said, "Tommy's a smart young man. He should do real well with the saw mill."

Jolly continued to carry the conversation. But as he spoke, he quietly studied the two grown ups and no ticed, as he had on his last few visits, that something had changed between them.

Again

They were right back where they started.

Or were they?

Jolly wasn't sure, but he suspected he knew what had happened. If his assumption was correct, if they were starting to care more than they cared to, then likely it would be only a matter of time before they were forced to face up to it. At least he hoped they would. Before it was too late. Before Kurt and Charlie had gone.

Finishing his meal, Jolly patted his full round belly, sighed, pushed back his chair, and said, "Charlie, come sit on my knee a minute."

Responding instantly, Charlie slipped out of his chair and hurried to climb up on Jolly's lap. Charlie leaned his head against Jolly's chest and his pale golden hair was smoothed by a weathered, wrinkled hand.

"Charlie, have I told you about the gumbo-cooking contest they hold every autumn up in Bay Minette?"

"No," Charlie said, "when is it? Will we go?"

The child never saw both his father and Helen frowning and shaking their heads no at Jolly. Jolly did, but he paid them no mind. "Every year in late September, folks from miles around go to Bay Minette for . . ."

Stroking Charlie's hair, Jolly talked at length about the upcoming gumbo cook-off, telling how he himself never missed it, since he cooked the best gumbo to be found anywhere in Baldwin County. Said he went to Bay Minette every September for three or four days. Said he always stayed for the whole shebang and it was more fun than anything. Said lots of boys Charlie's age would be there.

Helen could have pinched Jolly's white head off.

But when, lowering Charlie to his feet, Jolly rose and said he'd better be getting on home, Helen tried to get him to stay.

"Why, the sun's not completely down," she argued. "Stay and we'll get out the checkerboard."

Jolly couldn't be persuaded. He left for home. Charlie tagged after him as far as the shortcut through the woods. There they said good-bye and Jolly promised he'd be over again tomorrow.

Kurt had excused himself as soon as Jolly left. Helen cleared the table and cleaned up the kitchen.

As dusk descended, she stepped out onto the back porch and heard the sound of an ax striking wood. She shook her head. Kurt Northway was chopping more firewood. Never had she known a man to work as hard as he. He never stopped. Never rested for a minute. From dawn to dark he toiled as if obsessed.

Helen went down the steps and started toward the smokehouse. She was planning to bake several loaves of bread come morning, so she would need to bring in a big sack of flour. Swinging happily back and forth, Charlie spotted Helen, leaped out of the swing, and came racing over to her. He followed her into the shadowy smokehouse, asking questions, looking around at all the interesting things stored there.

"Oh, no!" Helen exclaimed, standing before the empty shelf where the extra sacks of flour were kept. "We're out of flour."

"Want me to go borrow some from Jolly? I know the shortcut by myself. He showed me."

"No. No, that won't be necessary. I guess I'll just put off my baking for a day or two. Come on, let's go."

Back outside, the mooing of the milk cow and the echoing ring of the ax hitting wood carried on the still evening air.

Helen stopped and, her brow knitting, said to Charlie, "Would you like to take old Bessie to the pasture?"

She didn't have to ask twice. Charlie raced away from her, heading for the cow pen, shouting Bessie's name. Helen waited a minute, took a deep breath, and headed down to where Kurt was chopping wood.

She paused a few feet away, studied him. Lines of weariness showed on his dark, handsome face. Drenched with sweat, he looked as if he were about to drop in his tracks and she had no doubt he was. What, she wondered, was he trying to prove?

Kurt became aware of her presence. He stopped the rhythmic swinging of the ax, lowered it slowly to the ground, leaned the handle against his leg. He lifted an arm, wiped the sweat from his eyes, and looked at her.

"Captain, I asked you to work hard. I didn't ask you to kill yourself," Helen said, moving closer. "You don't have to do everything at once."

"There's so much to be done," he said. He looked directly at her, then away. "I want to get everything finished before . . . before . . . ." He fell silent, shrugged wide shoulders.

"Before you leave?"

"Yes. Before we leave."

Chapter Thirty-four

"**T**ell the truth. You think she'll like it?"

Kurt gazed unblinkingly at the dazzling emerald cut stone, gave a low, long whistle, and said, "She'll love it. Any woman would."

Coop grinned, pleased. He took back the small velvet box, admired the glittering diamond for the thousandth time, snapped the box shut, and shoved it into his breast pocket.

Kurt Northway sat across the scarred desk from Sheriff Cooper at the county jail on Main. It was Friday, so Coop had been surprised when he'd looked up to see Kurt coming through the front door.

"You get your days mixed up?" he'd said, rising to shake hands with Kurt.

"No, but you know women. Last night Hel . . . Mrs. Courtney discovered she was out of flour." Smiling, Kurt shrugged. "Couldn't wait until Saturday. Had to have the flour today."

"Guess I'll soon be getting used to that kind of whimsical behavior," Coop had said, his face turning beet red.

And that was when he had pulled the tiny velvet box out of his pocket and showed Kurt the diamond engagement ring he'd bought for Em Ellicott.

"When is the big day?" Kurt asked now.

Sprawled comfortably in a barrel-backed chair, he

took the cigar Coop offered, lit it, slowly puffed it to life.

"That's up to Em," said Coop. "I'm afraid she'll want to make a big fuss . . . fancy church wedding and all. I suppose it'll take time to make all the arrangements."

Kurt nodded, drew on his newly lit cigar, and wished Coop every happiness. The two men smoked their cigars and drank strong black coffee, relaxing, enjoying each other's company. But the visit had to be a brief one. Coop was due in Mobile for a court hearing at one P.M.

The two men walked out onto the wooden sidewalk together, stood for a minute in the hot sunshine. They glanced across the street.

"You be careful, you hear?" Coop said without turning to look at Kurt. "The town appears to be full of troublemakers this morning."

His gaze resting on several rough-looking men lining the sidewalk outside the Red Rose Saloon, Kurt said, "Don't worry, Sheriff. I'm used to their jibes and insults." He turned, put out his hand, and shook with Coop. "Believe me, Sheriff, nothing they say or do can get to me." He smiled easily. "I'm one peace-loving son of a gun."

Coop nodded and smiled too. "Give my best to Helen and come 'round to visit next time you're in town."

"Will do."

Kurt stayed where he was as Coop mounted his big chestnut gelding and rode out of town. He drew on the burned-down stub of his cigar, then flicked it away into the street. He pulled his hat brim low over his eyes, stuck his thumbs into the waistband of his dark trousers, gave them a decisive yank upward, and stepped down off the wooden sidewalk.

Unhurriedly he crossed the dusty street. He stepped

up onto the sidewalk just outside the batwing double doors of the Red Rose Saloon.

"Excuse me . . . pardon . . . sorry . . ." he said, making his way through the groups of men loitering on the boardwalk.

He headed directly for Jake's General Store, ignoring the slurs and insults and vulgar names he was called. He passed the open door of Skeeter's Barbershop. Several men were inside. Jim Logan, the biggest of Niles Loveless's minions, yanked off his covering barber's cape, got up out of the chair, and walked outside. Half a dozen cronies followed.

Deaf to the hoots and heckles directed at him, Kurt continued on his way. But when he was only a few steps from Jake's General Store, he heard Helen's name followed by a shout of laughter.

Abruptly he stopped.

His forest-green eyes narrowing with rage, his jaw clenching tightly, Kurt turned and walked slowly back up the sidewalk. Jim Logan and the others watched him come.

Kurt reached the big ugly man and stopped directly before him.

His voice low, unemotional, Kurt said, "I admire wit and humor—same as the rest of you gentlemen." He pointedly looked from one grinning face to another. "Perhaps you'll share your jest with me."

"Why not?" replied Jim Logan with a smirk. "I said, it looks like Will Courtney died fighting the North just so his hot-blooded little widow could take herself a Yankee lover."

Kurt's right fist slammed into the surprised man's foul mouth with such ferocity Logan flew ten feet across the wooden sidewalk and slammed hard into the front wall of the barbershop. Stunned, Logan dabbed at the bright-red blood streaming from his left nostril. He called Kurt every conceivable name, then bellowed like a bull and came after him, screaming and swinging wildly.

Kurt moved just in time to dodge a mean round-house punch that would have taken his head off. Then he swiftly moved in, tagged Logan on the chin, and followed up with a hard one-two punch to the stomach. His breath momentarily lost, the big man bent forward gasping and clutching his belly. Kurt seized the opportunity, clipping Logan with an undercut to the chin that knocked his head back.

It was a violent, bloody, no-holds-barred fight. Kurt was outweighed by fifty pounds, but he was as tall as Logan and his reach matched that of his opponent's. His lean body was well muscled and hardened from the war and hard work. The two were evenly matched in pugilistic skills. But Kurt had one big advantage.

He was livid.

Fury flashed from his narrowed green eyes, surged through his blood, and guided his swinging fists. A man who'd been tightly coiled for far too long, Kurt slipped the choking bonds of reason and restraint. All his carefully reined-in anger and hatred and sorrow and passion poured out in a rash, ruthless assault on this despicable brute who dared sully Helen Courtney's good name.

The curious quickly spilled out of the saloons and businesses to watch the savage fight. Niles Loveless heard the commotion from down the street. He stepped outside his office in time to see Jim Logan hit Kurt so hard, blood spurted and Kurt flew backward out into the street. Logan followed, but Kurt was up in the wink of an eye and slamming into Logan so fiercely, the horses tied up at the hitchrail shied and whinnied. One broke loose and trotted down the street. Raider reared up on hind legs and put up a terrible racket as the two men rolled around on the ground beneath him.

"Kill the dirty Yankee bastard," somebody shouted. "Kill him, kill him!" others took up the chorus.

Most of the growing crowd was thoroughly enjoying the brutal, bloody fight. Not wanting to see it end, they even cheered when Kurt struggled to his feet. They roared when he landed a punch to Logan's ribs. They whistled when Logan quickly rallied and tagged Kurt with a bloody-knuckled fist to the chin. They stomped when Kurt came right back with a mean right cross. They cheered when big Jim Logan caught Kurt in a clench and delivered several damaging kidney punches.

The two men fought on and on, standing toe to toe until they were both so bruised and bloodied and beaten they could barely lift their tired arms. Jim Logan, spitting teeth and blood, finally sank to his knees, his eyes rolling back in his head. Gasping, still calling Kurt names, he knelt on the sidewalk.

Kurt remained unsteadily on his feet. His clothes were in tatters. His face, chest, arms, and hands were covered with dirt and blood. His right eye was swollen completely shut, his left was open, and a gash just below his eyebrow was dripping blood.

But he was still livid.

He reached down and dragged Logan to his feet so he could hit him again. Logan moaned in agony and tears streamed down his cheeks. Seeing that their crony was in trouble, a couple of big men came out of the crowd and grabbed Kurt's arms. Harry Boyd and Russ Carter held Kurt immobile while Logan, getting a second wind, stepped in and landed blow after punishing blow to Kurt's unprotected face and stomach.

Watching, Niles Loveless smiled with satisfaction. The arrogant Yankee was getting his face rearranged and nobody deserved it more. Maybe now he would have the good sense to get out of Alabama.

Niles's selfish pleasure was not shared by everyone.

Just outside Jake's General Store, the Livingston sisters watched, appalled and horrified.

"Dear me, this is terrible. Papa wouldn't have approved," said Caroline, shaking her head.

"It isn't right," echoed Celeste. "I don't care if the young man is a Yankee, this isn't right!"

"No, it isn't right," said Jake Autry, stepping up behind the sisters, a look of disgust on his face. "Not right at all."

The sisters nodded their agreement. "We've been unfair to Helen Courtney," lamented Caroline.

"And to the young man," added Celeste.

The grinning pair holding Kurt's arms abruptly released him. Kurt stood there swaying, fighting the waves of nausea and blackness washing over him. He was unsure of his surroundings, didn't know where he was.

Strange faces swam crazily before him and loud raucous laughter echoed in his aching head. Profanity was shouted at him from all around in a thunderous verbal attack meant to penetrate even the deep fog enveloping him.

Finally a jokester stepped up to him, kicked his weak legs out from under him, and Kurt crashed to the sidewalk with a groan of pain.

From his post outside his office, Niles Loveless gave an almost imperceptible nod to the gathering. At once Kurt was jerked up off the sidewalk by a couple of laughing men. They lifted him up into the saddle astride his tethered sorrel stallion. Neighing, his eyes wild, Raider started backing away as soon as he felt Kurt's weight. He was jerked back by several men yanking hard on the bridle. Laughing, the men looped the reins over the stallion's head and wrapped them around the saddle horn.

A tobacco planter then pulled off his straw hat, slapped the stallion on the rump, and a gambler drew his pistol and fired into the air as the big sorrel galloped out of town.

The faithful Raider set out at once for the farm. Kurt swayed dizzily in the saddle, barely aware of his surroundings. Weak from the loss of blood, hurting so badly he could hardly draw a breath, Kurt sagged forward to lean low over Raider's neck. Kurt clung to the stallion's long mane while lights flashed behind his eyes. He struggled to hang on as his blood dripped down the stallion's sleek withers.

The intelligent Raider, worried about his injured master, raced all the way back to the farm in a swift ground-eating gallop. Winded, lathered, he began to whinny loudly as soon as he exited the tree-bordered lane leading to the Burke farm. Helen and Charlie, outdoors in the garden gathering ripe yellow squash, heard the furious neighing. They paused and looked at each other, puzzled.

"Wonder who that could be?" Helen said.

Charlie's eyes grew round. "The man with the big black dog?"

"No. No, I don't think . . ." Helen rose to her feet, shaded her eyes with her hand. "It's . . . why, that's Raider. Raider's back and your father's—" She spotted the wet red blood dripping down Raider's sleek neck. Her eyes climbed to the man on his back. "Kurt!" Helen screamed. "Kurt! Kurt! No . . . noooo . . . oh, dear God, no!"

Helen was running then, tearing off her sunbonnet and work gloves as she went. She raced to meet the galloping stallion. Charlie, terrified, followed her, asking what was wrong. Helen gasped in horror when she reached Raider and the badly beaten Kurt.

"Charlie, go to Jolly's!" She shouted frantically. "Take the shortcut through the woods. Tell Jolly to get Dr. Ledet!"

Stunned, frightened, Charlie stood there staring at

his limp, bloodied father. Rooted to the spot, tears filling his wide eyes, he couldn't move.

"Quick!" Helen screamed, and Charlie flew into action.

Trembling, Helen gently touched Kurt's badly beaten face. "Kurt, can you hear me? It's Helen."

"Helen," he rasped, blood gurgling from his lips.

Fighting to control the sobs tearing at her tight throat, Helen said, "It's all right. You're home now. You're home, Kurt. We'll take care of you."

Her knees shaking so badly she could hardly stand, Helen grabbed Raider's bridle. Speaking softly to the winded stallion, she led him into the yard, around the house, and to the front gallery. Wondering how she could manage to get Kurt off the horse, up the front steps, and into the house, she gave a little sob of gratitude when the tired thoroughbred climbed the porch steps as if he knew exactly what was needed.

"Thank you, Raider, thank you," she murmured as he clomped right up to the front door. Helen started to reach up for Kurt, but Raider whinnied, then helpfully kneeled down on his two front forelegs.

Grateful, Helen was able to get her arms around Kurt's waist and pull him free of the saddle. She waited then while Raider rose fully to all four feet, turned, and moved out of the way.

"Can you walk?" Helen asked Kurt as she knelt on the porch, holding his head in her lap.

"I don't know," Kurt said truthfully. "Where are we?"

"On the porch," she told him, lifting her skirts to wipe some of the blood off his battered face.

"Can't I rest here for a while?" Kurt mumbled, barely able to speak. "I'm tired."

"I know," she whispered, "but we need to get you inside."

"I can't," he confessed, vainly attempting to open his eyes. "I can't make it."

"I'll help you," Helen said. "I'll get you inside, I promise."

And she did.

Straining to lift him, she managed to get him up into a half-sitting position. His head resting on her breast, she wrapped her arms tightly around him. Pressing her lips to his blood-tangled dark hair, she whispered, "We'll do this together. I'll stand up and you'll stand with me. We will go inside the house and to the guest bedroom."

Helen took a deep breath, draped Kurt's limp arms around her neck, slid her own around his back, and locked her hands. She struggled up onto one bent knee, bringing him with her. Then, calling on all the strength she possessed, she managed to rise to her feet and pull him up. Breathing hard, Helen stood there for a moment leaning against the house, fully supporting Kurt's weight, hoping she wouldn't fall.

Bracing herself on wide-spread feet, she backed into the open front door and literally dragged Kurt down the hall and into the guest room. Halfway across the room, she felt herself losing her balance. Instead of risking a hard, crashing fall which could further hurt the badly injured man, she sank slowly to the floor.

"We made it," she told him, gently laying him down on the thick, worn rug. "Stay just as you are," she whispered, then leaped up and dashed out of the room.

She was back in seconds carrying a basin of water and several clean white towels and washcloths. Her heart rose to her throat when she saw that Kurt hadn't moved a muscle. She set the basin on the floor, dropped the linens, and fell to her knees at his side. Picking up one of his badly skinned hands, she held it to her breast and anxiously called his name.

"Kurt, oh, Kurt, answer me. Please answer me."

His fingers tightened minutely on hers and his lips
stiffly moved. "I'm . . . not hurt," he managed weakly.
"Don't . . . worry."

"I'm not worried."

She was worried sick.

She wasn't surprised that something like this had
happened, but she was much too worried to be angry
with him for fighting. Praying the doctor would arrive
soon, Helen stripped away Kurt's tattered, bloodstained shirt and gently washed the wounds and bruises
covering his chest and shoulders and long arms. With
his help, she gingerly turned him over onto his side
and cleaned up his punished back. Carefully she
washed away the dried, crusted blood.

Dipping the cloth into the water, she squeezed it out,
then drew it slowly along the aging white scar slashing
around his side to his back. She sponged the blood
away from the satiny imperfection, talking softly as
she worked. Finally she tossed the stained cloth into
the basin of water and again turned him onto his back.

Helen rose and hurried to the bed. She drew back the
blue velvet counterpane and snatched it completely off,
dropping it to the rug at the foot of the four-poster. She
turned back the top sheet and coverlet, fluffed up a
couple of feather pillows, and returned to Kurt.

She removed his shoes and stockings, then unbuckled his belt. She made short work of the buttons
going down his fly. She considered stripping him of his
pants, decided it would be easier once she got him into
bed.

Puffing and breathing hard, Helen somehow got
Kurt off the floor and across the room. Using the little
stepping stool meant specifically for the purpose,
Helen climbed up onto the bed and pulled Kurt up with
her. She fell over backward onto the high feather mattress with him atop her. She rested for a split second,
then eased herself out from under him.

Within minutes she had his trousers off and the
snowy white sheet pulled up to his waist. His eyes
closed, he lay unmoving, looking so hurt and helpless
Helen wanted to cry. But she didn't.

She put her lips close to his bruised ear on the pillow and whispered, "I'll take care of you, Kurt. I will,
I promise. I'm right here."

She saw the tiniest fluttering of his thick lashes as if
he heard and understood. She swallowed hard, stepped
back, and began unbuttoning her bloodstained work
dress. She stepped out of the soiled dress, kicked it
aside, and considered leaving him for a moment, just
long enough to go to her room for a clean dress.

But he tried to speak and even though no sound
came, it was her name forming on his lips. He was trying to say her name.

"I'm here, Kurt, right here." She hurried back to the
bed, unconcerned about getting dressed. She laid a
cool hand to his hot cheek. Softly she touched his face,
his hair, his chest.

His left eye slitted open. He saw her leaning over
him. Again he tried to speak.

"Shhh," she cautioned. She laid a gentle finger to
his split, swollen lip. "You don't need to try and talk.
I know. I understand." She smiled at him.

Kurt's eye closed. He drew a ragged, rattling breath.
And passed out cold.

Chapter Thirty-five

The sun was setting across Mobile Bay and the stifling September heat had lost a little of its sting when Dr. Milton J. Ledet finally stepped out into the hall, closing the guest room door behind him.

The bearded, gray-haired doctor promptly announced to the three anxious people waiting in the shadowy corridor, "He has several broken ribs. Multiple cuts and contusions. Two fractured fingers on his left hand. A pulled ligament in his right leg. A badly sprained left ankle. A pair of black eyes. And a slight concussion."

"A concussion," Helen repeated, her face as pale as death. "Will he . . . is he . . ." She couldn't finish. She stood staring in horror at the doctor, one hand rising involuntarily to her breast.

"Now, Helen, it sounds bad, but he can make it." Dr. Ledet smiled, patted her shoulder reassuringly. "The young man has been badly beaten, but none of his injuries are of themselves life-threatening. Infection's the only thing that could kill . . . that could be dangerous, but his color is good. And his wounds—thanks to you, Helen—look clean."

"Praise the good Lord above," said Jolly, heaving a sigh of relief. Ruffling Charlie's blond hair, he said, "You hear that, my boy? Your father's going to be fine."

"Can I see my daddy?" Charlie looked up at the tall doctor with somber brown eyes.

"You may look in on him." Dr. Ledet began rolling down his shirtsleeves. "But he's sedated and presently he's sleeping, so be very careful not to disturb him. He needs all the rest he can get." The doctor carefully opened the bedroom door and motioned Charlie inside. Charlie stole softly into the room.

The three adults watched in silence as the little boy cautiously crossed the spacious bedroom lighted only by the eerie orange glow of the dying summer sun. Charlie reached the high feather bed. He pulled the footstool up close, climbed up onto it, and stood looking at the badly battered face of his sleeping father. Charlie didn't make a sound. But he reached out with short fingers and gently patted his father's bandaged left hand.

Helen and Jolly exchanged looks and smiles.

Charlie stayed only a minute. When he came back out, Dr. Ledet again closed the door. Then, ushering them all toward the back of the house, the doctor gave them their instructions regarding the care of his patient.

"You must keep him as quiet and as still as you can at all times. It won't be easy. He's in for a great deal of pain, I'm afraid. But remember, the more he thrashes about, the longer the healing process will take." From his black bag the doctor produced a vial of laudanum. He handed it to Helen. "He'll be needing this; a few drops at a time should ease him. Keep his bandages changed and his wounds clean, his temperature down. Think you can handle it?" He looked directly at Helen.

"Yes, we can," Helen was quick to respond. "Is there anything else we should do?"

"Yes." Dr. Ledet closed his black bag. "Make sure you keep him in bed until I say otherwise." He started

for the back door. "I'll look in on him in the next day
or two in case any infection should set in. If you need
me sooner, Jolly knows where to get me."

"Thanks so much for coming, Doctor," Helen said,
touching his shoulder. "We appreciate it."

"You're more than welcome, child," replied the aging bearded doctor whom Helen had known all her life.
He suddenly shook his graying head and said, "I'd like
to think what happened to the young man was nothing
more than a saloon brawl and horseplay."

"But you know better." Helen looked him straight in
the eye.

Dr. Ledet sighed, started to speak, but said nothing
more. He squeezed Helen's hand and went out. Jolly
walked the doctor out to his tethered horse while
Helen—with Charlie right behind her—headed back to
the guest room.

In the last gloaming of light, Helen and Charlie
stood unmoving at Kurt's bedside. Jolly came into the
room, glanced at the worried pair, and lit the coal-oil
lamp on the night table beside the bed. Then he too
came to the bed, looked thoughtfully at Kurt, and put
comforting arms around both Charlie and Helen.

The long bedside vigil had begun.

Jolly insisted he was staying the night. Helen
quickly agreed that the two of them could take turns
watching over Kurt. Charlie said he wanted to help
too. Helen told him he sure could. In fact he could go
gather up some of his things and move up to the house
until his father was well again. Charlie wasted no time
complying. He and Jolly went down to the quarters to
get Charlie's clothes.

Helen fixed Charlie a bed on the long blue velvet
chaise lounge so he could sleep right there in the room
with his injured father. Bedtime came and Charlie announced he wasn't going to bed. He was going to stay

at his father's bedside. Neither Helen nor Jolly argued with him.

But when the tall cased clock in the hall struck midnight, Charlie could no longer hold his eyes open. The sleepy little boy sank down onto his footstool and his head sagged on his chest. Jolly lifted him up in his arms and carried him to the chaise lounge, undressed him, and put him to bed.

Charlie slept while Helen and Jolly looked after Kurt. They bathed Kurt's face with cool clean cloths. They murmured soothingly when he became restless. They did all they possibly could to keep him comfortable.

And still.

It wasn't a simple task. At times it took both Helen and Jolly to hold Kurt down. Slightly feverish, in pain, slipping in and out of consciousness, he mumbled and thrashed and moaned. Sometime before dawn he settled down and fell into a less troubled slumber.

When the sun finally rose on a new day, Jolly was dozing in a chair. But Helen was wide awake. She hadn't been asleep. She might never sleep again. She felt responsible for what had happened to Kurt and she was determined to make it up to him. She would take care of him like no one ever had before. She would get him through this, do whatever was necessary, stay with him for as long as he needed her.

Worried, weary, her shoulders and head aching dully, Helen stood beside the bed as the pastel rays of the rising summer sun slanted into the room and across the dark, still face on the pillow. Her heart hurt as she looked at him. He was hardly recognizable. His handsome features were distorted by fierce swelling and ugly discoloration.

Her hand resting lightly on his bare, bruised shoulder, Helen silently told the prostrate man that she would get him well. She vowed to nurse him back to full vigorous health. She took a solemn oath that come harvest time, she would have him strong and fit and able to travel.

All the way back to his Maryland home.

Helen was gazing wistfully at him when all at once one of his blackened, swollen eyes slitted open. Helen's breath caught in her chest. Kurt looked up at her. He tried to speak, couldn't.

"Kurt," she whispered, leaning over him. "Oh, Kurt, it's Helen. I'm right here."

"Helen," he croaked through split, swollen lips. "You . . . you look tired." He weakly lifted his bandaged left hand from the bed.

Feeling like laughing and crying at the same time, Helen took his injured hand gently in both of her own and softly said, "No, dear. I'm not the least bit tired."

"You're . . . awfully . . . sweet," he murmured in a choked whisper, and his swollen eye again closed and his breathing became deep and slow.

Jolly took care of the morning chores Kurt usually handled; then, to Helen's surprise, he went home and they didn't see him for the rest of the day. Together Helen and Charlie began the long ordeal of patiently, caringly nursing Kurt back to health.

In the late afternoon of that first long tiring day, Helen efficiently changed Kurt's bandages, cleaned the abrasions on his chest, carefully retaped his cracked ribs, and soaked his sprained ankle in a basin of hot salt water she placed on the bed.

Kurt had awakened in the hottest part of the afternoon and she had spooned beef broth and hot tea down him. Charlie was there throughout, helping, touching, talking.

By bedtime Kurt appeared to be resting comfortably, so Helen turned to Charlie and said, "We both need to get some sleep. I'll be in my bedroom just next to this one. I'll leave my door open in case you need me. We'll keep the lamp burning beside your father's bed. Think you can sleep?"

Charlie yawned. "Can Dom sleep with me?"

Helen smiled. "If you can find him. Go on. Call him in."

Charlie raced from the room, down the hall, and out the front door. Helen returned to the bed to have one last look at Kurt. Charlie was back in a minute, wagging Dom.

" 'Night, now," Helen whispered to Charlie.

"That's not the way you say it," Charlie told her, dumping Dom on the chaise lounge.

"It isn't?" Helen reached out, cupped the back of his blond head. "How should I say good night?"

"You have to say, 'Nighty-night and don't let the bedbugs bite!' " Charlie grinned.

Helen smiled at him and said, "Nighty-night and don't let the bedbugs bite."

"I won't," he said, then turned, raced over to the high feather bed, and climbed up onto the footstool. The little boy leaned over and whispered to his sleeping father, "Nighty-night and don't let the bedbugs bite."

Helen swallowed hard and went to her room. Exhausted after more than twenty-four hours of work and worry, she undressed, drew her nightgown over her head, and fell into bed without even brushing her hair. She was asleep immediately.

It seemed to her only moments had passed when she was being awakened by Charlie standing beside her bed, calling her name and tugging on her hand.

"Charlie. . . ." she murmured groggily. "What is it? Can't you sleep?" Her eyes opened to bright morning sunlight.

"Daddy's sick!" he shouted. "I felt him and he's soooo hot."

Helen leaped out of bed and raced to Kurt's bedside, her heart hammering in her chest. She found him shaking with hard chills, his teeth chattering violently. Anxiously, she pressed her cheek to his. He was burning up with fever.

"Charlie," she said, never taking her eyes off Kurt, "does your father have any nightshirts?"

"Jolly gave him some," Charlie said, nodding, "but he never sleeps in them."

"Run down to the quarters, find those nightshirts, and bring them to me. Wait, Charlie . . . there's a big bottle of rubbing alcohol under the sink in the kitchen and a box of cotton balls. Bring those to me first. Then grab some towels and washcloths."

Jerking up the long tails of his nightshirt so he could run faster, Charlie dashed out of the room. Helen, trembling almost as violently as the man in the bed, whispered, "Can you hear me?"

"Cold," Kurt rasped. "I'm cold."

"I'll make you warm," she promised, then bit her bottom lip.

First she would have to freeze him half to death and she hated the thought of making him suffer. It couldn't be helped. She had to get his fever down. And fast.

Charlie returned with the clean towels, the alcohol, and cotton balls. He handed them to Helen and was gone again after the nightshirts. Helen laid everything on the night table. Then, murmuring softly, "I'm sorry, so sorry," she drew the bedcovers down to Kurt's waist. His left eye opened a little and he looked at her with such a pained, pleading expression she almost weakened.

She gritted her teeth and refused to let herself be swayed. Pulling her nightgown up to her knees, Helen climbed up onto the bed with him and began bathing Kurt's hot, jerking body with cotton balls dipped in alcohol. As she worked, she instructed Charlie to run out to the orchard and pull several handfuls of leaves from a peach tree. After he'd done that, he was to go out to the well and, if he could manage, draw a bucket of cool water.

As soon as he was gone, Helen stripped the covers all the way off Kurt. He lay there shuddering in his white underwear, trying to roll himself up into a ball on his side. She wouldn't let him.

"Stop it!" Helen's tone was sharp. She jerked on his arm and and ordered, "You lie still, you hear me? Just for a few minutes, that's all it will take."

Helen worked furiously, quickly, terrified by the real and present danger his high fever presented. With great effort and moans of agony from him, she managed to push Kurt over onto his stomach. She immediately curled her fingers around the waistband of his white linen underwear, hesitated for only a moment, then made short work of peeling the linen underpants over his firm brown buttocks, down his legs, and off.

She quickly climbed astride Kurt's waist and began patting the alcohol-soaked cotton across his back and down his arms. As she worked she crooned, "I'm so sorry, Kurt. I know you're cold. I'll warm you. I'll make you warm."

Her face pinkened as she spread the alcohol down the curve of his slim hips and over that part of him which was never exposed to the sun, yet was just as tanned as the rest of his lean body.

Helen heard Charlie noisily coming through the back door. She hurriedly got off the bed, drew the sheet back up over Kurt. Charlie came in struggling under the weight of the full oaken bucket, water sloshing over the rim, spilling onto the rug and him.

Helen thanked him for a job well done. Then she promptly came up with several more chores which needed to be done. Outside. Eager to be of help, Charlie hurriedly dressed in the parlor and went outdoors, with Dom accompanying him.

Helen again peeled the covers off Kurt, got back on the bed, and bathed his burning naked backside and long limbs with cold bracing water. He shuddered and squirmed and moaned in agony. She turned a deaf ear. She had to get his dangerously high temperature down.

When she had sponged all the bared flesh exposed to her, Helen realized she was in a bit of a dilemma. His cold bath was only half finished. The front of him—his chest and belly and navel and knees—needed bathing just as badly as his backside.

Maybe she could close her eyes and finish. No. That wouldn't work. Did she dare just turn him over and blithely continue with the bath as if her seeing him naked were an everyday occurrence? No. She couldn't do that either.

Helen's solution was to pull the sheet up over the prone, shivering Kurt. Then she struggled until she got him turned onto his back. By then the sheet was twisted around his body, so she tugged and pulled and finally got it loose. When she had it smoothed out and lying loosely over him, she folded it down to his waist. Then she yanked the bottom of the sheet free from the foot of the mattress and very carefully folded it up past his knees.

Kurt now lay on his back with the sheet preserving his modesty and hers. Helen went back to work. She bathed his chest and arms and legs. And reaching underneath the sheet, she swabbed and patted and bathed all the remaining burning flesh which she could not see.

The bath finished, she laid her cheek to his chest and sighed. He was still hot as fire, but perhaps a degree or two cooler than when she'd begun. She grabbed up one of the clean white nightshirts and managed to get it over Kurt's dark head. That was the easy part. Getting his long arms into the nightshirt sleeves seemed next to impossible.

But she did it.

Had anyone happened by the open bedroom door, they would have thought a wild wrestling match was taking place atop the high feather bed. And, in a way, it was. Helen and Kurt rolled and tumbled about, her striving to get the nightshirt on him, him fighting against it and trying to grab her and hold her close, seeking her body heat.

By the time she finally got both his arms in the sleeves and the nightshirt pulled down his hot, trembling body, her own nightgown was twisted up around her pale thighs and Kurt's injured hands were filled with the cheeks of her bottom. She was too tired to care. Her hands on his nightshirted shoulders, she laid her forehead on his chest for a minute to rest and get her breath.

Still panting from her labor, Helen extricated herself from Kurt, slid off the bed, righted her nightgown, and pulled the sheet and counterpane up over him, tucking both in around his shoulders and chin.

She rushed into the kitchen and brewed hot tea from the peach-tree leaves Charlie had gathered. Her Grandma Burke always swore by the brew, said nothing cooled a high fever like a cup of peach-tree-leaf tea.

She hurried back to Kurt, cradled his dark head in her arms, and forced most of the hot tea down him.

Still he shook and shivered.

Helen set the cup aside, snatched the downy hand-pieced quilt off Charlie's makeshift bed, and spread it over Kurt.

"There," she murmured, leaning close, stroking his hair. "Now, you see. That's better. Much better."

But the sick, freezing man in the bed continued to shudder and jerk with hard racking chills. His teeth chattered and his split, swollen lips formed the word, "Cold."

"Oh, my dear," she whispered in his ear, "I can't stand to see you freeze. I'll get you warm."

Without any further thought to propriety, Helen Courtney turned back the covers and got into bed with Kurt Northway.

Chapter Thirty-six

Helen wrapped her arms around the sick, shaking Kurt and held him close for half an hour. Until she heard Charlie coming in the back door. By the time the little boy entered the room, Helen was standing beside the bed.

"Did you gather the eggs?" she asked, smiling and pushing her tangled hair back off her face.

"Yes, only . . . only . . ." Charlie shrugged his narrow shoulders and caught his bottom lip between his teeth.

"Only what?"

"Two got broked and they squished all over the rest." He wrinkled his small button nose and added, "I think maybe Dom stepped on them."

"Sounds just like him, all right," Helen agreed, smiling. Then cheerfully she said, "I think your father is a little better."

"I'll see," Charlie told her, hurried forward, dragged up his footstool, and climbed on it. He leaned over and put his small palm on Kurt's forehead. "He's all wet," Charlie announced.

Helen laughed. "Yes, I know. He's perspiring, which means his fever has broken."

Charlie drew back his hand, wiped it on his trousers leg. "Want me to pull off the quilt?"

"No, let's keep him covered for a while. Let him work up a real good sweat." Helen started to the door.

She paused and said, "I'm going to clean up and get dressed now. You'll watch him?"

Charlie turned on his footstool, leaned back against the high mattress. He crossed his short arms over his chest and said, "I'll stay right here!"

By the time Helen was dressed, Dr. Ledet and Jolly had arrived. Jolly immediately headed down to the pasture to bring Bessie up for milking. The bearded doctor waved Charlie and Helen out of the room and examined Kurt.

Helen paced just outside the door. Her hands clasped behind her, she walked back and forth. Back and forth. Soon Charlie paced with her. Hands clasped behind his back, he walked back and forth. Back and forth. The Russian Blue sat unmoving in the sunlit corridor, observing the pacing pair with disdainful green eyes, silently letting them know he thought they were fools who had taken leave of their senses.

Dr. Ledet emerged, informing them that a slight infection had caused Kurt's fever to shoot up. He had carefully sterilized the contaminated wound and, hopefully, it should cause Kurt no further trouble.

The doctor praised Helen and Charlie. "Looks like you two have been taking real good care of him."

Nodding proudly, Charlie volunteered, "We sleep with him."

Helen nearly fainted. "What Charlie means," she was quick to explain, "is he's sleeping in his father's room at night."

The bearded doctor looked at Helen and chuckled. He put a hand on her shoulder and said, "Relax, child. I didn't really suppose one of you had climbed in the bed with my patient."

Helen could feel heat burning her cheeks. "No. No, of course not," she said, avoiding the doctor's eyes. Needlessly clearing her throat, she hurried on to tell

Dr. Ledet that she and Charlie had given Kurt an alcohol bath to get his fever down.

"Well, it worked," Dr. Ledet assured her.

The doctor soon left, promising to come again in a few days. Jolly stayed only long enough to handle some of the more pressing chores, then he too went home, mysteriously turning down Helen's invitation to stay for dinner. Helen had never known Jolly Grubbs to say no to a meal. She halfway wondered if he was not feeling well himself. She grew mildly concerned when Jolly didn't come around the next day.

Or the next.

Actually, Jolly Grubbs felt fine.

But he had ascertained that it would be good for just the three of them—Kurt, Helen, and Charlie—to be on their own together.

Kurt's bad whipping might just turn out to be a blessing in disguise, Jolly surmised. It could prove to be one of the best things that had ever happened to Kurt. Or to Helen. The pair had spent the entire summer avoiding one another, staying out of each other's way. Afraid of each other and of what might happen.

Well, by jeeters, they couldn't stay apart now.

Jolly chuckled to himself and wished he was a fly on the wall so he could see and hear what went on in that guest room at Helen's.

Helen didn't have a great deal of time to wonder and worry about why Jolly wasn't coming around. She was far too busy worrying over and taking care of Kurt.

Sheriff Cooper and Em Ellicott came to call, expressing their deep concern and bringing a big basket of food and a bouquet of freshly cut flowers. They looked in on Kurt, staying only a few minutes, not wishing to tire him. Coop stayed behind when Em and Helen left the room. Then after only a minute, he joined the woman out on the front gallery.

Helen poured icy lemonade from a glass pitcher,

handed the first glass to the tall red-haired sheriff. "Coop, did he tell you anything? Did he say what happened? Who beat him so badly?"

"No," Coop told her truthfully. "I asked who did it and why, but he wasn't forthcoming. Swore he's the one who started the fight." Coop leaned back against the porch railing, took a drink of lemonade.

Helen sighed. She turned and handed a glass to Em. Em purposely reached for it with her left hand. That's when Helen saw the sparkling diamond engagement ring and almost dropped the lemonade pitcher. She anxiously handed the heavy pitcher to Coop as Em, laughing, came up out of her chair.

The two young women hugged and laughed and jumped up and down while Coop stood there awkwardly holding the pitcher of lemonade, shaking his curly red head, and grinning.

Charlie stared at the women, totally puzzled. He looked up at the tall sheriff and said, "They sure act strange sometimes."

Coop chuckled and nodded. "They do for a fact, Charlie." But Coop's turquoise eyes sparkled as he looked at the laughing young women.

"I'm so happy for you both!" Helen exclaimed, stepping back to hold up Em's left hand and admire the dazzling stone. Then she whirled about, threw her arms around the surprised sheriff's trim waist, hugged him tightly while he held the pitcher out of harm's way, and said fervently, "Congratulations, Coop!"

"Thank you, Helen," Coop replied, awkwardly patting her back.

Helen released him as swiftly as she had grabbed him, turned back to Em, clasped her shoulders, and exclaimed, "Oh, Em, Em! It's wonderful! It's so wonderful!"

And then there was more hugging and tears and excited talk of a Christmastime wedding with Em in a long white satin dress and Helen in lush rose velvet as the matron of honor.

Soon Helen and Charlie were walking the happy engaged couple to their carriage, thanking them for coming, and waving as they drove off into the gathering dusk.

The long, languorous September days of Kurt's convalescence became—oddly enough—a pleasant period in his life and in Helen's. Like most women, Helen was a natural-born nurturer, so taking care of the injured Kurt was second nature; as soon as he was out of danger, she loved every minute of it.

Like most men, Kurt couldn't get enough of being cared for and pampered and fussed over by a sweet, pretty, bossy woman.

Charlie too enjoyed that special season of long, lazy days when the three of them were constantly together. He got to help Helen do everything. He was there to assist in the feeding of his father. He was right there with his own soapy washcloth when Helen gave his father a bed bath. He was there making faces and giving instructions when Helen shaved his father's whiskered cheeks and chin. He was there to see to it his father soaked his sprained ankle twice each day.

And in the quiet, still, scorching afternoons, he was there to wave a faded funeral-home fan back and forth before his father's warm face while Helen read aloud.

She had been reading every afternoon since casually asking, a couple of days after Kurt had been hurt, if he'd like her to read to him. When he had said yes, she had selected from the tall bookcase in the parlor one of the leather-bound works of Sir Walter Scott.

And so the afternoon reading quickly became a regular part of their routine, as did Kurt's morning bath. And the changing of his bandages. And serving his meals on a tray. And rubbing his back and legs while

he groaned with satisfaction. And a hundred other intimate little things the three of them shared daily.

It was during those first long anxious hours of worry
and the following calmer hours of watching Kurt re-
cover that Helen began to feel as if the three of them
were a family. She dearly loved the adorable Charlie.
She was falling in love with Charlie's brave, handsome
father.

She almost hated to see this sweet interlude come to
an end. She half wished that Kurt wasn't healing so
rapidly. Wished the long languid September days
would stretch on endlessly.

At times Helen stood on the gallery just outside
Kurt's room looking wistfully over the low flat fields
of her farm. Tall green cornstalks and golden summer
wheat shimmered in the strong sunlight. Wherever she
looked she saw the ripening bounty of all their hard labor.

Harvest time was just around the corner.

Harvest time and the crops would be sold and Kurt
would be back on his feet. And she would pay him
what she owed him and he would leave. And Charlie would leave. Both father and son would leave
her. They would ride out of Alabama and out of her
life. They would go back to Maryland.

Back to their home.

And she would be alone again.

Too quickly, the peaceful precious days were slipping by.

More than two weeks had passed since the brutal
beating and Kurt was on the mend. He was able to see
out of both eyes now. His broken ribs were no longer
painful except when he turned over too quickly. His
discoloring bruises had lightened. All but a couple of
abrasions were almost healed. The pulled ligament in
his right leg no longer bothered him and the fierce

swelling in his badly sprained left ankle had almost disappeared. The fractured fingers on his left hand— fore and middle fingers—were temporarily useless, but gave him little trouble.

Truth to tell, he felt rather guilty about continuing to lie in bed, but anytime he mentioned getting up, Helen promptly vetoed the notion. She had, she said emphatically, promised Doc Ledet that she wouldn't allow his patient to get out of bed until he, the doctor, okayed it. So there.

Kurt didn't argue the point all that much. He was enjoying the rest. What with the long hard years of the war, when he was constantly tired and hungry and dirty, it was rather nice to now be lying in a big feather bed and have a beautiful woman feed him hot meals from a tray and bathe him with soapy water and soft hands. A man could get used to such spoiling treatment.

Kurt sighed with lazy contentment one sultry afternoon, folded his arms beneath his head, and gazed contentedly out the open French doors. Beyond the broad white gallery and the tangled greenery cloaking the cliffs, the waters of the deep blue bay sparkled dazzlingly in the brilliant September sunlight.

Smiling, stretching, Kurt thought to himself that he could lie there forever looking out at that breathtakingly beautiful view.

The only thing which would make it better, he mused drowsily, would be to have Helen lying there beside him. He could almost feel her soft warmth enfolded in his eager arms. Could clearly envision her glorious golden hair fanned out on his naked chest. Could all too easily imagine his hands caressing—

The bedroom door opened and Kurt's head snapped around. Expecting to see Helen, his quickening heartbeat slowed and he fought the mild disappointment when Charlie skipped noisily into the quiet room.

Kurt smiled at his son and said, "Come keep me company. I'm lonesome."

"That's why I'm here," Charlie said. He dragged his footstool over to the bed and climbed up on it. He scaled the mattress like a nimble acrobat and crawled over to his father. Sitting back on his heels, Charlie said, "Helen's baking a surprise for you."

"Is she?" Kurt laid an affectionate hand on Charlie's bare knee. "What is it?"

Charlie squinted his eyes. "I can't tell. Helen said so."

Kurt nodded, then sniffed at the pleasant aroma wafting in from the kitchen. "Smells mighty good, whatever it is."

"Helen let me lick the bowl," Charlie said. Then, having heard Helen ask every afternoon about this time if Kurt would like her to read to him, he said, "Shall I read to you?"

"Please do," Kurt answered, just as he always did.

Charlie giggled, threw his arms up, and laced his hands atop his head. "Daddy, I can't read. Jolly hasn't teached me yet."

"Taught," his father gently corrected. "Well, that's all right. Why don't you tell me a story?"

"Tell you a story? What about?"

"Anything that comes to mind. Make up a good exciting tale and I'll just lie here and listen."

Charlie had an imagination. He began a colorful yarn, his eyes expressive, his hands gesturing.

Kurt listened for a time, lying back on the pillows, his eyes closed. But as the tale went on and on and grew more and more farfetched, his thoughts drifted to the day he and Charlie had first ridden onto Helen's farm. It seemed like just last week. It had been more than four months ago!

It was early spring then. Now it was early autumn. The fields had not been planted then. Now he was proud of the crops that would soon be ready for harvest, proud of the improvements he had been able to make in the run-down lowland farm.

Kurt smiled to himself. When the crops came in, Helen could easily pay her taxes and she would even have some extra money. Already she'd been talking about painting the house, getting new kitchen curtains, buying the beautiful lilac counterpane she had seen at the Bon Ton over in Mobile last winter.

Kurt's smile disappeared and his bare chest constricted. Yes, Helen would soon have money. Which meant she would pay him what he had earned and expect him to move on. To take Charlie and go home to Maryland.

Not so long ago that's all he had dreamed of. Going home to Maryland. Home to the Dunston horse farm. Home to where he would one day have his own farm, his own land, his own home.

But what was a home without a woman in it? Without Helen?

He didn't want to go back. He didn't want to leave Alabama. To leave her. His sweet, beautiful Helen.

And be alone again.

"... and then ... then this b-i-gggg monster ..." Charlie was still telling his story when Helen came into the room. Barefooted, her hair held atop her head with the mother-of-pearl clasp, she was carrying a tray with three glasses of chilled milk and three large slices of chocolate cake dripping with rich fudge icing.

Charlie immediately forgot about his storytelling. He clapped his hands when Helen handed the tray to Kurt and then climbed up onto the bed herself, crossing her legs beneath her and spreading her long skirts over her bare toes. Charlie thought it great fun for the three of them to sit there on the bed, talking, laughing, and enjoying the rich dark chocolate cake.

But as soon as he'd finished his cake, Charlie grew

restless. He was off the bed and gone, racing outside and shouting to Dom. At Kurt's insistence, Helen lingered.

Leaning back against the tall mahogany poster at the bed's foot, hugging her knees, she stayed and talked, relaxed, enjoying the easy closeness which had developed between them during Kurt's convalescence.

Listening as he spoke in a low, lulling voice, Helen studied his dark face, noting that it was almost back to normal. A little discoloration remained around his right eye and the cut just below his left eyebrow had not completely healed. But his handsomeness had been fully restored and in another week it would be impossible to tell that merciless blows had ever landed on those strong chiseled features.

Helen's gaze lowered to his chest, which was bare, his nightshirt having been discarded because of the relentless heat. As with his face, most of the bruises and cuts were now nearly invisible, save that worst deep cut directly below his heart—the one which had become infected. A small bandage covered it and Helen knew he would sport a small scar for the rest of his life.

Tempted to remove the clean white bandage and press her lips to the slow-healing wound, she said in soft, casual tones, "Tell me what happened."

Since they had been talking about something which had nothing to do with the fight, Kurt was puzzled by the question. "I don't . . . What do you mean?" He frowned and shrugged.

"The fight. What happened in town to cause the fight in which you were very nearly killed?"

"Now, Helen, do I look like a man who was almost killed?"

"Please tell me what happened."

"What happened? I got into a barroom brawl and got beat up. It's as simple as that." He smiled at her.

Helen smiled too. What a gallant liar he was. "With whom?" she prodded. "And who started it?"

"I didn't get the fellow's name," Kurt said evenly. "But I started it. I threw the first punch."

"You started the fight? You hit him first?" Kurt nodded. "But why? Why would you do such a thing?"

Kurt leaned back against the stack of pillows piled up against the headboard. Smiling, he said, "I had no choice, Helen."

"You didn't?" Her blue eyes grew wide. "Why?"

"You don't want to know." Kurt shook his dark head.

"I do. Yes, I do. Tell me."

"Well . . . the man—this big ugly brute—made an indelicate reference." Kurt cocked a dark eyebrow.

"Indelicate reference?" Helen repeated, frowning. "What exactly did he say?"

Impishly, Kurt grinned. "He called me a Yankee asshole."

Chapter Thirty-seven

Helen audibly winced and her blue eyes widened with shock. Her back stiffened and she was momentarily speechless. Her lips pursed, she stared at Kurt, astonished, totally taken aback.

But then she saw the self-deprecating grin on Kurt's handsome face and the devilment flashing in the depths of his forest-green eyes. She released her caught breath and smiled too, hesitantly at first, still a little tense and not quite certain that she should be smiling. Kurt's disarming smile broadened and so did hers.

And Helen started to laugh.

Kurt laughed with her. The two of them sat there on the feather bed and laughed uproariously. Suddenly the whole thing seemed incredibly hilarious and they laughed and laughed. Once they got started laughing, they couldn't stop.

Tears of laughter rolling down her cheeks, Helen clutched her aching stomach and fell weakly over onto her back at the foot of the bed. Eyes squeezed shut, she kicked her bare feet up and down like a child and continued to laugh.

When finally she started to calm and quiet a little, she opened her eyes, turned her head, and looked at Kurt. That brought on a new burst of explosive laughter. His bare shoulders shaking, Kurt leaned back against the tall pillowed headboard and coughed and

wiped the tears from his eyes. He slipped his left foot
out from under the sheet and gave Helen's hip a gentle
kick with his toes.

Giggling and gasping, she grabbed his ankle, forgetting it was the one he had sprained.

"Ooch," Kurt groaned dramatically, still laughing.
"Hey, that's my bad ankle."

"Oh, dear!" Helen released his foot immediately. The
laughter dying in her throat, she was up in a wink, tearing away the sheet and carefully examining his ankle.
"Have I hurt you badly, Kurt? I never meant to—"

"No, I was just teasing you," he quickly interrupted,
wiggling his toes and turning his foot this way, then
that. "See? The ankle's okay."

Helen's troubled gaze lifted to meet his. "You sure?
I'd just die if I thought I had stupidly hurt you."

Kurt looked into her beautiful eyes, saw the genuine
worry clouding them. He felt his heart kick against his
ribs. "Ah, sweetheart," he murmured, and instinctively
held out his arms to her. "Come here."

"I've been so worried about you," Helen said, spontaneously crawling toward him. "So worried and afraid
and I didn't know what to do and I . . . I wasn't sure I
could take care of you properly and . . . and . . . I felt
like you had gotten hurt because of me and I hated—"

"Oh, honey, honey," Kurt murmured softly, putting
his hands under her arms and gently pulling her to him.
He drew her into his close embrace, wrapping his long
arms protectively around her. Pressing her face to his
chest, he laid his cheek atop her head and his voice
was a low, warm caress when he said, "You've been
nothing short of an angel. Nobody could have done
more for me than you have and you'll never know how
much I appreciate it." One dark hand cradled her head
and the other—the one with the two fractured
fingers—moved soothingly, tenderly over her back and
slender shoulders.

Weak from all the giddy laughter, flushed and hot, Helen went limp against him, allowing him to hold her. Relaxing completely, she closed her eyes and sighed softly. Her lips against his bare warm shoulder, she said, "You really are feeling better, aren't you?"

"I never felt so good in my life," he said. Then Kurt sighed as she had sighed and pressed his lips to the silky golden hair which was pleasantly tickling his nose. His arms tightening slightly around her, he told her truthfully, "Earlier this afternoon I was thinking that I'd like to just lie here in this soft feather bed and look out at the white gallery and the jungle greenery and the wide blue bay beyond forever."

He paused, drew a deep slow breath, and considered revealing that his wishful desires had also included having her here in his arms just the way she was now, her soft slim body pressed close to his, her clean hair tickling him, delighting him, dizzying him.

He thought better of it and said simply, "Forever. Just like this."

Liking the feel of his warm chest gently vibrating beneath her cheek as he spoke, wishing just as he did that everything could go on "just like this forever," Helen exhaled slowly. Then she inhaled deeply, savoring the clean, masculine scent that was so uniquely his own, and said, "It is quiet and peaceful here, isn't it?"

The words were barely out of her mouth when the peace and quiet were shattered by the booming shouts of the approaching Jolly Grubbs and the excited squeals of Charlie as he ran to meet his beloved playmate.

Helen sprang away from Kurt as if she'd been cozying up to a red-hot stove. Kurt's arms felt instantly empty. He silently cursed both Jolly and his son, selfishly wishing at that moment that neither of them existed.

In a flash Helen was off the bed and smoothing her

hair and her skirts and at the same time anxiously stretching the rumpled sheet back down over Kurt's legs and feet.

Frowning, she gestured impatiently to the discarded white nightshirt peeking out from under the stacked pillows.

"Hurry! Get your nightshirt on!" she snapped irritably.

"But Helen, it's so hot and—"

"You heard me." She sounded almost frantic and Kurt knew that the sweet, innocent closeness of a moment ago had already become a regretted, guilty episode to her.

Kurt had the nightshirt on and Helen was seated in a chair by the bed with an open book in her lap well before Jolly and Charlie entered the room. The singular sound the pair made clomping down the hall was explained as they entered the doorway.

Charlie, facing Jolly, his short arms wrapped around Jolly's waist, was standing atop Jolly's feet. Jolly was doing all the work, Charlie was getting a free ride, and laughing with delight.

Helen smiled, recalling how she used to ride her Grandpa Burke's big feet the same way.

Nodding and smiling to Helen and Kurt, Jolly crossed the room. To Charlie, he said, "End of the line. All passengers off." Charlie jumped down and Jolly shook his white head and exclaimed, "You're growing like a toadstool!" Charlie nodded and stayed close to Jolly, hanging on his arm, happy to see him.

Helen was glad to see him too. Laying the book aside, she rose, hugged him, and said, "Where have you been? It's been three days since you were here last and we were all worried about you."

"Were you, now?" Jolly grinned, leaning over to shake Kurt's good hand. "Well, that's why I stayed away. Make you appreciate my company a little."

"I 'preciate you, Jolly," Charlie was quick to assure him.

"That's my boy." Jolly smiled, gave Charlie's ear a gentle tug, and said, "Since you 'preciate me, how about running out to the well and getting me a big dipper full of cool water? I'm powerful thirsty."

"Be right back!" Charlie shot from the room.

"Sit down, Jolly," Helen said. "While Charlie's getting the water I'll cut you a big slice of chocolate cake. Fresh baked this afternoon. How does that sound?"

"Sounds great, hon, but hold on a minute." Looking from her to Kurt, he said, "Ya'll remember me talking about the big gumbo-cooking contest they have every year over in Bay Minette, don't you?"

"I remember," Kurt said, nodding. "Sure."

Dear Lord, Helen silently agonized. She'd forgotten all about the gumbo cook-off. When was it? Soon? Right away? Was that why Jolly was here? To see if Kurt would let him take Charlie to Bay Minette for the four day affair? What if Kurt said yes? What if the two of them were left here all alone?

"Gumbo-cooking contest?" she said, the words choking her. "I recall something about it. But as you can see"—she gestured to Kurt—"we won't be going." She held her breath.

"How you really feeling, son?" Jolly asked Kurt. "You okay? Doc Ledet say when you can get up?"

"I could be up now," Kurt told him. "I should be up; I feel guilty about lying here as if I were helpless."

"Helen"—Jolly looked at her—"the doc say when he's coming out? When he means to let Kurt get up?"

"I expect Dr. Ledet either late this evening or tomorrow morning. But he won't be letting Kurt get out of bed just yet." She shook her head for emphasis. "And even if he did, a trip to Bay Minette anytime soon is out of the question."

"For you two it is," Jolly said, and smiled slyly. Ignoring Helen's knitted brow, he turned to Kurt and said, "You do look like you're feeling pretty good."

"As good as new," said Kurt, smiling.

"Mighty fine. I'm really glad to hear that." Jolly moved closer. "Now, before the sprig gets back in here, I want to ask you something."

"Fire away," said Kurt, and Helen gritted her teeth, afraid she knew what Jolly was going to ask.

"I want your permission to take Charlie with me to Bay Minette. I'd watch him real close, you wouldn't need to worry. The gumbo festival is just an excuse to get together. There'll be a whole passel of younguns for him to play with." Jolly paused and laid a weathered hand on Kurt's shoulder. "Son, that little boy needs to be around children his age. It's not right for him to never see anybody but the three of us, even if I am a big ole kid myself." He chuckled.

"I know," said Kurt, nodding, thoughtful. "We'll see about it. When the time comes."

"The time has come," Jolly said flatly. "I leave for Bay Minette the day after tomorrow. The big event begins on Friday. Sleep on it tonight if you must, but I'd really like to take him with me." He looked to Helen. "It would be good for Charlie to go, don't you think, Helen?"

"I suppose it would," she said grudgingly, shooting Jolly a quick daggered look that said she'd like to strangle him.

Jolly wasn't bothered by her obvious displeasure. Chuckling again, he turned back to Kurt. "Say yes now and Charlie and I will do up all the chores before we leave."

Kurt looked from Jolly to Helen. He said, "Helen, it's up to you. If you don't feel that Charlie should go, then I won't let him."

"You're his father," she said noncommittally. Knowing in her heart the trip would be very good for Charlie, that he would love it, and would have a wonderful time, she added, "The decision is yours." Again she held her breath.

"He can go," Kurt told Jolly decisively. "Sure, he can go, and thanks for wanting to take him. That's kind of you, my friend. He'll have the time of his life."

"That he will," Jolly said, beaming. "And so will I."

Charlie grew so excited when he heard the news, he could talk of nothing else. Hanging on to Jolly's chair as Jolly devoured a huge piece of chocolate cake, he chattered like a magpie, asking question after question. Eager for the adventure to begin, he asked why they couldn't leave right then, right that minute.

Jolly took the last bite of chocolate cake, released a loud sigh of satisfaction, complimented Helen on her baking, then told Charlie, "Because we have a lot to do before we leave." He rose, set his empty plate on the night table, pointed a finger at Charlie, and said, "Get some shoes on, scamp, and we'll get started on doing some of the chores."

The little boy followed the elderly man around for the rest of the afternoon. First they checked the cistern. It was full to the brim with soft Alabama rainwater. Then Jolly said they'd best lay in plenty of kindling and firewood and Charlie laughed and said it was too hot for fires. Jolly explained that Helen or even Kurt might want to bathe, so they would need wood for heating cistern water. They filled the woodbox by the cold fireplace and then stacked more logs on the back porch.

They drew pail after pail of fresh well water and carried them into the kitchen so Helen wouldn't have to do it. They milked Bessie—Charlie could actually get a few squirts of milk to come and he thought it a miracle. A funny miracle that made him laugh.

After a late supper and another piece of chocolate cake, Jolly went home. But he was back the next morning and he and Charlie went out to the vegetable garden and picked beans, peas, squash, okra, and tomatoes. Then they dug up onions and potatoes and stored them in the smokehouse. From the orchard they gathered ripe plums and golden pears and wine-red apples.

After that, they went "pecaning." With a long willow pole over his shoulder, Jolly led Charlie to the pecan grove bordering the orchard, where he beat the tall, leafy limbs, causing pecans to rain down to the ground, where Charlie eagerly picked them up.

Together they worked throughout the day, doing all they could think of to help Helen out while they were away. Helen worked too. She did the laundry so that Charlie would have plenty of clean clothes for his trip. That afternoon she ironed the freshly washed clothes, then carefully folded and packed them in the new valise Kurt had bought the day of the fair.

Dr. Ledet showed up in the late afternoon, examined Kurt, and announced that he would allow him to get out of bed starting tomorrow. "Let me get up now," Kurt begged, but the doctor refused. Tomorrow was soon enough, and even then he was to take it easy for a few days. Not overdo. Get lots of rest.

When the sun had set across the bay and the bullfrogs had started their evening clatter, Jolly sat on the broad front gallery, talking of the upcoming trip and peeling one of the apples they had brought from the orchard.

His brown eyes round, Charlie watched, amazed, as Jolly peeled the entire apple without a single break in the fruit's wine-red skin. He cut slices of the apple with his knife, gave one to Charlie, had one himself. After a while he looked over at Helen where she sat rocking silently.

"You're mighty quiet this evening, Helen, gal," he said, grinning like a cherub. "Something troubling you?"

"Not a thing," she said frostily, refusing to look at him.

"Well, I'm sure glad to hear that." He cut another slice of apple. "Kinda seemed to me like you were sitting over there all puffed up and looking like an old wet hen."

Helen ground her teeth. Then she looked at him, forced a smile, and said, "Why, you just couldn't be more wrong. As you're always saying, I'm 'as happy as a pig in mud.' "

Jolly handed Charlie the last apple slice. "Believe it or not, child, that's all I ever want you to be. Happy." He rose from his chair. "Time I get home and get to bed." He looked at Charlie. "I'll be here at sunrise tomorrow. Anybody that's not up and ready to go gets left behind."

"I'll be ready!" Charlie said anxiously, his eyes big. "Don't leave without me!"

"All right," said Jolly, "but you'd best turn in early tonight. We got a long ride ahead of us tomorrow."

Chapter Thirty-eight

Jolly and a very excited Charlie set out early the next morning for Bay Minette, leaving Kurt and Helen alone on the farm. They would be alone for at least four days.

And nights.

Helen dreaded it. Kurt looked forward to it. Helen was afraid of what might happen. Kurt was afraid of what might never happen. Helen was afraid she would weaken and allow him to be her lover. Kurt was afraid she might not weaken and allow him to make love to her.

Throughout that long hot day, Helen did everything possible to avoid Kurt. She was ingenious at thinking of things she had to do and places she had to be. Places where Kurt was not likely to come. Places where he couldn't find her.

Kurt missed her terribly. Since he'd been laid up, he had gotten used to having her in and out of his room all day, every day. He was half sorry that Doc Ledet had told him he could get out of bed.

Lost, lonely, Kurt roamed through the silent house and around the grounds looking for Helen. Yearning to see her smile. To hear her laugh. To have her say his name or touch him. He longed for the days just past when they had been so cozy and comfortable together. He wished those warm wonderful days hadn't ended so abruptly.

Night finally came and with it the *real* agony.
For them both.

Pretending a weariness she didn't actually feel,
Helen said good night and retired to her room shortly
after the sun went down. Carefully closing her bedroom door for the first time since Kurt and Charlie had
moved up to the house, she leaned back against its
solid hardness, wondering if she should search for the
key and lock it.

She immediately shook her head at such utter foolishness. There was no reason to lock her door. Nor
would she need to get down the pistol she had carefully unloaded and hidden in the top of the tall armoire
so Charlie wouldn't get hold of it. At the very beginning, Kurt had said, "I'm a Yankee, Mrs. Courtney, not
an animal. Sleep with a gun if you wish, but you won't
need it to protect yourself. At least not from me."

It was true. She hadn't needed the gun. She wouldn't
need it tonight. Kurt Northway was not some dangerous beast who had been lying in wait for this opportunity to brutally attack her.

Sighing, Helen pushed away from the door. She
wasn't afraid of Kurt. Face it, she was afraid of herself.
She was falling in love with Kurt Northway and because she was falling in love with him, she desired
him. She wanted him physically. Wanted to be in his
arms. Wanted him to make love to her.

Helen crossed the room, lifted the glass globe, lit the
lamp on the night table, and sat down on her bed. She
started unbuttoning the bodice of her faded gray work
dress and couldn't help wondering what it might be
like if it were Kurt's tanned hands that were unbuttoning the dress.

Helen shivered at the thought, sensing that Kurt
would be the consummate lover. When they had
danced on the moonlit gallery that hot night back in
July, he had executed the steps with ease—exuding

grace and confidence. And he had looked straight into her eyes as they danced, making her tingle from head to toe. Any man who was that sensual on the dance floor would surely be excitingly sensual in bed. There was about Kurt an easy self-assurance which intimated sexual maturity. No doubt, she mused, he also possessed the kind of emotional maturity necessary for an ideal romantic relationship.

But then Kurt Northway was not looking for an ideal romantic relationship. Certainly not with her. She would do well to remember—at all times—that this man she couldn't keep from wanting was still very much a Yankee. Born and bred in Maryland, he was eager to go back home.

Helen was no child. She understood fully that if she went to Kurt this very minute and asked him to take her in his arms, he wouldn't hesitate to make love to her. But neither would he hesitate to leave her come harvest time. Leave her without ever looking back.

Helen rose from the bed, blew out the lamp she'd just lit. In the shadows she finished undressing, drew her nightgown over her head, and let it fall slowly down over her bare, warm body. She released her heavy hair from the pins holding it, shook her head about, and got into bed.

She heard Kurt's bedroom door close, heard him cross the room.

Kurt entered the spacious guest room where he had spent the last two and a half weeks. He closed the door behind him, then smiled at the foolish irony of it. The door had not been closed before tonight. There was no need to close it now, yet he had.

Kurt crossed the darkened room. He moved to the open French doors and stood looking out at the bay, its calm waters silvered by the moonlight. He breathed deeply of the sweet magnolia-scented air.

After spending a summer in Spanish Fort, it was

easy to see why these Alabamians loved their state so much. There was a time he had thought no place on earth could compare with his native Maryland. He was wrong.

This land of the Mobile delta, stretching flat and unbroken to the white sands of the Gulf shore, had gotten a firm hold on him. Miles of beaches, dunes, swamps, palmetto, tall pines, and aged, moss-hung oaks created a world of tropical beauty. He would surely miss it.

Kurt exhaled slowly and his jaw tightened.

This lush land was not the only thing that had gotten a firm hold on him. The golden-haired beauty who unquestionably belonged here in this luxuriant lowland Eden had gotten a firm hold on him as well.

Helen Courtney was not simply an extraordinarily lovely young woman, although she was certainly that. She had the most magnificent blue eyes he'd ever seen and her alabaster skin was flawless. Her hair so silky and golden he could hardly keep his hands out of it and he felt sure that underneath her simple cotton work dresses was a soft, slender body of creamy perfection.

Helen was physically beautiful, but she was more, much more. She was intelligent, resourceful, and loyal. She was dependable and as brave as any woman he'd ever known. She was compassionate and understanding. She was nurturing and caring. She possessed all the traits that made a woman admirable and lovable.

She also possessed an innate sensuality which promised passionate lovemaking.

A muscle involuntarily danced in Kurt's tight jaw and he turned away from the silvered tropical splendor spread out below. In the darkened room he paced like a restless jungle cat, too edgy to consider getting any sleep.

He assumed that Helen was slumbering peacefully.

She wasn't.

Helen lay wide awake in the day-bright moonlight.

Tense, fidgety, she found it impossible to forget for a single second that Kurt—now healthy again—was in the very next room. Only a thin wall separated them. And there was no one else for miles around.

She had known from the minute Kurt said Charlie could go to Bay Minette that this was going to happen. That the two of them would be all alone together in this big silent house in the hot sultry night. And that it would be agony for her. It was even worse than she had imagined.

The damp, sticky nightgown clinging to her heated body, her mind awhirl, Helen wondered miserably what had come over her. The only man with whom she had ever made love had been her husband, Will. The two of them had made love with all the awkwardness, eagerness, and passion of youthful lovers.

Once he had gone, she had never once considered making love with anyone else. She had never looked at another man. Had wanted no other. Ever.

Until now.

Now she wanted Kurt Northway so badly it was all she could do to lie there. It was all she could do to stay away from that other room, that other bed, that dark, sensual man in whose strong arms she could once again be a complete woman.

Helen tossed and turned and wondered how Kurt would react if she got up the nerve to take that short, yet oh-so-long walk into his room. And into his arms.

She clutched at the sheeted mattress beneath her, guiltily hoping against hope that he would take the long walk. That he would come to her. That he would take her in his arms and make her forget for a little while there was anyone else in the world but the two of them. Or had ever been.

Helen knew he wouldn't come. She no longer heard him pacing. He was, she was sure, sound asleep.

She was wrong.

In the shadowy room next to hers, Kurt *had* stopped pacing. He had stripped, drew on one of the clean white nightshirts, and climbed into bed. But he wasn't asleep.

He couldn't rest knowing that the bed where he lay sleepless and edgy was dangerously close to the one in which Helen peacefully slumbered. Only a thin wall separated them. She was in the next room in her bed and there was nobody else for miles around.

It would be so simple, so easy to go to her. To kiss her awake and make love to her while she was still drowsy and warm with slumber. Instinct and his knowledge of women told him she might resist initially, but melting surrender would follow.

Kurt abruptly got up out of bed.

His strides long and determined, he stalked over to the open French doors. But he paused there in the portal, indecisive for the first time in his life. Then he heaved a great sigh of frustration, turned, and went back inside.

Hot and miserable, Kurt stripped off the long nightshirt and climbed, naked, back into the bed. Folding his hands behind his dark head, he lay there in the moonlight, his bare tense body covered with a fine sheen of perspiration.

Sweet temptation made his blood run hot. His body throbbed with the overwhelming impact of his desire. Teeth gritted, naked belly achingly tight, Kurt silently cursed himself for allowing Charlie to leave. He should have said no. Should have kept Charlie here so he wouldn't be suffering through this needless torment.

Jesus God, how was he going to make it through the next four days and nights without touching the bewitching beauty with whom he was helplessly, foolishly falling in love?

Chapter Thirty-nine

Morning finally dawned and two tired, jumpy people met in the kitchen and behaved like strangers. Breakfast was a strained affair with neither Helen nor Kurt saying anything. Both were relieved when the meal was finished.

Clearing her throat and rising, Helen said without looking at Kurt, "Dr. Ledet said you shouldn't overdo." She took his empty plate from in front of him. "If you'd like to rest this morning, I won't be disturbing you. I have plenty to do outdoors."

"I'm not tired," he lied. "I thought I might exercise Raider; he must wonder what's happened to me." He smiled stiffly and added, "after that maybe I'll do some hoeing. The weeds must be growing like weeds."

His laughter was forced. Helen didn't even smile. She set the empty plates on the cabinet. "If you're well enough for riding and hoeing, then . . . then perhaps this afternoon you'll feel like . . ." she paused, drew a spine-stiffening breath, held it, and continued, "perhaps it's time you . . . move back down to the quarters."

Kurt pushed back his chair and stood up. "Yes. Certainly. I'll remove my things—and Charlie's—from the guest room this afternoon." He went to the back door, paused, and without looking back, said, "I won't spend another night in the house." And then he was gone.

Helen released her held breath. From the window she watched him move quickly across the backyard, out the gate, and down the footpath to the stable. She continued to stand there, watching, until he led the saddled Raider out of the corral. The big stallion neighed and blew and nudged his master's shoulder affectionately, obviously overjoyed to see Kurt. It was just as obvious that Kurt was glad to see Raider.

Before mounting the big beast, he turned, wrapped an arm around the stallion's head, and pressed his smoothly shaven jaw to Raider's. Kurt whispered in the creature's ear and smiled and patted the sleek, quivering neck.

Raider suddenly shook his great head up and down rapidly, and Helen knew that Kurt had asked the stallion if he was ready to run. She couldn't keep from smiling at the thoroughbred's genuine excitement. She heard Kurt's shout of laughter as he looped the reins over Raider's neck and swung easily up into the saddle.

The stallion shot away from the corral like a streak of summer lightning. Long tail and mane flying, big body moving with incredible speed and grace, Raider raced away. He galloped down the narrow path between the garden and the orchard, heading straight for the freedom of the big northern field.

Smiling foolishly, Helen gazed after them, recalling the morning she had been atop the mighty stallion as he'd raced around the tree-bordered field. She remembered how thrilling it had been, how she had laughed and screamed and clung to the muscular arm wrapped tightly around her.

In seconds, horse and rider disappeared behind the orchard and the tall pines beyond.

Helen turned her attention to the morning chores. Kurt was out of sight. She would put him out of mind as well.

She glanced down curiously when something stirred her long skirts. A mournful Dom silently rubbed against her. Helen sat down on her heels and stroked the lonely feline.

"You missing Charlie already?" she cooed. His response, a soft, plaintive meow, sounded like the cry of a child. "I'm sorry, Dom. I miss him too. But he'll be back in a few days and then . . . then . . ."

Her words trailed off. Continuing to pet the silky-furred Russian Blue, Helen was sobered by the thought that if she and the cat missed Charlie when he'd been gone for only a few hours, what would it be like when he was gone for good? And Charlie's father too.

Swallowing hard, Helen rose, crooned to the forsaken cat, and poured some fresh thick cream into his saucer. She set it before him and waited. Dom looked at her, looked at the saucer of cream, sniffed it, but never dipped a tasting tongue into its creamy richness. He turned and forlornly walked away. Helen quietly followed, curious. Sure enough, Dom went straight to the guest room. He leaped up onto the chaise lounge where he slept each night with Charlie. Low sounds of misery coming from deep inside his throat, Dom curled up in the corner of the long chaise to feel sorry for himself.

"You'll get over it," Helen told the spoiled tom. But the statement was meant for herself as well as for Dom.

The best way to handle an aching heart was to replace it with an aching back, Grandma Burke always said. Hard physical labor. That's exactly what she needed. Helen grabbed up her sunbonnet and gloves and headed for her vegetable garden.

It hot and still. Dead calm. Not a hint of a breeze or a cloud in the sky. The sun shone down with a vengeance on her back and shoulders. In minutes she was damp with perspiration, but she continued to work.

She was laboring under the broiling sun when she looked up to see Kurt dismounting at the edge of her garden. He spoke softly to the big stallion and Raider didn't move a muscle as Kurt started toward her.

Slowly Helen came to her feet.

Kurt was smiling when he reached her.

He said, "Remember the morning Raider took us for a ride?"

After a long pause, Helen said, "Yes. I remember."

Kurt moved closer, so close she could see the pulse beating in his tanned throat.

"Let's do it again," Kurt said. He reached out, curled his lean fingers around the waistband of her worn skirt, and pulled her flush against him. He bent his head until his lips were almost touching hers. "Let's ride and laugh until we're so hot and tired we have to take a swim in the bay to cool off."

His lips hovered just above Helen's for a tension-filled moment. She started to speak—to say no—but Kurt swiftly covered her mouth with his own, smothering any protests. The instant his lips touched hers, Kurt's heart began to pound. His arms went around her and he crushed her to him. His eyes closed and he deepened the kiss, breaking the barrier of her teeth with his tongue.

Caught off guard, Helen's fiery response was instant and involuntary. She clung to Kurt and kissed him back, her heart beating wildly against his. They stood there in the garden, in the sunshine, kissing eagerly, hungrily. But when Kurt's hand moved up from Helen's waist to cup a swelling breast, she tore her burning lips from his.

"No," she breathed against his shoulder. "We can't ... do this ... please ..."

"Sweetheart, sweetheart," he murmured against her temple. "We can. We're alone and I want you and you want—"

"No, I ... I ..." she struggled, pushed him away. "I'm a married woman," she said.

"You are *not* a married woman, Helen," Kurt bit out, his green eyes narrowing, a muscle working his jaw. He grabbed her wrist, drew her back to him, and said, "You're coming with me."

"No! No, I'm not. Let me go!" Helen raised her voice as she clawed at the strong fingers imprisoning her wrist. "You let me go or so help me—"

Ignoring her threats, Kurt dragged her from the garden. He lifted her, struggling and squirming, up onto Raider's back and quickly swung up behind her, enclosing her in his arms.

"What do you think you're doing?" Helen, angry now, shouted into his dark, set face. "Where are you taking me?"

Kurt reined Raider about and the thoroughbred went into swift motion. Seated sideways across the saddle, Helen was immediately slammed back against Kurt's chest. She vainly attempted to lever herself up away from him. But without even glancing at her, Kurt tightened his arm around her, pressed her back in place.

In few short moments the big stallion came to a plunging halt at the far northern border of Helen's property. Kurt dropped to the ground and pulled Helen from Raider's back. His fingers again firmly wrapped around her wrist, he drew her along with him until they stood before three fresh graves marked with a wooden headstone.

Her lips rounded into an O, eyes flashing blue fire, Helen looked at the graves, then at Kurt.

"You see those graves?" he said. "Look at them. Read what the marker says. Read it aloud. Do it."

Helen swallowed hard. She glared at him, then stared at the graves of the Union soldiers. And finally in a shaky voice barely above a whisper, she read the epitaph:

"Yankee soldiers lie here in peace,
Guests of strangers,
Far from home,
They too died for their country"

Tears were already beginning to sting her eyes when Kurt said, "Like these unfortunate souls, your husband is buried in a grave somewhere in an alien field. Will Courtney is dead, Helen. He's dead, has been dead for years. He is never coming back. Say it. Say the words, 'Will is dead. He's dead and he's never coming back.'"

Helen's tears overflowed, spilled down her cheeks. But she shook her head in silent acknowledgment, and looking at the graves, she said, "Will is dead. He's dead and he's never coming back." She took a quick, tortured little breath, slowly raised her head, and looking directly into Kurt's eyes, added, "I am a widow."

Kurt instantly released her wrist. Nodding, he turned and led Raider away, leaving Helen behind. She stayed there alone for another half hour. And when once and for all she had finally said good-bye to the husband she had lost long ago, she dried her red, swollen eyes and returned to her work in the garden.

Helen was still in the garden late that morning when a lone horseman burst out of the tree-bordered lane, drawing her attention. She stood up, raised a hand, and squinted into the blinding sunlight. Kurt, hoeing in the cornfield, saw the rider too. He immediately threw down his hoe and donned his discarded work shirt.

Half worried that something might have happened to Jolly and Charlie, Helen hurried toward the house. Kurt met her there. He stood protectively beside her as the uniformed outrider jerked his lathered steed to a standstill.

"They've hoisted the storm warnings all the way from Pensacola to Pascagoula," the outrider shouted.

"The Lightship off Fort Morgan semaphored that a strong hurricane is just south of Dauphin Island and heading due north toward Mobile Bay."

"Any idea how far out the storm is? When it might come ashore?" Kurt asked.

"Hard to predict what these killer storms might do and when," said the soldier. "But unless it changes course, it will make landfall squarely at the mouth of the bay sometime in the next twelve hours. You'd best batten down the hatches and move quickly to higher ground. Don't wait too long. This storm is dangerous and it could hit by sunset!" The rider hauled back on the reins, jerking the bit tight against his mount's mouth, and wheeled him about in a semicircle. "Pass the word!" the messenger shouted, and galloped away.

Kurt immediately turned to Helen and gripped her slender shoulders. Looking directly into her eyes, he said, "I want you to go inside and throw a few things in a valise. When you're ready, ride Raider inland to higher ground. Go over to Bay Minette. Remain there with Jolly and Charlie until this storm has passed. I'll stay here and see if I can—"

"I'm going nowhere," Helen interrupted, decisively shaking her head. "Everything I have on earth is here in this farm!"

"I know that, Helen"—Kurt tried not to show his exasperation—"but this sounds like a dangerous hurricane. You heard the outrider. They're calling it a killer storm. I want you to be safe. Please take Raider and go."

"I'm not going to leave. I'm staying here to look after my home." She shrugged from his grasp and jerked her thumb in a westward direction. "But you're certainly free to go. It's not your farm, not your fight. Don't feel that you must stay here on my account. Go on."

Incredulous, Kurt said, "Woman, do you actually think I'd leave you here alone?"

"I've been left alone here for years, remember?" Helen smiled then and attempted to sound casual when she said, "I have ridden out tropical storms before. Alone. I can ride this one out alone."

It was the truth. She had weathered some severe storms in the past, but she had been extremely frightened. She was deathly afraid of hurricanes, had been since she was a child. Since an unexpected storm at sea had capsized the riverboat, carrying her young parents and all on board to their deaths. Hers was a deep-seated fear which she couldn't shake, couldn't master no matter how hard she tried. Now the very real prospect of a strong, destructive hurricane coming ashore absolutely terrified her, but she had no intention of letting Kurt know it.

Besides, there were several hurricane warnings posted every year in late summer and early autumn. Nothing much ever came of them other than a little wind and a lot of rain.

"Please go, Helen," Kurt tried again. "I promise I'll do all I can to look after your farm."

"You're not even completely well yet. Dr. Ledet said you're to take it easy."

"I'll take it easy after the storm hits," he said.

"Oh, really? Why, by then you'll—"

"If you insist on staying, let's don't argue," he interrupted. "We're wasting precious time. I'll go to the toolshed for the saw and hammer. There's enough lumber stacked against the smokehouse to board up all the windows of the house."

Helen nodded. "I'll gather more fruits and vegetables from the garden and bring in a ham from the smokehouse. Then I'll start moving the porch furniture inside and after that I'll . . ."

And so it went.

The pair spent the long, humid September day preparing for the coming tempest. Throughout the morning there was blinding sunshine, hot and hazy. But beyond the southern horizon, the sky was an angry-looking black.

And far out to sea a deadly hurricane was growing in diameter. Feeding hungrily on the ocean's summertime warmth, the building storm picked up speed. The seawater it had swallowed up condensed into rain and the thermal energy was quickly converted into awesomely powerful winds.

Those forceful winds were roaring at two hundred knots and the sea was howling like an enraged beast. Giant waves crashed high into the air, the sucked-up water leaving deep canyons in its wake.

Noon came and there hadn't been so much as a sprinkle of rain on Alabama's eastern shore. Kurt and Helen continued to ready the farm for a dangerous storm they hoped would never come. Hammering protective planks over the many windows of the farmhouse, Kurt worked tirelessly, sweating in the steamy heat, never looking up from the task at hand.

Helen worked too, moving quickly in and out of the house, taking care of the dozens of things that had to be completed before the storm came onshore. *If* it came onshore.

As she labored, she kept casting anxious glances at the southern horizon. What she saw looming out there in the distance made her grow increasingly nervous and fearful.

Concealed behind the thick wall of blackness which Helen saw was a howling sea being sucked up into a great seething dome several miles wide. Millions of tons of crashing waves being churned up into a writhing whirlpool, the gigantic maelstrom making its way steadily northward toward Mobile Bay.

By midafternoon the sun had completely disappeared and the first winds came. The storm was still hours away, but peripheral winds blew out of the dark sky in brief erratic bursts. The winds would hit, pass, and there would be total stillness again. Then shortly another quick burst of wind, slamming waves against the shore, ruffling the trees and jungle growth. Then again the eerie quiet, the dead calm, the fearsome night-black sky.

The first of the rains started in the late afternoon. Sporadic at first, huge diamond crystal drops peppered the trembling rosebushes, the branches of tall fragrant pines, and the bare tired back and shoulders of the laboring Kurt Northway.

Kurt paused for a minute, the hammer poised in his hand. He turned his hot face up to the sky. Smiling, he licked at the raindrops wetting his lips and welcomed the cool, fleeting respite from the sultry, oppressive heat.

Helen found nothing to smile about. She dashed up onto the side gallery as the first huge drops began to fall. Her face set, her mouth compressed into a tight line, she turned worried eyes toward the south. Her apprehension escalated with every passing hour. She nervously bit the inside of her bottom lip and wished she had taken Kurt's advice and left. She should have gone inland to where it was safe. Now it was too late.

The storm was imminent.

And too close for her to run.

At sunset there was no sunset. There was no sun to set. Only a sky so inky black it might have been midnight. But by eight P.M., the time when the sun should have been setting, everything had been done. All was ready.

Earlier Kurt had turned all the livestock loose, including his stallion, Raider. Giving Helen one last opportunity to reconsider and ride Raider to safety, he hadn't pressed it when she had again refused. He'd

sent the prized thoroughbred to higher ground, knowing the intelligent Raider would return when the storm
was over.

All the windows in the house had been boarded up.
The kitchen was full of food and fresh water. Low on
coal oil for the lamps, Helen produced dozens of long
white candles. Kurt agreed that they should save the
precious coal oil and burn the candles first.

There was nothing left to do.

Except wait.

The earlier squalls of intermittent rain had stopped.
The winds had calmed. It was very still. And it was
hot. Sticky hot. The tired pair sat on the darkened steps
of the front gallery, their damp clothes clinging to their
overwarm bodies, their nerves raw.

Especially Helen's.

She jumped when the first strong gust of wind hit.
After the initial shock, it felt good. It was cool and refreshing and she enjoyed its strong stroking relief. The
pleasure was short-lived. In seconds a gale-force wind
struck, sending them scrambling inside the safety of
the solid old farmhouse. Kurt bolted the heavy door
behind them.

It was very dark in the house. Kurt lit a half dozen
candles scattered about in the close, airless room.
Shadows danced on the darkened parlor's walls.

The winds stopped abruptly and all was still. Deathly still.

Helen paced anxiously. Trying hard to keep her rising fear firmly under control, she balled her hands into
fists at her sides and gritted her teeth and lectured herself.

Kurt carried a lit candle to the cold fireplace. He set
it down, turned about, and remained there. One long
arm resting on the high mantel, he watched Helen
pace, noting the rigid stiffness of her spine, her jerky
movements. She was badly frightened; he knew she

was. He wished he could reassure her, put her mind at
ease. He started to say something, but decided against
it. The times he had been badly on edge, the last thing
he wanted was to hear somebody tell him to "just relax."

Helen continued to pace, the tension mounting, her
heart drumming double time. The heat inside the still
room had become stifling. Almost unbearable. She felt
as if she could hardly get her breath. She longed to
rush back outside and into the cooling winds. Perspiration dotted her upper lip and hairline. She could feel
the moisture pooling between her breasts and behind
her knees.

Helen glanced at Kurt.

A trickle of sweat slipped slowly down his dark left
cheek. The hollow of his throat glistened wetly in the
flickering candlelight. Helen wiped her damp forehead
on the back of her hand and irritably tugged at her
wilted wrinkled skirts. Kurt pulled at the soaked shirt
sticking to his chest and blotted his shiny face on a
raised forearm.

"It's so hot," Helen finally murmured, pacing furiously. "So devilish hot!"

Kurt nodded understandingly, but said nothing.

For several more minutes Helen continued to prowl
restlessly, on the verge of hysterics, her fragile facade
about to crumble entirely. She stopped abruptly, looked
at Kurt with terrified eyes, and began to tremble un-
controllably.

"I'm frightened," she said truthfully, voice shaking
like her slender body. "God, I'm so scared!"

Chapter Forty

In the blink of an eye she was in his arms.

Kurt held her tightly against his tall, hard body, pressing her face into the curve of his neck and shoulder. Outside, the winds grew stronger and the bay surged higher. Great swells seethed under the powerful gusts of wind rolling across the water. Giant waves broke and crashed against the shore.

"Sweetheart, it's all right," Kurt told her gently, "I've got you. I'll never let you go."

"I'm sorry I'm such a coward," she cried, trembling violently. "I can't help it, I—"

"Helen, you're no coward," he murmured, his hand sweeping comfortingly over her shaking back. "I've never known a braver woman. Running this farm alone all those years. That took a great deal of courage."

"Just hold me tighter," she pleaded, her lips moving against his throat. "I don't want to die, Kurt. Not like this. Not in a storm. I'm so afraid of drowning and—"

"Shhh, baby. You're safe here in my arms," he promised, drawing her closer, holding her more tightly. "We'll be okay. We'll make it, sweetheart."

Her arms wrapped around him, Helen stood against Kurt's unyielding strength and squeezed him so fiercely his cracked ribs hurt, but he didn't let on. He just continued to talk to her in low, level tones, assuring her that the farmhouse was solid as a rock, that it would withstand the storm. They would be safe. Helen listened, more comforted by the sound of his deep familiar voice than by what he said.

Still, she was frightened as she'd never been before in her life. She was terrified that the monstrous power of the hurricane would wash great walls of water over the house. That they would be swept out to sea and this home she loved so dearly would become her coffin.

Her eyes squeezed shut, her heart pounding, Helen continued to tremble as the roaring crash of the storm surf became so deafening it drowned out the comforting words Kurt spoke in her ear.

Kurt knew she could no longer hear him, so he stopped speaking. In silence he held her protectively near, stroked her back, her shoulders, her hair. Helen clung so tightly to him, he could feel the gentle curves of her soft slender body pressed intimately close against him. And soon he too began to tremble.

But not with fear.

His lean fingers clutching her silky golden hair, Kurt gently urged Helen's head back, looked into her eyes, and said, "Helen, sweetheart."

"Y-yes?" she tried to stop the quivering of her lips. Couldn't.

Kurt's green-eyed gaze settled on her soft trembling lips. "Kiss me," he said, his dark head slowly bending to her. "Kiss me just this once."

His lips closed over hers and in an instant her soft trembling mouth answered the eager pressure of his own. Helen's tense, shaking body went limp against him and she kissed him with such surprising feeling, Kurt felt his knees buckle. Meaning to taste the honeyed sweetness of her lips for only a fleeting moment, he instinctively deepened the kiss.

While the roar of the crashing surf competed with the roar of the blood beating in his ears, Kurt softly groaned and pulled Helen even closer, crushing her slender body to his, urging her lips to part more fully beneath his own. Eager, willing, Helen's mouth anxiously opened wider. His teeth clashed with hers, their breaths mixed. Kurt thrust his tongue into the warm wetness of her mouth and shuddered when she met it with her own.

Hotly, hungrily they kissed, straining against each other, unable to get close enough. Pent-up passions too long denied erupted with a force which matched that of the storm. Kissing greedily, anxiously, as if they would never be allowed to kiss again, they gradually sank to their knees there on the parlor floor. Their mouths fused; their legs too weak to support them, they knelt together on the velvet plush rug, clinging to each other, kissing amorously in the flickering candlelight.

Outside the massive, mighty hurricane roared angrily onto shore and was pounding the cliffs just below the house. Great towering walls of wind-driven water surged up out of the boiling bay and lashed the land with deadly, devastating force. Winds strong enough to uproot big trees and completely blow buildings away rattled the boarded windows. Great sheets of torrential rain and hailstones hammered violently at the house's peaked roof, as well as the garden, the orchard, and the fields where the carefully planted crops were ripening.

Helen and Kurt never noticed.

Neither was distracted by the storm's fierce fury. Lost in each other, they kept kissing, each kiss growing longer, hotter, more desperate. Until finally kissing was no longer enough. As the powerful storm intensified and the howling winds escalated and tree branches struck loudly against the house, Helen breathlessly tore her lips from Kurt's. She laid her head on his supporting shoulder, no longer trembling with fear but with passion.

His lips in her hair, Kurt felt the hot sweat of desire run down his chest. His heart pounded violently, every fierce beat sending heated blood surging through his veins. His heaving breath choked off in his throat when Helen's soft hand lifted and she began unceremoniously unbuttoning his shirt. Her flushed cheek resting on his shoulder, she deftly undid the buttons all the way down his sweat-slick torso.

Then her head came up off his shoulder. She pulled back a little and looked at him. Unmistakable desire flashed in the depths of her beautiful blue eyes. Kurt tensed expectantly when she pushed the open shirt apart. He shuddered when she lowered her kiss-swollen lips to the flesh she had bared and boldly kissed his hot, wet chest.

"God ... baby, baby," he murmured, cupping her golden head in his hands, feeling as if his thudding heart would surely explode.

He whispered her name as she scattered kisses over the broad expanse of his chest and Kurt thought he must surely be in a dream. A hot, sweet dream. Here he was, kneeling in a candlelit parlor with this beautiful woman kissing his chest while outside a violent storm threatened to end both their lives. His eyes on the golden head bent to him, he knew that if he were going to die, he'd die a happy man.

When Helen raised her head, Kurt quickly kissed her again, tasting the salt of his own body on her soft dewy mouth. When their lips separated, he held her in place with fingers curled loosely around the back of her neck. His other hand moved directly to the buttons going down the center of her dress. He flipped the top one through its dainty buttonhole, then paused for a second, waiting for her to object.

She didn't.

And so, looking directly into her glowing eyes, Kurt swiftly unbuttoned the bodice down to her waist. As she had done, he pushed the opened dress apart.

The camisole she wore was plain white cotton, no lace, no frills, save for the ribbon tied into a small bow at the center top. Holding her gaze, Kurt tugged at one end of the bow. It came undone. One-handed he unfastened the camisole's tiny hooks, then gently, slowly pushed the open undergarment apart.

His breath became labored and shallow. Helen felt the heat of his eyes on her flesh and her bare breasts swelled under the intense scrutiny. She tensed expectantly when his dark head slowly lowered to her. A soft little whimper escaped her lips when his mouth touched the swell of her left breast directly below her collarbone. She shivered in sweet anticipation as his lips brushed sensuously back and forth. When his mouth opened and he pressed a fiery kiss to her warm tingling flesh, Helen's hands came up to tangle in the thick raven hair of his head.

Exhaling excitedly, she urged his dark face downward over the curve of her breast and at the same time she rose more fully to her knees.

"Kurt ... oh, Kurt," she breathed, eyes closing, as his lips warmly enclosed an erect nipple.

She felt the flick of his tongue against that diamond-hard point of sheer sensation and threw back her head in sweet ecstasy. A tiny sob broke from her throat as he drew her more deeply into his mouth and sucked on the throbbing nipple for a long thrilling moment.

"Helen, sweet Helen," he murmured against her burning flesh, brushed one last adoring caress to the under curve of her breast, lifted his head and kissed her waiting mouth.

In that long searing kiss was all his yearning, all his passion, all his love. It was answered in kind and when their burning lips finally broke apart, they wordlessly began undressing each other. Anxiously they stripped away damp clinging clothes from their hot shiny bodies. In seconds both were as bare as the day they were born.

Naked in the candlelight, they kissed once more,

their hands exploring slippery flesh, their hearts racing
wildly with unleashed passion. Kneeling on the velvet
plush rug in the middle of the parlor they held each
other close, Helen's slender arms twining around
Kurt's neck, playing over his muscular shoulders,
down his smooth clefted back. Her aching breasts flat-
tening against the solid wall of his chest, she felt his
awesome erection throbbing hotly against her bare
belly.

Kurt wished that he could wait a long patient time,
but knew he couldn't. He was so hot for this beautiful
golden-haired woman, he felt he was literally on fire.
Anxiously pressing her closer, he ran his hands freely
over her back, her hips, the twin mounds of her pale
buttocks. He kissed her, praying he wouldn't explode
in a premature climax from simply holding her naked
in his arms.

In danger of doing just that, Kurt put a stiffened arm
out and lowered them to the softness of the plush rug
as they kissed. They stretched out on the floor in the
firelight, facing each other. Kurt felt the trembling of
Helen's bare warm body as her passions swiftly rose to
match his own. His mouth covering hers, his tongue
searched for and found violent answer, a lustful licking, sucking response that made him shudder all the
way down to the soles of his bare brown feet.

There was no time to be the proficient, artful lover
she deserved. He could not control his raw response to
the clinging mouth, the tempting nakedness pressed so
intimately against him. He couldn't wait and slowly
woo her to sweet ecstasy as his heart would have him
do.

His blazing body overruled.

But Helen was just as eager, just as ready as he. The
reaction of her bare sensitive flesh to the hot hard
touch of his was quick, savage, electric. The raging

heat he ignited could be denied no longer. She wanted him, all of him. And she wanted him now.

In their shared hunger they came together after an economy of preliminaries. Helen eagerly stretched out on her back, with her arms, her body, and her soul laid open to Kurt. Looming just above, Kurt lay beside her, his weight supported on an elbow. His hand swept down over her flat stomach and to the triangle of golden curls between her pale thighs. He looked directly into her luminous eyes as his fingers raked through the angel curls, then slipped between to the sensitive slick feminine flesh. He found her burning hot and wet to his touch.

He spent only a few seconds caressing her. He dipped his forefinger into the silky wetness flowing from her and spread it over her burning flesh, readying her to comfortably accept him. Then he stroked and circled that tiny nubbin of ultrasensitive flesh and watched the changing expression on Helen's lovely face.

The shadowy candlelight could not conceal from him the look of exquisite agony that immediately claimed her. Her body surged up to meet his stroking fingers and her eyes fluttered restlessly and closed. Her lips parted and she drew a shallow, ragged breath, then moaned with mounting pleasure. Kurt soon withdrew his hand, urged her legs farther apart, and lithely moved between.

Helen's eyes came open and she looked into his. She felt his throbbing need pressed against the fiery spot where his fingers had touched her. He moved more fully into position and she felt the large swollen tip enter her. Her hands clasping his muscled forearms, her hips tipped upward to meet his first swift, deep thrusting.

Outside the storm raged.

Deadly destructive winds flogged Mobile Bay's eastern shore. Strong squalls of wind-driven rain pummeled the shingled roof and the walls of the house quaked under the hurricane's angry force.

But the writhing golden-haired woman being loved on the plush parlor rug never noticed. She was far too lost in the force of her dark lover's engulfing passion. *He* was the storm. *He* was the power. No longer afraid, Helen was swept into the powerful, pleasurable storm of Kurt's savagely sensual lovemaking.

Their sliding, slippery bodies came together fiercely, as if each had been starved for the other for a long painful time. Theirs was an urgent, primitive coupling. Wildly exciting and wonderful. Helen was buffeted helplessly about by the incredible physical joy Kurt was bringing her. His mouth was marvelous, his body was beautiful, and he knew how to use both to give pleasure. Her passion-glazed eyes caressing his dark handsome face, his powerful shoulders, she pressed her hands against the small of his back, urging him closer, deeper, longing to hold him to her—inside her— forever.

His own desire blazing out of control, Kurt made love to Helen with an untamed fury that matched that of the strong storm raking the shore. Pounding with deep driving strokes, he bent his head and spread fiery kisses over her flushed face and delicate shoulders and swollen breasts. Helen was just as wild, just as unbridled in her awakened ardor. Her pelvis lifted to meet every plunging thrust, every total immersion of his hard male flesh in her. She bucked savagely and ground her hips and gripped him tightly. She raked her nails over his shoulders and back. She licked his throat and nipped at his chest with sharp white teeth.

As the firelight bathed their rocking, reaching bodies, they climbed those last few golden steps toward total paradise.

"Kurt, oh . . . Kurt," Helen breathed, the heat building, spreading, pushing her dangerously close to the top. Her eyes wide, she clutched at his slick biceps and whispered, "I can't stop ... Kurt ... I want—" Her scream could be heard above the storm.

"Yes, sweetheart, yes," Kurt urged hoarsely, loudly, his own apex dangerously close. "Let it go, I've got you. Come with me now. That's it ... come, baby. Come!"

Helen gave herself up to the waves of exploding heat and overpowering pleasure, crying out when the throbbing fever pulsed and pulsed again, growing stronger and stronger still. The beginning of her violent climax brought on Kurt's. He held her to him, pumping furiously into her, ushering her toward total fulfillment. Going with her to that wished-for, other-worldly place found only when two naked joined lovers erupt in a blazing explosion of erotic joy.

Outside the winds roared like a mighty freight train.

Lightning flashed down from the blackened sky, splitting ancient oak trees in half. Thunder cracked and rumbled, shaking the very foundation of the old house. Blinding torrential rains and huge hailstones came with such velocity the sound was like bullets peppering the walls.

Helen and Kurt were not aware such a storm existed.

The fury of their own heated lovestorm was breaking over their heads. They were bursting in a deep, shuddering climax. They clung together as the violence of their shared zenith jolted though them, the buffeting waves of pure carnal pleasure radiating outward from that damp, heated place where their shuddering bodies were joined.

When finally it ended and they began floating back to earth, Kurt fell tiredly over onto the floor and drew Helen to his side.

Panting for breath, he smiled contentedly and

murmured, "Ah, baby, baby, I love you. I love you, Helen."

"And I love you," she gasped, struggling to get her breath back.

Kurt kissed her damp, flushed temple and said, "Jesus, honey, that was good." She nodded, said nothing. He exhaled loudly and asked finally, "You suppose that storm ever hit?"

Sighing happily, Helen snuggled closer, draped her arm over his hard waist. Grinning, she said, "What storm? I didn't hear a thing, did you?"

Chapter Forty-one

The storm was not yet over.

Outside or in.

Both persisted as the midnight hour came and went.

Outdoors, powerful winds and lashing hail and rain threatened to demolish everything in their path. While indoors, the rhythmic thrusting and bucking threatened to shatter the naked pair mating anxiously on the parlor floor.

Shuddering, panting, Helen was seated astride the reclining Kurt, her hands splayed on his sweat-slippery chest. Her unbound hair spilling loosely around her shoulders, she set the pace this time. She controlled the action. She made love to Kurt.

And she loved it.

Propelling her prostrate lover with rhythmic erotic movements meant to please both him and herself, Helen felt very powerful and at the same time helpless. Powerful because she was the dominant one. Helpless because she would do anything this dark lover might desire.

A sensual smile playing on her lips, Helen exercised her female power. She would slowly, skillfully rise up on her knees until Kurt's hot throbbing flesh was drawn nearly all the way out. Then, looking directly into his glowing green eyes, she would slide deliciously back down until he was again buried to the hilt.

A wanton grinding of her hips in a seductive circular

motion, and then slowly, teasingly back up onto her knees.

Kurt let her play, totally enchanted, wanting her to derive all the pleasure possible. He lay submissive with hands folded under his head, watching her.

Carefully controlling his own fierce need, he allowed *her* to make love to *him*. It was exquisite. The intense joy he derived from being up inside her hot tightness was enhanced tenfold by the sight of her undulating above him.

A naked pagan goddess, the radiance of her pale flawless flesh was heightened by the candle's flickering glow. She looked wild and cruelly demanding in her dominant position and it thrilled him beyond belief.

In the candlelight her long tangled hair appeared to be molten liquid gold as she whipped her head savagely about. Her small but perfectly shaped breasts swayed seductively with the movement of her rolling hips, the blush-rose nipples tightened into tempting twin peaks of dark wine-hued sweetness. His eyes fixed on their provocative dance, Kurt gritted his teeth and curbed the strong desire to rise up and capture one with his eager, watering mouth.

The creamy breasts swaying, nipples bobbing, Helen abruptly pushed her long tousled hair up onto her head. The movement of her arms lifted her delicate rib cage upward and stretched taut her flat stomach. Kurt tore his attention from her beautiful breasts to watch the sensual grinding movements of her bare belly and flaring hips. His heated gaze slid lower still, to where their bodies were joined.

Mesmerized, he stared unblinking at the mingling of the damp golden curls between her parted thighs with the raven-black crispness covering his groin. As he watched, Helen lifted slightly, giving him a treasured glimpse of her throbbing feminine sweetness sliding up the rigid slickness of his own pulsing flesh.

Highly erotic!

So exciting he could stand it for only a few seconds. Then Kurt's hands came from under his head and he reached for her. His fingers curling firmly around her upper arms, he drew her forcefully down to him and kissed her hotly. His tongue filling her mouth in rhythm with his plunging thrusts, he took quick, masterful control. When his burning mouth left hers, he captured a diamond-hard nipple and sucked vigorously while Helen moaned with delight.

He quickened the pace of his lovemaking, thrusting more rapidly. Faster and faster he drove, sending Helen spinning off into unbearable pleasure.

Kurt's lips left her breast. He pushed her back up into a sitting position astride and gave her everything he had. Within seconds her deep, wrenching climax began. Kurt smiled dreamily with proud satisfaction as she attained total ecstasy.

Helen screamed so loudly the sound of her joy rose above the storm's deafening din. Her eyes grew round with a mixture of wonder and fear.

Helen *was* frightened.

She reached peak after shocking peak and it was both wonderful and scary. Never before had she experienced such fierce physical joy. The ecstasy continued to escalate until finally it became so good it hurt. So incredible she could no longer stand it. And yet it continued. Tears welled up in her widened eyes and before she knew it, she was crying, very near to erotic hysteria.

Kurt drew her quickly down onto his broad chest and wrapped protective arms around her. Shaking violently, Helen clung to him in desperation, tears of elation spilling from her closed eyes. Only vaguely aware that his hot, hard body still labored to attain his own release, Helen clung to her lover, unable to help or to hinder him. Limply allowing Kurt to do what he would with her, she lay curled closely to him, her knees hugging his sides, hands clasping his upper arms. Even as he pumped and thrust into her, she began to calm, to stop crying.

A sweet serenity claiming her satiated body, Helen was soon rewarded with yet another deeply intimate joy. Since her own frenzied climax had passed, she was more fully aware of when Kurt's began. She was aware of the strong male hands firmly clasping her hips, forcing her pelvis down to meet the powerful surging of his. Aware of his heart hammering rapidly against her naked breasts.

Best of all, when his powerful climax came, she was gloriously aware of him filling her with the hot spurting liquid of love.

"My darling," she murmured when at last he went totally rigid, then limp. Lifting her head to press kisses to his open lips, she murmured, "Don't move, my love. Lie here and rest. Rest, darling. Let's stay just as we are." Helen continued to caress him, over and over again, raining kisses over his lips, his cheeks, his throat, his chest.

When finally Kurt could think and move and speak again, he stroked her slender back, her hips, her bare bottom.

Smiling, he said, "Baby, I couldn't move if you begged me."

"Good," Helen replied, and laid her head on his shoulder.

Listless from the fantastic loving, they sighed and moaned and rested in that position for several long minutes. Draped atop Kurt, her cheek against his shoulder, Helen now heard the storm winds howling outside, the heavy rains beating against the roof. She was aware that the full force of the hurricane had hit the Eastern Shore, that it was likely doing great damage. But for now, it somehow seemed that the storm had nothing to do with her. Snuggling comfortably closer to Kurt, Helen felt pleasantly groggy, yet she was far too excited for sleep. She didn't want to sleep. Not ever. At the very back of her mind was the nagging thought that this stormy night might well be the only one she would ever spend in the arms of this magnificent man. She didn't want to waste a second of it sleeping. Nor did she want her lover to sleep.

"Kurt." she put her lips close to his ear.

"Hmmmm." His eyes were closed; he was drowsy.

"I'm not going to let you go," she told him. "I'm going to stay here and keep you just like this until you want me again."

Completely spent, Kurt was forced to admit, "Sweetheart, I'm afraid you'll have a long wait."

"No," she said confidently. "I won't."

Then slowly, surely, Helen went about seducing the tired naked man beneath her. Clasping his flaccid flesh tightly inside her, she kissed his mouth, his throat, his chest.

And she whispered brazenly, "I want you, darling. I want to feel you moving inside me again." The tip of her tongue traced the interesting convolutions of his right ear while her naked breasts brushed against his face. "You allowed me to make love to you and it was wonderful." She playfully bit his earlobe, blew in his ear. "Now I'll allow you to make love to me and that will be wonderful too."

Helen continued to toy with him, to tempt him by pressing increasingly hotter kisses to his lips and whispering increasingly bolder suggestions in his ear.

Amazingly, within minutes Kurt felt himself swell and surge inside her. Helen slowly sat up, smiling with the same realization. Kurt's green eyes opened and he saw the triumphant look on her lovely face. He reached up and grabbed a handful of her tangled golden hair.

"You're a witch," he told her, "a cruel and beautiful witch wielding some magical power over me."

Keeping him prisoner with her strong gripping thighs, Helen threw back her head and laughed musically. "No," she said, "just a woman. A woman who demands your love."

"Not so." Twisting her heavy hair around his hand, Kurt said, "No mere woman could possibly bewitch me as you have." His hand tightened in her hair. "What must I do with you?"

"Make love to me," was her reply.

"Anything you say, sweet witch."

With incredible swiftness Kurt reversed their positions. Helen gasped and found herself on her back, her knees still hugging his sides. Kurt urged her slender legs up around his back. Then he rose to a kneeling position, sat back on his heels, and spread his knees wide.

Showing no mercy, his mouth was at her nipples, hot and eager, his hands guiding her up and down his rigid length. His penetration deep and getting deeper, he pushed high inside her, opening her, filling her to the fullest.

Her sharp nails scraping his shoulders and arms, her back arched, Helen felt his lips tugging forcefully at her aching nipple and his fierce male power throbbing insistently inside her. Her breath grew rapid and shallow. She threw back her head and closed her eyes, drowning in the torrents of white-hot splendor washing over her.

Roughly Kurt took her, knowing instinctively that's exactly the way she wanted it this time. Forcefully he loved her, thrilling her with his fiery aggression, exhibiting the fierce masculine strength which made him so exciting to her.

Kurt sensed her every need.

And so, giving no quarter, showing no mercy, Kurt held Helen astride his spread thighs and loved her with rugged, ruthless abandon. Helen squirmed and gasped and moaned, struggling against him, pushing on his chest, demanding that he let her go.

Kurt knew she didn't really want him to let her go. What she wanted was for him to set her free. To give her total fulfillment. That's exactly what he did. Holding her tightly, he started swiftly, skillfully pushing her toward complete carnal paradise.

In seconds Helen's release began.

Enraptured, she tingled from head to toe. Her heart fluttered in her breast. She felt herself melting in the burning heat radiating from her excitingly forceful lover. Stars exploded behind her closed eyelids. Spasming violently, she called Kurt's name in the throes of ecstasy.

When she floated back down to earth and could think again, and speak, she said breathlessly, "If I'm a witch, you're a devil."

Kurt laughed heartily. Then he set her back a little and pushed her golden hair off her flushed face. Cupping her cheeks in his hands, he looked into her shining blue eyes and asked worriedly, "Did I hurt you, sweetheart? Was I too rough?"

Helen smiled like the cat who got the cream. "Do I look like I've been hurt?"

"You look beautiful," he said.

"I look happy," she corrected. "I *am* happy." She impulsively threw her arms around his neck and crushed him to her, smothering his face against her throat.

"I love you, my darling," she murmured.

"I love you, Helen," he murmured, his arms closing around her.

They fell silent then, hugging each other tightly. For them both it was a moment which would forever live

in memory. The drumming of their mingled heartbeats,
the scent of their naked entwined bodies, the dying
glow of the candle flame, the rare peace and total contentment.

Too dear to lose.

Too sweet to last.

Chapter Forty-two

The powerful storm mercilessly raked the Gulf Coast, lasting throughout the long night. So did the passionate storm between the two lovers in the candlelit parlor.

At sunrise the mighty hurricane had finally blown itself out and a peaceful stillness and quiet returned to the battered Eastern Shore. An even more peaceful stillness and quiet had overtaken the tired, sated lovers inside the old farmhouse.

All the candles had burned out and sputtered to darkness, save one. The solitary white taper shone from atop the mantel. It no longer flickered and danced. Its tiny flame was stable and its pale illumination cast a soft honeyed light on the couple below.

Kurt lay on his stomach on the plush parlor rug, his face resting on his bent arm. Sleepy, tired, he sighed and groaned while Helen lazily traced with soft, exploring lips the slashing scar a razor-sharp saber had left across his lower back.

"I have wanted to do this," Helen whispered in the silence, "since the first time I saw this scar." She slowly slid her lips and tongue along the white satiny ribbon. "And I always wondered ... since it disappeared into the waistband of your trousers ... just where it led. And just where it stopped."

"Now you know," Kurt mumbled, stirring slightly under the teasing, taunting touch of her lips.

"Mmmm," she murmured, and kissed her way to the scar's termination, which was centered squarely between the cleft in his lean buttocks. When her lips met that concluding point but continued to move lower, Kurt's firm buttocks flexed, he quivered involuntarily, and he turned swiftly over.

"No, you don't," he warned. "It's my turn, baby. Let me enjoy what I've dreamed of doing since the first day I saw you standing in the field that morning in May."

Helen smiled at him. "What could you possibly have wanted to do to me that morning?"

"Just this," Kurt said, and stretched out fully on his back.

She too was instructed to lie down on her back, at right angles to him so that their bodies formed a T. Her head resting squarely on his stomach, her face was turned up toward the ceiling. Very slowly, very carefully Kurt spread her long golden hair out on his chest and belly and groin.

He laid back then with his head propped in his folded arms, enjoying the stunning sight and the tickling feel of her heavy hair swept out over his naked body like a giant golden fan.

"Kurt . . ." Helen began.

"Shhh," he warned. "Lie still, love."

Helen lay still.

In seconds both were asleep. Totally exhausted from the long night of loving, they fell quickly into a dreamless slumber. They slept the long hot day away together on the parlor floor.

When they awakened, it was late afternoon. They turned to each other, kissed, and wordlessly made love again. Kurt showed Helen just how tender, how gentle he could be, treating her as if she were some fragile treasure. A beautiful flesh-and-blood gem of priceless quality which he was allowed to possess. He paid homage to her with infinite patience and sincere adoration which was akin to reverence.

Purposely he prolonged the bliss, knowing that when it was over, reality would have to be faced. More than an hour went by from the time they awakened until the last little shudders of their loving had passed.

Dressing quickly then, they first checked on the Russian Blue. Feeling guilty for ignoring Dom for so long, Helen found the cat curled up on the blue velvet chaise where he had ridden out the storm. Cuddling him close, she apologized for her neglect.

She fed the hungry cat. Then she and Kurt ate a quick meal, ravenous after their night of highly physical lovemaking.

Finally Kurt said, "Sweetheart, stay here. I'll go out and have a look around, assess the storm's damage."

"I'm coming with you."

A heartbreaking sight awaited them.

Helen couldn't believe her eyes. Everywhere she looked was total destruction. All the outbuildings gone! Not so much as a single wall left standing or a plank of the corral fence in place.

Hand in hand, Helen and Kurt cautiously crossed the debris-covered backyard. Grandpa Burke's white settee was gone, as was Charlie's swing. But Helen was grateful the big oak tree had survived. Stripped clean of leaves, many of its limbs broken, it still stood.

Impulsively, Helen broke away from Kurt, went over and touched the tree's rough bark as if it were an old, dear friend whom she was delighted to see.

Bracing herself for what they might yet find, Helen squared her slender shoulders, again took Kurt's hand, and together they made a walking tour of the storm-punished farm. Helen could barely hold back her tears when she saw the destruction of all the farm's crops.

Gone.

All was gone.

What the demonic downpour and raging winds hadn't destroyed, the hail had.

Helen stood at the edge of the southern cornfield, staring sickly, shaking her head and biting her lip. The devastation was total.

There was nothing left. Nothing. All their hard back-breaking work had been wiped out in one single night. All those hours of plowing and planting and cultivating and hoeing under a broiling summer sun. After all that effort and struggle, there was to be no harvest this year. No ripe crops to take to market.

No money to save the farm.

Standing quietly at her side, Kurt saw the look on Helen's face and his heart ached for her. He knew what was going through her mind.

He moved closer, wrapped a long arm around Helen's narrow waist, and drew her to his side. "I'm sorry, sweetheart, so sorry." He kissed her temple. "We'll figure out something, some way to . . ." He sighed, shrugged, and said, "Everything will be all right."

Smiling bravely, Helen nodded. "I know it will."

But how? she asked herself, her worried blue eyes lingering on the desolation before her. Splintered wood and rubble littered every square inch of the farm. Up-rooted oaks, pines, and smaller trees lay on the ground. Not a single shrub or flower bush had survived.

Standing amid the ruin, both Helen and Kurt were already considering—separately—what could be done. What had to be done. It was then that both began to si-lently entertain a plan. A strategy to be kept from the other. A course of action that had to be taken as soon as possible.

In stunned silence they walked back toward the house. In the storm-ravaged front yard, Helen abruptly broke away from Kurt. She picked her way through the strewn rubble to the very edge of the cliff. She stopped, looked down, and the faintest of smiles touched her lips.

The new wooden stairway had miraculously withstood the storm!

"Kurt, come here," she called to him. He was at her side in a second. "Look," she said, marveling, "the steps are still there. Every single one!"

"Why, sure they are, honey," Kurt said evenly, although he was really as surprised as she. "I built them to last. Just like your grandfather built the house to last."

"I'm grateful for that," said Helen, smiling.

"Sweetheart, there's a lot to be grateful for," Kurt said thoughtfully. "Jolly and Charlie are safe and on high ground. You and I came through the storm untouched and the house still stands."

Helen turned to face him. Wearily she leaned her forehead against his chest. Placing her hands on his upper arms, she said, "I am grateful. Most of all I'm grateful you're here with me." She lifted her head to look up at him.

Kurt drew her closer. "Know what I'm most grateful for?"

"Tell me."

"For this sweet precious time you belong solely to me. No one can reach the farm for a while."

"No. No, they can't. All roads are surely flooded," Helen said. "It will take at least a couple of days for the high water to recede enough for anyone to come. Or for us to leave."

"No one can get here. No one can intrude." Kurt added, "We're alone. All alone."

Helen slid her arms up around his neck. "I hadn't thought about that." She tried to smile, but her blue eyes were filled with sorrow.

Softly, Kurt said, "Don't be so sad, my love. For the next couple of days, let's try and forget what the storm has done." He gently drew her closer, held her in his protective embrace. "We may never again be alone like this. Let's make the most of it."

He kissed her.

For the next forty-eight hours the pair did their best to shut out the harsh reality of the disaster. They were not entirely successful. Everywhere they looked were heartbreaking reminders of the near-total devastation.

But when they were in each other's arms the world with its worries faded away. Troubles were forgotten. The storm had never happened. There was only the two of them and the total bliss that comes from sweet love-making.

Forty-eight hours after the hurricane had come ashore, Raider showed up.

Late in the afternoon the big sorrel trotted out of the tree-bordered lane as the sun began to set, nickering and neighing loudly.

Kurt and Helen, rocking quietly on the front gallery, heard a noise, looked up, and saw the sleek thorough-bred heading determinedly toward the house.

"Raider." Kurt's tone was low, level, but his dark green eyes shone with relief.

"Yes! You were right," Helen said, leaping out of her rocker, "he's come home!"

It was a demonstrative reunion between horse and man. Smiling, watching the two, Helen realized anew just how much the sorrel thoroughbred meant to Kurt. He dearly loved the big stallion who'd been with him for so long. And he made no attempt to hide that affection.

Neither did Raider. While Kurt patted and hugged and spoke warmly to the horse, Raider nuzzled and whinnied and playfully nipped him.

Kurt explained to Raider, as if he were speaking to

a person, that the corral had been blown away in the hurricane.

"But that's all right, old friend"—Kurt stroked Raider's face—"we stored some oats and corn inside the house before the storm hit. You won't go hungry. Come with us." Kurt turned and reached for Helen's hand.

Raider followed Kurt and Helen up to the back porch, where they fed and watered him. While he feasted, they sat on the porch steps in the fading sunlight.

Thoughtfully, Kurt said to Helen, "The floodwaters are receding. The road will open soon. Charlie and Jolly will be coming back." He paused, looked at her, and added, "They could be back by tomorrow."

Nodding, Helen said, "Yes, I look for them. I know Jolly Grubbs. He'd never say anything to Charlie, but he's worried about us. He'll get here as soon as he can."

"I guess we'd better be watching for them," Kurt said.

"Yes, we'd better," Helen agreed. Her face flushed and she said, "No more going about naked or making love in the middle of the day." She hugged Kurt's arm.

"Damn," he said with a frown. "I like seeing you float about naked, looking like a naughty wood nymph. I'm going to miss our freedom."

"Mmmm, me too," Helen said, her smile fading.

A mischievous twinkle appeared in Kurt's green eyes and he said, "But it hasn't ended yet, has it?"

"No. We're perfectly safe until at least tomorrow afternoon." Helen smiled again, knowing what he was thinking.

Kurt looked into her eyes, captivated by her beauty and allure. "Why, then," he asked, lifting a hand to touch her hair, "don't you make me a happy man while there's still time?"

Charmed by his disarming smile, Helen said, "Gladly, my love. What would you have me do?"

"Undress, sweetheart. Here. Now."

Helen promptly released his arm, shot to her feet, and stripped off all her clothes while Kurt sat on the steps below, watching, enjoying. When she was naked, she unpinned her hair and let it spill down around her shoulders.

"Happy now?" she asked.

The fiery setting sun was kissing her pale golden hair and long smooth legs. She was any red-blooded man's dream of perfection. She was beautiful, she was sensual, she was uninhibited. And she was his.

At least for one more night.

Kurt allowed his gaze to take a slow, leisurely tour of the exquisite naked woman standing before him.

"I may never let you dress again," he said with quiet authority. "Just keep you as you are now and feast my eyes to my heart's content."

"What about me?" she said. "Gazing at your manly physique sans clothes is something I thoroughly enjoy."

Kurt came to his feet, began unbuttoning his shirt. In seconds he too was naked, his clothes lying discarded on the porch. He stood outlined against the blood-red sky, tall, dark, commanding.

"Examine me all you will," he said, grinning. "And since your behavior has been exemplary, you may even touch me—if you so desire."

Her gaze sweeping the length of his lean tanned body, Helen said approvingly, "My beautiful brown satyr. Come here."

Kurt moved toward her. He reached her, lifted his hands, and gently clasped her bare shoulders. "We have until noon tomorrow," he said. "Anything in particular you'd like to do before then?" His lids lowered over his eyes and a muscle danced in his jaw.

Helen surprised him when she asked, "Do you suppose Raider is terribly tired?"

Kurt's dark brows lifted in puzzlement. He glanced at the stallion, contentedly eating oats from a bucket on the bottom porch step.

"He's neither lathered or winded," Kurt said. "No. No, I don't think he's particularly tired. Why?"

"Remember the morning last spring when you took me for a wild ride on Raider?"

"I'll never forget."

"Could you take me for a ride on him again?" She lifted a hand to Kurt's chest, raked her fingers through the crisp dark hair. "Right now. Before the sun is gone?"

Kurt tilted his head to one side. "I thought you were going to stay naked until—"

"I am," she interrupted, smiling wickedly.

Without another word Kurt yanked his discarded shirt off the porch and whirled it up over Raider's back. Lithely he swung up astride the big beast and inclined his dark head for Helen to come to him. She hurried down the steps and squealed with delight when Kurt leaned down and easily plucked her from the ground. He sat her across the horse before him, enclosing her in his arms. He wrapped a portion of Raider's long mane around his hand, gave a gentle tug, and the responsive thoroughbred left his oats, turned in a semicircle, and took the two naked lovers on a wild romp in the dying sun.

Kurt purposely urged the stallion to run as fast as he could. Raider raced around the big northern field so swiftly the ground flashed dizzily by—making it nearly impossible to see the destruction and ruin left by the storm.

After the exhilarating ride, the lovers bathed, ate a late supper, and again sat out on the front gallery. This time without their clothes. In Helen's favorite armless

rocker, they made love while a billion stars came out
in the heavens.

Seated in the rocker with Helen draped astride, Kurt
rocked them to and fro, controlling the motion of the
rocker as well as the motion of their bodies. Murmuring endearments, making shocking proposals, whispering graphic words of love and lust, they made the most
of the total privacy they would soon lose.

A privacy that would end sooner than expected.

So soon they very nearly got caught in a most com-
promising position.

Chapter Forty-three

They stayed awake until the wee small hours, reluctant to see this final night of sweet seclusion come to an end. It was well past three in the morning before the pair finally fell into exhausted slumber in the guest room's rumpled four-poster.

There they lay, their naked bodies entwined in peaceful sleep, when a wagon emerged from the tree-bordered lane at shortly after ten A.M. Helen remained dead to the world as the wagon rumbled up the narrow road, but Kurt came awake with a start.

His dark head shot up off the pillow; he listened keenly and heard the wheels bumping over the road.

"Wake up!" He shook Helen. "Helen, wake up! Somebody's coming!"

"Dear God, no!" she choked, horrified, her eyes round. She quickly leaped off the bed and began frantically looking about for her clothes. "Where are my—"

Kurt had snatched a clean pair of trousers from the tall armoire and was hunching into them. "You have no clothes in here. Remember, we shed our things last night on the back porch." He buttoned his pants. "Jesus, we left them out there! I'd better go get them."

Her face a study in shame and misery, Helen shoved her hair behind her ears and dashed across the room after Kurt. In the hall he turned and paused for only a second.

"I'll gather the clothes from the back porch and hide them. I'll try and stall whoever is here while you get dressed."

"Oh, Lord, I'll just die if—"

"Don't worry!" he shouted as he raced down the long hall to the back door.

Fully dressed and looking totally at ease, Kurt was outside waiting to meet the approaching wagon.

"Daddy! Daddy!" Charlie called excitedly, his short arms outstretched well before the wagon reached the house. "It's me, Daddy! I'm home!"

"Charlie!" Kurt shouted, and his dark face broke into a wide grin. Walking fast, he hurried out to meet his son and Jolly Grubbs. "Am I glad to see you two," he said, nodding to Jolly and plucking Charlie from the high seat as soon as the wagon creaked to a stop.

Charlie wrapped his arms tightly around his father's neck, his legs around Kurt's ribs. "Daddy, I was afraid you blowed away!" he said, squeezing with all his might.

Kurt hugged him close, one hand patting Charlie's tiny behind. "I'm sorry you worried. I'm fine and so are Helen and Dom."

"Y'all made it all right, then?" Jolly said, his eyes on the house as he climbed down. He shook the hand Kurt extended.

"We did. We're fine."

"Thank merciful God for that. From what we saw coming down, I expect it got most of the crops."

"All of them." Kurt lowered Charlie to his feet, but kept an affectionate hand on him. "Nothing's left."

Jolly sighed wearily. "It's a cryin' shame is what it is. A cryin' shame."

"Spanish Fort?" Kurt inquired. "Much damage there?"

"Not a bit." Jolly looked toward the house. "Where's Helen gal? Now, she's not hurt and you're keeping it from me, are you?"

"No, no," Kurt quickly assured him. "Not a scratch. Either of us. She'll be along any minute."

The sentence was no sooner finished than Helen came flying out the back door, smiling and calling their names. The minute Charlie saw her, he raced to meet her.

They met at the spot where the back gate had been before the winds blew everything away. Laughing, delighted to see him, Helen went down on her knees and flung her arms open wide. Charlie flew straight into them. He put his own short arms around her neck and hugged her so tightly Helen felt a squeezing in her heart.

"Charlie, oh, Charlie," she crooned, "I'm so glad to see you, I've missed you so much!"

"Me too," he said. "I was scared the wind blowed you away and I'd never see you again. I love you, Helen."

Helen swallowed hard. "And I love you, darling."

She hugged him more tightly, but Charlie fidgeted, clearly ready to be released.

"I have to find Dom," he explained, and Helen let him go. He looked worriedly at her and said, "Will he remember me?"

Laughing, Helen rose to her feet, ruffled his blond hair, and told him, "Certainly. You're Dom's best friend. He missed you almost as much as your father and I."

Charlie grinned, then dashed away shouting, "Dom, I'm home! Dom, you come here to me!"

Dom came. A streak of blue fur, the cat raced to meet Charlie as Helen gave Jolly a hug. Charlie fell to his knees and Dom rose up on his hind legs. Charlie lovingly squeezed the cat. Dom, his sharp claws carefully retracted, laid his paws on Charlie's chest and affectionately butted his head against Charlie's chin.

Then, squealing happily, Charlie shot to his feet and the pair disappeared around the house.

Helen anxiously inquired about the safety of friends and neighbors. Jolly assured her that everybody was all right. He said he and Charlie had talked with folks when they came through town that morning. The only real concern was for her and others who lived down along the shore.

As they stood in the sun talking, Charlie, with Dom sprinting ahead of him, came flying back to them.

Excitedly, he shouted, "Daddy, they didn't blow away! The steps to the water! They're there, they're there!"

"Well, I'll be switched," said Jolly.

They all laughed and started to go inside, but another wagon turned out of the lane. Helen couldn't hide her surprise when Jake Autry climbed down. Food and supplies were piled high on the wagon bed.

The owner of Jake's General Store said simply, "I figured folks out this way might need a little help." He climbed down, smiling. "We were blessed; the storm didn't hit Spanish Fort."

"Why, Jake,"—Helen was gracious—"how thoughtful of you. We're very grateful for your kindness."

Looking sheepish, Jake turned to Kurt, put out his hand. "Captain Northway, I don't mind admitting that I'm ashamed of the way I've acted. Treatin' you so bad and all. I don't have nothing against you personally."

"I know you don't, Jake." Kurt shook his hand.

"I was real sorry about you gettin' beat up in town that day. I think lots of other folks was too."

Kurt smiled. "Don't worry about it. I'm fine."

"Well, anyway, I just want you to know from now on you're welcome in my store anytime."

Jake was leaving when Sheriff Cooper and Em Ellicott arrived. Relieved to find Helen and Kurt unhurt, Coop and Em were both wearing work clothes, ready to pitch in and help put the place back in order.

They had been there less than half an hour when a long wagon piled high with new lumber pulled up to the house. A half dozen men with axes, rakes, hammers, and saws rode atop the stacked lumber. Helen recognized them all. They were men she had known all her life. Most were war veterans. Their presence stated clearly what they couldn't bring themselves to say. They were ready to put the war—and their animosity toward her for having a Yankee captain on her farm—behind them.

Helen was speechless when at exactly twelve noon the ladies of the sewing bee showed up en masse. Em was at Helen's side as the chattering ladies approached. Her hands on her hips, a gleam of warning in her eyes, Em silently dared any of them to make one false move.

The banker's wife, pink-faced Hattie Price, was the first to alight. The middle-aged widow of Colonel Tyson B. Riddle, Mary Lou, was right behind Hattie. Rose Lacey. Betsy Reed. Kitty Fay Pepper and her mother. All the sewing bee ladies were there. Except Yasmine Parnell.

They carried straw hampers filled with sliced roast beef, cole slaw, string beans, fresh-baked bread, and several kinds of dessert.

Mary Lou Riddle elbowed Hattie Price out of the way, stepped up to Helen, and said, "Child, it's no secret that we've disapproved of you having that Yankee here, but—"

"Mary Lou, will you let me say it, please?" Hattie Price took over. To Helen she said, "We never said anything bad about you. We were just all very concerned about your safety."

"That's not quite true." The young bride, Kitty Fay Pepper, stepped forward. Smiling, she said, "Helen, your ears must have burned all summer long. The whole town has talked of nothing else and we—all of us—" she looked around at the other ladies, "have gossiped mercilessly about you."

"Really?" Helen smiled and placed a restraining hand on Em's arm. "I'm not surprised."

"Of course you're not," Kitty Fay said. "But maybe you'll be surprised to hear that we're ashamed of ourselves." Kitty Fay again looked about. "Aren't we, ladies?"

"We are," they murmured in unison.

Em spoke for the first time. "Well, you ought to be! You owe Helen an apology."

"We apologize." Again in unison.

"Accepted," said Helen.

Everyone laughed with relief then and Helen asked, "But where's Yasmine Parnell? Isn't she one of your regulars at the sewing bee?"

"You haven't heard?" said Mary Lou Riddle, eyebrows lifted.

"Now, Mary Lou," scolded Hattie Price, "we will do no more gossiping." She laughed and added, "At least not for the rest of the day!"

And then there was a great flurry of activity as the sewing bee ladies fed the working men the picnic lunch they had brought. They spread the noon meal on the broad front gallery and everyone ate, including the ladies. They sat in the chairs, along the railing, and on the front steps.

Helen, across the porch from Kurt, noticed how the ladies were quick to offer him more roast beef, another helping of cole slaw, and always with a smile.

It was then, surrounded by old friends and with the Alabama sun warm on her face, that the profundity of her loss hit Helen. Suddenly she wanted to weep and scream and rail at the cruel fates for taking everything away from her. Heartsick, she continued to smile graciously and make small talk.

The men went back to work as soon as they finished and by two-thirty the sewing bee ladies were departing, making Helen promise to call on them if there was anything she needed. The dust had hardly settled behind their departing carriages when yet another conveyance appeared.

The Livingston sisters arrived in an antique coach which had been garaged in the old carriage house behind their home for years. Atop the box, dressed in threadbare livery, was the white-haired old black retainer who had once been the Livingston family driver.

Neither coach nor driver had been out on the road for a decade.

The tiny twittering sisters embraced Helen and told her how very relieved they were to see that she hadn't been lost or hurt in the storm.

Caroline, the older of the two, said, "Helen, Sister and I know you need help now and that's what we're here for."

"We were so worried about you, dear," said Celeste, the younger sister. Her face colored as she added, "We acted so mean that day last spring when we saw you in Spanish Fort."

"We did, and Papa would just roll over in his grave if he knew about it," put in Caroline. "Can you ever forgive us?"

"Of course," said Helen. "I forgive you."

"Thank you, child," said Celeste. "We want to make amends. We're going to help you."

Helen smiled at the withered pair, wondering what they thought they could possibly do to help. "Your unexpected and very welcome visit is help enough."

The little ladies started smiling then as if they had a secret too good to keep. Caroline made a big show of pulling open the drawstrings of her reticule. She dipped her gloved hand inside and brought out a lace-edged handkerchief in which something was wrapped.

Carefully she peeled away the folds of the handkerchief until finally the two shiny twenty-dollar gold pieces were revealed.

"Take it," Caroline said, "take the gold and fix up your place."

"Buy whatever you need," said Celeste.

"Oh, my dears," said Helen, deeply touched, "I could never take your money, but you will never know what your generous offer means to me."

The sisters tried to persuade her, but Helen continued to gracefully refuse. They left with their gold still in Caroline's reticule, relieved that Helen had turned it down, but feeling very good about themselves for offering their entire fortune.

Helen felt good about them as well.

The shadows lengthened and the tired townsmen went home.

"Helen, is there anything—anything at all—I can do for you?" Em asked her best friend after everyone had gone.

"Yes," Helen said. "Yes, there is. Go to Niles Loveless's office either this afternoon or in the morning. Niles—and you—must keep this in strict confidence. Tell him I will sell him my farm and timberlands."

"No!" Em protested. "Helen, you can't do that."

"Tell Niles I will be there tomorrow afternoon with the deed," Helen went on as if Em hadn't spoken. "Come out here—alone—and take me into town."

"Helen, please . . . please think it over for a—"

"I've thought it over. If you're my friend you'll do what I ask. And Em, don't you dare tell Coop!"

"I won't tell anyone, but I do wish . . ."

While the two young women argued, Coop and Kurt walked tiredly up toward the house. Jolly and Charlie followed several yards behind.

"Coop," Kurt said levelly, "do me a favor. Tell Niles

Loveless I'm ready to sell Raider to him now. Tell him to have the last figure he offered waiting. In cash. Gold. I'll be in his office tomorrow afternoon and turn Raider over to him."

"You sure you want to do that, Captain?"

"I'm sure. And, Coop," Kurt said, "not a word to Em."

Chapter Forty-four

At half-past ten the next morning, Niles Loveless sat down behind his massive mahogany desk in his office on Spanish Fort's Main Street.

Niles Loveless was in a morose mood. He was not a happy man. But his despondency had nothing to do with the destructive hurricane which had raked the Eastern Shore. The storm had done no damage to Niles's palatial palace or to the acres of manicured grounds surrounding the huge white mansion. His countless stables of blooded thoroughbreds had come through unscathed. His vast estate had not suffered so much as a broken windowpane or a felled live oak.

In Niles Loveless's considered opinion, that was just as it should be. He was a rich aristocratic country gentleman and shouldn't be bothered with the annoying little problems and setbacks that plagued lesser men. He took it as his due and always had. Never in his life had he been called on to tolerate the troubles and disappointments others regularly endured.

Until now.

Niles Loveless uttered an oath and slammed his fist down on his mahogany desk.

He couldn't believe it. It could not be true!

Niles leaned forward and put his head in his hands and groaned. He felt like he was going to cry. His world was crashing down around his ears and nobody

seemed to give a tinker's damn. The last twenty-four
hours had been a living nightmare.

It had all begun when, out of the blue, his pampered
wife Patsy had awakened yesterday morning, turned to
him in their enormous bed, and coolly told him she
was having the servants move all his things down the
hall to one of the guest rooms. She said she had continued to share his bed these past few years because
she wanted a larger family. But now that she was getting older, she'd decided two children were quite
enough. And that since he was getting older as well,
perhaps one woman would be enough for him. She
said that for years she suspected he was sleeping with
Yasmine Parnell, but didn't want to admit it. Now she
no longer cared. In fact, she insisted he expend all his
sexual energy on Yasmine and *never* touch her again.

No amount of denying or cajoling or pleading could
change Patsy's mind. He would, she blithely told him,
stay married to her for as long as it suited her. If it
didn't suit him, well, that was too bad. It was actually
her mansion, her land, her blooded racehorses, her
money. He wouldn't, she promised, get one penny of
the McClelland fortune if he ever left her.

Stunned, hurt, Niles had ridden into Spanish Fort
consoling himself with the knowledge that at least his
mistress loved and desired him even if his wife did not.
He could hardly wait to pour out his heart to his beloved.

He had not seen his beautiful Yasmine for nearly
three weeks and he needed her badly. She had gone
down to Point Clear for a long holiday, had fled the
coastal resort only days ahead of the hurricane. There
had been no opportunity for them to meet since her return. Finally she had sent word that she would come to
his office that afternoon.

He had waited all day for her to show up.

At last, at four o'clock, she had breezed in, looking

lovelier than he'd ever seen her. He had eagerly tried to take her in his arms, but Yasmine had stopped him.

Sounding just as cool as Patsy, she said, "Niles, darling, you've meant so much to me. And for that reason, I felt I had to come here to explain it to you in person."

"Explain what?" he had felt his heart drop.

"You mean you haven't heard?" Yasmine pursed her red lips. "Darling Niles, I naturally supposed that someone had told you. No? Well, the fact is I met the finest gentleman at Point Clear. He's a wealthy Philadelphia banker and he's simply mad about me. Oh, I know what you're thinking, that I've found myself another rich old man to marry, but that isn't the case this time." Yasmine giggled then and happily exclaimed, "He's seven years younger than I. He's tall, muscular, extremely good-looking, and his prowess as a lover . . . well, nothing compares with youth, now, does it? Anyway, dearest, this absolutely gorgeous young man has convinced me to become his bride!"

"His what?"

"We marry tomorrow in New Orleans. Then it's off to Europe for a six-month honeymoon. Say you're happy for me, darling!"

Say you're happy for me, darling!

That sentence now repeated itself in Niles's head, a litany that was driving him crazy. He again beat on his desk with his fists. That bitch! That shallow, two-timing, ungrateful tart!

All those years he had devoted to Yasmine, putting her happiness before his own. Then she up and says she's marrying a young boy and that, no, she can't allow him—after having ruined his marriage—to make love to her ever again! The high-handed refusal had been her departing statement.

"Dammit to hell!" Niles Loveless said aloud now, frustrated, miserable as he'd never been in his life.

In agony he leaned back in his chair, closed his eyes,

opened them, and glanced listlessly out the front office windows. He immediately straightened and stared, his eyes wide with hope. A well-dressed, dark-haired woman was coming across the street toward his office. Could it be? Had Yasmine come to her senses?

Niles sighed with disappointment when he recognized Em Ellicott. Em came into Niles's office wearing a frown that matched his own. Niles didn't bother to rise.

"What do you want, Miss Ellicott? I'm a busy man."

"I've a message for you, Niles." Em glared at him. "Helen Courtney is willing to sell you her farm."

Niles pushed back his chair and jumped to his feet. "There is a God!" he said, flinging his arms heavenward, his handsome face quickly transformed. "Hallelujah!" He clapped his hands like an excited child. "When? When do I get my property?"

"Helen will be at your office around three this afternoon with the deed. And Niles, she wants this kept confidential." Em's tone was as cold as her eyes and she quickly turned away.

"I'll be waiting!" said Niles. "And thank you so much— "

But Em had already gone.

Excited, feeling like his old self again, Niles rubbed his hands together in anticipation and paced eagerly back and forth. To hell with Yasmine Parnell! Who needed her? He was about to become the undisputed largest single landowner in all Alabama! He'd find himself a new, prettier, younger mistress. And as for Patsy, well, he'd been tired of her for years.

Niles was still pacing and planning a half hour later when Sheriff Cooper stepped into the door of his office.

Smiling sunnily at the tall lawman, Niles said, "Come in, Coop! Come in! What can I do for you this fine September morning? A bourbon? A Cuban cigar?"

Coop shook his red head. Thumbs hooked into gun belt, booted feet apart, he stood framed in the doorway, refusing to move inside.

"I've a message for you, Niles," Coop said softly.

"It's already been delivered, my friend," Niles smilingly announced. "Your little sweetheart was in here a while ago. She told me the good news."

Coop frowned. "How could she? Em knows nothing about it."

"You're wrong, Coop. She knows. She said Helen Courtney is ready to sell me her farm! Now. Today."

For a long second Coop didn't speak. "I see," he said finally, his frown deepening. "Well, I have another message for you. Captain Northway will sell you his sorrel thoroughbred. Said he will accept your last offer."

"God almighty, will wonders never cease!" Niles exclaimed. "This is too good to be true. When? When can I get my hands on that magnificent stallion?"

"The captain will bring him this afternoon." Coop's tone was clipped. He backed away.

"Thanks a million, Coop!" Niles gushed, "I sure appreciate this and—"

But Coop was already gone.

Chapter Forty-five

Had it been a dream?

Helen considered that possibility as she carefully dressed for her trip into town to meet with Niles Loveless.

It seemed so unreal now.

As if it had never happened.

As if she had never known the wonder of his arms, the thrill of his kiss. Could it actually be that she and Kurt had gone about naked as if they were Adam and Eve before sin? Had they really made love on the parlor floor? And in the big four-poster? And in her armless rocker on the front porch? And atop Raider's back?

Helen sat down on her bed. She laid the new sky-blue piqué dress across her lap.

It *had* happened.

She had been as intimate with Kurt Northway as a woman can possibly be with a man. And she wasn't sorry. She loved him, loved him with all her heart, with all her soul. Loved him now. Would love him tomorrow and next year. Loved him so much it hurt.

While they were alone, Kurt had said he loved her, and she believed him. But maybe she had just wanted to believe him.

She was no naive child. Kurt had told her he loved her, but those words were spoken in the heat of passion. When he made love to her, he had murmured the sweetest of endearments and told her repeatedly how much he loved her.

But did he?

Jolly and Charlie's early arrival back at the farm had cut short their tryst. Almost caught in bed together, there had been no time for last kisses, or promises, or whispered reassurances. No chance for either of them to say "I love you" in the naked light of day.

Since then there had not been a single opportunity for them to be alone. The farm had been a flurry of activity with people constantly coming and going. Even last evening when darkness had fallen, Jolly was still there. Exhausted, he had accepted her invitation to stay over.

So Jolly had spent the night. Charlie had slept in the four-poster with his father. And she had lain awake in her lonely room, missing the loving splendor she'd known less than twenty fours before.

During the long night alone she had gone back over the events of the day. Not once had Kurt looked at her in a way that said he loved her. He had made no move to get her alone. He had behaved exactly as he had before he'd ever touched her.

Helen sighed.

She had been a fool to suppose he really loved her. She *was* a fool. Kurt Northway wasn't in love with her. Kurt had probably made love to lots of women. Women far more beautiful and experienced than she. Their brief little fling had likely meant little or nothing to him. Who was she to suppose that she was someone special to a man like Kurt Northway?

She hadn't been special, she had simply been available. She had fallen into his arms practically begging him to make love to her.

Miserable, unsure, Helen sighed and rose from the bed.

She owed Kurt Northway for the summer's work.

Nothing could change that fact. She owed him and she paid her debts. She would pay this one.

Helen began pulling the blue piqué dress over her head. Bottom lip caught between her teeth, she managed to fasten the tiny hooks going down her back. She hastily brushed her hair and wound it into a shiny rope which she anchored in place with the treasured mother-of-pearl clasp.

She winced softly, recalling the last time she had worn the clasp.

And nothing else.

Shaking off the painful reverie, Helen slipped her stockinged feet into a pair of worn slippers and reached for her reticule. With steady hand she took from the bureau's top drawer a folded packet of yellowing papers which were tied with a frayed gold cord.

The deed to the Burke farm.

Up and out at work since sunup, Kurt had not been near the house all day. Jake Autry and a crew from Spanish Fort were back again, helping out. Everyone labored throughout the morning on building a new corral. They all stopped working just long enough to eat the thick roast beef sandwiches Charlie and Jolly brought down at noon.

Then shortly after lunch, Jake and his men left. Kurt and Jolly continued working, Jolly measuring and sawing lumber, Kurt hammering it into place. Charlie did his part too, bringing them dippers of cool water from the well and gathering scattered debris left by the storm.

At midafternoon, Jolly said he'd had it. He took out a big red bandanna, mopped his ruddy face, and announced it was time for a little nap on the shaded front porch.

Kurt, perched astride the new corral fence, lowered his hammer, swung his long leg over the top rung, and dropped to the ground. He looked about, spotted Charlie playing with Dom up where the back gate had once stood.

"Jolly, there's something I have to do." Kurt looked the older man in the eye. "Could you mind Charlie for a couple of hours? Keep him out of Helen's way?"

"Helen's not here, son. She went off with Em Ellicott a while ago," Jolly said, a deep frown on his face. "I'll watch the sprite, you go on."

"Thanks."

Kurt saddled Raider, looped the long reins over his neck, and told the horse to follow him up to the house. Raider patiently waited while Kurt went inside and washed up. He came out in a clean white shirt, navy twill trousers, and black cowboy boots. He swung up into the saddle and rode away, smiling and waving to Jolly and Charlie.

The smile disappeared as soon as Kurt was out of sight.

He wondered where Helen was.

He wondered what she was doing.

He wondered if he had ever really held her in his arms. Really made love to her through the long sultry nights. Really slept in the bed with her. Really felt her soft bare body—warm with slumber—pressed against his.

Was the haunting sound of her voice calling his name in ecstasy nothing but a longed-for fantasy? A beautiful daydream which had nothing to do with reality?

Helen had told him she loved him, but the words were whispered in the throes of passion. Had she meant it? Even if she had loved him then, did she love him now? Now that the real world had caught up with them? Or was she filled with remorse?

Kurt had found no chance to see Helen alone. He had no way of knowing what she was thinking or how she felt about him. She treated him no differently than she had before they ever made love. She gave no indication she cared about him.

Kurt ground his teeth.

The one and only thing he was sure of was that Helen cared about her farm. The farm meant more to Helen than anything or anyone. It was everything to her. And whether she loved him or not, he loved her and he was not going to let her lose her farm.

The clock in the Methodist church tower struck four P.M.

Helen and Em sat in the deserted dining room of the Bayside Hotel. Upon arriving in Spanish Fort, Em had persuaded Helen to go there for a cool refreshing glass of lemonade before she met with Niles Loveless. Helen had reluctantly agreed, knowing that Em was stalling, playing for time, hoping to change her mind about selling the farm to Niles.

"I have no other choice," Helen repeated, looking across the table at her best friend. "The facts are these, Em. I owe Kurt Northway for working my place all summer. I intended to pay him with profit from the autumn harvest. Thanks to the hurricane, there will be no harvest. No profit. But there is still the debt." She took the last sip of her lemonade, set the glass down, and rose. "I'm going to walk down to Niles's office. I'll meet you at the jail afterward."

"Oh, Helen, I do wish—"

"I do too."

The two women exited the dining room. Em hurried to the county jail as Helen resolutely made her way toward Niles Loveless's Main Street office.

Em rushed into the jail, motioning Coop to join her at the front window. Miserably she told Coop what was happening. He shook his red head regretfully.

Helen marched determinedly down the sidewalk,

nodding to people, smiling bravely. A condemned prisoner on her way to the gallows. The yellowing deed clutched tightly in her hand, she forced herself to go forward to meet her doom.

Kurt rode into Spanish Fort as Helen was taking that slow, tortured walk to Niles Loveless's office. With single-minded purpose, Kurt cantered his beloved stallion toward the very same office.

The pair were less than a block apart when Kurt looked up, saw Helen, and stared in puzzlement, momentarily speechless. She looked as lovely as a summer day in her sky-blue dress. Her hair was swept up atop her head, held in place with the mother-of-pearl clasp he had given to her. Her lips were smiling, but her beautiful eyes were not.

In her hand she carried a rolled-up document.

It took only a second for her intent to dawn on him.

"Helen, no!" Kurt shouted loudly, stopping her in her tracks and attracting the attention of the people on the street. "No! I won't let you do it!"

Helen stood frozen in place.

"Kurt." She stared disbelieving. "What are you doing here? Why are you . . ." Before he could speak again, it hit her. "No!" she screamed at the top of her lungs, and started running toward him. "No! You are not selling Raider to Loveless!"

Helen's shrill scream pierced the lazy afternoon silence. Passersby stopped and gaped. Gamblers poured out of the poker parlor. Drinkers spilled out of the Red Rose Saloon. Ladies peered out of the millinery shop windows and shoppers hurried from Jake's General Store.

Helen and Kurt were oblivious to the gathering crowd.

Blue skirts billowing, heart pounding, Helen raced down the street toward the man she loved.

A broad smile on his dark face, his pulse hammering, Kurt eagerly kneed Raider forward to intercept the woman he loved.

They met in the dusty center of Main, and Kurt, laughing now, leaned down from the saddle and swept Helen up off the ground. The deed clutched tightly in her hand, she threw her arms around his neck as he set her across the saddle before him.

Stares and gasps from the startled spectators quickly changed to laughter, applause, and whistles.

Hearing the commotion, Niles Loveless came hurrying out of his office. He was just in time to see Kurt give Helen a kiss and wheel the big stallion around.

Bewildered, Niles shouted, "Hey, come back here this minute!" He stepped anxiously out into the street. "Where's the deed to my property, Helen?" He started running, following the mounted pair. "Dammit, Northway, get off my thoroughbred stallion!"

Laughing, the lovers never looked back. They never heard him. Eyes only for the golden-haired beauty enclosed in his arms, Kurt couldn't believe his good fortune. This remarkable woman was willing to sell her beloved farm for his sake. Helen was just as dazzled. This magnificent man was willing to give up his prized stallion for her.

Watching from the window of the county jail, Em and Coop laughed as well. It was an amusing, highly satisfying sight to see Niles Loveless, crimson-faced, puffing for breath, foolishly chasing down the street, shouting empty threats, cursing, making a spectacle of himself before the entire population of Spanish Fort.

Raider pranced grandly down Main as if aware that a happy drama was unfolding and he was an important part of it.

On the back of the proud stallion, Kurt and Helen were breathless from kissing. The kisses began as soon as Kurt turned Raider southward and continued until

the last dwellings on the outskirts of town had been
left far behind.

Helen finally tore her lips from Kurt's, pulled back
a little, and scolded, "Kurtis Northway! You were going to sell Raider to Niles Loveless! Dear Lord, what
am I going to do with you?"

"Try marrying me," was Kurt's grinning reply.

"Yes!" Helen exclaimed. "Yes, of course! That's exactly what I'll try!"

"I love you, Helen Courtney." Kurt said the words
she wanted to hear. Said them in the naked light of day.
"I love you, baby, and I just couldn't allow you to sell
your farm to Loveless."

Helen kissed him again. "I love you too, my darling.
My kind, caring, unselfish darling. Oh, Kurt, I love
you more than you'll ever know." In a symbolic gesture, she grabbed a portion Raider's long mane with
one hand, held the yellowing deed up in the other, and
said, "If we should live to be very old and during our
years together you give me countless precious gifts,
none will ever mean as much to me as the one you've
given me today."

"God, you're so sweet and good," said Kurt. "You
deserve better, Helen."

"There is none better than you!"

Kurt smiled, but his eyes turned wistful. "You're
wrong, sweetheart. I love you, you know that, and I
want to marry you. I'm *going* to marry you. But love
doesn't change the fact that I have no prospects, no ex-
pectations, no resources, no money. Right now, I don't
know how I'm going to take care of you and Charlie."

"I've an idea, but . . . I'm not sure . . . darling, you
don't mind staying down here?" Helen asked soberly.
"You won't be unhappy if you don't go back to Maryland? Back home?" She looked directly into his forest-
green eyes.

"Home is where you are," Kurt said softly. "My home's in Alabama."

A smile as bright as the September sun lit Helen's happy face as she said quickly, "I've been giving it some serious thought lately and I . . . you know those dense woods ringing the farm?" Kurt nodded. "All the land that Grandpa Burke meant to clear and plant in crops one day. It's part of the farm. Six hundred acres of piney woods."

"You own six hundred acres of timberland?" Kurt's dark brows lifted.

"No. We own six hundred acres of timberland. You, me, and Charlie. Then there are Jolly's timberlands too and . . . what would you think about starting a sawmill and going into the lumber business? You heard Jolly telling about our old family friend over in Bay Minette who owns a sawmill. He's prospering and I'm sure we could do as well. Construction's going on all over the South and the price of lumber is rising. . . ."

Between kisses and laughter, the pair laid plans. They spoke of a bright and happy future. And touched briefly on the past, remembering those who were now dear, if fading, memories.

The love they had found together was not the first for either of them.

But it would be the last.

They were losing the sun by the time they turned into the tree-bordered lane of home, and Helen, cuddling close to Kurt, felt the faintest tinge of autumn chill in the air. She shivered deliciously.

Anytime now the leaves would start to fall and the days would begin to grow short. The sunny autumn afternoons would give way to crisp clear evenings. Soon the fireplace in the parlor would blaze brightly to warm the cold starry nights. And she and Kurt and Charlie and Jolly would sit around the cozy fire on long winter evenings, snug as bugs in a rug.

And then later, when all the lights were out and the old house was dark and silent, she and Kurt would snuggle warmly in their big four-poster bed. Husband and wife alone at last.

Charlie, with Dom following, ran out hollering when they reached the house. Jolly was right behind him. Both were full of questions which Helen and Kurt were all too glad to answer. They mentioned the idea of the lumber mill and Jolly was enthusiastic.

All talking at once, they moved around the house to the front gallery.

There a radiant Helen hugged Dom, Charlie, Jolly, and Kurt in turn and cautioned them all to stay outside on the porch until she called them in.

She pulled from Kurt's arms and went inside, going directly to the dining room. Cheeks flushed with excitement, she hurried to the heavy rosewood sideboard. She began carefully unpacking her Grandmother Burke's fine bone china and fragile crystal.

She shook her head in amazement and relief. Not one single piece had been shattered in the storm.

Covering the long dining table with an aging white lace-and-damask cloth, Helen hummed as she set the table for a very special evening meal. She placed a fragile china plate at the head of the table, tilted her head to one side, and studied its position. She reached down and moved the plate a half inch forward from the table's edge, then laughed at herself. She'd seen her grandma do the same thing at least a thousand times.

Helen's blue eyes suddenly filled with tears of happiness and she pressed a hand to her full heart.

Tonight, at last, that long-awaited homecoming.